The Oldest Cold Case in Port Cabrillo

A Hunter Triplets Mystery

Beverly M. Kelley

Get-a-Clue Publications

Published by *Get-a-Clue Publications*
September 2013
Paperback Edition
Copyright 2013 Beverly M. Kelley

ISBN-13: 978-0615893471

Printed in the United States of America

Get-a-Clue Publications
516 Island View Circle
Port Hueneme, CA 93041
beverlymkelley.com

Aerodynamically,
the bumblebee should not be able to fly.
But since the bumblebee doesn't know this,
he takes off anyway.
This book is dedicated to my favorite
human bumblebee.
His name is Brendan

ACKNOWLEDGEMENTS

The author wishes to express her great appreciation to her proofreader Marianne Ratcliff, her beta readers Cathy Thomason, Donna Breeze, Barbara Burnett, her sister Jeanne Cannon, and her favorite husband Jonathan Sharkey, for all of their thoughtful comments, brilliant suggestions, and much-appreciated encouragement. Thanks also to Guido Henkel for his most instructive blog on eBook formatting and Joleene Naylor for her step-by-step articles on cover creation.

Contents

Chapter 1: A Star, But No Moon

August 28, 1971

It couldn't possibly have been Marilyn Monroe, but there she was—lolling in front of a sleazy nightclub directly across the alley from the restaurant. The innocent white of her outfit stood out in harsh contrast to the flaking brown enamel on the door.

Since neither a subway nor a subway grate existed in all of Port Cabrillo, theorized Cesar, there was certainly no chance her pleated skirt would be heading heavenward any time soon. He couldn't recall the name of the movie in which Ms. Monroe wore the cocktail dress with the plunging halter-top, but he remembered it had made her into a Hollywood icon.

What was it she said when the wind blew up her dress? Something about the breeze from the subway being delicious? But she didn't actually say the word "delicious"—it was more like she exhaled it.

Around eight every evening, Cesar took his break in his Volkswagen. Since parking was at a premium during the dinner rush, Felix Gutierrez asked his employees to find space for their rides elsewhere. Cesar had turned up the perfect spot out by the backdoor. Even though Cesar's mother kept predicting that a pitch-black alley would attract car thieves, Cesar didn't believe that anybody would steal his eight-year-old Bug—despite the new paint job.

Maria Elena, the owner's wife, tried to press a heaping plate of the bistro's "Saturday Night Special" on him, but he declined. While Cesar drooled at the thought of her green corn seafood tamales, he had a very strict rule about eating in his car. Yet, realizing that his wife might enjoy the special treat, he reconsidered—thanking Maria Elena and packing the tamales in a clamshell container to take home to Maricela.

While eating may have been taboo, smoking in his car was perfectly acceptable—"even though it's a filthy and expensive habit" according to his young bride. He really tried—but he just couldn't quit—not even when she brought up the effects of secondhand smoke on eight-month-old Cesarito. Maricela didn't hesitate to fight dirty. Guilt, in fact, was her preferred weapon of choice.

While a day job in construction and nights serving Mexican dinners provided Cesar's nineteen-year old physique with the equivalent of a hard-body workout, it was his brain that craved stimulation. Cesar, unfortunately, was forced to forfeit his football scholarship when Señor Gutierrez refused to give him Saturday afternoons off.

While Cesar had comforted himself with plans to eventually attend night school, he realized he would need something else to keep from succumbing to total boredom. Then it came to him. He would distract himself by mimicking the Jimmy Stewart character in *Rear Window*.

Even though Cesar was not a photographer convalescing with a broken leg, he found spying on his neighbors during his dinner break as amusing as did the protagonist in the classic Hitchcock film. Cesar needed no high-rise apartment as a vantage point; he peeped from the shadowy interior of his parked automobile. Nor did he require a zoom lens to enhance his surveillance; the nightly parade performed less than fifty feet away. In fact, during the past month or so, Cesar found guilty pleasure in surreptitiously observing what Señor Gutierrez termed "the who-knows-what" going on right across the alley from his family restaurant.

Cesar owed his success—as a vehicle-bound voyeur, that is—to a couple of factors. First, he couldn't have been dressed better for the part. His waiter's uniform consisted of black pants, black shirt, and a full-length black cotton apron. In fact, the stealth-friendly garb—combined with his black curly hair and milk chocolate skin—made him, in his humble opinion, virtually invisible once the sun went down.

Second, the burned-out lamp over the restaurant's backdoor didn't hurt either. Despite months of Maria Elena's nagging, Gutierrez still hadn't gotten around to replacing it. Without it, the sole source of illumination along the entire two-block alleyway was the single caged lamp over the nightclub exit. Just a few minutes ago, it was providing an exquisite halo spotlight for Marilyn Monroe's platinum curls.

Cesar may have wanted to believe his dusky appearance defied detection, but the movie star had no trouble spotting him. In fact, she made a beeline across the alley—her oh-so-kissable cherry lips and voluptuously curvy body suddenly within spitting distance of the very married man. "How about a light?" she inquired. *That sultry voice—it was unmistakable.*

Cesar still had no words, even after Monroe thanked him for firing up his Zippo on her behalf. In fact, he would have remained permanently mute had she not next behaved in a manner he next found both rude and reprehensible. In an effort to adjust her ankle strap, Monroe had managed to scrape the pointed toe of her silver high heel against the side of his newly painted vehicle. The resulting scuffmark caused Cesar to go ballistic. "Get the hell away from my car," he screeched. When that didn't work, he added, "Are you nuts?" Before Monroe could respond to Cesar's rather impertinent question, however, the portal with the peeling paint opened halfway. Nobody emerged, but a reedy tenor announced, "Hey Norm, you're on."

Monroe acknowledged her stage call with a high-pitched giggle and jiggled her way back to her place of employment—but not without first showing Cesar the appropriate finger.

Cesar continued to mutter obscenities under his breath as he plotted his next move. What he really wanted to do was pop the trunk, withdraw a container of car polish, and rub away at the violated area. That wasn't going to happen. He had left the wax at home after detailing his mother's Buick. Instead, he decided to focus on the slightly built blond teenager who had wandered over into his sightline.

It was a chilly night yet the young man wore no jacket. He was shifting his weight from one square-toed shoe to the other as he stood outside the corroded door that had allowed Monroe to escape Cesar's invective. He looked to be about Cesar's age, but Cesar didn't peg him as a fellow working stiff. His clothes—an overpriced madras shirt and khaki pants—indicated he might be a college student.

Was he enrolled at Santa Lucia University? That's where Cesar had dropped out, and where Cruz, his twin brother, reigned as the star quarterback. Cruz wouldn't have been caught dead sporting the preppy look, and certainly not because it was all the rage at the private school. Cruz was his own man.

This kid, however, was quite desperate to fit in. He had taken great care to invest in just the right wardrobe, wear his blonde hair six inches too long, and cultivate a moustache. Unfortunately, his feeble effort at growing facial hair wasn't going to fool anybody. College Kid was clearly not old enough to gain admission to the disreputable nightspot. He was probably waiting for somebody on the inside to crack open the rusty door and sneak him in.

Cesar couldn't have been more wrong. College Kid was waving at a chunky, older chap. He stood well over six feet and was leisurely strolling down the alley from the eastern end. Cesar judged him to be a thirtyish Anglo with a weakness for carbohydrates. He was dressed in a corduroy jacket, white tee, and jeans so freshly ironed that the crease still appeared to be knife-sharp.

He also seemed to be toting something at his side—a long cylindrical object. At first, Cesar supposed it to be a conventional baseball bat, but the item, which Big Guy was now knocking against his open palm, was nowhere near regulation size—nor was it made of light-blond wood. In fact, it seemed more like a bulky stick than a Louisville Slugger—and the color was an odd brownish-black.

Cesar tried to eavesdrop as the pair conversed in hushed tones. While the teenager seemed quite animated—at times gesturing almost ferociously—Big Guy was mostly mum. He only occasionally offered a grunt or a nod—that is, when he wasn't smoothing his thick straw-colored moustache or shrugging his obviously padded shoulders.

Just in the short time it took for Cesar to settle back into his imitation-leather seat, the alleyway had grown so dark he could barely make out the two ebony silhouettes across the way. It hadn't mattered that the moon was waxing gibbous that evening; the ocean fog had already rolled in with a vengeance—hauling with it, the stinging stink of dead seaweed. He also noted that the asphalt now glittered with precipitation. Soon, the foghorn at the Cabrillo Lighthouse, located only two blocks away, would bellow its warning.

The two males kept their backs to him. Whatever the topic of their discussion—it seemed to mean a great deal more to the younger man. When Big Guy pointed the bat at him, however, College Kid's demeanor underwent a total transformation. In fact, he went mute while his whole body became as rigid as the Juan Rodriguez Cabrillo statue at City Hall.

Cesar had become so engrossed he hadn't checked his wristwatch. His break had been over for some time now. He would really have to psych himself up to return to work. *Only a few more hours to go.* Once he finished his shift, he could escape to the bachelor party. Just before his hand moved to pull down the door handle, though, he heard a dull thwack from across the alley's inky expanse.

Like a computer, Cesar's brain ran through possible permutations of what had just occurred. Without even a slim shaft of moonlight for illumination, however, Cesar could only guess.

Had Big Guy turned his bat into a weapon? He could only imagine a fat crimson arc of blood flying out from College's Kid's face.

Then, as if in answer to Cesar's question, Big Guy turned his mug head-on into the light. Supersized incisors seemed to gleam an eerie pearl white, and Big Guy's lips appeared frozen into an extra-large shit-eating grin. There was no more to see after Big Guy pivoted back into the shadows to face the boy.

Cesar imagined that College Kid's front teeth were probably lying somewhere on the pavement in front of him. With a blow like that, the club must have left a gaping hole in the boy's sweet, unsuspecting face. Still, Cesar couldn't help but marvel. Despite the substantial wallop, College Kid had managed to remain upright. *Why didn't he run?* Cesar suspected that the enormity of Big Guy's savage act had simply thunderstruck the young man into silent submission.

Now, the boy took his turn in the low-wattage spotlight. Cesar could see that his nose, while leaning wildly to the left, was still intact. Ribbons of red, however, soaked the front of his plaid shirt. Cesar would not soon forget his eyes. They were crazed in absolute terror. Big Guy, however, just stood there—as if expecting College Kid to retaliate.

College Kid's quivering hands moved from clearing his eyes of blood to assuming a defensive posture—as if his slender fingers could somehow protect a visage that now resembled ground round. In addition, the only force holding up his spindly legs seemed to be sheer willpower.

The boy's refusal to fall to pieces after the initial assault must have really pissed off Big Guy because he just kept pacing back and forth while stabbing the head of his truncheon into the pavement.

Conflicting emotions ripped through Cesar's gut. He may have been revolted, yet he found himself intentionally stifling his screams. He should have demanded that Big Guy's attacks stop but Cesar's amygdala, the portion of the brain instrumental in identifying danger as well as promoting self-preservation, had already taken over. If Cesar had surrendered to his altruistic feelings and attempted to intervene, he would be merely marking himself as Target No. 2. *Besides, it's much too late for College Kid now. I don't think my protests would really change anything.*

Suddenly, the image of Maricela cradling Cesarito at her breast appeared in his mind's eye. The fear of losing the two of them caused Cesar to slink even farther down into his hidey-hole.

Perhaps Cruz, an *hombre* who actually relished the limelight, might have responded differently. Yet a family man like Cesar had no alternative. He had to embrace the anonymity the darkness provided.

The scraping sound of the push-bar unlocking the restaurant door caused Cesar to look away. *Was somebody else coming out on a break?* When nobody materialized from behind the red door, however, Cesar returned his gaze to the other side of the alley. College Kid was no longer on his feet. In fact, his body was sprawled facedown on the pavement with his assailant looming over him, chuckling softly.

Cesar sat horrified as Big Guy, humming an unidentifiable tune, took the club in both hands, raised it high above his head, and drove it straight down—squarely hitting the back of the young man's skull. Cesar, imagining even more gore exploding across the asphalt, was positive he would later find human tissue on his own automobile's exterior.

Subsequently, and this baffled Cesar, Big Guy struck College Kid three more times—with each blow seemingly more out of control than the one preceding—yet always landing on the same spot. It was as if Big Guy had painted a bull's eye on the back of College Kid's head and was earning points for each direct hit.

Big Guy may have initially wanted to stop College Kid's words, but now, by battering the back of his head, he seemed to be going after his thoughts as well. He guessed that unless something distracted Big Guy, he would keep on bashing College Kid's skull until his brain tissue became one with the blacktop. But Cesar would provide neither the distraction nor would he engage in any further handwringing. His only hope for survival, he told himself, was to escape—undetected. If only Big Guy would leave.

While he was waiting, Cesar put his nimble brain to work spinning out various exit strategies. Just as a viable plan was beginning to take shape, though, Cesar's body started trembling violently. He tried, but he couldn't stop shaking.

If Big Guy detected the sound of his now squeaking seat, he would, like College Kid, be history. He was beginning to feel like the horror-movie victim who cleverly conceals her petite frame under the kitchen sink but gives herself away by uncontrollably sobbing. *If only I could roll up my car window, I could keep the sound inside. No, it's a little too late for that now.*

He was actually considering a request for divine guidance, but the words to every prayer he had ever learned had already vaporized like ocean haze on a sun-drenched day. *Too bad Father Valdez had never covered anything like this in confirmation class.*

Not only was he now totally alone, but also totally vulnerable. Narrowing his eyes into slits, he attempted to read the future in the purple mist swirling in front of him. He had to puzzle out exactly what Big Guy would do next if he had any hope of getting away.

At that moment, Cesar sensed a significant drop in temperature from across the alley. Apparently, Big Guy's rage had released him as swiftly as it had taken over. He must have grasped the fact that his victim was dead. *Nobody could have survived after losing so much blood.* The thick, dark-colored liquid outlining the young man's body had grown to the size of a plastic wading pool.

Next, as if on cue, Big Guy paused and extracted an aerosol can from his left jacket pocket. He sprayed a single word on the ground next to the body. Cesar sat in his car in horrified silence, wondering why Big Guy kept staring at the grisly scene. Why waste so much precious time? Somebody could walk out of the nightclub or the restaurant at any moment. *What could Big Guy be thinking?*

But the killer was clearly in no hurry to take his leave. He slowly sat back on his haunches and began to assess his handiwork. Apparently the result pleased him because he started humming again. Finally, he reached over and soundlessly placed what appeared to be the murder weapon on the pavement next to a spray-painted message. Cesar watched without blinking as Big Guy slowly removed his bloody gloves, carefully turned each finger inside out, and methodically rolled up each glove before stuffing the pair into his right jacket pocket.

As the murderer turned to shuffle down the eastern end of the alley, he stopped abruptly in front of the Volkswagen. He seemed to be examining the pitch-black interior of the vehicle. *Can he see me?* Cesar tried not to breathe.

When Big Guy finally melted away into the night, Cesar kept mumbling hoarsely, "He saw nothing—nothing at all." He kept repeating those same six words until he was finally ready to believe them.

Big Guy may not have seen Cesar but Cesar had definitely seen Big Guy. During the few moments the caged lamp had illuminated Big Guy's face, Cesar hadn't been able to put a name to the glowing teeth and demonic grin. Since then, however, not only had Cesar's brain been whirring away, but it was also good and ready to spit out the killer's identity.

At the exact moment Big Guy's name dawned on Cesar, however, it arrived with both a psychological sock to the stomach, as well as a perplexing question. Cesar eventually recovered from the former, but he had no idea how to react to the latter. After this singularly gruesome evening, however, "What the hell should I do now?" seemed perfect as his new mantra.

Chapter 2: The Mother of Triplets Seemed Nonchalant

January 3, 2011

Anne Hunter thought she could hear her muscles weeping with fatigue. A thin sheen of sweat glossed her face. After spending an entire week cleaning her mother's Victorian mansion, she had frittered away the last twenty minutes—twenty minutes she couldn't afford—sweeping the broad wraparound porch.

As she tidied up, she found her thoughts hijacked by an image of her usually staid mother caught up in a fit of the giggles. Carina had been perusing her bank statement when the titters started. Eventually she regained control, and as she wiped her eyes she explained, "You know, Anne, there's more than enough loot in here to hire a team of painters every single year for the rest of my life."

Before the royalty checks from Carina's first bestseller had arrived, Carina and Anne had been compelled to do all of the restoration work by themselves. They had managed to fix up the interior but the two acrophobes were not about to take on painting the mansion's three-story exterior—even with scaffolding.

Anne paused for a moment to study the porch's slender spindles and lacey latticework in the morning sun. After diligently consulting her research materials, Carina had finally settled on a robin's egg blue for the siding and a rich creamy eggshell for the trim. While the painting professionals had worked their magic several times over the years, Anne considered it high time to call them back again. She was just about to inform her mother, when she stopped, took a deep breath, and shook her head. Carina was gone. She had been gone since the day after Christmas. Anne had forgotten again.

Anne walked over to the white wicker chaise longue, still ideally positioned to provide Carina with an unobstructed view of the Pacific. True to its name, the indigo-hued ocean seemed to instill an immediate sense of peace, but this morning Anne didn't have time to savor the relaxing sight.

Draping the soft purple afghan she had crocheted herself over the backrest, Anne couldn't bear to look at it—not only because it no longer warmed her mother's too-slender shoulders, but also because she couldn't help focusing, laser-like, on the barely detectable void indicating where she had dropped a stitch.

During the last few years, Carina would laze in the inviting warmth of the morning sun while Anne worked on a jigsaw puzzle or read to her. A rickety TV tray still held a nearly completed depiction of clouds and gulls—unfinished only because key puzzle pieces had gone missing. Facedown, on a nearby wicker chair rested a dog-eared copy of *Little Women,* which, according to the meticulous penmanship on the title page, had been "presented to Carina Dahl by her loving parents on the occasion of her tenth birthday." Anne, who never tired of caressing its worn leather binding or fingering the barely intact gilt lettering, had only gotten through two-thirds of her mother's favorite novel before Carina closed her eyes for the final time. The bookmark remained at "Tender Troubles," the chapter in which Louisa May Alcott hints at the grownup gentleman Laurie will become, thanks to his unselfish ministering to Beth.

As she retrieved the treasured book, a long rectangle of mustard-yellow newsprint escaped from inside the back cover and pirouetted to the floorboards. Even though she could hear the to-do list thundering for her attention, she found herself skimming a *Los Angeles Herald-Chronicle* feature story dated January 22, 1962 and headlined "Birthday Stork Triples Family's January Joy."

"Born within ten minutes of each other, the Hunter triplets, named after the literary Bronte sisters, arrived at Port Cabrillo Hospital about a month premature," the article began.

"Charlotte, the firstborn, was the smallest, at three pounds, eleven ounces. Emily, identical in appearance to Charlotte, weighed four pounds, one ounce. Anne, the fraternal triplet, was shorter, darker-haired, and tipped the scales at four pounds, four ounces.

While mother Carina was thrilled at having delivered three healthy babies," noted the reporter, "she appeared nonchalant when reminded that the blessed event had occurred on her nineteenth birthday."

"The proud father is Morgan Hunter, an English professor at Santa Lucia University, where he teaches courses in creative writing as well as Victorian and pre-Victorian literature. Professor Hunter, who is a Harvard graduate, is currently at work on a much-anticipated historical novel set in nineteenth century London."

"The couple will make their home in Port Cabrillo. When they aren't busy changing diapers, they are working to restore

Thomas House, a six-bedroom Victorian perched on Spyglass Hill."

Anne found herself feeling more than mildly perturbed. Apparently, if the journalist were to be believed, even as a newborn, she had been nothing like her sisters. She had already learned from the baby books that while Charlotte and Emily smiled, crawled, and walked earlier than she did, not only didn't she speak until she was nearly four, but when she did finally open her mouth, she stuttered.

While Charlotte and Emily had eventually clambered to the top of their respective fields, Anne had never risen above the entry-level rank of a mystery manuscript reader. Furthermore, not only had she managed to get sacked by a third-rate publishing house, but her former employer also saw to it that she would never work in her chosen profession again.

Publishers receive all sorts of unsolicited novels, and while many reputable firms simply ship them back to would-be authors unopened, Anne's employer did not. "They are loath to miss out on the next alphabet mystery maven," was how Anne's immediate supervisor put it.

Anne had been content to punch a time clock at Get-A-Clue Publications for nearly ten years. While she could barely afford the oversized closet she rented in Brooklyn, she actually looked forward to devouring the manuscripts assigned to her—even the really bad ones—and most of them were really bad. Yet what pleasured her most was filling out the standard review form. While most manuscript readers detested that part of the job— summarizing the book's contents, commenting on plot and characters, and making a publication recommendation—to Anne, it was like Christmas morning every time she opened a new submission.

Anne's unique gifts became immediately obvious to her boss. Not only could she accurately speed-read, but she was also able to determine sales potential. Within a few months, Anne was permitted to sign rejection letters. While manuscript readers were supposed to stick to the standard "thanks for thinking of us" boilerplate, Anne preferred to preface her response with at least one compliment. Sometimes the only positive she could find, however, was that a manuscript was neatly typed.

Everything had been going well until that ill-fated day she was unexpectedly called into the office of the president. "Good morning, Mr. Deets," said Anne, rather meekly.

Deets returned her greeting by waving a piece of correspondence in front of her face. "What is this?" he demanded, in a voice rivaling an air horn.

"That appears to be the memo I wrote to Ms. Cannon."

"In fact, it's the memo in which you accuse Lottie Mallory of plagiarism. Do you know who Ms. Mallory is?"

"Yes, sir, she's the author of the Chrystal C. Chandler series."

"And do you know how many books she's sold?"

"No, sir, I don't."

"Every single one has hit the 100,000 copy mark."

"I see."

"So what makes you think you can accuse a best-selling author of plagiarizing her books?"

"Not *all* her books."

"Not *all* her books?" he sneered.

"No, just *The Cat was Blacker than Midnight*. The plot and most of the characters were lifted from an unsolicited manuscript I reviewed five years ago."

"So you're telling me that you can remember, word for word, a manuscript you read five years ago?" Since Anne didn't know how to respond, she remained silent while Deets continued his harangue. "I'll tell you what you have. You have five minutes to pack up your things and get out of here. You're fired. And don't even think about applying for another reader job in New York—or anywhere else for that matter."

Actually, Anne did possess a photographic memory, but she realized that Mr. Deets just didn't care. As a matter of fact, Anne could still recall, in vivid detail, the unique features of the novel submitted by Caroline Harper—a self-diagnosed ailurophile and domestic goddess from Newark, New Jersey. Anne would have been able, had Deets given her the opportunity, to produce a copy of the rejection letter she had sent to Ms. Harper as well. Anne's "We're going to pass on this" missive indicated that while Harper's book was not polished enough for publication, her work had shown considerable promise, and she was recommending Harper revise and resubmit.

Instead, Harper, who was not only totally inexperienced as a writer, but also dreadfully naïve, had forwarded her manuscript to her favorite author. When Harper finally figured out that Mallory had published what was essentially her novel, she engaged an attorney. Her lawyer explained that while Mallory had, indeed, plagiarized Harper's work, he would have a devil of a time proving it in court. Even if Anne agreed to testify, he told Harper, Anne's credibility would evaporate once opposing counsel painted her as a disgruntled ex-employee instead of an altruistic whistle-blower.

Fortuitously for Harper, Mallory was persuaded to offer Harper a generous settlement. And Harper took it. Regrettably for Anne, Deets had seen to it that she was blacklisted. She would, however, eventually find personal fulfillment in caring for her dying mother.

Her sisters Charlotte and Emily, physically mirror images of each other, were big believers in what Anne called "the all-multiples-are-gifted-with-ESP nonsense." Not only did Anne poo-poo the paranormal, but, as she would often remind her sisters, "Even though we share the same birthdate, I am not, thank you very much, identical to anybody. I am Anne. And that's enough— or at least it should be."

Anne squeezed her eyelids shut and attempted to banish a migraine that seemed intent on putting her out of commission. It didn't help that the doorbell had been chiming all morning. Now, as she opened the stainless steel side-by-side refrigerator and attempted to insert but another casserole, she caught a whiff of dill pickle juice—usually undetectable unless the glass jar had broken. "Oh sh-sh-shit," she stammered. "I have one hour to get to the church. Why does this always happen to me?"

A dazzling assortment of cakes, pies, and cookies—fragrant with exotic spices—occupied every square inch of counter space. Ordinarily at the sight of all those confections, Anne would have gone on a sampling spree, but this morning, the cloyingly sweet scent of sugar-laden desserts made her feel queasy. In addition, the heady perfume of six bouquets of fresh-cut flowers—all awaiting water, proper vases, and hands more skillful than hers at flower arranging—had turned into a case of vertigo.

Anne picked up a dog brush and absentmindedly ran it through her hair. *Wait a minute, what am I doing?* she asked herself for the third time that morning. She turned instead and called to Chloe. The five-pound gold and silver Yorkshire terrier was probably hiding under Carina's ornately carved four-poster bed. While the pup had mastered all manner of dog tricks, the only thing she wouldn't do, at least consistently, was "come" on command. Whenever she heard the groan of the refrigerator door, behind which delectable liverwurst was kept, Chloe was "Yorkie-on-the-spot." So why didn't she show up when her name was called?

Carina's theory had been that Chloe was simply too smart. She figured out that every time she heard the words, "Come, Chloe"—a bath or comb-out or tooth-brushing loomed in her immediate future. Yet Chloe's curiosity always got the best of her. Once she emerged from her "safety zone," all Carina or Anne had to do was point a finger and "freeze" Chloe in place. No matter what hygienic torture was in store for her, the Yorkie was forced to gird her hairy little loins and soldier on.

Anne never told anyone, but she and Chloe shared a special secret. Anne could rarely eat without spilling something down her front. Unlike her sisters, Anne possessed an ample bosom and it invariably doubled as a crumb-catching shelf. While snuggling into the warmth of her embrace, Chloe would regularly "clean up" Anne—her tongue proving more effective at eradicating the evidence than any pre-moistened wipe.

"Oh, here you are," said Anne in a matter-of-fact voice. "So what do you think your Mommy is doing now?" she said, referring to Carina. While Chloe possessed a limited vocabulary, whenever a query was addressed to her, she would cock her little head—first to the right and then to the left—as if concentrating intently on summoning up the appropriate response. Apparently Chloe felt the best comeback to the "Mommy question" was to make a leap in the air in front of Anne's chest, trusting that Anne would snatch her to safety. "I can never figure out how you do that, Chloe. Do you have springs hidden somewhere in those tiny legs?"

Chloe cocked her head to the right again, and proceeded to gently but thoroughly lick Anne's asymmetrical face. "That's not going to be good enough, little girl. I'd better grab a real shower now or I am going to catch all sorts of hell from Charlotte and Emily."

Anne had no doubt that Charlotte would deliver the eulogy. The dresser in Charlotte's childhood bedroom groaned under the weight of all the trophies she had been awarded at high school speech competitions. Charlotte's maiden oration had been particularly memorable—not just because it was a well-argued address—but because, having practiced so many times the night before, Charlotte woke up with laryngitis. Yet, despite, or because of her sexy whisper, she ended up winning the tournament.

Charlotte had also been an unparalleled prosecutor in San Diego—racking up an astonishing ninety percent win rate. Now, however, she spent her time—something like sixty hours a week—locked up in a plush corner office as the Los Angeles district attorney's second-in-command. Anne knew Charlotte didn't really miss San Diego. While she had enjoyed the victory bottles of champagne, she didn't also relish having to rub elbows with an ex-husband.

Charlotte's marriage to Austen had ended abruptly after she discovered her hubby had no intention of coming to terms with his gambling addiction. In fact, they'd been wed for only six months when he got in trouble with a loan shark. Her first clue had been the disappearance of their most expensive wedding presents. Yet only after Austin came through the door with broken ribs and a face striped with purple bruises, would he admit he owed a staggering $10,000 to some goon with his own personal enforcement squad.

Her paternal grandparents came to the rescue. When Austin wouldn't step up, however, Charlotte insisted on repaying every dime—but she never got serious about a man again. In fact, she rarely dated, despite finding herself feeling genuine affection for Peter Burnett, her accountant/financial planner. Thanks to his guidance, Charlotte owned, free and clear, a red Porsche 911 Cabriolet, a well-appointed city-view loft, and a full-privileges membership at the venerated Los Angeles County Club.

Further, Charlotte's little black dress would undoubtedly come from a chic boutique only stocking up-and-coming designers—and whose names Anne couldn't recognize on a bet. She could, however, have successfully wagered on Charlotte's choice of shoes. They'd be suede peep-toe pumps with lipstick-red soles—her sister's trademark.

Anne guessed that Emily, Charlotte's monozygotic twin, would arrive at the service attired in her dress police uniform. It hadn't been easy for Emily—especially having to start out as a beat cop in Watts. She gradually worked her way up the Los Angeles Police Department hierarchy—despite all the "boys-in-blue-only" chauvinism, unexpected backstabbing by ambitious female colleagues, and the tension-filled drama that accompanies the unwritten forty-eight-hour deadline whenever an Angeleno becomes a homicide statistic.

Anne's favorite "Emily story" occurred on the first day her sister was elevated to a patrol car. As she and partner Joe Munday were cruising a particularly sketchy neighborhood, Emily thought she saw (out of the corner of her eye) a man shove a woman's leg back into the trunk of a late-model Ford. When she first told Munday, he laughed it off. But when Emily wouldn't let the matter slide, he agreed to circle the block—maintaining that if her claim proved to be nothing, he could still get significant razzing mileage out of what he believed to be a case of first-day jitters.

By the time Emily and Joe caught up to the suspect, he was carrying a quart of booze in one hand and set of car keys in the other. Since Joe and Emily didn't possess a warrant, they couldn't search his car. But that didn't stop Emily. She edged up to the suspect, flashed her million-dollar smile, and warned him about what would happen if law enforcement found an open container of alcohol in his car. She would be happy, she sweetly informed him, to help him stow the booze in the trunk. Before he realized what was happening, Emily had his keys.

"And in the guy's trunk," Anne could recite right along with Emily, "I found plenty of room for the bottle—right next to a shovel and his wife's body."

Carina's struggle with cancer was the final shove Emily needed to resign as chief of detectives once she realized that an impenetrable glass ceiling was as much in evidence at the LAPD headquarters in 2001 as it had been twenty years earlier. After five years as chief, it dawned on Emily she had risen as far as she could. She applied for the chief of police position in Port Cabrillo, and to her astonishment, not only got the nod as top cop, but a place in the local history books as well. Emily Hunter became the first female police chief in San Perdido County.

In addition to her innate ability to cause men to fall all over themselves, Emily was also blessed with an angelic soprano voice. How Carina had managed to eke out eight years of vocal lessons from an already strained-to-the-max budget still mystifies the triplets, but, as their mother was fond of saying: "There's a huge difference between a luxury and a necessity. Emily's singing lessons are a necessity."

Carina requested two songs at her funeral service: "Bridge Over Troubled Water" and "It Is Well With My Soul." Emily was well acquainted with the former. She had practically worn out her personal copy of the Simon and Garfunkel album. The second selection, however, seemed an odd choice. But Carina, as usual, had her reasons. "If you listen closely to the lyrics, my darlings, you should be reminded of Job—you know, from the Bible?"

All three had nodded in agreement.

"In the course of two short years, Horatio Spafford, the man who wrote this hymn, lost everything. His only son was taken by scarlet fever, his finances were ruined by the Great Chicago Fire, and to top it off, his four daughters drowned at sea."

Carina paused as she focused on three sets of cerulean-blue eyes. "So I don't have to spell out why these particular lyrics struck a chord—if you'll excuse the ham-handed pun."

The girls understood. They had been only nine years old when their father walked out. After writing "The Letter," Morgan never communicated with any of them again. The legal-sized envelope embossed with the name of a prominent Los Angeles attorney contained a quitclaim deed to Thomas House as well as a signed marital settlement agreement handing Carina sole legal and physical custody. What Morgan hadn't provided was an explanation for his unexpected departure. All the missive revealed was that he no longer desired to be married and was philosophically opposed to providing either alimony or child support.

Carina, who lacked the financial resources to fight Morgan in court, was forced to sign on the dotted line. The dissolution of their marriage was granted without any further participation on her part.

In just nineteen days, we will be celebrating our fiftieth birthday. Five decades. Although Anne had previously suggested that their half-century milestone warranted some sort of festivity, neither her sisters nor her mother had agreed with her. With Carina's death at Christmas, Anne was even more convinced that the triplets needed something special to keep from drifting further apart. *But Carina's memorial service might not be the best place to broach the subject,* she correctly speculated. Regrettably, she couldn't bring herself to attempt triplet telepathy—even though her cause was just and her heart was pure.

Yet while Anne didn't hold with extrasensory perception, she had no trouble conjuring up an imaginary fairy godmother (armed with the customary three wishes) from childhood. Wish No. 1 had always been for beautiful hair. While Charlotte and Emily had been blessed with bouncy blonde curls, Anne would regularly complain that she had been cursed with locks "the color of hamster turds," as she so tastefully put it. And, to make the situation even worse, her hair was so fine and straight that not even a "stylist to the stars" could have made a difference.

When her sisters first discovered silver threads among the gold, they carefully instructed their hairdressers to re-gild the outliers. Not Anne. Her mop, which was still considerably more pepper than salt, would never, she swore hand-on-heart, see the inside of a beauty parlor. She had also obstinately insisted on cutting her hair herself ever since she could hold the kitchen shears. Yet even her sisters had to admit that they admired the way her whimsical bangs and feathered sides framed her chubby cheeks.

Since she couldn't see the back of her hair to trim it, she allowed it to hang straight down or pulled it up, hit-or-miss, into a ponytail. A memorial service does warrant something special she thought, as she considered a black velvet ribbon. She was quite sure that Chloe would have one she could borrow.

Feeling every one of her forty-nine years, Anne trudged upstairs. As she headed for her bedroom, all she could think about was doing a face-plant on her therapeutic mattress. She just needed to give her busy brain the opportunity to wander or perhaps drift into that special snooze zone between beta waves and total REM sleep. Anne's bedroom, however, was hardly conducive to slumber. Multicolored pieces of clothing covered every flat surface like the back of a kaleidoscope. And most emitted, she hated to admit, a bouquet best dubbed as "needs-to-be-laundered."

As she surveyed her closet, she unearthed a clean black blouse that had fallen to the floor. She smoothed it out, shrugged it on, and buttoned it up. She didn't own a black skirt so Charlotte and Emily would just have to get over the disgrace of Anne wearing slacks to church.

Anne didn't realize, as she jerked her pants off their clothespin-like fasteners, that a hanger could possess a mind of its own. She watched, mouth agape, as it helicoptered straight up into the air, ricocheted off her prominent nose, and finally skittered under the bed—landing right next to her only pair of dressy heels. "Thanks, Mommy," said Anne, "But did you really think I would wear flip-flops to your funeral?"

Chapter 3: Time to Say Adios

August 28, 1971

Still shivering in the balmy night air, Cesar thanked the nameless guardian angel staying his hand before he pulled down the door handle. Had he opened it—even a sliver—the dome light would have illuminated his face. He didn't want to think about what might have happened had Big Guy spotted that.

A few minutes later, as Cesar continued to play ghost, he heard a deep-throated car engine roar to life. The sound had clearly originated at the eastern end of the alley. Looking into the rearview mirror, though, Cesar could barely make out the glow of headlights. *It couldn't possibly be Big Guy.*

Cesar was already emotionally wrung out—not only with trying to wrap his mind around the carnage Big Guy had wrought, but also with attempting to process the shame, culpability, terror, and indecision he was feeling. Moreover, while his brain might be screaming, "I don't know what to do," he'd better figure it out. *Think Cesar. Put your brain in analysis mode.*

Even if Big Guy guessed somebody was sitting in the Volkswagen, he may not have realized it was Cesar. On the other hand, he had been able to identify Big Guy. *Why, I've even worked at his house.* The first time they met, Cesar had immediately sized him up as somebody who paid scant attention to "the help." To Big Guy, Cesar was just some nameless Mexican. Being too unimportant to remember actually brought a modicum of comfort to Cesar. It had been a good eight years since Big Guy had last slapped a wrinkled-up five-dollar bill into his palm. *That's all Big Guy figured a full day of backbreaking chores was worth. Still, this wasn't exactly the time to be strolling down Memory Lane.*

When, at last, Cesar willed himself to glance back into the rear view mirror, the alley had grown so dazzlingly bright he could actually make out the license plate on the approaching car. The front plate on the brand-new black Mercedes 350 SL read 365AXY. *Big Guy. Selir de aqui. It's time to say adios.*

Although Cesar's engine cranked over immediately, Volkswagens are not known for the ability to zoom from zero to sixty—despite Cesar's most urgent need to do so. But the car's lack of get-up-and-go was not what was worrying the teenager.

What if Big Guy planned to smash his Mercedes into the Bug?
Cesar would end up every bit as lifeless as College Kid.

Cesar had barely shifted into first when he felt the impact.
While the jolt seemed intense enough to jar a filling loose, he
seemed to be physically okay. More importantly, his car was still
running. The only problem was—it wasn't under his control.

Yet in that same moment, Cesar became conscious of the fact
that Big Guy had really screwed up. If his goal had been to squash
the Beetle and its contents, he failed miserably. The murderer
should have targeted the Beetle's left flank and shoved the
diminutive car against the brick wall of the restaurant. The skimpy
aluminum side panels would have collapsed like a beverage
container being compacted for recycling. And Cesar would have
been just so much gory collateral damage.

Instead, Big Guy rammed the rear where the engine afforded
Cesar some protection. Furthermore, instead of hitting the back
bumper dead-on, Big Guy caught the left side. This caused Cesar's
car to swing widely to the right and aimed the vehicle straight at
the spot west of the restaurant where a narrow walkway met the
alley. Gravity did the rest, causing the lightweight car to roll
downhill and subsequently out of Big Guy's reach.

Whether or not this means of escape qualified as divine
intervention, the perfectly positioned pedestrian path gave Cesar
access to Via Pacifica, one of the most heavily trafficked streets in
Port Cabrillo. As the town's main drag stretched out before him,
however, Cesar was faced with a *bona fide* dilemma. If he turned
right, he could easily blend into the steady stream of cars traveling
eastbound—but that would be exactly the move Big Guy expected.
If he turned left, however, he would have to wait until a space
opened up on both sides of the road.

Cesar's best bet, as far as he was concerned, was to return to
the alley. He threw the engine into reverse and crabbed his way
back up the walkway. At the top, he gave the steering wheel a hard
jerk to the right and sighed. In less than a minute, the Volkswagen
had returned to its original parking space.

Yet Cesar was so rattled; he had to tell himself to shut off the
engine. *Okay, okay, what's next?* The next step was to calm down.

Cesar's breathing finally started slowing. He could tell it had
become less rasping and ragged. *I'm going to survive.*

"E-e-e-e-eek!" The door at the back of the restaurant
creaked open, and a garbage can inched out—seemingly all by
itself. Cesar's blood pressure had already entered "stroke range." A

second garbage can followed closely behind the first. Finally, a busboy with a black crew cut and a filthy white shirt emerged from behind the red metal door. "Hey, Cesar," he called out in an adenoidal soprano. "Break's over. Old Man Gutierrez is looking for you."

Cesar tried to respond, but found insufficient saliva to lubricate his tongue. After a few seconds of lip-licking, though, he was finally able to sputter, "Emilio, it's you!"

"That's right, *Verga.*"

"I've just been trying to get up enough strength to return to work," said Cesar.

Emilio rolled his eyes.

"Do me a favor, *por favor,* and tell Señor Gutierrez that I've got a real bad case of the flu. I don't think I can finish my shift."

"That's a load of bullshit," said Emilio. "I happen to know that you're going to Hector's bachelor party tonight."

Cesar grunted.

"And that's why you are in such a hurry to get out of here."

Cesar raised his hands in the air. "You got me, Emilio."

"So what's the rush, *Verga?* Are you afraid you won't get there in time to see the stripper?"

"Yeah, that's right," said Cesar. "Come on, Emilio. Just cover for me. *En el peligro se conoce el amigo.* Be a friend to me, and I'll return the favor one day."

Emilio didn't say a word. He just turned and walked away. After the restaurant door slammed behind him, he giggled like a little girl. *Cesar may think he's smarter than me, but he don't know everything.* What Cesar didn't know was that the old man had already called it a night. The entire wait staff had been ordered to punch out at eight o'clock. Emilio, however, who had not been invited to Hector's party, opted to keep this information to himself.

Cesar started up the VW for the second time. A throbbing pain blistered the nape of his neck. And as he gripped the steering wheel more tightly, he found the stinging sensation migrating to his shoulders as well. *Never mind how I feel. Where am I going?*

While he would eventually end up in his own neighborhood, for now, he would snake along a complicated labyrinth of side streets at the opposite end of town. *No way Big Guy will be able to follow me home.* Pushing back his gold-rimmed glasses, he reached over and switched on the radio. Just before the Bee Gees wondered how one could mend a broken heart, Cesar reconsidered. *I don't need any further distractions.* He reached over and turned off the radio. *Besides K-BOP insists on playing the same song every fifteen minutes.* Cesar was admittedly more of a James Taylor fan. It was Maricela who couldn't get enough of the Brothers Gee. In fact, hearing their saccharine lyrics would cause her to cloud up and rain all over his shoulder.

Cesar rolled down the car window. He could smell the unmistakable odor of new car paint. Cesar had availed himself of an Earl Scheib—"any car, any color"—paint job for $29.95. It was the first step in the plan to rehabilitate his 1963 Volkswagen. The Southern California sun had transformed the original gulf blue color into the anemic hue of skim milk. Custom wheels and furry dice would come later.

Sanding out the rust spots, pulling out the dents, and filling in the dings had taken months—largely because he had so little free time to devote to his very first automobile. With the arduous preparation work completed, however, Cesar next found himself totally intimidated by Earl Scheib's seemingly unlimited choice of colors. While the stock VW paint for 1963 included black, pearl white, ruby red, anthracite, beryl green and gulf blue, Cesar finally ruled out all but the last two. "What would really turn me on," he eagerly informed the Earl Scheib paint specialist "is a shade exactly midway between gulf blue and beryl green."

The middle-aged man nodded.

"Oh, and it also must have, if you can manage it, just a touch of silver—like the diamond sparkles in the ocean right before sunset," Cesar said. The specialist paused, scratched his chin, and scribbled "metallic blue-green" on the order form.

As Cesar completed the right-hand turn onto Starboard Lane, he made a mental note to rid the ashtray of cigarette butts before Monday morning. He had learned the hard way that nothing escaped Cruz's notice. Since Cruz would not hesitate to narc him out to his mother (whom the boys affectionately called J*efa*) he had to eliminate the evidence. *I don't need any more nagging from the Maricela-Angelica tag team.* His self-esteem had already endured a big enough hit when he was forced to forfeit his college scholarship.

How he wished he could prevent the jealousy ogre from rearing up and revealing its ugly green mug whenever he saw his twin brother sprinting joyfully down the football field or heard him sharing a provocative idea from a textbook. Cesar hated to admit it, but he would have exchanged lives with Cruz in a New York minute—especially whenever he saw that damned clipping from the *Port Cabrillo Pilot* posted on the refrigerator door. To Angelica Castillo, the headline "Castillo Twins Win Full Ride to Santa Lucia University" still managed to warm the cockles of her heart. It had precisely the opposite effect on Cesar.

And as if the stupid article weren't enough, *Jefa* had to employ his handmade seagull to affix it to the refrigerator. *Why in the world would she embarrass me like that?* The last thing he wanted to think about was that afternoon, back in 1963, when Father Valdez decided to get artistic with his confirmation class. The good padre had directed the six-graders to shape a dove out of salt dough, paint it, and attach a magnet to its backside.

Cesar had never seen a dove, but he had plenty of up-close-and-personal experiences with seagulls. Besides, as he had argued with Father Valdez, nobody actually knew what the Holy Spirit looked like. "Isn't theology," he asked, "simply a matter of interpretation?"

When his question didn't receive the answer he expected, Cesar pressed on: "Couldn't God choose to appear in the guise of a seagull if He really wanted to?"

"Stop clowning around and get to work," responded Vargas. Cesar got so incensed, he threatened to stop attending confirmation class but *Jefa* wouldn't hear of it. *You never won a pissing match with Jefa.* Both Cesar and Cruz were duly confirmed, and that was that. Cesar, however, stopped attending Mass after tenth grade.

While Cesar usually remained on the building site during the thirty-minute lunch break, occasionally Eduardo Gomez, the construction company owner, would give the crew an extra half hour while he shopped for materials at the wholesale lumberyard. That's when Cesar would head for Surfside Drive. He would park *Señor Escarabajo* (his pet name for his Volkswagen) next to the broad white sand beach that was deliberately devoid of development. He was personally grateful to the Port Cabrillo City Council for keeping the two acres of sand as a park—even during the recession when it looked like the municipality might go belly-up.

The tangy salt air also added a certain ambience to the simple bologna sandwich, tortilla chips, and apple included by Maricela in Cesar's brown-bag lunch. Unlike the other construction workers' wives, she froze the sandwich so it tasted freshly made and typically included a love note from either herself or the baby.

Cesar may have felt the Port Cabrillo Chamber of Commerce made too big of a deal out of the annual number of sunny skies, but the town of 22,000 souls did enjoy a nearly perfect climate. In fact, the Chamber's oversized thermometer at City Hall only bore numerical markings between sixty-eight and seventy-two degrees. That's all that was usually needed to keep track of Port Cabrillo's daily temperature.

Cesar, however, found himself most attracted to the beach when nobody else was willing to venture out—especially on days when stiff western winds whipped up whitecaps and banks of black nimbus clouds blotted out the sun. On those occasions, Cesar took long walks along the shoreline all by himself—declining to invite even his brother along.

Even though Cesar hadn't encountered another car for nearly thirty minutes, the illusory image of the Mercedes never left his rearview mirror. And whenever he would look up; the shaking would start all over again. In fact, his elbow was trembling so violently, he accidentally dislodged a snapshot clipped to his visor.

The informal family portrait fluttered all the way down to the floor mat before he could retrieve it. The photo featured Angelica with overpermed locks dyed an unnatural shade of red as she curved her flabby arm around the waif-thin shoulder of Maricela.

At first glance, Cesar's wife seemed to be all hair. She must have spent hours curling her crowning glory into the stylish shag that she claimed made her look like a Hispanic Farrah Fawcett. When Cesar first saw the photo, he wished that her coal-black eyeliner had been applied with a less heavy hand, but he still worshipped her—as much, if not more, than on the day she first caught his eye.

While the women in the photo had made an attempt to smile, Cruz had captured the eight-month-old baby on the verge of a major meltdown. Not only had Cesarito's lower lip descended low enough to reveal a pink tongue quivering with rage, but the baby's black-fringed eyes were also brimming with moisture.

The only person missing from the photo had, of course, been the photographer, but Cesar felt his twin present in the bespectacled image of himself—as usual, standing alone as if waiting for a bus to arrive.

Most folks couldn't tell them apart. They were taller than most Mexicans, well muscled, and usually (unintentionally) decked out in exactly the same colors—mostly black, but dark brown or midnight navy if they were feeling especially flamboyant that day.

In fact, Angelica was frequently puzzled as to whose garments were whose, as she washed and folded their laundry every Monday morning. She had been thinking of labeling their apparel with a permanent marker, but the twins, for obvious reasons, put their kibosh on her plan.

When Cesar finally reached Seabright Avenue, he glanced down at his hands. They were so rigidly locked at ten and two o'clock, his knuckles glowed as white as parchment. *Isn't it about time I released my death grip on the steering wheel?* He was also sweating profusely. Wet semi-circles appeared under each arm.

Facing death was not something Cesar was prepared to do. He considered himself invincible—just as every nineteen-year-old does. Sheer terror, however, felt like a weight crushing his chest. "Cool it," he said, and kept repeating the words like some silly New Age chant. He had to lighten up if he was going to manage his panic. *If I can control the fear,* he told himself, *I will make the smart choice.* The smart choice, he already realized, might also define the difference between life and death.

Lamaze exercises might help him get control of himself. He and Maricela had enrolled in a natural childbirth class. *Natural childbirth.* As far as he was concerned, there was nothing natural about childbirth. And while he didn't doubt that labor pains could be agonizing, he felt Maricela crossed the line with the few well-chosen *maldiciones* she called him in front of the doctor and *Jefa.*

When he first met the love of his life, it was her self-assurance that impressed him. He thought of her as some sort of aloof Madonna. She seemed to possess an internal strength that allowed her to confront any demons that showed up after her mother's untimely passing. In fact, she reminded him of his favorite Mexican boxing champion. The celebrated fighter didn't need to punch anybody out in order to win respect from his peers. His presence alone demonstrated sufficient evidence of his power.

When Maricela surrendered to her labor pains, however, Cesar was more disappointed than he should have been. He couldn't stand the idea that his little *novia* was transmuting from a formidable spiritual warrior to an out-of-control hysteric in a few short hours.

No, Maricela, he wanted to say, *you aren't starring in "Daughters of Darkness" tonight.* He wanted to say even more, but Maricela wouldn't give up the floor. When she wasn't shrieking, she was rattling off the litany of indignities that she'd been forced to endure during the past forty weeks.

What happened to the devoted wife who wrote me sweet nothings on flowered stationery? Where was the bride who was so thrilled to become a mother? During the pregnancy, even while neighbor ladies shared horror stories about childbirth, Maricela remained serene. The night of her delivery, however, she could have been starring in *Friday, the Thirteenth*.

He realized the last trimester had been taxing—especially after having to deal with the mother of all aching backs, false-yet-alarming Braxton-Hicks contractions, and ballooning up to the size of his car. Yet precisely when the newlyweds were poised to welcome baby Cesarito into the world, she insisted on playing the blame game. And Maricela had been quite explicit; she had sized him up as a man, and found him wanting. Moreover, as she told everybody within earshot, she held him personally responsible for getting her into "this condition." Cesar feared all of Port Cabrillo heard her cry *"ir al infierno"* as he tried to coach her labor.

As Cesar replayed the scene in his mind, however, he had to admit that the tableau wasn't without humor. In fact, he could discern a chuckle already starting low in his throat. It built up slowly, until Cesar—eyes closed, face upturned, and mouth open wide—allowed it to utterly fill the interior of his car. *What a satisfying release it is to laugh from the center of one's belly.* He could hardly keep from shouting, *"Todo es bueno."* It is all good.

As Cesar left Beacon Boulevard and traveled the entire length of Neptune Place, he guessed, quite correctly, there would be no place to park. Hector Gomez had made the acquaintance of nearly every male under the age of thirty in Port Cabrillo, and they all considered him *"mi mejor amigo."*

Hector had not only been a buddy of Cesar and Cruz since grade school, but his father was also Cesar's boss. He'd worked two summers with Eduardo Gomez even before he had turned sixteen. Cesar relished working with his hands, and Gomez, a burly man with infinite patience, showed him how to become fast and accurate with the hammer—as well as most of the other tools in the chest. In addition, climbing up and down ladders and hauling around heavy building materials managed to put more muscle on Cesar than the SLU weight room ever had Cruz.

Approaching a familiar cyclone fence, Cesar stopped the car. If there had been an imaginary light bulb over Cesar's head, it would have clicked on. Gomez and Sons Construction Company would provide the solution to Cesar's most pressing problem. While Big Guy might not have known his name, he definitely knew his car. The construction site, however, could provide a safe hideaway for *Señor Escarabajo* that wouldn't be visible from the street. Furthermore, nobody at work would even question the auto's presence on the lot. If they did, he'd just plead car trouble—as usual. Everybody knew that the eight-year-old VW constantly caused him grief. Now all he had to do was unlock the gate.

Fortunately, just a week earlier, Gomez had tapped Cesar to accept a weekend delivery. A shipment of rebar had been promised the previous Friday morning but a tornado in Oklahoma kept the cross-country trucker from making his deadline. He did, however, promise Gomez that he would arrive promptly at eight o'clock on Sunday morning.

Since Cesar usually watched little Cesarito while Maricela and *Jefa* attended Mass, he tried to beg off, but he didn't get much sympathy from the father of ten. "*No problemo*," Gomez had said, "just bring the kid with you. That's why God invented car seats."

An eight-foot chain-link fence and a pit bull facetiously named "Tinkerbelle" protected the building site. In addition, Eduardo had invested "a shitload of cash" into a galvanized steel gate that only swung open after the correct three-number combination was dialed in.

Eduardo was quick to inform anybody who would listen that "this little beauty isn't some cheap lock used to secure a storage shed or a school locker. It's a heavy-duty double-sided combination deadbolt," he would declare, and wait patiently for the listener to be suitably impressed. "Besides," he would add, "it has been permanently welded to the gate. In twenty years," Gomez would next pause dramatically for effect, "I have never lost a saw or a screw."

In Cesar's humble opinion, the dog was much more of an anti-deterrent than the lock—double-sided or not—since Eduardo had given the combination to pretty much everybody. The magic numbers were the month, date, and year of his wife Irma's birth.

Two weeks ago, though, one of the workmen inadvertently mentioned to Irma that the combination was 11/21/26 and her wrath went unabated for three days. Irma, as Eduardo failed to acknowledge, was more than a little sensitive about her age. In fact, she was Eduardo's senior by eight years, and felt he was morally obligated to keep her confidential information, confidential. "Not share it with every *pendejo* you work with" was exactly how she put it.

So Eduardo dutifully reprogrammed the lock. He told Irma that instead of her birthday, he would use the date his favorite canine—a loopy Irish setter named *Rojo*—entered his life. What Eduardo neglected to add was that he found said pooch on Irma's thirty-ninth birthday. He figured she would be none the wiser, while the staff—and Eduardo—would only have to memorize one new number.

Cesar decided to park the Bug behind a five-foot mound of red clay—but before he did so, he removed his full-length black apron, folded it neatly, and deposited it into the trunk. Luckily the construction site was only a mile away from Casa Gomez, where the bachelor party was being held. Taking this as an omen as well as an opportunity for a little aerobic exercise, Cesar broke into a run. Despite having to abandon his position as halfback for the Vikings, he was pleased to find himself still in pretty good shape. Only eight minutes elapsed between the time he left Spinnaker Drive and arrived at Neptune Place. According to his new Swatch, it was not even ten o'clock yet. He smiled as he realized he had beat the stripper by two full hours.

Over the years, the Castillo twins were frequent guests of Hector's—even before Gomez converted the garage into an oak-paneled mecca for every teenage jock or wannabe in Port Cabrillo. Next to a small weight room where Hector and his friends used to sweat all over the Joe Weider body building equipment, Gomez built a "sports lounge"—a sixteen-by-twenty-foot male-only sanctuary.

Four twenty-one-inch television sets were mounted in the corners of the rectangular room. Each could be tuned to a different channel—but the choice was invariably a sporting event. Neon signs advertising various Mexican beers decorated the walls. The focal point of the room, however, was the full-service bar that included adult beverages as well as the usual bill of fare at a Fifties-era soda fountain.

The line of eight stools had been rescued from the Dumpster behind Fernando's Place on Anchor Road. Not only did the owner's wife consider black Naugahyde passé, but she also believed that her proposed fern-and-light-oak decor might attract clientele more cultured than the beer-guzzling regulars.

Cesar took the empty seat next to Cruz. Hector's older brother Miguel, who was playing bartender for the night, requested his drink order.

"Cerveza."

"Lime?"

Cesar nodded. He took a full minute to shove the green citrus wedge all the way down the neck of the bottle. Cruz just sat watching, bemusement curling up the sides of his generous mouth. "Say, Bro," chirped Cruz, "no offense, but you smell like you just played all four quarters at this afternoon's football game."

Cesar didn't respond to the crack, even though irritation at his brother skittered along nerve endings already frayed by the night's events. As he reached for his beer, though, he paused to appreciate the cool damp of the condensation on his sweaty palm. Taking a long draw from the longneck, his lips moved as he counted the dead soldiers already lined up in front of Cruz. "I see you didn't wait," said Cesar in a flat voice.

"I wasn't expecting you until midnight," said Cruz, as he blotted the beer stain on his navy polo shirt. "What did you do, get fired?" Cruz, as usual, was indulging himself at Cesar's expense. When no comeback, witty or otherwise, seemed to be forthcoming, Cruz searched his brother's countenance. He was not quite ready for the look of terror that suddenly swept across Cesar's face. And then, just as suddenly, it disappeared.

Not knowing what to say, Cruz tipped back on his stool, smoothed his forehead with two fingers, and tried to formulate a question that wouldn't offend his brother's sensibilities. Cesar had been, to put it mildly, prickly of late. The last thing Cruz wanted to do was to cause him further distress. Still, his short-lived peek into Cesar's panic was not something he could ignore for long.

Cruz pivoted on his seat and looked long and hard at Cesar. The move was enough to provoke an abrupt attitude adjustment on Cesar's part. Not only did Cesar's customary twinkle return, but he also treated Cruz to one of his luminous smiles.

Yet Cruz placed his hands on the knees of his Levis and continued to stare. The shaking was almost imperceptible at first. In no time at all, however, the jerky movement had become quite pronounced. Cruz didn't say a word. He grabbed his letterman's jacket off the bar and gripped Cesar's shoulder—propelling him toward the door. "We're going to get some air," Cruz announced.

They rambled down the six-block length of Neptune Place until Cesar felt secure enough to open his mouth. He had planned on disclosing only the *Reader's Digest* version of his evening, but soon realized that Cruz wouldn't settle for anything less than the full narrative. While Cesar had always been a bottom-line sort of guy, Cruz overflowed with questions. Consequently, he frequently interrupted the story—requesting that Cesar back up and provide a little more detail with each new revelation. "So we have to assume," Cruz finally said in an unsteady voice, "that Big Guy not only knows your car but he also knows your identity?"

"Yeah, I guess so."

Both brothers fell silent as they continued down the sidewalk. One question, however, Cruz never thought to ask Cesar. He never asked if Cesar knew Big Guy's identity. He had no way of knowing it would be a fatal mistake.

After they turned right on Ocean View Place, Cesar stopped in his tracks, stuck out his right arm, and blocked Cruz from taking another step. Despite the name of the street, the ocean wasn't actually visible from the Castillo family domicile. Originally, Casa Castillo had been little more than a fairytale cottage. Over the years, however, "rooms were tacked on here or there," Angelica used to say, in a voice thick with pride, "to accommodate our family of seven."

In addition to her five sons, Angelica was most proud of her roses. Rare vintage bushes edged either side of the front walkway, outlined the kidney-shaped patio in the rear, and climbed the arbor archway serving as the front gate. The especially fruity-sweet smelling Zepherine Drouhins offered an all-senses-pleasing introduction to the modest property.

The driveway was empty, but that wasn't unusual for a Saturday night. This particular evening, Cesar had taken the Volkswagen to work, while Cruz had borrowed his mother's brand new Skylark. He certainly could have walked the six-and-a-half blocks to the bachelor party, but when Angelica made the offer, Cruz refused to stand on ceremony. His football scholarship had not included an automobile allowance and he envied Cesar the freedom his set of wheels provided.

"I rarely go out on weekends," Angelica admitted. She much preferred to stay home and watch TV with Maricela and the baby. What she didn't say was how elated she had been when Cesar brought home the daughter Angelica had been denied.

While Cesar literally fell in love with the girl next door, the couple did not enjoy much of a history together. In fact, they first met only three years earlier, when unpaid hospital bills forced Maricela's father to sell the family home after Maricela's mother died. Her father had no choice but to move in with his parents on Ocean View Place. Maricela wasn't happy about spending her senior year at a new high school, but she had little control in the matter.

The only good thing about relocating to Port Cabrillo had been meeting Angelica—and then Cesar. Although Maricela had been a frequent visitor to the Castillo house, the first time Cesar noticed her, she was wearing an orchid corsage—and hanging on the arm of an older neighbor boy who had invited her to his prom.

Cesar was so overwhelmed by her singularly exquisite face he couldn't remember his own name—something that didn't fail to escape his brother's notice. In fact, for the next few months, Cruz's constant teasing defined Cesar's life. Once Cesar was finally able to screw up enough courage to ask Maricela out, though, the couple became inseparable. They married two months after their senior prom.

Cruz, still puzzled about being restrained, was losing patience. He decided to follow Cesar's line of sight—which took him to the middle of the white-lined asphalt. Nobody, not even Cruz, could have missed the black Mercedes that was idling right in front of their house.

Chapter 4: Carina's Big Send-off

January 3, 2011

As Anne glanced over the memorial program, she was still disappointed with the cover. Granted, it featured the most recent portrait of Carina, but the emaciated face wasn't the way Anne wanted anybody to remember their mother. Carina had only praised the portrait because Charlotte had caught her award-winning roses in the background. They had been dining *alfresco* on their last collective birthday even though it had been pouring rain. Carina, insisting that they on eat out on the front porch, had said, "We can have the ocean as the first course."

In the photo, Carina had been attired in a rose-colored *Pashmina* shawl that fell into graceful folds over her lavender cashmere sweater. With no makeup, save a hurried dab of pink lipstick, Carina had struck a pose with her right cheek resting against the curve of her right hand. As usual, she declined to smile. Anne recalled that just before Charlotte snapped the picture, Carina took a second to comb her arthritic fingers through tresses cropped at chin-level. Anne had been amazed when the skillfully cut hairdo instantly fell back into a becoming platinum crown.

Anne's favorite photo, however, appeared on the back cover. All through high school, Carina had performed folk dances with a Scandinavian troupe. On this particular occasion, her father Dolph had suspended her in time following an extraordinarily strenuous routine. Birgitta Dahl, the grandmother the triplets had never met, also performed as a teen. When the time came for Carina to compete, Birgitta was so determined to create the perfect costume she traveled all the way to Stockholm to purchase the decorative ribbon. Carina's mother sewed yards and yards of the red, white and black diamond-patterned trim to her daughter's black cotton skirt as well as down the front of the bright-red bodice. In the photo, although tendrils of white-blonde hair escaped coiled braids decorated with wildflowers and the white eyelet apron had lost most of its starch—Carina appeared radiant. Anne couldn't help but grin at Carina's obvious bliss after a flawless performance.

When the introductory chords to "Bridge Over Troubled Water" cascaded down an unseen keyboard, the audience quieted, even though most of them thought they were merely listening to a recording. Once, however, Emily's silvery voice rang out with the poignant lyric, a small gasp went up and echoed throughout the church. Emily had prevailed upon Jane Summers, a police dispatcher who also moonlighted at the local steak joint, to accompany her. Since they wanted the focus to be on Carina's songs, they concealed themselves in the choir loft. Scores of handkerchiefs fluttered out of pockets and handbags by the time Emily's disembodied voice reached the final "it is well with my soul."

The mourners took nearly an hour to make their way to Thomas House. Although they were traveling less than a mile along Lighthouse Drive and Reef Street, once the line of cars tried to crawl up the single lane driveway, they met with instant gridlock. Yet while their engine idled, many took the opportunity to appreciate the fragrant night-blooming jasmine, Roman chamomile, sweet woodruff, and scented geraniums planted by Carina on either side of the driveway.

Spyglass didn't qualify as much of a hill after Colonel Scott A. Thomas lopped off the top to provide a level foundation for the Victorian mansion. The house was constructed in 1878 as a wedding gift for his son Scotty. Thomas, himself, laid the flagstone path to the back door of the kitchen. He also built the freestanding barn that was later converted into a garage. Carina, however, hoarded so much Victoriana; there was no room for a bicycle, much less an automobile, in its generous interior.

The wraparound front porch looked out over a sloping dichondra lawn. A wide, glittering outcrop of lava rock, apparently originating somewhere beneath the Pacific Ocean, edged the back of the lot. The bustling wharf and a six-block commercial area on Reef Street was visible from the north-facing windows, while hundreds of domiciles—occupied by shopkeepers, young families, retired folks and beach-lovers—punctuated a regimented grid of nautically named streets to the east. Each morning, the dawn would transform the houses, whatever their original exterior pigment, into an explosion of cerise-colored Monopoly pieces.

No gathering held at Thomas House ever saw as many attendees as the celebration of Carina's life. The throng of grievers overflowed the first floor, porch and front lawn. During the three-hour reception, the dining room provided the perfect venue for wall-to-wall guests to trade personal reminiscences of Carina as they piled their plates from a blossom-bedecked potluck buffet.

"You did a bang-up job on the eulogy, Charlotte," said Anne, as she and Emily migrated, dirty dishes in hand, to the kitchen. Instead of pitching in, however, Charlotte seemed content to whine about how much effort it took to make 200 people feel at home.

"And your singing brought tears to my eyes, Emily," continued Anne. Emily nodded. She was attempting to balance a couple of empty casserole dishes while simultaneously nudging the swinging kitchen doors open with her hip—a hip bearing a holstered firearm.

"What's with the gun?" asked Charlotte, her brassy voice momentarily stopping the chatter in the dining room.

"A better question, Charlotte, might be, 'Is it loaded?' "

"Is it?" asked Anne, nervously.

"Yes, and so are my arms—so how about a little help here, Charlotte?" asked Emily.

"You know, listening to all those warmhearted words about Carina got me to wondering," said Charlotte, ignoring Emily's plea for assistance. "Do you think she ever regretted dropping out of college to take care of us?"

As Charlotte pulled a dishtowel off the seat of a kitchen chair, Emily raised her eyebrows in anticipation. But instead of taking her turn at drying the dishes, Charlotte had been merely relocating the towel in order to sit down.

"Well, as she always said," began Anne.

"As she always said," said Emily, scraping leftovers into a bag for the compost heap, "it was far more important that *we* got our degrees."

"And once we got them, she was there to applaud each of us," said Charlotte, helping herself to a cookie. "Didn't she have to travel to three different universities on the very same Saturday?"

"She d-d-delivered—" started Anne.

"She delivered the commencement address at your school, Charlotte," said Emily, refilling the creamer. "We were all so proud. An honorary degree from USC."

"She deserved it. She is, uh, was, after all, a best-selling author."

"But don't you th-th-th-think—" Anne tried again.

"But wasn't she," said Emily, "more proud of restoring this house? Yes, I'd say so."

"She just loved everything about the Victorian Age—from the arts to the architecture," said Charlotte, as she uncorked another bottle of wine and poured herself a generous glass.

"Remember when she confessed her most secret desire? You know, wanting to be a lady-in-waiting to Queen Victoria?"

"M-m-maybe—" stuttered Ann.

"Maybe she was—in another life, of course," said Charlotte.

"That's what Aniston, her college chum, reported at the service," said Emily. "Didn't you just love the hilarious stories she told? Especially about Carina's attempts to write raunchy romances? She had all the mourners in stitches."

"F-f-fortunately—" began Anne.

"Fortunately, for the three of us, Aniston convinced Carina to turn her writing into groceries," said Charlotte.

"Except having to deliver a two-hundred-page bodice-ripper every four weeks couldn't have been easy."

"B-B-But," stammered Anne.

"But that didn't stop her. She churned out dozens of them."

Anne threw up her hands, walked over to the staircase, and headed up to the second floor. She would hunt for backup supplies. Even though she had ordered sixty folding chairs from a rental company, there wasn't nearly enough seating. In addition, the eager eaters had swiftly exhausted her stock of plates—both china and paper. In fact, somebody was going to have to wash dishes in order to provide clean tableware for everyone who desired food. Anne, however, didn't believe that somebody would ever be Charlotte.

"I loved it when—" said Charlotte, still sipping wine. The noise from the tap as Emily refilled the sink with suds required that Charlotte raise her voice. "Aniston commented about the erotic predicaments in which Carina placed her heroines. She said, and I quote, 'not only were they highly improbable, but also physically impossible.' "

"Modulate your voice, Charlotte. We still have company."

"So exactly where did Carina get her inspiration? For all the sex scenes, I mean."

"I wouldn't go there, dear sister. Carina had neither the time nor the inclination for romance in her life. Don't you remember when her girlfriends would try to fix her up with some really nice guy? She just wasn't interested."

"I don't blame her. Relationships take trust, and trust has been a tough issue for all of us."

Since Charlotte didn't believe there was enough alcohol in the entire mansion to continue a discussion of trust, she changed the subject. "What did you think of Marilee Masters?"

"Which one was she?"

"She was wearing the old-fashioned tweed suit, brown pumps, and oversized glasses."

"Oh, yes, I remember her. She was Carina's editor. At the first mystery house."

"Editor? She looked more like a Marian-the-librarian type to me."

"Well, Carina's circle of friends did include an inordinate number of librarians."

"Thank God, I say, for Marilee Masters. She decided to take a chance on Carina because she saw," and, at that precise moment, Charlotte was attacked by a series of sneezes, "the literary potential in her writing." Charlotte suffered allergy attacks whenever she found herself around cleaning supplies.

"Even in all those bawdy books she wrote?"

"Especially those books. It's not easy to find new and different ways to write about sex. In addition, Marilee, knowing Carina didn't have a degree, decided that Carina might profit from an extensive reading list—a sort of an 'everything you ever wanted to know about literature but were afraid to ask' list. "

"She must have—profited I mean. After finishing all her reading, she came up with, according to Marilee, 'a very marketable whodunit.' "

"That must have been the first book featuring Inspector Meadow."

Inspector C. F. Meadow, as Carina's devoted fans would happily tell you, was no ordinary detective. Carina's female protagonist faced a tricky challenge during the early nineteenth century when a woman's place was (only) in the home.

She had always aspired to work at Scotland Yard but was effectively barred, as were all other females, from the solely male bastion. Her only option was to pass herself off as a proper English gentleman. The fact that she did so with inordinate success and singular style for twenty years was a credit to Carina's ingenuity as a writer.

"I l-l-liked L-L-Louisa's words the b-b-best," said Anne, returning to the kitchen with an unopened package of paper plates.

"Who was she?" asked Charlotte, now rubbing an expensive lotion into her palms.

Anne tried to spit out a reply, but Emily had already grabbed the floor, "The woman in the pink suit. Carina's favorite editor— Louisa Mayer."

"Didn't she say Carina modeled her protagonist on a real-life London detective?' " asked Emily.

"That's right. But Carina's detective became more famous than the actual private eye had ever been," said Anne, finally getting in the last word—and all without a single stammer.

"Well done, Anne," said Emily.

"But I think Louisa got the most laughs," said Charlotte, ignoring Anne's big moment, "when she provided the inside scoop on Carina's tenth book."

"*The Whitechapel Copycat*?" asked Emily. Her sister nodded. According to Mayer, Carina had grown understandably bored with her plucky protagonist and yearned to explore other options as a writer.

"So that's the moment when Carina decided to kill off Meadow," concluded Charlotte. After the release of *The Whitechapel Copycat*, however, Carina's publisher received bushels of angry letters and telegrams. In fact, Mayer's superiors demanded that she immediately bring Carina to a "Come-To-Jesus" meeting in the conference room. "I would have loved to have been there to represent Carina," added Charlotte.

"Too bad you hadn't yet passed the bar."

After her *The Whitechapel Copycat* experience, Mayer confessed in her wheezy voice, she would never attempt crystal ball-reading again. When it came to predicting that day's events, she had been wrong—twice. Not only did the top brass offer Carina an unprecedented ten-book contract if she would bring Inspector Meadow back to life but Carina, herself, immediately agreed to the deal—without any conditions.

The money, Carina later admitted to Mayer, had just been too good for a single mother to pass up. After she handed in her final Meadow manuscript, *Unmasked at Last*, though, Carina carted her typewriter up to the attic and announced to nobody in particular that she would never write again—not even to finish her history of Thomas House.

As Anne picked up the last remaining dirty casserole, a tear traveled down her cosmetic-free cheek. Eighty-seven-year-old Anglica Castillo had sent word through Maricela that although she couldn't be there in person, she was dispatching a batch of her mouth-watering tamales instead. If their "second mother" had been there, fumed Anne, still harboring a boatload of pent-up frustration, she would have never allowed Charlotte to tease her.

Angelica had entered the triplets' lives right after the christening. Once Stanfield and Eugenie Hunter took a look at the chaos descending on the second-floor nursery, they decided that not only was Carina understandably overwhelmed, but their son Morgan was also going to prove absolutely useless. Since the grandparents constantly traveled, they couldn't exactly lend a hand, but, as they insisted, "We can hire somebody to help out."

The Santa Lucia University faculty wives were all gushing about Mrs. Castillo's childcare skills. In fact, her name topped everybody's babysitter list. Eugenie, however, was most drawn to Angelica because she was successfully raising a set of twins. In fact, Cesar and Cruz celebrated their eighth birthday during the first month Angelica started working at Thomas House.

And nobody was surprised when, despite their cultural differences, Carina and Angelica became fast friends. After Morgan announced he would reside elsewhere, Carina didn't know what she would have done had Angelica not shown up at the front door with a bouquet of homegrown roses, a piping hot plate of enchiladas, and a good bottle of chardonnay.

"You know, *mija*," Angelica had quietly confided, "I suspected something was wrong when Professor Hunter called so late to ask me to watch the girls." Morgan, fearing that Carina might engage in hysterics in reaction to his news, opted to announce his imminent departure at a restaurant.

"I thought he wanted to celebrate our tenth anniversary," said Carina, sobbing over the wine. "What a naïve fool I was. I was so thrilled at the prospect of a romantic night out—I got all gussied up. Full war paint and his favorite cocktail dress. I guess all abandoned wives say the same thing, but you know, Angelica, I never saw it coming."

Chapter 5: Concord, A Living History Book

March 1952

Big Guy acquired the nickname "Duke" when an early growth spurt caused him to tower over his classmates at Haines Academy. His affluent parents shipped him off to Concord, Massachusetts even before his sixth birthday. He was a twelve-month resident at the prestigious boarding school during the next thirteen years.

Every Halloween at the Sleepy Hollow Cemetery, a new batch of Haines kids—easily identifiable by their green blazers and black corduroy pants—would be apprehended by Concord's finest. The post-curfew temptation to fool around among the gravestones of Ralph Waldo Emerson, Henry David Thoreau, Nathaniel Hawthorne and Louisa May Alcott proved all too attractive—especially on All Hallows Eve.

Duke got into considerable trouble not merely for instigating just such an excursion, but for what he did to "Mourning Victory," a memorial chiseled by Daniel Chester French—the artist best known for his larger-than-life likeness of Abraham Lincoln in the nation's capital. Encouraged by his posse of miscreants, Duke had clambered to the top of the sculpture to recite verbatim, as well as with an exaggerated lisp, the William Ellery Channing poem for which the cemetery was named. His admirers howled their appreciation when he decided to augment his performance by taking human feces and desecrating his marble perch.

The good citizens of Concord were justifiably upset, but Duke escaped being expelled after Matthew Andrews, his writing teacher, showed up to plead his case. For his penance, in addition to eight weeks of Saturday School, the headmaster assigned Duke an essay to be entitled "Concord, A Living History Book."

Duke, who had already enjoyed nearly every Haines Academy field trip, didn't have to hole up in any library to research his subject. Already enamored with the Revolutionary War battle sites in what is now Minuteman National Park, Duke could speak with considerable expertise about the War for Independence—starting with the opening salvo at the Old North Bridge. In addition, he'd accompanied Mr. Andrews on so many tours of the three landmark houses within walking distance of the school, he could have served as a docent himself.

The "Old Manse" on Monument Street, where Emerson drafted his celebrated "Nature" essay at an upstairs bedroom desk, was always the first stop. Like every visiting student, Duke had read the poetry that Hawthorne and his wife Sophia etched on the windowpanes, strolled through the heirloom vegetable garden planted by Thoreau as a wedding present, and tried to envision such leading Transcendentalists as Bronson Alcott, Thoreau, and Margaret Fuller discussing the issues of the day in the handsomely furnished parlor.

"The Wayside," according to Duke's essay, had not only served as "home sweet home" to such high-profile individuals as Minuteman Samuel Whitney, Harvard President John Winthrop, Nathaniel Hawthorne, and Harriet Lothrop (*Five Little Peppers* series), but also, while Bronson Alcott was in residence, operated as a well-known stop on the Underground Railroad.

"Orchard House," so named because forty mature apple trees were included with the deed, was also an Alcott family abode. The manor house featured the shelf desk where Louisa May Alcott penned her classic novels as well as the irises painted on doorframes by May Alcott, Louisa's inspiration for Amy March in *Little Women*.

While most American high school students are required to read *Walden or Life in the Woods,* Haines Academy pupils could actually boast of being there. It was during a field trip to Walden Pond that Duke lured Jules Glass to his death.

Jules had always looked up to Duke—and not just because of his height. Yet, without even trying, Jules managed to best Duke with respect to grades, sports, and—just last week—being named editor of *The Chameleon.* Losing the editorship gravely disturbed the balance in Duke's psyche. His perception was that he had been treacherously betrayed—and by his best friend.

Worn wipers scraped across the windshield of the bus that rainy Friday afternoon in March. Mr. Sparks was energized as he drove two-dozen students the few miles down Route 126 to the shore of the lake. He had already lectured on glacial retreat, the extreme depth of the pond, and Frederick Tudor —the man who would become a millionaire simply by harvesting lake ice every winter. The pond was ice-free today, but the water temperature was cold enough to trigger hypothermia.

Duke had discovered the forsaken canoe when he, bored beyond belief by Sparks' history lesson, wandered off. Although he guessed the badly weathered craft had been abandoned around

Thanksgiving, it still appeared watertight. While most boats that far north are usually stored onshore during the winter, nobody seemed to care about this particular canoe.

Duke waited until his classmates had moved to a recreation of Thoreau's cabin before making his pitch to Jules. The students had already viewed Thoreau's original bed, chair, and desk at the Concord Museum. Now, they were snapping photos of each other in front of a huge sign that read: "I went to the woods because I wished to live deliberately, to front only the essential facts of life, and see if I could not learn what it had to teach, and not, when I came to die, discover that I had not lived."

It didn't take much to talk Jules into escaping from what Duke characterized as "death by ennui." After snickering their way through an awkward boarding of the tippy canoe, they allowed the vessel to float out a few yards from the shore. The lake seemed placid, and even Jules grew less agitated as they chatted up all manner of topics as intellectually matched comrades often do. Duke even congratulated Jules on his latest achievement, and then, as if momentarily caught by surprise, pointed to what was obviously a small rubber chameleon peering up at them from the bottom of the canoe.

Jules chuckled, but as he playfully reached over to pick up the replica of the school's mascot, Duke turned and savagely knocked it out of his hand. The rubber figure landed on one of the wooden slats, halfway between the bow and stern seats they'd been occupying. Duke stomped as hard as he could on the chameleon. "This is what you get for trying to stow away aboard our canoe," he thundered dramatically.

Jules stopped laughing. He could see water pooling around the spot where the rubber chameleon had been shoved through the canvas shell, courtesy of Duke's steel-toed hiking boot. Reaching for the lone paddle, Jules found it had seemingly dematerialized. When he attempted to employ his snow-jacket-clad arms to propel the small craft toward land, the icy water soon rendered them paralyzed. Jules said he was afraid that they had allowed the boat to drift out too far. Duke made no comment.

Jules looked around the canoe. He hated to panic but the water had already inched its way up to the gunwale. When Jules turned back to ask his hero to perform a Red Cross carry, Duke was gone. In fact, he was nearly halfway to the shore. The paddle was tucked securely under his arm and he was shouting:

"Swimming, Jules. That's the one thing I am better at than you are."

As Duke glanced toward the far end of the lake, however, he caught sight of a lone figure standing silently between two aspens. The rest of the class, who had discovered a gift shop conveniently located nearby, were entering the doorway with their usual high-decibel level of exhilaration. Duke wondered how much of the canoe incident had been witnessed by the slender young man. Although he was too far away to be positively identified, Duke had a pretty good idea who he was.

The other students called him Spook, but his given name was David Neiriker Reed. His pasty-white complexion and almost colorless grey eyes hinted at the origin of his nickname, but it was his eerie ability to become seemingly transparent at will that actually made it stick.

Spook seemed to possess the uncanny ability to blend in with the furniture whenever he wanted. Boys, who would suddenly look up while studying, would find Spook silently standing in the middle of their rooms. They would scratch their heads and wonder how this strange boy had managed to invade their privacy without making a sound. Spook never spoke; he just watched and waited for somebody, anybody, to befriend him. He especially yearned to be included in Duke's clique—but remained clueless as to how to secure an invitation.

Duke's first inclination had been to get his precious derriere on dry land, but it had to appear he had made a genuine effort to save Jules. Everybody knew Jules couldn't swim. Like all seniors, Jules had been required to take the mandatory proficiency test in the indoor pool before he could graduate. Yet, despite lesson after lesson—Jules always sank like a stone. The freezing water at Walden Pond hadn't improved his chances—even though a life-or-death situation like this should have fired up enough adrenalin in Jules to outpace the school's entire aquatic team.

After attempting to keep his head above water for what seemed like an eternity, Jules finally gave himself permission to briefly shut his eyes. He told himself he was only going to rest momentarily. Regrettably, keeping his arms and legs moving in the frigid water had completely worn him out.

Before sleep could overtake him, though, Jules forced himself to open his eyes one more time. He marveled at the splendor of the oak, hickory, and chestnut trees lining the lake; listened briefly to the familiar song of a Townsend warbler; inhaled air deeply scented with white pine; and eventually released himself to the tranquility waiting at the bottom of the pond.

To his amazement, he found himself quite willing to continue his downward trajectory—despite its conclusion at a terminus from which he would never return. A few hours later, though, Jules *would* return. A wet-suited diver would be hauling his ice-cold corpse to the surface.

Duke watched Jules go under for the last time. He was pleasantly surprised that he felt nothing—not even a twinge of conscience—at his role in his best friend's death. And although Duke worried about what Spook might have observed, it wasn't his major concern at the moment. Right now he needed to figure out what he could do to avoid succumbing to hypothermia himself. He splashed wildly while simultaneously yelling for help.

After five minutes however, the best Cyrano in the history of Haines Academy found that keeping his pronounced nose aloft was becoming nearly impossible. When struck with the realization that he was in actual peril, his mind turned to the old bromide, "If you are bent on revenge, dig two graves." The words contained, he was now aware, more than a grain of truth.

Duke was in serious trouble. His arms and legs proved too heavy to lift. His abundant energy reserves had all but evaporated. He felt dizzy and disoriented. The chill from water and wind had invaded the innermost reaches of his body. And, if he continued to thrash around any longer, his bones threatened to crack like dried-out twigs.

What is that? Is somebody calling my name? The sounds seemed to be coming from the bottom of the lake. While the gravity of his situation had more than dawned on Duke, at this precise moment, he didn't know to what to do. Not only had his mind gone blank but his confidence had also deserted him. Yet just as his air supply had dwindled to nothing, he felt two brawny arms pulling him free. With the glacial cold numbing his brain, he never realized that his legs had become entangled in the underwater weeds.

Mr. Sparks spun Duke around, positioned him in the crook of his arm, and swiftly closed the distance between Duke's would-be watery grave and the dock. Six smaller arms tugged him up over the side. Duke immediately broke into convulsive sobs. All Mr. Sparks' questions would have to wait.

Duke, relieved by his teacher's silence, took in as much life-giving oxygen as possible. As the engine on the school bus growled awake, unseen hands removed his wet clothes, and, as if out of the blue, a dry towel appeared and tried to rub him raw. He next felt himself covered by jackets or sweaters that had, only moments before, warmed his classmates. Even though he was being continually reassured that he was, indeed, safe, Duke couldn't help bawling like a newborn. He had no way of knowing that two short weeks later, school authorities would chalk up Jules's drowning to a childish prank gone awry. Duke, understandably, would be asked to finish out his senior year elsewhere.

As for Spook, Duke's gang would dissolve without inviting him to join, but he would bronze in the afterglow of public recognition. His quick thinking would earn him a special medal for heroism. Award in hand, any suspicions about Duke's role in the murder at Walden Pond were immediately expunged from Spook's memory. And since Spook chose to step to an indifferent drummer, Duke learned a life-shaping lesson—the piper didn't always have to be paid.

Chapter 6: The Most Thoughtful Gift

January 31, 1961

"The diaper delivery truck is out front," yelled an indignant Morgan.

"So show him to the nursery," said Angelica.

Morgan was stunned. He couldn't believe a housekeeper would presume to issue him orders. In fact, he made a big display out of ignoring her as he retreated to his study to sulk. The scholar was supposedly completing a novel, but the clicking of typewriter keys rarely emanated from his sanctuary on the third floor.

Stanfield and Eugenie, as Morgan frequently reminded Carina, were the Newport Beach Hunters—but they were far from ideal parents. His father, an investment banker, was rarely home. His mother, who found herself locked into a loveless marriage, gave her son too much of everything. Morgan was the poster child for narcissism.

Although he graduated from the Chadwick School in Rancho Palos Verdes, his high school academic record was far from remarkable. In fact, he only made it into Harvard as a legacy. Outside of literature and writing classes, he put absolutely no effort into his university coursework, claiming his real education took place in the Cambridge pubs.

Morgan was actually refused admission into the creative writing doctoral program—that is, until his father made a sizable donation to the old *alma mater*. Although Morgan's Ph.D. advisor initially took him on because of an extraordinary collection of short stories written as an undergrad, Professor David Shell soon discovered his literary *wunderkind* lacked both the discipline and desire to complete a dissertation.

When Harvard asked Morgan to withdraw, he shrugged his shoulders and announced he would try his hand at teaching. Without a terminal degree in his discipline, however, the only position offered him was from Santa Lucia University. While not an ideal starting point for the academic fast lane, Morgan envisioned SLU as a springboard to a more prestigious institution once his novel was published.

Angelica found Carina in the nursery, gliding back and forth on the Eastlake platform rocker and reading aloud from a framed piece of calligraphy created especially for her by one of the faculty wives. The plaque held an apt quotation from Mark Twain: "Sufficient unto the day is one baby. As long as you are in your right mind, don't you ever pray for twins. Twins amount to a permanent riot; and there ain't any real difference between triplets and an insurrection."

Angelica, who found Carina's cheeks were wet with tears, offered her a clean diaper to wipe them away, "Now, what's the matter?"

"What's the matter?" repeated Carina, emphasizing every syllable with equal force. "I fancied these triplets a great deal more when they were merely a possibility."

"Ah, I know what you mean."

"Do you ever think about traveling back in time, Angelica?"

"Back in time? No, I never look back, *mija*."

"That's probably very wise, but I can't help wanting to live some days all over again."

"What's the first one you would choose, Carina?"

"The day of my baby shower. That was the last time, me—and my big belly, of course—were the center of attention." A radiant smile spread across her blotchy red face. "Did I ever tell you about the shower?"

"No, *mija.*"

"It was such an elegant affair. Elizabeth Toliver, the president of the Faculty Wives Club, opened her home for the occasion. Would you believe that thirty-five women showed up to honor me?"

"Why wouldn't they?"

"Well, everybody knew how to count, Angelica. It was no secret I delivered the triplets only six months after our wedding date, but they all still made me feel so welcome.

"Tell me about the food." Food, to Angelica, was always the highlight of any party.

"We nibbled on finger sandwiches and drank tea out of English bone china cups. And you would have loved the miniature éclairs and light-as-air cream puffs."

"Sounds *muy perfecta*, Carina."

"It was. We played silly games, and, oh, the presents …"

"I only wish I could have been there with you."

"Me, too, dear friend."

"Is that where you got the swings?" Angelica blessed the trio of wind-up baby swings every single day. All three colicky babies morphed into slumbering angels the minute they started moving back and forth. When the weather warmed up, Angelica planned on dragging the swings out to the front porch. The fresh ocean air might coax the girls into finally sleeping through the night. She knew, as far as Carina was concerned, that red-letter day couldn't arrive soon enough.

"They were a gift from the English Department faculty," said Carina. "I think they all pitched in."

"They definitely get my vote as 'Best Gift.' Of course, there were all those freebies as well." said Angelica. The novelty of triplets being born in San Perdido County brought triple rewards from merchants who catered to kids. The Hunter daughters were treated to matching outfits in sizes 0 though 3T from a national chain store, three oak cribs with Winnie the Pooh blankets and sheets from a mail-order house, a customized triple baby stroller, thirty cases of canned baby food, and a year's supply of formula.

"*My* favorite gift," said Carina, "came from my congregation at Holy Trinity."

"The year's diaper service was a real blessing," said Angelica, and they both laughed at her play on words.

"Which reminds me, we are down to the last dozen diapers."

"Don't worry, Carina. The delivery guy was just here. We're all set for another week."

The girls went through more than one hundred diapers a week, and every day started with either Angelica or Carina preparing twenty-seven bottles of formula. Their commercial-sized washer and dryer churned out fresh laundry eight hours a day. Neither Carina nor Angelica looked forward to the time when the girls would be eating solid food. Feeding them three meals a day loomed as a monumental logistics problem.

"Maybe I can enlist my twins to help out," Angelica had told Carina, shoving aside, for the moment, the probability of her husband's strenuous objections. Like many Hispanic men, he held inflexible views about what *did* and what *did not* constitute suitable work for the male of the species.

Carina rose and placed the plaque on its little nail above the changing table. She couldn't help but appreciate Elizabeth Toliver's thoughtfulness. Not only did she create the gift with her own hands, but it cleverly acknowledged Carina's love of literature as well.

Actually, the only black cloud hovering overhead had been the conspicuous absence of Birgitta Dahl at the shower. Carina told herself she shouldn't have been surprised when her mother hadn't bothered to show up. Neither parent made an appearance at her wedding. Whenever anybody asked why, Carina would just laugh and say "Religious differences."

Religious differences—as if that explained anything. Dolph and Birgitta, whose political views were decidedly to the right of Attila the Hun, always maintained that they sent their only child to Santa Lucia University for two reasons.

First, Carina had to be protected from "those liberal crazies teaching at godless institutions of higher education."

Second, even though the Dahls claimed to be Lutheran, they favored a legalistic view of the Bible over Martin Luther's doctrine of grace.

Being all about rules, Dolph and Birgitta were attracted to a school that required freshmen to live on campus in gender-segregated housing, enforced a zero-tolerance policy toward alcohol and drugs, and required at least three religion classes of every graduate.

It was not surprising that finding Carina with child even before the end of her freshman year would turn their world upside down. "Of course, there will be a wedding," they sputtered, "and you will schedule it as quickly and quietly as possible."

Carina wasn't at all sure that Morgan would agree to walk her down the aisle—as contemptuous as he was of matrimony. He was quite vocal, in fact, in condemning the convention as "outdated and meaningless." He agreed only to tie the knot after a drinking buddy in the Philosophy Department convinced him that marriage was Morgan's only alternative to the unemployment line.

But the groom, who was really not in a dominant bargaining position, decided to toss two grenades (disguised as ultimatums) into the wedding negotiations. "I will only agree to a civil ceremony and only if it is performed at City Hall," he announced to the Dahls. To his way of thinking, his embrace of atheism should garner as much deference as their rigid religious views. Carina being married in their home church by their Lutheran pastor, however, turned out to be a non-negotiable for the Dahls.

On July 15, 1960, Morgan and Carina became man and wife. Their wedding was a rather informal affair—no bridesmaids, groomsmen, flowers, or white dress. The wedding party included the happy couple, the bridegroom's parents, and the city clerk who conducted the brief ceremony. Nobody remembered to bring a camera.

Chapter 7: Plan B

August 28, 1971

The Castillo twins turned tail and ran for their lives. When they finally squinted behind them—no Mercedes appeared to be following them up Neptune Drive.

"We may have outrun him tonight, but the man in the black Mercedes is not going to give up. He will keep on looking for you."

"To do what?"

"Isn't it obvious? Now's the time to implement our plan."

"*Our* plan?"

"We have to make Big Guy believe that you are dead. If we can do that—that will be the end of it. He will stop looking. More importantly, he will leave the rest of us alone."

"I don't understand."

"We have to figure out a way for you to vanish."

"What do you mean, vanish? I can't vanish. I have a family to support."

"Look Cesar, you don't really have to disappear. It just has to seem as though you have. Bro, it's simple."

"Simple?"

"All we have to do is get rid of your car. After that, we can ship you off somewhere for a little 'vacation.' "

"A vacation? You can't be serious."

"I'm quite serious."

Cesar chewed on Cruz's plan for a few moments. When he was finished, he had only one question, "What would you do with my car?"

"We can use the bulldozer—from the building site. You must know where Gomez keeps the key."

"And do what?"

"Well, first, we would dig a big hole."

"And then?"

"And then, *tonto del culo*, we'll bury it."

"You want me to bury '*Señor Escarabajo?*' What are you thinking? You want me to put my little Bug in the ground—to rot?" The pitch and volume of Cesar's voice rose with every syllable.

"Cesar," begged Cruz, but the agony eating away at his brother was also starting to burrow into his own heart.

Cesar turned his back on Cruz, and exited his mother's vehicle, spitting out "*Me vuelves loco,*" before slamming the door.

"Not as crazy as that hombre in the big black car," Cruz shouted after him. "He's already tried to kill you once, Cesar. He will succeed the second time. You've got to act; not react."

Cesar nodded, but refused to look at Cruz. Finally, as he turned and faced his brother, he was struck by the panic now darkening Cruz's eyes. "He knows where we live, Bro," said Cruz.

The last remark caught Cesar up short. He paused, cleared his throat, and shook his head. "What do you want me to do, Cruz?" he said, in a voice both low and gravelly.

"Your car is a small price to pay."

"Why should I have to pay any price, *ese?*"

"Okay, okay, I know how much '*Señor Escarabajo*' means to you, but consider this. What if Big Guy decides to kidnap your wife and child?" Cruz swallowed hard and added, "or kill them. Or *Jefa*? Or me?"

Cesar returned to the car and sat very still in the dark. He realized that an easy solution to his dilemma just didn't exist. It didn't matter that none of this was his fault. The safety of *la familia*, as he well knew, was the only thing that did matter.

When Cesar finally turned and looked at his brother, he made no effort to hide the wet lines etching his brown cheeks. Even though Cesar tried to appear calm and cool—it was no use. "Okay, we will get rid of the car," agreed Cesar, "but I will not bury '*Señor Escarabajo*' "

"So exactly what would you suggest? Remember, you have to convince Big Guy that you are, for all intents and purposes, gone. Gone for good."

Cesar looked at Cruz, and smiled. "I've got it under control."

"And by that, do you mean that you have a Plan B?"

"Do you remember that old mining town that *Papi* took us to see the year before he died?" Cruz shook his head. "Come on, Cruz. You must remember. It's only about an hour's drive from here." His twin furrowed his brow as he tried to figure out what town Cesar was talking about. "Shit, Cruz, you have to know. We weren't up there all that long ago. Why can't I remember the goddamn name?"

"All I recall is the ghost town we saw with Enrique."

"No, that's Bodie. That's miles away. You know, up near Lake Tahoe. This ghost town is in Lockwood Valley."

"Oh, why didn't you say so? You mean Lexington."

"Lexington. Yeah, that's the name," said Cesar, looking relieved. He hated it when he couldn't remember something as simple as a name. He was far too young to be suffering with memory issues—like somebody's *abuela*. He'd just chalk this slipup to stress. "Nothing much up there to see but a whole lot of parched earth and discarded mining equipment," he said as he perused a mental photograph of the place that included a rusted-out ore car, a couple of abandoned automobiles, and five ramshackle structures that used to be home to somebody.

"Do you remember the mining shack, Bro? So deteriorated, it was falling to pieces. I swear, I could have pushed the wall down with my little finger."

"I'm surprised that you didn't do just that."

"Right, and have *Papi* on my case? Don't you remember how paranoid he was about the abandoned gold mine? He told us, more than once, I might add, to stay the hell away from it."

"Ah si, *mina de oro*."

"So are you planning to disregard our father's sage counsel?"

"I do. The gold mine, you see, is going to be my secret hiding place for '*Señor Escarabajo.*'"

"Get real."

"No, this is as real as it gets. And don't worry, Cruz. I am pretty sure I can find Lexington. Even without a map. It's at the end of an unpaved road, if I remember correctly, that meanders up into the hills."

"But what about the bachelor party?"

"It should take us no more than a couple of hours to get there, do our thing, and return to Port Cabrillo. Nobody will even miss us."

"But Bro, the Lexington road is gravel. Are you sure your little tin can will be able to handle the pounding?"

"I'd be more concerned with how you are going to clean up *Jefa's* Skylark once we get back. If you hand her the keys to a filthy car, she's going to want to know how it got that way— especially since you supposedly only drove a few blocks to Casa Gomez."

Fortunately, except for Tinkerbelle barking and setting off all the other canines in the neighborhood, the twins had no trouble getting the Volkswagen out of the company yard. Both vehicles were on the road in five minutes—and all without being seen. The twenty-minute drive to San Perdido was also uneventful. The twins soon found themselves on the turnoff to Highway 33, where the next leg of the trip—a straight shot to Lockwood Valley—turned out to be just another thirty miles of dark, empty asphalt. So far, Plan B was working without a hitch. Both brothers brimmed with optimism as they turned off Lockwood Valley Road and rattled their way toward Lexington. As they turned into the parking area, they found the pint-sized ghost town even more rundown than they had remembered.

Bodie, on the other hand, was Lexington's polar opposite. When big brother Enrique invited the twelve-year-old twins to join his family on a weeklong tour of California, they had been downright giddy. Enrique managed to squeeze a couple of missions, the state capitol, and a train museum into their itinerary as well.

During their tour, the six-member Castillo entourage joined dozens of other curious tourists as they peeked into windows and tried to imagine what life had been like circa 1870. The ghost town provided dozens of structures to see—from a cabin furnished with a butter churn and a spinning wheel to a gaudy saloon decked out in crystal chandeliers and red-velvet cushions to a general store fully stocked with mining equipment, shelved cans, and boxes of foodstuffs. Bodie even possessed a bank—complete with a walk-in vault—that tickled Enrique (who managed the Haltom City Bank) to no end.

All ghost towns are supposed to possess ghosts, and Bodie was no exception. Cesar would never forget the guide's chilling story about the woman in Gay Nineties garb who haunted the saloon. When Cesar claimed he saw her too, Cruz informed him, in no uncertain terms, that he must have a screw loose. Yet what Cruz remembered most about Bodie was what the park ranger had called "the state of arrested decay."

The California State Parks Department decided to maintain the surviving buildings in the same condition that had existed in 1962 when the government acquired the property. Consequently, every summer, work crews labored to shore up walls, repair roofs, and replace smashed windows. Lexington, on the other hand, simply didn't draw enough visitors to warrant any upkeep whatsoever, even though it was located an hour's drive from Los Angeles.

"Okay, so what's next, Bro?"

Cesar laid out Plan B in four steps.

First, they would pry the Jeffrey pine boards off the beams framing the gold mine entrance.

Second, Cesar would drive the Volkswagen into the tunnel as far as possible, park, and carefully walk back out.

Third, they would re-nail the boards across the mouth of the mine. According to Cesar's optimistic estimate, in less than fifteen minutes, they would be back on their merry way—returning to the party well before midnight.

"Sounds doable," said Cruz. "All the implements we need to complete your checklist can be found in the trunk of *Jefa*'s car."

Angelica always carried the Ladies Tool Kit they had given her last Christmas. Although they loathed the Pepto-Bismol color, the case did contain nearly one hundred items useful for minor home or car repairs. While a crowbar wasn't one of the useful items, the weathered eight-inch boards framing the mine entrance did not put up much of a fight. Outside of getting themselves and their mother's vehicle really dusty, all went exceptionally well. Executing Plan B couldn't have been easier.

The fourth step, of course, involved putting Cesar on a bus to New Mexico, where he would surprise a distant cousin with an unannounced visit. Even if Big Guy hired a private detective to locate Cesar, this particular familial relationship would not pop up on anybody's radar including the police. Cesar would remain in Albuquerque for a month or so.

The biggest difficulty, as far as Cesar was concerned, was being separated from his family. He didn't know how long he would be forced to stay away—but even thirty days seemed interminable to the new father and husband.

As he informed Cruz, every single day Maricela seemed to be celebrating some new Cesarito "first" that she faithfully logged into his baby book. Even during Cesarito's short eight months on the planet, she had already recorded four—his first smile, tooth, bite of solid food, and step. But now, who knew how many milestones Cesar might miss while he was hiding out? He could feel tears welling up for the third time that evening.

"Don't worry, Bro. I have an idea," Cruz had said.

Chapter 8: Heard It Through the Grapevine

September 4, 1971

Big Guy shook open the *Port Cabrillo Pilot*. He had been expecting a moving van to pick up his few sticks of furniture, cardboard wardrobe crammed with classy apparel, and two-dozen heavy cartons.

Although Big Guy customarily subscribed to three daily newspapers, he rarely had the time to read them all. Today, it looked like he would be able to tackle each one from cover to cover.

After the Cabrillo Movers' boys finally arrived and carted away his belongings, he headed over to Mike's Car Repair to pick up his Mercedes. Mike's estimate for the bodywork had been over a thousand dollars, but Morgan couldn't very well ask his insurance carrier to pick up the tab. When Big Guy realized he hadn't been alone in the alley, getting rid of the witness in the Volkswagen had become a top priority.

Since he was exhausted from all the physical exertion and didn't really relish recycling the gore-covered baseball bat, Big Guy decided to allow his '71 SL to do the job instead. It seemed easy enough—just ram the hell out of the fragile Bug and its nosy driver would end up in the morgue—right alongside Truman Carpenter.

As he re-envisioned the witness's kiddie car departing down a walkway instead of succumbing to the deathblow by his mighty Mercedes, Big Guy found himself quivering in exasperation. *It was only sheer dumb luck*, he told himself, and then got even more pissed off as he thought about it. *On top of everything else, I have to foot the bill for the repairs. I just can't seem to catch a break.*

While "Brother of Viking Quarterback Vanishes" caught his eye, it was the description of the missing teenager's car that really riveted Big Guy's attention. During the past few days, he had scoured Port Cabrillo and surrounding environs for the VW. Now some local newspaper reporter named Raul Rodriguez was describing the same car. *Metallic blue-green. Check. 1963 model. Check. Chrome-plated wheels. Check.* So the witness he was looking for, according to the *Port Cabrillo Pilot*, had vanished without a trace. *Now wasn't that a real shame?*

Rodriguez had also thoughtfully provided the name of the driver: Cesar Castillo. He would remember that. Then, about two paragraphs down, the reporter added, "Police have also been unable to track down Cabrillo's 1963 Volkswagen." *So the police can't find his car either.* But his joy was not yet quite complete.

The final paragraph told him everything else he needed to know. According to Chief Tony Ortega of the Port Cabrillo Police Department, the police hadn't, as yet, uncovered any reason to suspect foul play. "Mr. Castillo is missing," Ortega had told Rodriguez. "We simply don't have enough information to proceed, but that doesn't mean we don't fully intend to keep investigating."

In other words, the cops have no leads, and there's nothing else to link this kid to the Carpenter murder. He grinned like an obese Cheshire with an overbite. *If this Cesar Castillo is gone for good, I may no longer have a problem.*

Chapter 9: Thomas House

Summer, 1960

On their wedding day, Stanfield Hunter presented Morgan and Carina with a sizeable check. The blushing bride put the unanticipated windfall to immediate use. She had previously discovered a Victorian mansion in Port Cabrillo that had fallen into disrepair. The house on Spyglass Hill could be theirs, free and clear, Carina learned if—they paid the back taxes owed the county in full and brought the plumbing and electrical wiring up to code. Enough money would remain in their checking account to make a good start on restoring the parlor and dining room.

The first time Carina toured the rooms on the first floor, she wept. Every one of them, with the exception of the twenty-by-fourteen-foot kitchen, had been thoroughly trashed. Her extensive research had already revealed that ever since the Civil War, properties owned by Colonel Scott A. Thomas had been unlawfully occupied by trespassers. This mansion, Carina had learned, had been no exception.

In fact, when Thomas R. Berylwood, known to Port Cabrillo residents as "The Honorable," had served as Thomas's agent, he spent most of his time disabusing homesteaders of the belief that the land on which they were squatting wasn't theirs for the taking. The Homestead Act, as "The Honorable" explained, didn't apply to private property. Even when he showed them Colonel Thomas's deeds of sale, Mexican land grants, and property titles, most refused to relocate. Luckily, Berylwood had been trained in the law by a retired Pennsylvania Supreme Court justice. The bright young man invariably prevailed in court.

Although the Port Cabrillo cops suspected vagrants were responsible for the damage to Thomas House, it was only after the greenhouse was set on fire that they thought to board up the windows and change the locks. It was too late, however, to save the reception hall, parlor, living room, and dining room. The unlawful residents had rendered all four rooms completely uninhabitable. In addition, every vintage doorknob and antique drawer pull had been removed and presumably sold to purchase drugs. Graffiti covered the carved-oak chair rails as well as the antique-flocked wallpaper. Carina removed twenty garbage bags of trash from the living room alone.

With the liberal application of soap, water, and a little elbow grease, though, the rooms on the second and third floors—including six bedrooms, two full baths, a laundry room, nursery, and study—suited her instant family of five just fine.

Carina, who spent months investigating the history of her new home at City Hall and the town library, was astonished to learn that Thomas House had played a pivotal role in the early development of both the Port of Cabrillo and the sleepy beach town that grew up around it.

Colonel Thomas, according to Carina's notes, built the mansion in 1878 as a wedding present for his only son. Perched one hundred feet above sea level, the three-story edifice enjoyed a panoramic view of ocean, wharves, downtown, and the residential area to the east. Not only was Spyglass Hill the highest elevation in Port Cabrillo, but was also the only four acres in San Perdido County that didn't belong to Berylwood.

When Colonel Thomas lost his wife Edith in childbirth, he lavished too much affection and attention on little Scotty. Eighteen years later, after an elaborate ceremony united Scott A. Thomas, Jr. and Miss Constance Seabridge, Colonel Thomas took the couple aside and admonished them to fill every single room with children. Unfortunately, they were blessed with only a single son whom they christened Scott A. Thomas III.

On the day Trey turned twenty-one, he married Claire Berylwood, the youngest of "The Honorable's" four daughters. After five years elapsed without a single infant bawling in the nursery, Claire found herself wallowing in self-pity. She grew so despondent that she decided to consult a fortuneteller. She had heard that the nearest psychic had been camped out near Nordoff—a four-hour carriage ride away.

According to entries from her diary, Claire arrived at the gypsy campsite decked out in a large Peter Pan hat that had been extravagantly trimmed in black tulle and peacock feathers. She had also chosen that day to wear a fashionable lampshade tunic trimmed in oriental black braid over a burgundy hobble skirt. Generous pleats of champagne-colored material fell from the empire waist of the bodice—skimming her hips in front but dipping below her knees in the back. Her outfit was topped off with a black lace jabot at the neck.

Carina could scarcely imagine a more uncomfortable ensemble—especially considering the August heat that grew even more intolerable as one traveled inland from the seashore.

Since Claire's narrow skirt didn't allow her to climb up the wooden stairs at the back of Madame Adelphia's gaily-painted wagon, the two women conducted their business on a rough-hewn bench near the fire pit. Claire had noted that the hearthstone still reeked of roasted goat and that before she could remove her traveling gloves, Madame Adelphia, garbed in a leather skirt edged in mud-caked fringe, had gripped her veiled face in both hands and whispered, "I know why you are here."

As shocked as she was, Claire continued to pull off her gloves—laying each one, palm down, on her lap. While Claire had expected Adelphia to pick up her right hand and trace her heart, head, and life-lines, the gypsy calmly explained that palmistry wasn't necessary to determine what had been ailing Claire.

What Claire hadn't realized was that her unlined face, her expensive wedding band, and her arrival without a husband already told Adelphia everything she needed to know. "Not only are you a recent bride, but you are quite accustomed to getting your own way," said the gypsy. Further, it was common knowledge that a woman with a suckling infant could not absent herself from home for more than three hours. The condition of Claire's horse and buggy indicated that she had been on the road for most of the day. To Adelphia, only one problem merited such a lengthy and taxing trip—Claire hadn't been able to conceive.

Yet if she wanted her to continue, Adelphia warned Claire, she had better not consider her a mere fortuneteller. "Closely observing and drawing conclusions—that's how these false prophets operate," she said quite solemnly in a heavily accented voice. "I, on the other hand, am quite different. I only see the truth about my clients when I shut her eyes."

When Adelphia touched another human being, she felt a pulse of energy that sometimes produced a grainy image in her mind's eye—"much like a daguerreotype," she told Claire.

"I possess," Adelphia explained, "second sight. While I have no idea how my gift works—any more than my mother before me—what I have, is far more powerful than anything those charlatans could ever imagine."

Claire noted in her journal that not only was the bench on which she was seated growing harder by the minute, but her feet had begun aching unmercifully. She had purchased her high-top boots two sizes too small. Like most women in her social set, Claire operated under the mistaken impression that small feet reflected gentility and good breeding.

While Claire desired more than anything to loosen the laces on her boots, she kept hearing the words of her mother echoing in her brain. Esther Berylwood must have said a thousand times, "Giving in to discomfort is most unladylike behavior." Instead Claire attempted to distract herself by studying the tiny gold cross around Adelphia's neck.

In fact, she hadn't been paying attention at all as Adelphia hissed, "You've got to stop praying to get pregnant."

When the gypsy's words finally got through, an exasperated Claire could only sputter, "Why?"

Adelphia closed her eyes. She sat very still until something— maybe the sudden appearance of a vision—caused her dark-fringed lids to fly open. As Adelphia's face grew increasingly more rigid, she told Claire she would soon discover something far worse than being barren.

Claire, of course, refused to believe her, but she couldn't return home—not just yet.

"Do you really want to know what I see in your future, Mrs. Thomas?" asked Madame Adelphia. When Claire nodded her head affirmatively, Adelphia added softly, "You will rue this day.

"I'll be the judge of that," said Claire and instructed Adelphia to continue. The gypsy closed her eyes tightly, and began to prophesy.

Claire, according to the clairvoyant, would soon become a mother. During the next six years, she would give birth to four strapping sons. Claire could hardly contain her joy. Yet when Adelphia caught a glimpse of Claire's ear-to-ear grin, she added without cruelty, "But—there will be no grandchildren to cuddle in your arms."

At this point, according to Claire's diary, not only did her hands begin to tremble, but she also became most desperate to return to Port Cabrillo. As she gently loosened the black lace jabot around her neck, Claire found it soaked in perspiration.

Adelphia decided to wait for Claire to regain her composure. "Are you ready to hear the rest?" When Claire nodded up and down, Adelphia continued without emotion, "Before a single son can take a wife, all four will perish. And, Claire, they will all die on exactly the same day in exactly the same place."

Weeping, Claire refused to hear any more. Yet she could scarcely depart without receiving the entire message—no matter how horrifying it might prove to be. According to her journal, Claire pulled an embroidered handkerchief from her sleeve and pressed it to her lips. When the quivering didn't cease, she went after her hat---adjusting it this way and that. Finally, when, at last, she felt in control, she gestured for Adelphia to resume.

"For you, the worst part will be," said Adelphia, turning to conceal her own tears, "that you will never be allowed to say 'good-bye.' And you will be forever changed."

The clairvoyant would prove accurate in every single detail. Within six years, Claire gave birth to Tiberius, Thaddeus, Timothy and Theodore. After Pearl Harbor, all four enlisted in the Army. Claire couldn't dissuade them, no matter how hard she tried. On D-Day, all four ended up making the ultimate sacrifice at Normandy. And, as the fortuneteller had predicted, without closure, Claire would never be the same.

Both Trey and Claire Thomas passed away in 1950—within three months of each other as is often the case with couples as devoted as they were. They were laid to rest, side by side, in the Port Cabrillo Cemetery. Thomas House would remain vacant until 1962, when Carina would come to its rescue. She and Anne would spend the next thirty years restoring the Victorian mansion to its original grace and charm.

Thomas House was a Queen Anne—the so-called "Painted Lady" that Victorian enthusiasts seem to favor. Any architectural authority worth his or her salt, however, would insist on adding two key descriptors to the classification—first, "Eastlake" because of the lacy ornamental detail on the exterior and second, "Stick Style" because of the exposed trusses or stick-work beneath the eaves.

During the late nineteenth century, when Charles Eastlake published his *Hints on Household Taste in Furniture, Upholstery, and Other Details,* he hadn't intended on ushering in an architectural movement. His goal had been to merely persuade woodworkers to return to a higher standard of craftsmanship. The irony, however, had been, in response to popular demand for Eastlake-style furniture as well as the extensive exterior decoration now referred to as Victorian "gingerbread," the geometric ornaments, spindles, low-relief carvings, and incised lines featured in his book would be mass-produced by machines—instead of talented craftsmen.

Carina fell in love with her noble manor from the first moment she saw the top story floating on the wreath of fog that usually nestled around Spyglass Hill. She considered Thomas House to be her "Castle in the Clouds," and after investigating the lives of its former occupants, she believed she had been called upon by a higher power to save the remarkable relic from ruin.

While Carina had shared most of Claire's diary with her husband and children, she deliberately held back Madame Adelphia's final warning. "And one more thing," the gypsy had whispered to Claire, "Your house will never allow anybody it loves to leave."

Chapter 10: Point Me in the Direction of Albuquerque

August 28, 1971

Cesar's wallet was fat with cash since he'd received weekly wages from both his employers. He took a deep breath and noted that the first three steps of Plan B had unfolded without incident. Now, Cruz was pulling the Skylark into the bus station parking lot. Step Four should be a breeze.

It wasn't yet midnight, but the twins had expected to see somebody waiting at the ticket counter. Even though it appeared that the next bus to Albuquerque wouldn't depart until morning, surely he'd arrive at his destination by Monday at the latest. He told his brother not to bother waiting with him—he'd be just fine.

Watching the Skylark pull out of the parking lot, he considered what he might say to Ernesto Herrera, a second cousin (once removed) on his father's side, once he arrived in New Mexico. Despite absolutely no communication between *Papi* and Ernesto during the last ten years, Cesar knew Ernesto would not turn him away. Come to think of it, he doubted that Ernesto was even aware that his father had died. He would have to tell him about *Papi's* failure to make a go of the family grocery store, his ensuing mental breakdown, and the twin's discovery of their father's corpse in the garage.

Maria's Market had been a fifty-year-old institution in Port Cabrillo even before Angelica married Emilio—her "very own Ricardo Montalban," she liked to say. Furthermore, it was the only family grocery store that managed to survive after the big chains came in. Emilio worked fourteen-hour days, but his mother Maria, the eldest daughter of the store's original Maria, seemed to lack confidence in his management skills. She feared he wouldn't know what to do after she passed away so her plan was simple: she would live forever. The family business went bankrupt only two years after her untimely demise.

But he wouldn't tell the whole story. He'd leave out the part where the cops assumed that *Papi* had taken his own life. Besides, the authorities were forced to let their suspicions slide once the *médico de familia* listed the cause of death as "acute myocardial infarction."

Although Dr. Muños believed that Emilio had deliberately ingested some sort of toxic plant, he signed the death certificate anyway, advising the family to refuse an autopsy. The physician had ruled out oleander, the ubiquitous median plant blooming along most freeways in Southern California, as the source of the toxin. He suspected *Aconitum napellus*—also known as monkshood or wolfsbane. Emilio's death, he informed the Castillo males only, would not have been easy. He would have spent several hours vomiting violently before the deadly brew finally caused his heart to beat at warp speed. Eventually the overworked organ had simply given out.

By Dr. Muños not telling the whole truth—that Emilio's cardiac arrest had been drug-induced—not only would *Jefa* be allowed to bury Emilio in the Catholic cemetery, but she would also be able to collect on his paltry life-insurance policy.

Angelica, who had always maintained that her husband died of a broken heart, came closest to the truth. She managed to accept her widowhood with grace and faith. *Y así siguen las cosas. And so it goes.*

She babysat and cleaned houses to cover the inevitable end-of-the-month gap between expenses and income while the twins mowed lawns and washed cars for extras she couldn't afford. With financial assistance from her out-of-the-nest offspring, Angelica was able to make the mortgage payments and keep the refrigerator filled.

*****

Sunday morning saw the Castillo household in complete chaos. Angelica had already spread the alarm, family-wide, even before the crack of dawn. Although she immediately reported her son missing, the police told her they couldn't begin their investigation for forty-eight hours.

Maricela, who hadn't gone to bed, was slumped on the sofa, rocking little Cesarito in her arms, and insisting there was something wrong with the clock. Since Cesar still hadn't returned from the bachelor party, she maintained it couldn't be Sunday morning.

While Enrique, the eldest, had booked a late-afternoon flight from Dallas, Raphael and Jorge showed up around noon to offer, in their words, "emotional support and advice."

Rafael and Jorge had flown the coop even before *Papi's* demise. Impatient with the glacial pace of night school, and anticipating failure in their father's future, they opted to apprentice with a family friend who installed tile for a living. After a couple of years, they were able to start a successful flooring business of their own. While their heavily muscled shoulders strained the seams of their red Castillo Brothers' Flooring Company shirts, the bulge swelling over their belts spoke volumes about their addiction to both CJ burgers and *cerveza*.

As Angelica looked at Raphael and Jorge, though, she shook her head and sighed. She no longer put much stock in their so-called "assistance." Today would be no different. If the balding bachelors weren't wrapped up in television sports in the den, they were surreptitiously removing cans of beer from her refrigerator.

Maricela had wept three facial tissue boxes empty as she continued her surveillance from the front picture window. Every few minutes, she would search between the wavy raindrop stripes for the familiar Volkswagen. Ever since she found Cesar's side of the bed empty, she had attempted to will her husband to walk through the front door. She told herself that she wouldn't say a word—not even if the explanation he offered seemed totally lame. The "why" no longer mattered. She knew that Cesar would never willingly abandon her and the baby, *but where was he?* She even tried praying. More than anything, Cesar *had* to be alive. If he came back to her, she promised the Virgin, she would stop nagging him—even about his cancer sticks. "But you know this," she told the Mother of Jesus. "They will kill him eventually."

On Monday, Señor Gomez and Señor Gutierrez called to inquire as to Cesar's whereabouts. Of course, he hadn't shown up at either job. When both men spoke the same words in response to the news, however, Angelica took it as some sort of an omen. Yet what they said was far from unexpected. "How could he be missing?" they asked. "He was here on Saturday."

Ed Spencer of the Port Cabrillo Police Department arrived Tuesday afternoon around two o'clock. The patrol officer stood a good four inches taller than any member of the Cabrillo family and although he served a city with a substantial Latino population, he had never bothered to learn Spanish.

His nose, which had clearly been broken more than once, presided over heavy purple lips. Doughy bags underlined his eyes and he smelled of Ulster soap. His loyal patronage of the fried fish stand on Beach Boulevard had caused his uniform shirt to be more than flatteringly snug. Two of the brass buttons, in fact, threatened to depart from service at any moment.

In his spare time, Spencer liked to head out to the shooting range near Point Magu. He had grown up in Bozeman, Montana, where felling your first elk was a sacred rite of passage. These days, however, he didn't really do much hunting, unless you count knocking off the occasional cheeky gopher trying to tunnel its way into his back yard. He and some officers from Santa Paula used to jaw about going after wild boar up in Kern County, but that's all it ever was—just a lot of talk.

While Port Cabrillo was able to retain its own police department despite serious economic challenges, most of the other San Perdido County cities contracted with the sheriff. Not much of a tax base existed in Port Cabrillo—other than that generated by tourism and the Port of Cabrillo. Without the means to compete financially with other cities, the PCPD wasn't always able to attract the best and the brightest. In fact, the only guys who seemed to apply were either fresh-faced grads of the San Perdido County Police Academy or over-the-hill officers looking to retire, sooner rather than later. The latter, especially those who had spent most of their careers in high-crime urban areas like Spencer, didn't lose much sleep over offenses committed against people of color.

Spencer took out his notepad and a cheap black pen. "I want to talk to Cruz Castillo first," he told Angelica in a guttural growl.

She stared at his wide black belt, the holstered gun on his right hip, the side-stick on his left, and sent up a silent prayer to the Virgin. When she called out to Cruz, there was a noticeable tremor in her voice. "Please come out of the kitchen and meet Officer Spencer."

"Are you here about my brother?" the twin asked, looking Spencer right in the eye.

"Yeah—Cesar is it? When was the last time you saw him?"

"Well, it was Saturday night—actually Sunday morning, by then—at the bachelor party."

"What was the address of this bachelor party?"

"The party was given in honor of Hector Gomez—242 Neptune Place—about six blocks from here."

Spencer jotted down the name and address. "What time did you last see Mr. Castillo?"

"I'm not exactly sure since I don't own a watch. I do remember, though, we were all pretty excited."

"Why was that?

"Because the exotic dancer had finally arrived."

"Finally?"

"She was supposed to show up at the stroke of midnight, but apparently she had car trouble. I remember when she telephoned Hector to say she would be late."

"So it was some time after midnight?"

"Yeah, probably closer to one o'clock."

Spencer wrote down the time. "Do you know the name of this stripper?"

"I think her name was Destiny."

He wrote down "Destiny." "Do you know her last name?"

"Nope, she didn't say. She just threw her red feather boa around my neck, pulled my head in close, and blew in my ear. 'My name is Destiny,' she said. 'What's yours, *Provocativo?*' "

His brothers, who had just wandered into the living room, started hooting. Officer Spencer looked confused. "What's so funny?" he blurted out. His question merely prompted another round of braying.

"Everybody thought calling me *Provocativo* was pretty humorous. Even my brother cracked up."

"So, your brother was present when the stripper arrived?"

"Yes, we both watched her dance. I thought Destiny's routine was pretty bitchin' but my brother—being a married man and all— he was trying really hard to avert his eyes." The brothers howled at this. "So after her routine was over, I decided to call it a night."

"Why just you? Why not your brother, too?"

"I played football all Saturday afternoon. I was dead tired by the time I arrived at the party." Spencer wrote "football game" on his pad.

"Before I left, though, I told my brother I'd see him at home."

"And you drove?"

"My mother's car."

"A 1971 Buick Skylark," Angelica chimed in. "It's out there in the driveway." Luckily, a late season rain had showered off the accumulated grime—leaving little or no evidence of the excursion to Lexington. Officer Spencer, however, didn't seem at all interested in taking a look at the Buick. The more pressing question, to his way of thinking, was "Why didn't you drive home in the same car?"

"Well, Cesar works from five to eleven o'clock at night, so he couldn't get to Hector's until after his shift was over. My mother generously offered the use of her car last night, so I drove the Buick."

"What kind of car does Mr. Castillo drive?"

"A Volkswagen."

Spencer was now scratching away furiously. "Year?"

"1963"

"Color?"

This wasn't going to be an easy question for Cruz to answer. "Officer Spencer," he said in a strangled voice. "It's hard to say. The VW just got a new paint job, but it's not really a standard color . . . "

"For a Volkswagen?"

"Uh, huh."

"Well, how would you describe it?"

"The color definitely had silver in it."

"Okay."

"But it wasn't really green and it wasn't really blue. How would you describe it, *Jefa?*"

Angelica reflected for a moment before opening her mouth—not exactly standard operating procedure for the impulsive woman, but she had already decided that her answer could be critical to the investigation. "Well, it was more blue than turquoise, but I really wouldn't call it teal or cyan."

Spencer was drumming his fingers on his gun. Angelica looked at Spencer, and Spencer looked at Angelica. Spencer decided to leave the space for 'color of the vehicle' blank.

"Don't forget the custom wheels," reminded Jorge, who had been keenly observing the interview. Raphael nodded his head in agreement.

"Right." Since Spencer didn't see a space for "wheels," he decided to jump back to the timeline. "So you got home and then what did you do?"

"I fell into bed. I was exhausted."

"What time did you realize Cesar was missing?"

"My mother came in at daybreak. She told me Maricela was hysterical."

"Why?"

"Because Cesar hadn't been home all night."

"Had that ever happened before?"

"Never."

"Does your brother have any enemies?"

"Nah, everybody loves Cesar."

"Well, maybe somebody at work?"

"No. Nobody."

"What about financial problems?"

"He had a full college scholarship to Santa Lucia University."

"But he was forced to drop out," added Angelica.

"What does a scholarship have to do with his finances?"

"His school tuition depended on a football scholarship. But he had to forfeit it—the scholarship, I mean."

"I see."

"But you don't see. Mr. Gutierrez wouldn't give him the time off to play football. He was stuck. In order to support Maricela and baby, he *had* to take on a second job. The only second job he could get was as a waiter at Gutierrez's restaurant."

"Second to what?"

"Second to his construction job. Life wasn't easy for Cesar, but he took responsibility."

"Okay."

"Okay, nothing. You don't understand how hard it was for him. When he found out he couldn't make a decent living with just a high school diploma, he knew he had made a huge mistake. You know, by dropping out of college. He was making arrangements to start night school, but you know how *that* goes."

Spencer didn't write any of this down. Instead, he changed the subject. "Would there be any reason he might consider taking his own life?"

"Take his life? Are you *loco,* Officer Spencer?" interrupted Angelica. "Look at his *bonita* wife and *bonito* baby. He wasn't depressed. He was tired—bone-tired. You would be, too. He was trying to be a good father and husband. Why aren't you out there looking for his car? Shouldn't you be issuing an APB or something?"

"We will, Mrs. Castillo, we will. This is the earliest we can fill out a missing person's report." Angelica was livid, but she tried to calm down. Jorge started gently rubbing her back. "Please allow me to continue with my interview," said Officer Spencer to Angelica and then turned and faced the twin. "Did Cesar have any scars or tattoos?"

"Now, it's tattoos," said Angelica. She stepped in as closely as any five-foot woman could to a man standing more than a foot taller. With her face in front of Spencer's chest, she asked, cranking up the volume so that all of Ocean View Place got an earful, "Why would you need to know about tattoos?"

"You've got to cool it, *Jefa*," said Jorge quietly. "The policeman is just trying to do his job."

"No son of mine has a tattoo. Or a scar, for that matter. I'm a good mother. I take good care of my sons."

"We just need to know," said Officer Spencer, "in case we have to identify the body."

"The body," yelped Maricela, suddenly abandoning her vigil at the window. "He isn't dead. Cesar isn't dead. He can't be. Why on earth would you say that?"

She didn't wait for Spencer to answer. She merely shot daggers at his face, handed the baby over to Angelica, and snuffled her way toward her bedroom.

"But I need to talk to Maricela Castillo next," said Officer Spencer, his pitch rising with each word. "I need to find out if they have been having any marital problems . . ."

"Look," said Jorge, "just leave Maricela alone for now. No, there were no marital problems. Cesar and Maricela are very happy. They love each other and they love the baby. You couldn't find a better father than Cesar anywhere."

"Or husband, either," added Angelica. "You know what, Officer Spencer? I think it's time for you to leave."

Later as he typed up his report, Officer Spencer had to admit—the questioning hadn't gone as well as he had anticipated.

"You were so calm," Angelica would tell her youngest son. As she examined his face, however, her motherly suspicions got the best of her. "Were you telling that stuck-up *hombre* the truth?"

"Of course I was."

Neither twin had ever lied to his mother, so he wasn't feeling at all comfortable reciting the fairy tale they had concocted before parting company with his brother at the bus depot.

He felt really bad—in fact, as he noticed his mother's tired eyes now ringed in red, and the worry furrow between them deepened by her emotional pain, the temptation to tell *Jefa* everything became overwhelming. Yet, he did find the strength to resist—only after he reminded himself that Big Guy knew where they lived.

He looked at the clock. It was too late to go to class. Maybe he should get some fresh air. The shopping center was only a few blocks away. He could use the pay phone at the filling station.

After placing the receiver back into its corroded cradle, he extended his right hand over his eyes. It was a futile effort to deflect all the gruesome images he didn't want his imagination conjuring up. He was still having trouble comprehending Ernesto Herrera's response. When he asked to speak to his brother, Ernesto had said he wasn't there. Apparently he had never made it to Albuquerque. Implementing Step No. 4 hadn't been quite as simple or easy as Cesar had planned.

Chapter 11: Anne is a Little Different

Angelica was the first to notice that Anne was a little different from her sisters, and not just because she looked nothing like them. She couldn't exactly put her finger on what was so odd about her—but that didn't keep her from trying.

Angelica knew kids. She had mothered other people's children as well as her own five sons for the last three decades. She had to admit that she had never observed such behavior in a baby before. The infant with the dark brown fuzz seemed to stiffen when Angelica held her, and her big blue eyes darted back and forth, refusing to meet Angelica's, no matter which way she turned the baby's face. Anne also developed what Angelica called *peculiaridades*. She would repeatedly roll her tongue into a tube, blink her eyes, or bite her bottom lip. While the frequency of these mannerisms proved annoying to others, Angelica noticed they seemed to calm Anne down. She, Angelica decided, must be one of those bashful kids who just needs more attention and affection. Angelica made it a point of giving both to her—in spades.

When Carina first placed Anne in the oversized playpen with her sisters, her face reddened with rage. In fact, she continued to shriek until relocated to the hardwood floor by herself. She refused to have anything to do with Charlotte and Emily. After she started crawling, though, Carina couldn't allow her the run of the room, so she purchased a second playpen just for Anne.

In addition, Anne didn't play like her sisters did. Anne's concept of fun was silently sorting her toys into piles according to color or shape. She would sometimes place her hands over her ears when confronted with a loud noise. And while Charlotte and Emily requested dolls from Santa, Anne asked for nothing.

Instead of the childhood make-believe engaged in by her siblings, Anne much preferred wallpapering with her mother, or adding a couple of more entries to her annotated "Books Read" list. All that pretend stuff with tea parties or Malibu mansions bored her silly. Besides, other children—especially her sisters—weren't interested in spending time with her. They called her names or mocked her repetitive mannerisms. The Port Cabrillo librarian became Anne's closest friend.

When the triplets outgrew the nursery, each was given her choice of a private space. Charlotte and Emily agreed on a pair of east-facing rooms on the second floor because of the secret passage between the closets. Anne, however, refused to move, despite Carina's claim on the nursery as "the perfect place to write." In fact, in protest she formed an immovable X in the doorframe and declared, "I will st-st-stay here f-f-forever."

Carina, who could be even more stubborn than her daughter, eventually offered a compromise that proved mutually acceptable. Carina would convert the nursery into an office, but Anne would be allowed to move into the west-facing bedroom upstairs.

Once her father moved out, Anne also took over his study as well. As she entered puberty, the chamber provided the perfect venue for "melancholy princess" fantasies. Her once-upon-a-time storylines invariably began with being banished to the tower for displeasing the king. She imagined herself toiling on her ancient loom in a purple velvet gown, while, at mealtime, a silver tray holding only moldy bread and a small goblet of water would be shoved through an opening at the bottom of the nail-studded door. A single candle in a pewter holder and a single log in the fireplace—even during winter, when nights were long and the moat iced over—was all she was ever allowed. From time to time, she would gaze out across the imaginary moat, hoping to see her prince patiently waiting on the other side. Her savior would be instantly recognizable, Anne knew. His hair would be blond, his eyes blue, and his cap festooned with a feather the exact shade of purple as her gown.

Before Morgan left, however, he witnessed six-year-old Anne falling in love with seagulls. She spent the entire summer learning everything she could about them. She filled notebooks with pencil drawings of gulls soaring above the waves. She even created a seagull merry-go-round to illustrate their rise and fall as they rode the thermals outside her mullioned window.

When she finally exhausted all the library's resources about gulls, she turned to ornithology in general. Anne's obsession was so well known that whenever a library within an hour's drive received a new book on birds they gave Thomas House a call.

When she turned eight, baseball replaced all things avian. It all started when she discovered four old baseball bats in the attic. No, not the flying mammals usually associated with belfries, but those celebrated hickory sticks that little boys used to whack a baseball. Since none of the bats bore a trademark, the owner of a baseball memorabilia shop in San Perdido judged them worthless. When she wrote Alex, her pen pal from Boston, about her find, however, his next letter contained a photo featuring Alex posing with a Louisville Slugger. He claimed the bat had been once employed by the Sultan of Swat to hit a homerun.

With that Anne burned to acquire the bat personally created for Arlie Latham after she read about it in *Baseball Magazine*. Latham was the former third baseman for the St. Louis Browns and her favorite player. According to the article, when Latham broke his favorite in St. Louis, he decided to commission a replacement. At a woodworking shop located near his hotel, seventeen-year-old Bud Hillerich—also an amateur ballplayer—created the first Louisville Slugger for Arlie. Hillerich turned the bat on his father's lathe from a perfect specimen of Kentucky white ash.

Anne discovered Latham after immersing herself in baseball card collecting. Her father Morgan had gotten her started by buying her several fillable albums—not just for the twentieth-century trading variety that accompanied chewing gum, but also for the thin slips of paper bearing player likenesses that tobacco companies included with their products. Anne's most treasured find, by far, was a trio of these from 1910 featuring Latham as a New York Giant.

Anne was also smitten with Alex. When he disclosed a longing for a genuine artifact from the earliest days of baseball, she became fixated on fulfilling his heart's desire. Finding a baseball bat from the period when professionals whittled their own—and shape or length varied from player to player—wasn't going to be easy.

"You are only a hour's drive from Santa Barbara," he had written. "That's where, according to my research, the New York Volunteer Regiment used to bat around a cowhide-covered ball with a stick made from a mesquite branch. Surely, you can make my dream come true."

Neither of her parents, however, would agree to drive her all the way to Santa Barbara on what they characterized as "some wild goose chase for a boy you've never met." Morgan, however, got her pretty excited about Charley Hall, a local San Perdido County legend first picked up by the Cincinnati Reds.

Anne not only sent Hall's Boston Red Sox player card to Alex as a Christmas gift, but also promised to contact Hall's relatives about any baseball equipment he might have left behind. In fact, she spent months tracking down family members only to discover that Hall's last sibling succumbed to cancer in 1963.

In desperation, Anne wrote to Christopher Kendal, a sports journalist who spent the better part of his career writing about Hall. Kendal provided the name of a grandson "who might still reside in Santa Barbara." After calling all the Halls in the Santa Barbara directory, however, Anne was forced to concede defeat. She never heard from Alex again.

Chapter 12: The Reading of the Will

January 10, 2011

Stan Gardner, Carina's attorney, asked his secretary to call the Hunter triplets. "Just tell them," he instructed her, "to be present at the reading of the will on January 21st."

Charlotte immediately begged off. "Puh-lease, Della," she complained. "The reading of the will? Are you for real? My schedule is impossible—especially during the next three weeks. I'll tell you what. Why don't you just pop a copy in the mail?"

Emily gave the same "thanks, but no thanks" response. "Della, don't you realize that my job as police chief is 24/7?" asked Emily. She suggested that Della fax her mother's last will and testament to the station.

Only Anne had been willing to come. But, of course, she was the only one with an ulterior motive—a motive based on her two biggest fears.

Fear No. 1 was being forced to leave Thomas House. Assuming that Carina bequeathed the Victorian to all three of them, Anne was quite sure that Charlotte and Emily would immediately put the mansion on the market—and divvy up the profits as soon as it sold. Since none of their sweat had gone into the thirty-year restoration, they had no emotional equity to protect.

Anne was barely four the first time she shrugged into 4T overalls and asked, in a toddler-pitched voice, "Me, help?" Her mother had placed a sandpaper-covered block into her tiny palm, and led her to the master bedroom. The room, which had been emptied of all its furnishings, measured sixteen-by-twelve-feet. "We are going to sand one plank at a time. Okay, Sweetie?"

Anne nodded happily. Undaunted by the adult-sized task, Anne kept returning, day after day.

Mother and daughter would eventually replace rotten fir floorboards, install stained glass windows, recreate ceiling medallions, shingle the roof, paint the ceilings, wallpaper the walls, repair the crown molding, and refinish the English oak woodwork. While uncovering six fireplaces concealed behind walls or paneling proved quite an adventure, neither mother nor daughter would ever forget the "Riddle of the Hair."

During the removal of plaster from the servant's passageway to the dining room, Anne discovered human hair in the walls—and not just a single shade of hair. There were strands of blond, brunette, and auburn. Naturally, Carina and Anne allowed their writer's minds to run wild.

Anne's pet theory consisted of a psychopath luring hungry homeless women into the kitchen where he slashed their throats, covered their bodies in quicklime, and stashed them between the studs. She was positive the vile serial killer had secreted dozens of bodies within the plastered walls.

Carina, however, remained unconvinced. "Answer me this, dearest daughter. Why would your killer go through all this effort when he could just throw the bodies into the ocean? Isn't our yard essentially the Pacific?"

As they hacked and sifted through chunks of chalky lime, they continued to banter back and forth—spinning out dueling hypotheses that soon approached the outermost limits of absurdity. Each attempt to top the other was followed by peals of laughter. Once the demolition was finally complete, both were disappointed to find no further human remains remaining.

Only after making the acquaintance of Clarence Gates, a Victorian homeowner from Santa Paula, were they able to unravel the mystery of the leftover locks. Gates apprised them of an interesting yet obscure fact about interior walls during the late 1800s. It seems that workmen mixed in hair clippings from local barbershops to strengthen the plaster.

"What's more," Gates recounted in his professorial voice, "the sale of hair clippings became as lucrative a sideline to shearers and shavers as bleeding patients and pulling teeth had been during the Dark Ages. Now I have a question for you, little girl," he said, turning to Anne. "Do you know why the barber pole is always painted red and white?"

Anne took a wild guess. "Is it because of the candy canes, you know, that the barber gives to the kids who sit still and don't cry?"

"Well," said Gates, "according to the history books, the red and white colors symbolize, respectively, the letting of blood and the extraction of teeth. Yet, and I think your mother will concur with me here, you've come up with a much sweeter answer."

Fear No. 2 for Anne was being forced to work at an unfulfilling job. She had been so thrilled when Marilee Masters, her mother's former editor, provided her with a position as a manuscript reader in New York. It had seemed the perfect fit. Not only was Anne addicted to reading books, but mysteries were her own personal cocaine.

Certainly Anne fulfilled the minimum educational requirements for the job. She held an AA from Port Cabrillo Community College and a BA in literature from UCLA. Higher education had offered both peaks and valleys to Anne. While she shone in classes requiring scholarly papers or independent research, low marks clouded her record when oral communication skills were demanded. Fortunately, despite her speech impediment, she still managed to graduate with honors.

A stellar grade point average, however, didn't translate into a stellar job. While her well-written resume would usually land her an interview, the inability to maintain eye contact, speak without stuttering, and appear sublimely self-confident, kept her from receiving a lucrative job offer. As a result, Anne ended up cycling through a series of mindless entry-level job posts. In fact, her self-esteem was circling the drain by the time Carina sent her to Dr. Jean Benton.

Anne couldn't have been more impressed with Dr. Benton. At their first meeting, the psychologist had been impeccably dressed in a charcoal skirt, an understated white silk blouse, and a soft cashmere sweater—the exact shade as her skirt—draped across posture-perfect shoulders. Yet it was Dr. Benton's sympathetic blue eyes, accepting smile, and crown of white curls—reminding Anne of the snowy egrets in Bubbling Springs Park—that proved most disarming to the emotionally vulnerable girl.

Dr. Benton administered a series of tests over the next two meetings. Anne was so anxious about the results; she almost didn't show up for the final session. Yet she needn't have worried. Benton, unlike other psychologists, spent most of the hour lauding her strengths. Anne, according to Benton, enjoyed an above-average IQ, an excellent sense of recall, and had scored in the ninetieth percentile on questions dealing with intellectual curiosity, attention to detail, ability to focus, and sense of right and wrong.

When Benton mentioned right and wrong, Anne was reminded of a job interview with the Port Cabrillo Police Department. Apparently, in response to the "Have you ever been convicted of a crime?" question, Anne had related, in mind-numbing detail, a story about stealing a candy bar.

Not only had Carina insisted that five-year-old Anne return her ill-gotten gains, but that she'd also have to confess to the grocery storeowner in person. The store's proprietor, not realizing how hypersensitive Anne was, decided, instead, to teach the wannabe thief a life lesson. He invited a neighborhood patrol officer, who was quite willing to play along, to join in the fun. But it wasn't much fun for Anne when the cop threatened to put the kindergartener in jail. Anne, apparently, was so traumatized, she hasn't been able to set foot in Tom's Mini-Mart to this day.

It wasn't that Dr. Benton had been blind to Anne's lack of social skills. The psychologist did share her notes with her patient concerning limited communication competence, insistence on processing information linearly, and an inability to discern being lied to or taken advantage of—vulnerabilities that would keep attracting emotional predators into Anne's life. What Dr. Benton tried to emphasize was that her disability had no inherent power to limit Anne in any significant way.

Anne was able to invest so much trust in Dr. Benton that she even disclosed the humiliation she suffered at the hands of junior-high-school bullies—something she had never even told her mother. The psychologist wisely suggested that Anne regularly journal her feelings—not only to exorcise her demons, but to also explore her obvious gift for writing. Ever since then, on the first day of every January, Anne starts a brand-new black-and-white composition book—and fills it with musings, short stories, drawings, and lists, during the rest of the year.

While most people admit to keeping some sort of "bucket list"—goals to accomplish or places to visit before one shuffles off this mortal coil—Anne, on the other hand, seems driven to record, for example, all the songs with the word "moon" in the title, or all the dog breeds with white fur, or all the news broadcasters with obvious hairpieces. Anne never knew when the compulsion to begin a new inventory—favorite Jackie Chan movies, ingredients that do not belong on pizza, undetectable poisons—might arise, but she always feels duty-bound to respond.

Dr. Benton also suggested specific career choices that played to Anne's gifts. After dismissing the first twenty as "boring," Anne fixated on "proof-reader," and despite her lack of training and journalistic experience, she applied for a position on the *Port Cabrillo Pilot* copy desk. When she passed the AP test on the first try, Old Man Lewis hired her on the spot. Ironically, No. 26 on Benton's list was "manuscript reader."

Even if Get-A-Clue Publications hadn't dismissed Anne, she still would have flown to Carina's side when summoned. Not only was Anne more than happy to serve as her mother's caretaker and companion, but she would also prove invaluable as a healthcare advocate. In fact, she so immersed herself into researching Carina's cancer, she became almost as knowledgeable as Carina's physicians themselves.

A diagnosis of a terminal illness forces most people to review their lives and Carina was no exception. She was forced to admit that her trio of little women hadn't turned out anything like the fictional March sisters. Without putting too fine a point on the metaphor, you could say Carina's relationship with Charlotte, Emily and Anne needed more restoration than her Victorian mansion.

While the triplets did show up for dinner a couple of times a year, they did so reluctantly. Carina was so intent on recapturing happier times, though, she invariably brought up one or another of the combination birthday/costume parties they held before Morgan's abrupt departure.

The triplets would just roll their eyes as Carina insisted on sharing memories of the over-the-top affairs that were not necessarily exorbitant, but always imaginative and unforgettable. The entire class—the triplets refused to be separated during their elementary school years—would be invited to the mansion for an enchanted afternoon. And beforehand, on New Year's Eve, the four of them would sit down and hash out their ideas for the upcoming party.

Carina's favorite brainstorming session occurred before their ninth and last birthday bash. The triplets, gathered under the Victorian chandelier in the dining room, couldn't wait to explore the creative possibilities the popular *Popeye* television cartoons provided as a party theme and couldn't help all talking at once.

"We could give prizes for costume categories," said Emily. "How about 'the most realistic?' "

"I'd really like to see an award for 'most original,' " said Charlotte.

" 'M-m-most h-h-humorous?' "

"And there's always 'most labor-intensive," added Carina.

"D-d-don't f-f-forget 'most unforgettable.' " They all laughed. "Well, how about turning 'Pin the Tail on the Donkey' into 'Pin the Anchor on Popeye's Arm?' "

"Uh, how do I say this, Annie-Fanny? Okay, three words: 'lame, lame, lame.' "

"Be civil, Charlotte," reprimanded Carina.

"But do you know what might be better?" asked Charlotte, ignoring the admonishment.

"No what?" asked Emily.

"How about we give every kid a henna tattoo?"

"So they could look like real sailors?" asked Emily.

"I don't think their parents would appreciate tattoos," said Carina.

"Henna is not permanent, you know."

"Yes, I know, Charlotte. I'll tell you what. I'll agree to henna tattoos if every guest brings me a signed permission slip."

"Well, you can forget about that. It's only fun when you do something your parents hate."

"So how about a 'Popeye' variation on a scavenger hunt?" asked Emily.

"No, Em. Scavenger hunts are boring."

"No, that's not true, Charlotte. We could make it a 'Save the Damsel in Distress' hunt, said Anne without stuttering.

"Like what?"

"Well, we could pose the question, 'Where did Bluto take Olive Oyl?' "

"Sheesh. Can't you do any better than that?"

"Okay, how about this? We could play 'Hot Potato'—with Swee'pea as 'the potato'?"

"No, Emily, that's child abuse."

"What all the kids would love is some kind of contest."

"Like what?"

"How about a 'How Fast Can You Diaper Swee'pea" contest?"

"Really, Emily—diapers?"

"And the prize can be—"

"I know. I know. One of those cool fake turds."

"Charlotte, is this how I raised you?"

"What about the music? There are some really cool songs in the cartoons."

"You are wise to do something with music, Emily. How about the best alternative lyrics to 'Popeye the Sailor Man'?" asked Carina.

"Are you serious?" said all three—in unison.

Anne, now turning to the birthday menu, exclaimed, "We absolutely have to have W-w-w-wimpy burgers."

"Absolutely."

"C-c-c-could the cake also be in the shape of Popeye's sailor hat?"

"I guess so."

"And we could serve it with green pistachio ice cream. Green, you know, like spinach?"

"Great idea, Emily."

"Maybe I could make up a Popeye word search as a party favor. What do you think?"

"I think that's perfect, Anne."

"I bet we could turn the entire second floor into Sweet Haven."

"How would we do that, Charlotte?"

"We could put signs on each door indicating whose residence it might be."

"Sure, we would have a door for Popeye."

"And Bluto and Geezil."

"Hmm, maybe a door for Ham Gravy?"

"And definitely for Olive Oyl and Swee'pea."

The guests' mothers even took it upon themselves to tailor their presents to the party theme as well. They emptied spinach cans of their original contents, washed them out, and refilled them with such coveted girly booty as a pretend compact and lipstick or a ball and jacks set or a coiled-up jump rope.

Carina considered it odd when Morgan, who always appeared as "The Handsome Prince" no matter what the actual party theme, was a no-show that year. In fact, he remained cloistered in his university office all afternoon. The triplets were terribly crushed, but their misery would only worsen seven short months later when he officially walked out of their lives.

When the triplets refused to celebrate birthday No. 10, Carina was devastated. "Is it because of your father?" she said, hoping it wasn't.

"Well, I don't know why you would ask that," said Emily, in an uncharacteristically brittle voice, "when he didn't bother to show up last year."

"No, it's not him," said Anne, but she wouldn't elaborate.

"Since Daddy doesn't care about us, I don't care about him," said Charlotte as she twirled a golden curl around her index finger.

"So what is it, my darlings?" said Carina, with equal parts alarm and dismay.

No one said a word. Charlotte surveyed the table. Blank looks all around. She knew she would have to be the one to speak up.

"Why do we always have to have one big party?" she inquired with a meaningful sigh.

Carina was puzzled. *Was it because it's my birthday as well? Did that fact take something away from the triplets' celebration? I don't even put my name on the birthday cake,* she thought to herself.

Emily looked at the chandelier. Anne looked at her shoes. Only Charlotte was willing to damn the hurt feelings and charge full speed ahead. "I don't want to share my birthday. I don't want to share my friends. I'm not just a Hunter triplet. I'm Charlotte. I just want it to be Charlotte's birthday. That's all I want."

Once more, Anne's eyes dropped down to her shoes. She couldn't meet her mother's eyes—she saw so much hurt in them. Emily started to say something, but after noticing Carina's crestfallen face, thought better of it. Yet both Anne and Emily agreed with Charlotte. They felt exactly the same way. They just lacked her intestinal fortitude—and her glorious way with words.

Carina's cheeks burned with embarrassment. She was just about to unload her own feelings on her thankless brood, but as she looked around, she decided her best course of action was simply to exit the room. She knew she wouldn't have been able to rein in her anger and frustration once she got started anyway.

While Carina had stopped dressing the triplets in identical outfits once the freebie clothes ran out, she had to admit she often thought of them as a unit—an unholy trinity, as it were.

She'd never realized that she might be unconsciously damaging their sense of individuality. And while she knew intellectually that Emily and Charlotte were unique human beings, she rarely, as Charlotte's complaint correctly alleged, dug underneath their physically identical exteriors to honor the considerable differences in their personalities, interests, and gifts.

Because Anne's peculiarities were off-putting to Charlotte and Emily, they never developed much of a relationship with her. Carina had been guilty of rarely challenging Anne's solitary puttering or periodic withdrawals to her room that had permitted Anne to carve out the life of an only child.

In fact, as an only child herself, Carina had especially envied the interdependence between Charlotte and Emily. She just couldn't understand their drive in adolescence to separate from each other. While they hadn't asked to change bedrooms, the secret passage no longer concealed clandestine twin business. Their secret twin vocabulary had also disappeared. And while she had expected their taste in clothes to diverge at some point—she was shocked when they started to acquire different friends. Yet what seemed to upset Carina the most was the cycle of bickering that developed as competition replaced collaboration in their relationship.

And although the Hunter triplets claimed that calling a halt to their collective birthday parties had nothing to do with Morgan, Carina simply didn't believe them.

By the time the triplets were ready for college, Carina held no expectation that they would attend the same university. Why should they? They were financially free to choose any school they fancied—their paternal grandparents had already agreed to pick up the tab. Nor was Carina surprised when none of them even considered Santa Lucia University.

Jeanne Tolliver, who regularly kept in touch with Carina, recently reported that while Morgan's novel was still a "work in progress," the promise of its publication—a false promise as it turned out—had earned him tenure.

The administration had also been impressed with Morgan's Oxford program, which entailed overseeing twenty seniors studying pre-Victorian literature abroad. Not only did the Oxford program provide an opportunity for Morgan to get out of the country every spring, but also out from under the steely eye of Dr. Bonita Burnett, the nervous English Department chair. When she finally realized that rumors of Morgan's dalliances with female students were probably not merely rumors, she had been unable to uncover sufficient evidence to take proper action.

While Carina was eventually able to let go of her failed marriage, she could still get herself worked up over his insensitivity to his daughters' feelings. A recent case in point involved Morgan and school photographs. The triplets had innocently requested that Carina address an envelope for them. They had decided to gift their father with their grade-school portraits. The envelope, however, was returned, unopened, with "return to sender," scrawled across the front—in the red ink Morgan routinely used to grade papers.

Carina, of course, rang up Eugenie, who agreed that an immediate mother-son lunch was in order. Morgan calmly informed his mother that he was sorry, but he simply wasn't cut out to be a father. "I'm an author," he said. "Finishing my novel is the top priority in my life. If you feel the need to be close to the triplets, feel free to do so. Just leave me out of it. I'm just not interested."

Early in their marriage, Carina realized that Morgan was "just not interested" in teaching as well. He found his students to be "provincial and parochial"—except for the few who hung out at his favorite watering hole, or who were bright enough to take him on during a debate. Although he relished a lively discussion about gun control or ending the war in Vietnam, his favorite subject, by far, was religious hypocrisy.

In fact, Morgan led a group of newly hired faculty members into recommending that Santa Lucia University abandon its religious roots. The professors, who came primarily from the sciences, argued that secularization, especially at a time when religious institutions of higher education were being shuttered all across the country, would be the only way to keep SLU from going belly-up.

Yet the administration and board of regents stuck fast to the mission statement. They were convinced that enough parents would be willing to fork over hefty tuition checks, if the university would adopt two relatively easy fixes: 1) to strictly enforce campus regulations against underage drinking and premarital sex and 2) to offer a money-back guarantee that a degree at SLU would take no more than four years. As a result, Santa Lucia University not only remained afloat; it garnered impressive scores by university-ranking entities.

Carina wondered what her life might have been like if she had graduated in 1964 as planned. Instead, finding herself pregnant with triplets, she opted to sacrifice everything—her relationship with her parents, her education, and her future as an English professor. Yet despite making the tough choice then, there was no subsequent payoff now. Carina was alienated from her children, and they, in turn, were alienated from each other.

The end of her life, now closer by days rather than years, was pushing Carina to make things right. Her attorney, Stan Gardner threw up his hands at the questionable codicil she insisted on adding to her will. While the legal language stipulated that although her daughters would still inherit the bulk of her estate, they would not be able to liquidate her stock portfolio, empty her bank accounts, or sell her mansion *until all three of them had resided in Thomas House for no fewer than twenty-four months.*

Carina's daughters had no idea how wealthy a woman she really was. Even after the Inspector Meadow series took off, she refused to abandon her penny-pinching ways. To Carina's way of thinking, royalty checks could cease as swiftly as they had commenced. She never would have dreamt that her publisher would still be making payments to her estate for more than two decades following her death. Carina had invested so well, albeit conservatively, that her present portfolio, even without the sale of her beloved Victorian mansion, would make each of her little women multi-millionaires.

When Stan informed Carina that the codicil she had in mind would not only be unenforceable, but it would, in all certainty, lose to the feeblest of court challenges, Carina instructed him to mind his own business. She signed the amended document and added three sealed envelopes to her file.

"I want you to call my daughters to your office, read my last will and testament with as much authority as you can muster, and solemnly hand each daughter her envelope. Do you understand my wishes, Stanley?"

The attorney nodded, yet couldn't help thinking that her clumsy attempt at manipulation, even if backed up by a multimillion-dollar incentive, still wouldn't glue her Humpty Dumpty family back together again.

Yet, with Carina dead and buried, he had enacted, as instructed, the first phrase of her eleventh-hour family restoration project. Unfortunately, by refusing to attend the reading of the will, Emily and Charlotte had essentially pre-empted the rest of Carina's plan.

Stan felt her pain.

Chapter 13: Happy Valentine's Day

February 14, 1972

Sergeant Michael Miller may have flunked the detective test twice, but he ended up as the top case-closer in San Perdido County.

He was so highly regarded by county prosecutors because his testimony could always be counted on to be solid and irrefutable. He never got rattled while being questioned—no matter how snarky the insinuations or bullying the tactics of the defense attorney. Miller liked to believe that his innate honesty was self-evident to every member of the jury.

Miller, who tried for a forceful yet noncombative demeanor whenever he appeared on the stand, had been visibly shocked when, in open court, a public defender called him "a self-righteous prig." Miller would later chalk up the name-calling to sheer desperation. *The attorney* thought Miller, *must have realized that his client was as guilty as sin.*

Miller also deliberately patterned his delivery after the "just the facts, ma'am" detective on *Dragnet*—although his police colleagues weren't hip enough to appreciate his homage to Jack Webb. Very few people knew that his fondest childhood memories arose from play-acting with the bespectacled ten-year-old Danny Gillespie who played Officer Frank Smith to his Joe Friday.

Whenever Miller testified in court, he donned a black wool suit, a white cotton shirt with French cuffs, and a tasteful yet conservative tie. Since he had been grilled only this morning, that's exactly what he was wearing as he ordered a BLT at the courthouse coffee shop. As he waited for his sandwich, he found himself absentmindedly fingering his lucky cufflinks—twirling the left one around so that the engraved MM faced forward. He wondered when the verdict would be returned.

Andres Aguilar was being tried on two counts of first-degree murder. The first charge was for the premeditated killing of Truman Carpenter. While the jury had been shown photos of the Santa Lucia sophomore's brutally beaten body, the bloody baseball bat left behind the nightclub that featured female impersonators, and the word "faggot" spray-painted on the asphalt, there was really insufficient evidence to convict. The killer had left no forensic evidence and no witnesses had come forward.

During the investigation, Miller had become increasingly more frustrated. Every would-be lead resulted in a dead end. His luck would turn one week later, however, when Aguilar chose to attack another homosexual in exactly the same location. He and a couple of his buddies had gotten tanked up at Fernando's Place on Anchor Road, jumped into Aguilar's rusted-out pickup truck, and set out to "troll for queers." Once again, Aguilar had armed himself with a baseball bat.

Felipe Gutierrez, whose family restaurant was located directly across the alley from the first murder scene, had the police station number on his speed dial. The second the man dressed as Marilyn Monroe started screaming, Gutierrez sprang into action. A squad car arrived within five minutes. The officers apprehended Aguilar "red-handed," so to speak—still swinging the blood-stained Louisville slugger. Aguilar's friends, who had been egging him on during the assault, attempted, unsuccessfully, to flee the scene. They ended up testifying against Aguilar in exchange for immunity from prosecution.

Although Aguilar denied having anything to do with the college student, when Norman Mortenson, AKA "Marilyn," died en route to the hospital, the deputy district attorney tacked on a second count of premeditated murder. Miller figured that Lindy Lindstrom should be thanking his lucky stars for being handed such a slam-dunk case. While only circumstantial evidence linked Aguilar to the first homicide, being able to serve up police officers as eyewitnesses to the second, played exceedingly well with the jury. Lindstrom was so confident in the outcome, he requested the death penalty.

What Lindstrom couldn't predict was that California would take a four-year hiatus from executions—due to unconstitutionality rulings by both U.S. and California Supreme Courts. Still, to the San Perdido County prosecutor, being able to slap Aguilar with two consecutive life terms wasn't exactly the makings of a worst-case scenario.

Despite having solved both the Carpenter and Mortensen homicides, Miller was still getting nowhere on the Cesar Castillo case. When Officer Spencer finally handed the missing persons file over to Miller, it held a single sheet of paper. To Miller's way of thinking, Spencer's missing-persons report was missing a report.

Spencer had neglected to collect information concerning Castillo's vital statistics, what he was last seen wearing, and any distinguishing physical characteristics. Not only didn't he check for Cesar's fingerprints on file, but hadn't bothered to interview Cesar's wife, the rest of the Castillo family, the guests at the bachelor party, or either of Cesar's employers. He made no requests for bank account information, credit card statements, or telephone records. Worst of all, he hadn't even obtained the license plate number on Cesar's car.

It seemed obvious to Miller that Spencer had already retired; he just hadn't gotten around to filing the paperwork. Miller, on the other hand, was no slacker. He became as agitated as an OCD victim stepping in doggie doo doo when he wasn't able to fill in every single blank or question every possible source.

The first thing Miller did when he took over the case was to consult the arrest files. He was pretty sure that due to his ethnicity, Spencer had written off Castillo as just another gang-banger. Miller, however, wasn't at all surprised to learn that both twins were squeaky clean—not even a late book fine at the local library.

When Miller conducted his follow-up sessions at the Castillo home, Maricela was more than willing to chat; she just didn't have anything new to disclose. As far as she was concerned, her marriage to Cesar was all lollipops and roses. There were no credit card balances because there were no credit cards. A savings account holding $1,200 had been earmarked as a down payment on a house. "For the present," she had said, "We pay Angelica four hundred dollars a month rent." Not only did they own the 1963 Volkswagen free and clear, but the registration, license and insurance were also up-to-date.

Eduardo Gomez told Miller couldn't understand why Cesar hadn't shown up for work on Monday. The last time he saw him, Gomez told Miller, was Friday, around four o'clock. He considered the twins "part of the family," and as Miller recalled, when Gomez said "family," he actually choked up. "Cesar has been working for me ever since he could correctly identify a crescent wrench," Gomez said, wiping a tear from his eye. "He could do no wrong as far as I am concerned."

Gutierrez reported seeing Cesar arrive on time Saturday afternoon but did not see him leave after he dismissed the entire wait staff at eight p.m. He also told Miller about having to lay down the law concerning football but "after our little talk," said Gutierrez, "Cesar finally got his head screwed on straight." Miller took his words to mean that Cesar had finally acquiesced to Gutierrez's authority—relinquishing his football scholarship in order to retain a tips-only position at the restaurant.

"I understand, Mr. Gutierrez," said Miller, but what the detective, who had also worked his way through college, understood—was what an SOB Gutierrez was. It seemed to Miller that Gutierrez resented Cesar for going after a diploma—as if Cesar wanting to better himself was somehow personally offensive to the old man.

Miller also contacted every bachelor party guest. They all remembered seeing one or both twins, off and on during the evening, but for the most part, nobody "was in any condition (wink, wink, nod, nod) to keep track." Even after thirty interviews, Miller learned nothing new.

As to Destiny Rodriguez, she told Miller that she did, indeed, arrive around one o'clock. She also admitted that she always flirted with her feather boa.

"Pretty mild stuff," she said in her honeyed voice. She had already figured out "that going overboard in the come-on department—especially with a bunch of drunks—was asking for trouble." She could only recall two names. The groom's she had learned for obvious reasons, but there was also this good-looking Latino. As she told Miller, before pivoting on her five-inch stiletto heels to leave, "I'm attracted to handsome dudes—but only those who don't realize how handsome they really are."

"So how did you know he didn't realize how handsome he really was?" the detective persisted in his Joe Friday monotone.

"Because," she said, "he turned the same shade of red as my feathers when I called him '*Provocativo*.' "

"With *Provocativo*," the detective burst out laughing. "And his name was?"

"Cesar," she said.

*****

Back at his office, Miller was just about to sit at his desk when the phone rang. *Why would the executive director at the Port of Cabrillo wish to speak with me?* He waited patiently as the secretary clicked over to her boss's inside line.

"This Philip Berylwood," announced a rich baritone.

"Any relation to 'The Honorable?' " asked Miller.

The Honorable Thomas R. Berylwood was probably better known to the residents of San Perdido County than the retired railroad tycoon who built Thomas House. In 1868, Berylwood purchased more than 21, 000 acres from Colonel Thomas, most of which he would subdivide and sell at a tidy profit. The remainder was either farmed or became the city of Port Cabrillo, which Berylwood named for the Portuguese explorer who landed there in 1542.

The two men, indirectly related by marriage, had both been employed by the Pennsylvania railroad—one as the president and the other as an agent—but their paths didn't cross until the War Between the States when Berylwood's courage and competence so impressed Colonel Thomas, he later hired him to supervise his business interests in California, even though he was twenty years younger and held no management experience.

Berylwood's first task was to acquire an array of oil-drilling machinery. The equipment, originally manufactured in New York, was to be transported by ship around Cape Horn and then up the coast to the Port of San Francisco.

Once in San Francisco, the gear would be loaded on a smaller ship and sailed back down the coast to San Perdido, where large rafts would surf the heavy machinery to shore. It made no sense to Berylwood to waste so much time and money, but since Southern California lacked a deep-water port, he possessed no alternative.

Berylwood, however, would soon hear about a thousand-foot submarine canyon with what was essentially an underwater river running through it—just off the coast of Port Cabrillo. The real attraction for Berylwood would be the ability to construct a silt-free harbor without costly annual dredging fees, thanks to Mother Nature.

While Berylwood would complete the Cabrillo Wharf in 1872, he left development of the port to his eldest son. Richard Berylwood would spend the next fourteen years attempting to realize his father's dream by negotiating with Washington D.C., persuading the family to deed over the required acreage, and convincing the good people of San Perdido County to pass a million-dollar construction bond.

"I'm sorry, but I just had to ask," said Miller.

"Don't be sorry. Everybody asks—especially now, Detective, that I'm in this job."

"So how do you like Port Cabrillo?"

"I must say "The Welcoming Little City by the Sea" is more than a public-relations slogan. Everybody has been incredibly friendly."

"So how you are related to Thomas R. Berylwood?"

"My father was the youngest of his eight children. I'm named Archibald, after him."

"But I thought you said your name was Philip."

"I did, but neither my father nor I were very fond of the name 'Archibald.' "

"Was your father also involved with the Port?"

"Not in the least, Detective Miller. He was a physiologist. He specialized in the brain."

"The brain, you say?"

"My father headed the Department of Physiology at the Harvard Medical School. After his first wife died, he remarried. She was a colleague from Johns Hopkins. I was born a year later."

"So you didn't follow in your father's footsteps?"

"Hell, no—far from it. Apparently, I was a big disappointment in that regard. No white lab coat for me. At thirteen, I fell in love with a Mercedes-Benz at the Port of Baltimore. In truth, I received the lion's share of my vocational education just by hanging out there."

"At the Port of Baltimore?"

"That's where most Mercedes-Benz automobiles enter this country. And that's when I told my father I would be running a port by the time I turned twenty-one."

"And what did he say to that?"

"He said he wanted to examine my cerebral cortex. Personally."

"But, said Miller laughing, "That still doesn't explain how you ended up in California."

"I worked most of the ports up and down the Atlantic coast, trying to beef up the administrative experience portion of my resume. Last year, I was named executive director at New Bedford."

"But you're still not in Port Cabrillo yet, Mr. Berylwood."

"You're right. I'd only been in Massachusetts for about six months when a headhunter dropped by and asked if I'd be interested in relocating to the West Coast. To Port Cabrillo, to be exact."

"And you said, 'I don't mind if I do.'"

Now it was Berylwood's turn to laugh.

"Since you answered all my questions, Mr. Berylwood, please let me know what I can do for you."

"No, Detective Miller, it's what I can do for you. We have managed to locate a 'drowned' Volkswagen. It's halfway across the channel from Berth Three."

"So, you must have heard that I've been looking for a '63 VW? Tell me, Berylwood, is yours metallic blue-green?"

"We won't be able to identify the color or the year until the crane pulls it up. Would you like to be there?"

"You bet your sweet . . . yes. One thing, though, how did you locate the car if it was underwater?"

"That's another story."

"Don't tell me a ship ran into it."

"Oh no, thank goodness for that. It happened when we were dredging—well, not so much dredging."

"Wait a minute," Miller interrupted, "as I understand it, the whole point of building a deep water port at Port Cabrillo was to take advantage of the silt-free harbor. 'The Honorable' wasn't mistaken about that, was he?"

"Absolutely not. What we removed wasn't silt at all. It was lead paint residue left by all the ships docking here during the past forty years."

"And here I assumed that the safety experts only worried about toddlers snacking on lead-painted windowsills."

"That's what ship owners also wanted to believe. They prefer painting their hulls with lead because it dries faster and lasts longer."

"So what's the big deal about a few paint chips at the bottom of the sea?"

"Ah, Detective, haven't you heard that lead can be just as toxic to aquatic life as it is to human beings?"

"And since we eat seafood?"

"Exactly, Detective."

"But rest assured, I'm still not giving up my fish tacos."

"And I wouldn't blame you," said Berylwood, "See you soon."

*****

Seagulls seemed to appear and disappear as they wheeled through the intermittent overcast overhead. The stench of diesel oil and decaying tires was giving Miller a headache, but he was more concerned with balancing his 180 pounds on the uneven riprap. Even after a few minutes of practice, he still didn't feel secure. Fierce winds were likewise doing their best to propel him into the drink, but the jetty provided, undeniably, the best seat in the house.

Besides, to Miller, an afternoon spent on the waterfront was a welcome change from his windowless cubicle at the police station. Miller's colleagues knew better than to get him started on "that unsightly architectural monstrosity" that was City Hall. In addition to the police station, City Hall housed the Hall of Records, the City Council chambers, and various municipal offices.

Binoculars weren't necessary for Miller to spot the U.S. Coast Guard diver, even though he was attired in a black wetsuit and black mask. His neon-yellow oxygen tanks glowed like a psychedelic poster under black light. Miller watched as the diver secured a thick cable to the VW from the fifty-ton dock crane that would haul it out of the water. A curious harbor seal swam by just as the diver's long black fins flipped straight up in the air and then descended forty-two feet below.

When the water was calm, an observer like Miller could spot bonito and barracuda rummaging around the sunken breakwater rocks for lunch. Today, though, the water in front of Wharf 1 was awash in whitecaps and the Weather Service had clocked the winds at forty miles per hour. Perhaps it had been an equally breezy day when the Bug rolled off the pier. That's the only explanation Miller could come up with for a VW submerged so far out in the channel.

No Beetle is actually airtight, but as anybody who has ever owned one knows, you have to open the window if you intend to slam the door shut. Actually, the Beetle gained its reputation for staying afloat thanks to a clever advertising campaign launched during the Sixties. In the commercial, the driver plunges his Volkswagen straight into a lake. As the vehicle glides along the shore, the driver rolls down the window, leans his head out and asks, "Now, what other car gives you this kind of quality, for this kind of price?"

Still a Volkswagen cannot float forever—despite the improbable moat scene in *Castle Keep*. Miller estimated it took a good forty minutes for the vehicle to drift across the channel. Within an hour, however, the car would have completely filled with seawater, slowly bubbled its way down to the bottom, and ultimately snuggled into the mire.

A metallic glint of reflected sunlight caught Miller's attention. He waited impatiently for the roof of the VW to break through the surface of the water. Torrents of mud and water drained from every aperture. Miller had to admit he was impressed as the crane effortlessly swung the car over and deposited it on the dock. The vehicle was positioned front end first, so the license plate was not immediately visible. *It's time to get a closer look.*

The diver who first discovered the car reported that there was no body inside and a seatbelt had been tied to the steering wheel. Since Miller knew that a Volkswagen trunk was far too small to conceal a corpse, he was hoping that the glove compartment, at least, might yield a new lead. *Finally, I can see the license plate. Well, almost all of it.* Unfortunately, mud covered the final digit. *ABF 14. Hmm, that's an exact match—so far.*

The last time Detective Miller had received a token of affection on February 14th, he was in middle school. His mother had sprung for a humorous valentine from the local drugstore— something she hadn't done before or since. She had purchased the greeting card, she said, because the punch line made her laugh out loud and she figured her son might need cheering up now that Danny Gillespie had moved away. It had been a thoughtful gesture on her part and Miller had never really expressed his appreciation. *But if this license plate actually checks out, it would be the best Valentine's Day gift, ever.*

Chapter 14: For Sale by Owner

January 2, 1971

Adolf Hitler maintained that a "People's Car" should be available for easy purchase across the Fatherland. He ordered Ferdinand Porsche to design something that was fuel-efficient, cost no more than a motorcycle, could comfortably transport two adults and three children, and was able to attain least sixty-two miles per hour. The last qualification was added to allow travel on Hitler's greatest public works project, the Autobahn.

In 1938, Hitler officially christened his automobile the KDF-Wagen—KDF standing for *Kraft durch Freude* or "powered by joy." Yet it was hardly a joy to operate such a minimalist vehicle. The driver stopped the car with mechanical drum brakes, turned over the air-cooled engine with a starting crank, indicated which direction he was turning with mechanical flaps, changed gears without synchromesh, squinted to see out of postage-stamp-sized windows, backed up without benefit of a rearview mirror, and sat on an unpadded seat. As to the number of cup holders, don't even ask.

Legend has it the Feds proposed that Henry Ford II take over the VW Works after World War II at absolutely no cost to him. Ford's right-hand man Ernest Breech advised, "What we're being offered here, Mr. Ford, isn't worth a damn." Yet despite its many shortcomings, the "People's Car" still holds the record as most-manufactured automobile of a single design anywhere on the planet.

Cesar Castillo, however, didn't know any of this when he went car-shopping. He just thought it would be cool to own a Beetle. For several weeks, he worried the classified ads from three different newspapers. Finally, the *Los Angeles Herald-Chronicle* yielded a used-car advertisement bonanza: "By owner, 1963 Volkswagen, 80K miles, leatherette upholstery, $500, or best offer."

"What do you think, Cruz?"

"Hell, Bro. That's a Beverly Hills phone number. That's too far to go for a used car."

"Look, *Jefa* will let us take the Skylark, and you aren't really doing anything today. It's exactly what I have been looking for. Don't be such a *tonto del culo*."

Cruz decided not to be such a *tonto del culo* and got out his map. When the twins finally arrived at the Oakhurst Apartments, they felt they were on the set of a Doris Day movie. For openers, the stucco on the front of the structure was tinted a flamingo pink. A black-and-white-striped awning protected the entrance. And the palm trees in the parkway provided absolutely no shade.

Charity Russell lived in Apt. 204, which required a climb up a black winding staircase. She told Cesar on the phone that she was nurse and needed to leave for work by three o'clock. The Castillo twins arrived around two-fifteen.

"I didn't see any Volkswagens parked on the street."

"This is Beverly Hills," said Cesar, in his know-it-all voice. "She probably keeps the car in a covered space in the back."

When Charity opened the door, the irresistible fragrance of scalloped ham, onion, and potato casserole not only tickled Cesar's nostrils but also reminded him that he hadn't eaten since breakfast. He said, "Hi," and the substantial black woman in blue scrubs responded in kind.

He noticed that her hair had been chemically straightened and pulled back into a short pageboy—the sides tucked behind generous ears decorated with small gold hoops. She ushered him in and asked if he wanted anything to drink—an offer that didn't include, Cesar noted with disappointment, a portion of casserole.

Charity was just about to close the door when she caught sight of Cruz, who had been delayed by a protracted search for a parking spot. Her dark, almost plum-colored face broke into a toothy grin. "So you are twins," she said, barely able to contain a chuckle.

"Yes, I'm Cruz. It's only Cesar, though, who is in the market for a car."

"Don't worry, my sister's VW is not for sale." At that particular moment, as if on cue, a young woman, the mirror image of Charity, sauntered out into the living room. The only difference between the two was their attire. Charity's twin was dressed in blue jeans and a UCLA sweatshirt.

"H-e-e-re's Hope," said Charity, as if introducing the host of *The Tonight Show*. The two boys tried not to laugh, but they were totally unsuccessful.

Still chuckling, Cruz cracked, "Apparently we have arrived at the residence of the Double Mint twins."

"Oh, how I wish that were true," said Hope. "But then I would have supposed that you two got the call first."

"Nope, not even a postcard from Mr. Wrigley," said Cruz, now flashing his pearly whites. "So exactly what are the odds of a random meeting between two sets of identical twins?"

"Actually pretty good," said Charity. "More than three sets of twins come along in every one-hundred births."

"And Charity ought to know," said Hope. "She delivers babies for a living."

"Actually we're both pediatric nurses," explained Charity.

"You said on the phone," said Cesar, checking his Swatch, "you have to leave in about twenty-five minutes. Do you have to travel far?"

"I'm at the Children's Hospital at Vermont and Sunset. Hope works at UCLA."

"Regrettably, when we both finished our training," said Charity, tugging her loose top down over her ample rear, "we were unable to secure employment at the same hospital."

"So that's why we chose Oakhurst. It's centrally located—exactly halfway between both hospitals."

"That's nice. Isn't that nice, Cesar?"

Charity made a face at Cruz. "I'd just love to continue chatting with you guys, but I've really got to get to work."

"So let's see this car."

The vehicle was parked in a numbered space at the back of the building. It was the stock VW gulf blue with seats upholstered in silver-beige faux leather. The plastic steering wheel, in Cruz's opinion, could have used a bit more Bon Ami.

When Cesar asked if he could start up the car, Charity handed him a key fob in the shape of the letter "C"—perfect for somebody named Cesar had it not been covered in rhinestones. He fired up the engine. It sounded like a gas lawnmower, but as he allowed the engine to idle, he was pleased to find it solidly chugging along. *Always a good sign when the engine doesn't die right away.* Depressing the clutch, he engaged the four forward gears as well as reverse. *No problem in the transmission department, either, as far as I can tell.*

While the exterior was not exactly in pristine condition—having suffered eight years of benign neglect—it was still acceptable. The mileage appeared to be exactly as advertised. While the standard black hubcaps would have to go, and the original paint was badly faded, it was still a steal of a deal. Still the bargain-hunter in Cesar prickled to do better. "Would you take $400?"

"No, I'm afraid not. My asking price is already one hundred dollars below Blue Book as it is." Cesar knew she was right, but his dickering gene would not be denied. Besides, the advertisement had specifically said, "or best offer." Still she might just walk away if he insulted her any further, so he decided to take a different tack, "Are you the original owner?"

"Yes, both Hope and I were given brand-new Volkswagens the day we graduated college. Hope's Beetle is parked five stalls down. The only difference is the last number on the license plate." *And needing an auto mechanic as a boyfriend*, Charity thought to herself. Her car was a lemon and she would be greatly relieved to be rid of it.

"My plate number is ABF 144 and Charity's is ABF 145," said Hope.

"A graduation gift from your parents?" said Cesar. "How bitchin' is that?"

"Well, not from both of our parents. Our mother—her name was Faith—is deceased.

"Sorry to hear that," said Cruz, who shot Cesar a "stifle that snicker" look. "And your father?"

"Daddy is still around. He's a physician practicing up in Santa Barbara. That's where we grew up."

"So why did he choose a VW?"

"Daddy knew we would be needing an economical car. The Volkswagens cost $1500 each, but that was back in 1963. We actually asked for convertibles, but Daddy wouldn't hear of it."

"While we did appreciate the great gas mileage, I think Daddy chose these two in particular because neither came equipped with a radio. He believed that listening to music while driving was distracting."

"In fact, he constantly harped about the number of rock-and-roll-lovers who ended up in his ER."

"Good thing he never saw us applying *mascara* while we were behind the wheel."

"So why don't you want to hang on to this car?" said Cesar. "Is there something wrong with it?"

"Well, the vehicle is eight years old, but I've always kept up the routine maintenance."

"Anything else?" said Cesar, not catching Charity's evasion.

"The car has given me absolutely no trouble," she finally responded, which was, of course, an outright lie.

Cesar, who gave Charity credibility points for her open face, nurturing vocation, and first name, however, was sold. "Are you prepared to sign over the pink slip today?"

Cruz remained uncharacteristically silent—but only because he realized Cesar was madly in love with the car.

"Why, yes, I am," said Charity, without so much as a blink. "It's right here in my pocket."

Her twin Hope, however, would soon have reason to wish she had also put her car up for sale. One week later, in broad daylight, somebody would pinch her VW from the hospital parking lot.

The police officer taking her stolen vehicle report couldn't help himself, "There's not enough faith, hope, or charity in all of Beverly Hills to bring that little Bug back to you," he quipped. The Volkswagen, according to the cop, was especially popular among car thieves, and he had no doubt that it would end up at a chop shop being cannibalized for parts.

The police officer couldn't have been more wrong. Hope's Beetle ended up being drowned—at the bottom of the harbor in Port Cabrillo.

Chapter 15: Emily Always Had a Thing for Dogs

January 21, 2011

While both Charlotte and Emily requested Barbies for their seventh birthdays, Charlotte stipulated the attorney version while Emily only had eyes for the law-enforcement doll. In the midst of perusing the Barbie section at the local toy store, Carina not only wondered what sort of judge would have welcomed a wasp-waisted lawyer in a micro-miniskirt into his courtroom, but also if Mattel might just be hedging its bet with Police Officer Barbie—the box containing her navy blue uniform also held an elegant champagne-colored cocktail dress.

While Emily had a tough time fitting her doll's curly blonde locks under the snug-fitting uniform cap—something she would experience as a real-life policewoman—she was tickled silly with the authentic uniform, handcuffs, and other tools of the trade. What she couldn't understand was why her parents had confiscated the doll's gun. Yet neither Morgan nor Carina would be swayed. No firearms would be allowed in their home—no matter how minuscule. *End of discussion.*

While girlfriends would tell Emily, who was reed-thin at 115 pounds, how fortunate she was, Emily would invariably respond that she would have gladly exchanged her tastefully small breasts for Barbie's more ostentatious display of pulchritude. And although Emily had always been athletic, when she entered the police academy, she discovered she couldn't lift as much weight, jump as high, or run as fast as the men. Refusing, however, to hold a pity party for herself or settling for some lower female standard, she invested all her free time in working out. In a few short months, her physical fitness marks were as respectable as her male colleagues.

Emily discovered three important insights during her academy days. First, the bad guy wasn't going to handicap himself so she could catch him—she would have to sprint quicker than any perp. Second, she wasn't the only recruit having issues with numbers. She discovered that men of color, because of their ethnic diets, had just as much trouble meeting minimum standards for BMI and blood pressure as she did with her PT scores. Third, once Emily began thinking of her gym time as an opportunity to network and establish professional relationships, her resentment evaporated as quickly as her limitations. Now, nearly twenty-five years later, the twenty-two male police officers under her command wouldn't, in their wildest dreams, confuse Emily with Police Officer Barbie.

Emily announced that her No. 1 priority as the top cop in Port Cabrillo would be building up the K-9 unit. Even as a youngster, Emily had a thing for dogs—even though Carina proved allergic to canine dander. After a tiny (she could snooze inside Carina's bedroom slipper) Yorkie pup followed her home, Emily researched hypoallergenic breeds at the Port Cabrillo Library. With the news that Yorkshire Terriers don't produce dander, all Tiffy had to do to win Carina's heart was crawl into her lap and start snoring. That very afternoon, the parsimonious Carina purchased a designer leash and harness from a high-end pet shop downtown.

Although Emily dutifully tacked up "Found Dog" signs around the neighborhood, when nobody came forward to claim Tiffy (*Breakfast at Tiffany's* being Emily's favorite movie), she became the first of three Yorkies to call Thomas House home.

Tiffy took to training like a Jerusalem artichoke to sunshine. Within a week, she was housebroken. Within two weeks, she grasped the idea that once she climbed inside Emily's purse she was to go into stealth mode—silent and invisible. As long as she complied, heavenly manna in the form of dog treats dropped into the carrier. Tiffy was eventually smuggled into restaurants, movie theaters, and stores—even church, on a couple of occasions.

Emily continued to teach her new dog old tricks. Tiffy would act out heart-wrenching death scenes when shot by Emily's finger, provide vocal accompaniment to Carina's piano playing, and fetch specific toys (squeaky ball, stuffed bunny, rubber veterinarian) on command. Emily even coaxed Tiffy into fetching the newspaper—no mean feet for a canine that weighed far less than the Sunday edition.

A dog, Emily used to say, marked both the beginning and end of her four-year marriage. She met Michael Harrigan on Santa Catalina Island. The dazzlingly robust outdoorsman with curly blond hair had been urging his Jeep up a hill when she got her first look. He seemed attractive enough, but his desirability quotient got a big boost once she spotted a beautiful black Labrador retriever on his passenger seat. She hadn't, however, anticipated what would happen once he whipped off his designer shades. Her knees nearly buckled as she lost herself in his glacial blue eyes.

Michael was attached to the Los Angeles Sheriff's Department but had been assigned the enviable task of patrolling the so-called "Island of Romance," located, if you believe the Four Preps, "twenty-six miles across the sea." It was his task that particular morning to drive Emily from Catalina's celebrated Airport in the Sky to an at-risk youth camp on the far side of the island.

After a whirlwind courtship, and despite Carina's words of caution, the couple wed and took up residence in San Pedro. Lucy and Heather, a terrier-mix rescued by Emily after her master became a homicide victim, cohabited with the couple. The two canines got on famously, both accompanying Mike to Catalina whenever Emily taught a special leadership class in New York.

After a particularly grueling week on the East Coast, Emily couldn't wait to get back to her hubby and the "kids." If ninety-degree heat and ninety percent humidity hadn't brought out Emily's grouchy side, a couple of petulant students did. She was looking forward to spending a romantic night under the stars. When Emily arrived at the secluded campground, however, only Lucy romped out to greet her. "Where's Heather?" she asked Michael.

"I'm sorry, Em, I don't know how to tell you this," he said, strangling on the last word. Finally, after finding the painful silence between them unbearable, he croaked, "She's dead."

"She's dead? What happened?" Emily's voice and hands were shaking.

"I, uh, I guess you would say that she drowned."

"Drowned?" Her voice had dropped so low he could hardly hear her. "What are you talking about?" she tried to say calmly. "Heather won't go anywhere near the water. And the ocean—you know how much hates the ocean."

"I had to tie her to a pier piling."

"Why would you do that?" said Emily, still refusing to raise her voice.

"I couldn't take her with me. I guess I just didn't think about the tide. I mean I didn't think it would come in, you know, before I returned."

"You didn't think the tide would come in?" Emily was getting the picture now, and her outrage was definitely getting the upper hand. "What the hell are you talking about, Michael?"

"Well, there was this young lady . . . "

"A young lady? Are you serious?"

"Well, she was sunbathing on her daddy's yacht and she invited me onboard for a little drink."

"A drink? While you were on duty?"

"Well, yeah—just one. Then I guess—. Well, you know how it is. One thing led to another," he admitted sheepishly. "And—"

"And? And I can hardly believe you are telling me this. How could you, Michael?"

Michael may have had nothing more to say, but Emily did. "Good job," she seethed. "I hope you realize just what you did."

Michael just stared at her. There wasn't an smidgen of remorse in his glacial blue eyes.

"You killed my dog," she said, "and our marriage—all on the same day."

Before Emily took over the department in Port Cabrillo, a single black and tan Doberman assisted Officer Anthony Trueblood in the field. But Emily had again done her research, and in a twenty-page proposal to the Port Cabrillo City Council, she argued that acquiring four more dogs would be the productivity-increasing equivalent of adding four new officers to the force.

While the initial investment would be steep—$20,000 to purchase and train each dog—officers of the canine variety, she maintained, would not have to be compensated with a $60,000 base salary or comprehensive heath insurance or a hefty pension after retirement. All a police dog would require was a bowl of kibble, weekly baths, and the occasional kind word.

Since no line item for increasing the K-9 unit existed in the budget, though, Emily was forced to go forth, uniform hat in hand, and beg for donations. And that was exactly what she was doing on that rainy day in January. Having passionately introduced her topic, Emily picked out a few sympathetic faces in the audience and started speaking directly to them. She had charmed the members of the Harbor Commission (who had already funded three dogs via grant money from Homeland Security) into hosting a public event where she might wrangle contributions for a fifth K-9.

"Ranger is an extremely intelligent German shepherd," she told the 175 citizens assembled in the crowded meeting room. She displayed a poster-sized photograph of the red and black dog. "He caught my eye at Gold Coast K-9 in San Perdido—a local company that searches for specially bred and trained dogs from Germany, the Netherlands and Czechoslovakia."

"When a cop pursues a suspect, especially at night," said Officer Carver, taking up his microphone, "he or she is at a big disadvantage—especially if the hunt ends up in an enclosed space like an alley or a darkened room. These occasions are precisely the time when a police dog can prove invaluable to law enforcement."

"Exactly," said Emily, "with their enhanced senses of smell and hearing, their superior ground speed during a chase, and the sheer intimidation factor that comes with a ferocious growl or sharp teeth, dogs like Ranger or Phantom provide an extra layer of protection between the criminal and the officer. I would love to equip every single cop on our force with a canine complement."

"Do you always send the K-9 out first?" asked an obviously worried dog-lover.

"Most of the time," Emily continued, filling the room with her dulcet tones, "we don't even have to dispatch the dog. We just tell the offender, 'don't run, or we'll send the canine,' and any criminal who is at all smart or reasonable, will decide that he or she doesn't want to risk getting bitten. They usually surrender without incident."

"Recently," picked up Carver, "we had an armed-robbery suspect who was hiding in the bushes. The patrol officer could not see him, but the dog caught his scent and brought him out—providing a peaceful ending to what could have been a very dangerous situation."

"Who takes care of the dogs?" asked an elderly man.

"Officers assigned a K-9 must adopt the animal into the family," Emily said. "It's just like adopting a child—only the child is very hairy and weighs ninety pounds."

"While the dogs can find bad guys and protect the officers," Carver resumed, "the biggest advantage is that they prevent the suspect from fleeing or fighting. We can count on this happening every single night we patrol."

"While most of the dogs are used to search buildings or backyards too dangerous for officers to enter alone, today, we are going to show you a black Lab named Phantom. He sniffs out narcotics—even if stored in airtight containers. Before you arrived, Officer Carver planted cocaine somewhere in this room. Would you like to see Phantom do his thing?"

The audience was clapping enthusiastically, but hushed the moment Emily bent down to release Phantom's leash. She gave the Dutch command for "seek" and the dog took off. When she glanced over at Carver, however, the officer was looking genuinely upset. Apparently, he had expected the dog to run toward the back of the room.

Typically during such demonstrations, Carver stowed a plastic case filled with cocaine directly underneath the refreshment table. This afternoon, however, Phantom's paws were headed in the opposite direction. He was loping over to a man wearing a heavy black leather jacket even though the temperature in the jam-packed space had reached ninety degrees. When Phantom quietly sat down at his feet, the shaggy-bearded gentleman jumped up, pulled a Saturday-night special from the back of his jeans, and threatened the crowd with his weapon.

Officer Carver and Chief Hunter, who had already brandished their firearms, ordered him to drop his revolver. The highly agitated man, however, refused to comply. In fact, he managed to fire off a shot before Phantom knocked the gun out of his hand.

The audience didn't know what to think. Either they had been witnessing an elaborate skit staged for their benefit or they had been glued to a reality television show—without the television part. When Chief Hunter dropped to her knees and clutched at her calf, however, they instantly surmised the situation was all too real. Within sixty seconds, however, Carver not only had the gunman cuffed and seated in a squad car, but had also called for an ambulance to speed Emily to the ER.

While Charlotte had been listed as Emily's primary emergency contact, when she failed to pick up the phone, the police dispatcher rang up Thomas House. Anne would amaze everybody—including herself—at her unruffled response to the news that Emily had been shot.

As she pulled her mother's Mustang convertible into the hospital parking lot, she thought about the condition in which she might find her sister. Although she could claim no expertise in the treatment of gunshot wounds, she had already guessed, correctly, that Emily's regulation steel-toe boots had prevented any damage to the twenty-six bones in her foot. And with the bullet hitting her calf, Anne prayed that the wound would prove to be a "through-and-through"—entirely missing the fibula or tibia. *Surgeons can do amazing things, these days, with metal screws and titanium rods*, she thought. *While, it might take awhile, Emily will eventually be able to return to the job she loves. Yet if she's immobilized for any length of time, I could volunteer to be "her legs." If she lets me.*

Anne started making plans as waited for her sister to get out of surgery. *And if Emily gets blue, we could even tackle "Project Cold Case."* Although Emily had won a grant to reexamine evidence in decades-old cases that might benefit from modern technology or DNA analysis, the major obstacle to getting the unit launched had been the uncooperative chair of the SLU Criminal Justice department. Dr. Donald Doyle told Emily he preferred sending interns to bigger and more prestigious law-enforcement agencies—"to better to enhance their resumes," he said.

Too bad Emily had never told Doyle about her high school internship with Detective Colin Samuels. He was the reason Emily decided to pursue a career in law enforcement.

In 1979, Emily helped Samuels solve—without a single fingerprint or DNA profile—the celebrated Tracy Cox homicide. The irony was that the Ms. Cox's murderer, who turned out to be a clergyman from San Perdido, wouldn't have shown up in CODIS anyway—even if DNA analysis, which was still eight years into the future, had been available.

DNA wouldn't put a killer behind bars in California until 1989, when investigators from the San Perdido County Sheriff's Department discovered a hair with an intact follicle at a crime scene and shipped it off to a Maryland lab for testing. In fact, during the ensuing eleven years—when the Sheriff's Department would finally get its own lab—DNA was rarely tested in San Perdido County. Local law enforcement relied on old-school forensics. "I still believe," Emily had told Anne, "there's a great deal to be learned by skillful interrogation and good old-fashioned deductive logic—you know, the kind your beloved Sherlock Holmes used to employ."

As Anne was turning the corner toward Emily's room, she found herself playing an involuntary round of "What If?" *What if Chloe had been the drug-seeking dog at the demonstration?*

Her first response was to grin, but before she realized it, an involuntary nasal hoot had quickly followed. Snorting would be next, she knew, if she didn't immediately take control. Yet by the time the second hoot arrived, Anne realized it was already too late.

A dainty little ladylike laugh—that's the second request Anne would have made of her fairy godmother, if she had one. In fact, she would have settled for a hearty chuckle or even a high-pitched titter—anything but this humiliating cycle of hooting and snorting. She headed into the nearest restroom until the cycle had run its course.

The joke, Anne realized, was that Emily would have been perfectly safe with Chloe. The only substance the little Yorkie could track with her nose alone was liverwurst, and Anne sincerely doubted that any person who concealed Braunschweiger on their person—would also be toting a gun. *A nice rye bread perhaps; but no gun.*

Charlotte had missed the call from the hospital because she was already on the line with the Los Angeles Fire Department. Apparently while battling a blaze in the loft above hers, enough water had puddled under the floorboards to cause her eighteen-foot suspended bedroom ceiling to collapse.

Charlotte's residence was one of forty-four recently renovated city-view lofts in an Italian Renaissance building constructed during the Roaring Twenties. The original builder had lined the lobby with marble pillars, imported granite and limestone for the facade, hired muralists to decorate the roof's interior, found artisans to install intricate mosaic tiles, and, as the signature architectural feature, wrapped the entire exterior in a Lucca Della Robbia-style frieze.

Every window framed a breathtaking view. Sometimes on weekends, when the weather was mild, Charlotte would enjoy a cappuccino and a freshly toasted bagel out on the balcony.

Charlotte would often stand and admire the vast expanse of granite counters, the six-foot walls of antique glass cabinet fronts, and state-of-the-art appliances that defined the enormous cooking/dining/entertainment area.

"No itty-bitty wood-burning stove for me," she had told her mother.

Maybe next New Years Eve she would throw a big bash—inviting everybody she had ever met. She would also hire somebody who worked all the A-list parties to plan the whole thing. *The best part would be the watching—watching all of them as they envied me this spectacular space.*

Charlotte's heart almost stopped, though, when she heard from the Fire Department. Her first call should have been to her sisters, reassuring them that she was safe, but she dialed Peter Burnett, her accountant/financial planner, instead.

Charlotte had forgotten the deductible on the house insurance, but she knew the amount had to be quite sizeable in order to make the monthly premiums affordable. The figure $50,000 came to mind, but she immediately banished it to the place where she sent all bad news. *Why wasn't Peter answering his phone? He couldn't possibly have planned for this calamity, but I have always been able to count on him. If he tells me everything is going to be all right, I will believe him.*

Burnett, fifteen years her senior, was as dark-haired as Morgan Hunter had been blond. And while Peter maintained his tan and fit body by playing tennis, her father, the last time she saw him, had been satisfied with the pasty-white bulk of an inactive academic. With Morgan, there had never been the long hours of playful conversation she shared with Peter. Morgan had been as stingy with his time as he had been with his money and affection.

Actually, it might be better if Peter did not answer his phone, thought Charlotte. At this particular moment she just wasn't up to playing her part in a rehash of the dialogue they'd kept repeating of late.

"Haven't you already accumulated the equivalent of two years of vacation?" he would say. He never seemed to skip ahead to the good part.

"Yes," she would respond, in the most resigned voice she could muster.

"Are you determined to kill yourself?" Now his patter would take on a singsong cadence.

"No."

"Do you think Stephen Chamberlain cares how exhausted you are?"

"No." Why couldn't she get that little girl pout out of her voice?

"Have you considered that the universe might be speaking to you?"

"Yes," she would confess. She really didn't know how the universe spoke to people, but admittedly, a collapsed ceiling was quite an attention-getter.

"Would you like the key to my place on Kauai?" That was the good part, or at least it could have been, had he offered to accompany her.

"I'm sorry, Peter," she said without fail, "I'd really like to go but I just can't seem to find the time."

Whenever Peter spoke about his mist-shrouded villa, his eyes would close and a blissful smile would transform his face. He would recount breakfasting on macadamia-nut pancakes with fresh mango, being awed by the 360-degree view from the top of his mountain, or being rocked in his hammock by the gentle trade winds.

Charlotte, though, wasn't about to be seduced by Peter's romanticized word pictures; her practical nature invariably reigned supreme. If she had really desired a stunning ocean view—without all the Hawaiian humidity and a four-hour plane ride, that is—her mother's hilltop mansion in Port Cabrillo would clearly present the better option.

And this being a global society and all, surely at least one grocery store in the sleepy little beach town stocked fresh mango and macadamia nut pancake mix.

Finally, if she spent a few weeks at Thomas House, Charlotte could still be close enough to work via laptop or car and still be far enough away to dodge the distracting construction work on her loft. Charlotte grabbed the key to her Porsche, started humming "Little Grass Shack," and hit the road.

As the sun ducked under that barely discernible purple thread existing between sky and sea, all three of the triplets found themselves back in Port Cabrillo. As the trio gazed out of Emily's hospital window at the purple, pink and orange sunset unfolding in front of them, they experienced—simultaneously—their first moment of triplet telepathy.

Now this is a birthday party I will never forget.

Chapter 16: Dinner and a Cold Case

January 31, 2011

As the winter storm rumbled its way out of the coastal city and veered toward the inland portion of San Perdido County, it seemed like old times in the cozy Hunter dining room—except in place of three adolescents in pigtails chattering beneath the ornate Victorian chandelier, three laptop computers sat open, ostensibly conversing among themselves.

The night sky was only one shade of charcoal darker than it had been during the daylong downpour. Without sunlight streaming through the stained-glass windows, the jewel-like bevels and glimmering olive, red, and amber leaded cuts had taken on the flat appearance of a paint-by-numbers panel.

Charlotte, Emily and Anne had abandoned their computers on the antique mahogany table in order to forage in the kitchen for sustenance. Their hope had been that together, they might be able to produce a respectable dinner.

Emily discovered six half-filled cartons of Chinese takeout that successfully passed her sniff test, and gave each a turn in a microwave rescued from Emily's apartment.

Anne, who had already whipped up a citrus salad with garlic and ginger dressing, was stir-frying fresh vegetables on the wood-burning stovetop.

Charlotte had managed to unearth three pairs of chopsticks in the silverware drawer. She also found can of crunchy noodles as well as a bright-pink box of almond cookies in the pantry.

"The house is beginning to take on the fragrance," said Anne, her mouth otherwise engaged with a juicy mandarin orange section, "of a Chinese dumpling factory."

*****

Dinner was accompanied by giggles and gossip, but all three Hunters deeply felt the absence of their mother. Still, if Carina had had her way, no Wi-Fi, much less a PC would have been welcome in Thomas House. Fortunately, Anne, who was an early adopter of new technology, managed to convince Carina, who was a proudly stubborn Luddite, to change her mind. Anne's most persuasive argument hinged on the point that it was much more efficient to research health issues online, rather than have Anne trudge to the library and leave Carina alone to fend for herself.

During exploratory surgery at Port Cabrillo Hospital, Carina, whose cancer had been staged at III, underwent a total hysterectomy. "With no real method to screen for ovarian cancer," Carina's gynecologist had said, "by the time most women learn they have the disease, it's far too advanced to cure."

Carina was subsequently assigned a UCLA oncologist named Dr. Andrea Mitchell, who had warned: "Ovarian cancer cells aren't easy to eradicate—they can spread quickly into the abdomen or even find new places to hide. Your surgeon was only able to remove a portion of the tumor cells."

"So how many are left?" asked Carina in a wobbly voice.

"Millions may have been left behind, but we're not finished putting up a fight. The second line of attack will be chemotherapy."

"Chemicals? I don't know if I want chemicals in my body. Which ones are you talking about?"

"Typically we combine a platinum-based drug such as *carboplatin* or *cisplatin* with a taxane such as *paclitaxel* or *docetaxel*." Carina looked as if Dr. Mitchell were speaking Klingon.

"Don't worry about remembering the names of all these pharmaceuticals. I will provide you with handouts for each drug I'm including in your custom cocktail. I just want you to agree to partner with me in this battle. We are going to battle it together, but it's up to you whether or not we're going to win."

Anne shot her mother a reassuring glance and asked, "How will the drugs be administered?"

"This is going to be a double-pronged assault," said the oncologist. "You will receive the cocktail intravenously in cycles. That means you'll get the drug for a few weeks and then you'll get a rest. In all, you will receive a total of six three-week cycles of chemotherapy during the next eighteen weeks."

Carina moaned and turned to Anne. Her daughter patiently patted her hand and directed her to keep listening.

"But your surgeon also placed a tube in your stomach," the oncologist continued. "The tube is attached to a port that makes it easier to deliver the drugs into the abdomen each time an intraperitoneal treatment is given."

"What does intraperitoneal mean?" asked Anne, clearly enunciating each syllable.

"Intraperitoneal refers to the abdominal area where we bathe the cancer cells in cancer-killing drugs."

"How long do I have?" asked Carina, finally spitting out the only real question she had for the doctor.

"In a study published in the *New England Journal of Medicine*, this one-two punch therapy enabled women to live sixteen months longer than IV chemotherapy alone."

Carina wrinkled her forehead while closing her eyes.

"That's huge," added the oncologist. "This method has the longest survival rate that's ever made its way into the scientific journals."

"In a case of ovarian cancer this advanced?"

"Yes. Exactly the same as yours, Stage III."

"What about side effects? Will I go bald?"

"The short answer," said the doctor, "is 'it depends.' Everybody responds to chemotherapy differently. You may not lose your hair."

As it turned out, the oncologist was right. Carina didn't go bald, but she did take up a new hobby—smoking marijuana. She decided, however, to keep this information from both of the law-and-order officials in the family. Since neither of them resided at home, she had no trouble implementing her "don't ask, don't tell" policy.

Although Anne knew that smoking weed kept the nausea and pain down to a manageable level, she couldn't resist, from time to time, to calling her mother "The Stoner" when nobody else was around. As it turned out, Carina would remain alive for ten more years after her initial diagnosis.

*****

"Okay, what's going on with 'Project Cold Case?' " asked Anne. "Which file did you choose for us to start with?"

"Hold on, hold on, Annie-Fanny. You are not exactly a professional like Emily and I are. Why don't you just be a good girl and make sure that those of us who make our living in law enforcement remain well-fed."

"Why does 'Project Cold Case' require professionals?"

"Because amateur detectives don't know what they are doing," said Charlotte, carefully applying a new shade of lip gloss.

"But you're not a detective."

"What do you mean?"

"Don't you rely on the police to do the investigating for you?"

"She's got you there, Charlotte," said Emily, in her sweetest voice.

"Well, the way I look at it, it's up to the cops to find the murderer; but it's up to me to put him behind bars," she said tartly, fluffing out her hair and studying her image in her compact mirror. "We work as a team."

"But I can work as a team."

"I can work as a team?" Charlotte mocked.

"You know what I mean."

"My question is, 'what do you actually know about crime?' "

"I've read hundreds, if not thousands of mystery novels."

"So?"

"So, I can usually figure out the murderer by the end of the third or fourth chapter."

"Figuring out a killer's identity in a fictional whodunit isn't the same thing as figuring out the killer's identity in the real world," said Charlotte, zipping up her cosmetics kit and tucking it into her designer bag.

"Well, I don't know why not."

"Because real life is messy and complicated. And when rank amateurs get themselves involved, murderers can get away with murder."

"What do you mean?"

"Well, what if it's you who does or doesn't do something that allows the killer to get off—let's say, on a technicality?"

"But I wouldn't do that."

"You wouldn't intentionally do that, but solving crimes is a business best left to those who have actually studied the law."

"Tell me how you think I might allow a murderer to go free. Give me an example."

"I can think of three possible legal scenarios right off the top of my head."

"Like what?"

"First, you might search a suspect's house without obtaining a warrant beforehand. Without a warrant, anything you find can't be used in court. Second, you could inadvertently contaminate the evidence by not securing it in an evidence bag. A judge will entertain a motion to suppress evidence even where there's only a mere possibility that it might have been compromised. Third, you might break the chain of custody—"

"How?"

"By, say, accidentally leaving it unattended, and then—"

"I know, I know. And then everything will have to be thrown out," said Anne, with a deep sigh.

"So, my dear sister, with just the three cases I outlined, if the only proof the prosecution possesses is eliminated through your stupid mistake, the killer will walk."

"Except these are cold cases—right, Em? We will be looking at old evidence, evidence already collected by somebody else."

"That's correct, Annie."

"Then I can't possibly be guilty of any of the violations you cited, Charlotte."

Emily chortled while Charlotte reddened.

"Just remember, Anne," added Emily, settling back in her wheelchair. "Charlotte doesn't always speak for me."

"Hell, Em, mark my words," said Charlotte, her lips pursed in an unflattering pout. "You are going to be very sorry you allowed Annie-Fanny to work with us."

"No, Charlotte, I'll be happy to take all the help I can get. Who knows? Anne might be the one to solve this case."

"Yeah, right." Then turning toward Anne, Charlotte asked, "So what does the professional mystery reader think? Did the butler do it?"

"Well, Charlotte, your question is quite irrelevant since our first case isn't going to be an unsolved homicide." said Emily.

"It's not?" said Charlotte, her eyes reflecting irritation.

"I wanted to give our fledgling Cold Case Unit every advantage, and a forty-year-old homicide would be a huge stretch for us."

"So all cold cases aren't homicides?" asked Anne.

"Many are missing persons cases."

"I'll bet you are thinking of Cesar Castillo," said Charlotte, hoping Emily would be impressed with her clairvoyance.

"As a matter of fact I was," said Emily, turning her computer around so that they could all see a photograph of the missing nineteen-year-old. "Especially after I received not one, but two phone calls about Cesar Castillo today."

"One must have been from Angelica."

"Since she's our second mother," said Emily—her voice full of feeling, "I couldn't exactly ignore her request to look into his disappearance."

"Wait a minute, won't our personal connection to the Castillo family be considered a conflict of interest?" asked Charlotte.

"I don't see why it would be," said Emily. "Port Cabrillo is such a small town—everybody knows everybody anyway and since the three of us grew up here, we were bound to have known the victim. In fact, I believe I was hired to head up the Police Department precisely because I was the hometown girl."

"You still should give some consideration to the conflict-of-interest issue. Did you ever think to mention this to the San Perdido County district attorney?" asked Charlotte. "Because bias is the first thing any good defense attorney will try to establish."

"Except this is not a murder case and we have no idea if the outcome will even lead to criminal charges."

"Well, okay. You are just going to have to keep in mind that that's the way my mind works."

"You mean once a prosecutor, always a prosecutor?"

"I guess so. You see the only time my office deals with a missing person is when the missing person has been murdered."

"What about the second call you mentioned?" said Anne, easing up the top on her laptop. A fetching photo of Chloe served as wallpaper.

"I also heard from the detective who worked the case back in 1971. His name is Michael Miller. He told me that every year on the anniversary of Cesar's disappearance, he checks the morgue files on unclaimed bodies—just to see if any of the John Does match Cesar's physical characteristics. He claimed he never found a corpse that even came close. He did ask that we consider the Castillo case as a personal favor to him."

"Bias aside," said Charlotte, extending her hand so she could admire the soft coral polish applied by her manicurist, "we will be more likely to locate a missing person than crack an unsolved murder case so I, for one, vote 'yes.' "

"I won't deny that the likelihood for success also remains paramount in my mind. Our first case can't end in failure. And scientific technology has come a long way since Cesar disappeared."

"Like DNA?" asked Anne, enthused by the prospect of learning real-world forensics.

"That's right, Anne. And of course local, state and national agencies now share information electronically these days."

"Isn't there a national data base for missing persons?"

"That's correct."

"I also read somewhere about special software that can 'age' a photograph," said Anne. You can see exactly how the missing person might look today."

"Oh, Annie, that's an intriguing idea. Aging software might be especially helpful in this case. I'll look into it. Most importantly, Cesar Castillo's disappearance remains the oldest cold case in the files. In fact, the fortieth anniversary will be on August 28. If we can get the newspapers involved, maybe we can persuade the public to assist us as well."

"If you could solve the case by the anniversary date, Emily, it would be quite a public relations coup," said Charlotte. "And afterward, you would have no trouble getting the City Council to see things your way."

"Or the grant people either—when it's time to ask for more funding."

"So tell us what you already know," said Anne eagerly.

"Since the station went paperless, all the photographic evidence, interviews and reports have been digitized. They're all readily available on computer. That's a plus."

"Is there any DNA or fingerprint evidence?" asked Charlotte.

"Well, nothing like the bloody murder weapon, if that's what you're asking. In fact, there was never any evidence of foul play. We could, however, enter Cesar's DNA into the national database and see what happens."

"Sheesh, Emily, wouldn't Cesar be an old man by now?"

"Not quite the elderly coot you must be envisioning—he was only nineteen at the time of his disappearance. Depending on when his birthday falls—I still need to get up to speed on the specific details—he'd be fifty-eight or fifty-nine now."

"I remember that Cesar and Cruz, who were eight years old when Grandma hired Angelica, would do odd jobs around Thomas House," said Anne. "In fact, Angelica claimed that when we were babies, they even changed our diapers."

"Changed our diapers?"

"What's so hard to believe, Charlotte?" chimed in Emily. "That an eight-year-old changed your diaper, or that you used to poop in your pants?"

"Puh-lease, Anne. I never pooped in my pants."

"Well, I just emailed you the files," said Emily, "so after we all get caught up, I'd like us to brainstorm like we used to. Perhaps we can come up with a new angle—something the original detective missed or didn't think to explore."

"What do you know about this Detective Miller?" asked Charlotte.

"He did the best he could with this case," said Emily. "I know you will be impressed with how thorough he was. Especially with gathering documentation and conducting interviews. He literally left no stone unturned in his search for Cesar."

"But he never found him," pointed out Anne.

"Never even came close," said Charlotte, with a condescending look.

"Well, he almost came close," shot back Emily. She couldn't help instinctively backing fellow police officers.

"What happened?" asked Anne.

"About six months after Cesar disappeared, Miller believed that he had located Cesar's car. In fact, he was standing on the shoreline when the Coast Guard fished a 1963 Volkswagen out of the Port of Cabrillo."

"But it wasn't Cesar's car, was it?"

"No, but you aren't going to believe this. The license-plate number of the vehicle they dragged out of the drink was only one number away from Cesar's."

"Crap," said Charlotte, picking at an errant wad of mascara from under her left eye.

"I'd have said 'shit' had I been Miller," confessed Emily.

"I'd have said, 'Blessed is he who expects nothing, for he shall never be disappointed,' " said Anne, yawning dramatically as she rose from the table.

"Ah," said Emily. "A good word from Alexander Pope. Goodnight, Mr. Pope."

"Goodnight, John Boy," added Charlotte.

Chapter 17: Forty Years Later

February 7, 2011

Angelica had been listening to Cruz and Maricela quarrel for the past forty years. Apparently, on this particular occasion, her son had committed the unpardonable sin of lighting up a cigarette. Maricela, in an effort to gain the upper hand, had thrown two questions at Cruz: 1) "Are you *loco?*" and 2) "Have you forgotten the oxygen tank in the next room?"

Angelica knew from experience that Maricela had no intention of listening to his answers.

Instead, Angelica relished the serenity she felt alone on the patio. Occasionally a bird would twitter and break the silence, but even the chatter produced by dozens of her feathered friends would never prove as intrusive as the epithets hurled during Cruz and Maricela's forty-year power struggle.

She laid her head back on the lounge chair and exhaled. Gone, she thought, was the luxurious head of hair she had always insisted on coloring Lucille Ball red. At present, only a few wisps of white remained to tuck under her well-worn Dodgers baseball cap. She felt every day of her eighty-seven years. She missed being in charge of her own kitchen. She missed driving her car to the shopping mall. Most of all, she missed Carina. The two of them would have managed to chuckle over the latest episode of the Cruz and Maricela *telenovela*. Perhaps she was reaching back with selective memory, but she couldn't recall Cesar and Maricela ever fighting this much.

It had been forty years since Cesar had disappeared, and now Emily Hunter was going to reopen the investigation. She was positive that Carina had something to do with it, but Emily said that couldn't be true—her mother died two months before she decided to activate the Cold Case Unit. Still, nobody could convince Angelica that Carina had not reached out from beyond the grave to aid her best friend.

Angelica lamented no longer being able to identify each of her twenty-six varieties of roses by fragrance alone. Her lungs had deteriorated so badly with emphysema that her doctor now had her tethered to an oxygen tank.

Because summer seemed to be the only season in Southern California, Angelica made a point of choosing roses that bloomed continuously. She had planted every single bush herself, including the delicate pink April Loves lining the front walkway. Anybody strolling down Pacific View Drive found the air perfumed with an exquisite scent uniquely reminiscent of vanilla, strawberries and myrrh.

The spent pink, red, orange, white and lavender petals in the rear gardens needed raking and bagging, but she no longer possessed the stamina. She had reminded Cruz more than once to help her tidy up the rose beds, but he could never spare the time. While Cruz knew how important his mother's garden was to her, Maricela kept him constantly occupied with repairs to her day-care center or attendance at social events. Rather than nagging, she decided to wait for Cesarito to pay a visit. She knew he would agree to lend her a hand.

Even though she often felt frustrated, Angelica was quicker to count her blessings. Among them were eleven great-grandchildren nearly ready to take their place in the world. Five were the offspring of Cesarito and Liliana. Unfortunately, history had repeated itself with those two. Liliana got pregnant while she and Cesarito were still in high school. Instead of attending college with the money his parents had saved, Cesarito bought a share in Jorge and Rafael's flooring business. Everybody seemed happy with the arrangement, especially Cesarito, who, realized by the time he hit junior high school that, unlike his stepfather, he was simply no scholar.

When the front door slammed for the second time, Angelica knew she had the house all to herself. The reporter from the *Port Cabrillo Pilot* wasn't due for another hour. She wanted to show him the treasured family album, but she couldn't remember where she put it. *Think, Angelica. You better not have that Alzheimer's disease that Maricela and Cruz keep talking about.* Although Angelica insisted that she was fully capable of living on her own, they had also been adamant about returning to Ocean View Place to care for her.

When Maricela first entered her life, Angelica couldn't have loved her any more than if she had been her own daughter, but now Angelica was having trouble recognizing this new-and-not-improved version of Maricela. As Cesar's bride, she had been sweet and generous—especially to her brand-new husband. Yet now as Cruz's *esposa* of three decades, she was never pleased with anything he did. Angelica suspected that some underlying resentment was keeping them at each other's throats, but exactly what that was, she couldn't say. She continued to pray to the Virgin for understanding—and patience.

When the doorbell rang, Angelica pulled herself up and the photo album slid off her lap. *That's where it's been all along*, she thought, as the heavy book slid across the patio pavers and nearly plunged into the koi pond. Finally, after retrieving the book and tucking it securely under her arm, she made her way to the front door—her oxygen tank bumping along behind her. She didn't want to keep her special guest waiting.

"Come in. Come in," said Angelica, breathing with considerable effort. "What did you say your name was?"

"Raul Rodriguez. Junior. My father was the reporter who first wrote about your son's disappearance in 1971." The black-haired man who towered over Angelica was the spitting image of his father, who was, in Angelica's opinion, the second most strikingly handsome man she ever met. The first, of course, was her own husband.

"*Ay dios mio*," said Angelica, as she crossed herself. "Is your father still with us?"

"Yes, he is, although he retired as a journalist seventeen years ago. In fact, he sends his regards," Raul said, his voice reminiscent of Edward James Olmos.

"Tell him '*muchas gracias*.' "

"I will. But first, I want to thank you for inviting me into your home, and for being willing to talk to me about a subject that must still bring pain to your heart."

"Mr. Rodriguez, your parents raised you well. Such good manners. And so rare in young people these days. Would you care for *café con conela* and *pastel de café?*"

"It's Raul, *por favor*, and coffee with cinnamon would be very nice. Did you bake the coffee cake yourself? It certainly smells heavenly."

Despite his effusive praise, Angelica seemed close to tears. She had placed her face in both palms. Raul said nothing more but positioned his well-muscled arm around her stooped shoulder as he assisted her to the old-fashioned Formica and chrome table. The blaring of the TV was already giving him a headache.

"Who puts a big screen in the kitchen?" Angelica asked. She grabbed the remote from the table and hit the button to silence the TV. "That foolish noise box is on morning, noon, and night."

"That's much better," said Raul, as he reached into his backpack and brought out a digital tape recorder. "Do you mind if

I record this?" When Angelica nodded "no," he flipped the switch and placed it in front of her. A tablet computer also made its way out of his backpack.

"When your father sat down at this same table forty years ago, all he required was a notebook and a pencil," said Angelica. Raul grinned. "And as for me," she continued, "I never dreamed I would be heating up *la torta de café* in a microwave or using some ridiculously expensive contraption to make a single cup of coffee."

Raul laughed as he placed his cellphone on vibrate mode. "I think the easiest way to get through this is for us to make our way through your family album. That way you can introduce me to the entire cast of characters, one by one, and catch me up with what's been happening to them since the disappearance."

"Excellent idea, *mijo*. Then that's exactly what we will do. The album is right here on my lap."

"Since Dad provided me with his notes from 1971, I also know what you told him then so I promise we won't go over the same ground. Are you ready to get started?"

The first page held Angelica and Emilio's black-and-white wedding photo. Raul could neither appreciate the bride's fiery red hair nor her oversized bouquet of crimson velvet roses but he smiled as Angelica kissed the tip of her finger and transferred the kiss to Emilio's lips in the photo. "Emilio died the year before Cesar disappeared."

The next six pages held baby pictures. To Raul, all of the infants looked exactly alike—dressed in what must have been the same blue crocheted cap, sweater, and booties. Angelica identified the first image as Enrique. "When he retired as president of the Haltom City Bank last year," said Angelica proudly, "he and Elodia relocated to Dallas. Gabriel and Guliana, their kids, are happily married and have presented me," she said, with an evident degree of self-satisfaction, "with six great-grandchildren."

"Really, where do they live now?"

"Everybody but Enrique and Elodia live in Fort Worth."

"Since Texas is so far away," said Raul, "how often to you get to see them?"

"Not very often, but they do keep in touch by phone."

"When I talked to Enrique yesterday, I noticed he's acquired quite a heavy Texas drawl."

"I have a hard time understanding him too," Angelica admitted, "but Elodia, who was also born in Port Cabrillo, never picked up an accent at all. I really don't understand why Enrique did, but when I asked him about it, he says it was good for business."

"Now let me get this straight. Enrique was the one who put up the $10,000 retainer to hire the private detective. Right?"

"Yes, that's correct. The investigator was Ken Milhoune. I can't believe I still remember his name. He was this Anglo *hombre* with a sickly white complexion. He had no hair—but, as I recall, he kept rubbing his bald *cabeza* while he was talking. When he found a promising lead in East Los Angeles, we all got pretty excited but, in the end, it just didn't pan out."

"Do you remember what was promising about it?"

"Something about a Social Security number. He reported that Cesar had been working under another name not long after he disappeared. But after the restaurant job, the trail got cold really fast. Still, we were lucky."

"Why do you say that?"

"Milhoune was, I would have to say, an honorable man— even if he wasn't all that successful. I remember when he announced in this gravelly voice (which Angelica skillfully imitated) 'I'm giving up, and I advise you to do the same.' I guess he could have milked us for a lot more money but he didn't. I respected him for that."

As Raul came to the photos of Rafael and Jorge, Angelica couldn't help spending a full five minutes bragging about Castillo Brothers Flooring. Raul tried to look suitably impressed and even congratulated her on her achievement as a mother but in response, Angelica felt compelled to launch into a five-minute diatribe about Rafael and Jorge's shortcomings as well. She was clearly distressed that neither brother—eighteen months apart in age—had found a suitable wife. "Work isn't everything," she said, making disparaging clicks with her tongue. "Are you married, Raul?"

"Who is this?" responded the journalist, deftly deflecting her question. They had arrived at another image of an infant—only this baby's eyes were closed.

"Oh that's Santiago, my little angel."

"Angel?"

"He left us before he was even seven days old. 'A congenital heart defect,' the doctor had said. Cesar and Cruz, in fact, were conceived the night Santiago passed away. Emilio just wanted to comfort me," said Angelica, shooting Raul a knowing look. He just patted her hand. "I had been so unhappy over the loss, I couldn't eat or sleep. Then a miracle happened. Nine months later, I wasn't holding just one baby in my arms—I was holding two."

"The twins. They are certainly identical in every way. How were you ever able to tell them apart?"

"A mother always knows—but Cesar and Cruz claimed they could fool their teachers."

"Their teachers?"

"Yes, sometimes they would switch, you know, on test days. Like if one of them hadn't studied." Raul nodded understandingly. "Then there was this time when Cruz was trying to date two girls simultaneously."

"So," laughed Raul, "Cesar deceived one of the girls into believing he was Cruz?"

"I think she was still suspicious. She asked him how he had gotten to be such a good kisser."

Raul howled with laughter. "So what did Cesar say?"

"He told her he had read a couple of good books on the subject."

"That's funny. But being so close and all, Cesar's disappearance must have been really tough on Cruz. How would you characterize his reaction to losing his brother?"

"He was devastated. He started doing badly in football and wanted to quit. In fact, he even talked about dropping out of college. We sat him down—each of us—and finally convinced him that leaving school would have been the last thing Cesar would have wanted."

"Wasn't he also concerned about Cesarito and Maricela? Their welfare, I mean."

"We all were. Cesar had been working two jobs to pay the bills. Then, after Cesar disappeared, the older brothers—they all had good jobs by then—well, they just stepped up. I didn't even have to ask. They wouldn't hear of Cruz dropping out of college. Each one of them wrote a generous check every month. And Maricela started babysitting at home—just a few kids, at first."

"Now that's interesting. Doesn't Maricela *own* a day-care center these days?"

"Yes, but she had to prepare by taking classes at night. Eventually she earned her degree. After she and Cruz married, they found a six-bedroom house with a fenced-in yard on Whitecap Avenue. It's theirs now, free and clear, and fifty children— from newborn to four-year-olds—are enrolled at Los Niños Place."

"When did Maricela and Cruz get married?"

"Maricela wasn't free to wed until Cesar had been declared legally dead. Not only was it a very difficult decision for Maricela, but also for the entire family. She finally filed the papers in 1981. Cruz and Maricela eloped six months after that."

"Cruz told my father that he didn't believe his brother was dead. He said, and let me get this right, 'that he would have felt the loss in his soul.' He claimed that being twins and all, he just would have known. Did you ever hear him say something like that?"

"Yes, many times. But who can argue about matters of the spirit? Still, I know that Cruz loves Maricela and Cesarito with all his heart. He says that all he ever wanted was for the three of them to be a family. But deep down inside, with Cruz—I don't know how to put this in words—there are two opposing forces—and they keep trying to tear Cruz apart. On one hand Cruz had to admit Cesar was dead in order to marry Maricela and become Cesarito's father, but on the other, I don't think he ever really believed it."

"Yet, time was ticking away."

"He couldn't keep waiting for Cesar to show up. On the tenth anniversary of Cesar's disappearance—that's the day he made up his mind."

"He was teaching at the high school by then."

"That's right. I am so proud of Cruz. He earned a teaching credential and then secured employment at Cabrillo High. He still teaches history and coaches the baseball team there. He says that he has never been happier, but, as his mother, I know in my heart that he misses his brother every single day. All of us do."

"Cruz told me that Cesar's disappearance still baffles him. He wonders, even after all this time, what happened to Cesar and his car. Do you have a theory about what happened to Cesar after the bachelor party?"

"I really have no idea. All I know is that if God wills it, I will see my son. If not, He has His reasons. Our Heavenly Father doesn't have to tell me what He decides. I've finally been able to put the matter in His hands. He does what's best for all of us and that's all I need to know."

"Cruz also said that although he's moved on with his life, certain memories of Cesar still haunt him. Do you have any special memories of Cesar?"

"You can see that I'm wearing an old Dodgers cap. It was Cesar's. One of the best nights of his life, he used to say, was spent with 56,000 other fans at Dodger Stadium."

"What was so special about it?"

"That was the night he got to see Sandy Koufax pitch the fourth game of the 1963 World Series. No other team had ever clobbered the Yankees 'so elegantly,' as he put it. Since Cesar loved the Dodgers, I love the Dodgers."

"Do you also hate the Yankees as much as Cesar did?"

"Damn straight. The Yankees? I spit on them."

"Okay, okay." Raul had to pause to rid his mind of that particularly disturbing image. "Enrique told me that all he, Rafael and Jorge want now—is closure. They believe that a memorial service with flowers and music might help to bring that about. How do you feel about that?"

"If they really want to hold a memorial service, they should just go ahead and do it. They don't need my permission. But as they already know, I won't be attending."

Chapter 18: Researching at the Morgue

April 14, 2011

Old Man Lewis was a diminutive gnome of a man—with a bent nose, thick white hair, and a chin the size of a little green apple. Anne found him hunched over his rolltop desk with his drugstore reading glasses on top of his head. He was using them to restrain an errant silver forelock that kept insisting on impairing his vision. He was also fouling the air with a nasty-smelling cheese sandwich.

Actually, he was the *second* Old Man Lewis to serve as publisher of the *Port Cabrillo Pilot*. His father Brendan had started the weekly newspaper in 1958—with a $500 loan and a dream that refused to be rebuffed. The Honorable's son Thomas made the first Old Man Lewis an offer he couldn't refuse—a ninety-nine-year lease on an empty warehouse located on the wrong side of Reef Street. The rent? The princely sum of one dollar a year.

Lewis took possession of the space on a showery day in January and invited members of the Port Cabrillo Chamber of Commerce to assist him with the cleanup. Together, they erased twenty years of accrued grime before giving the headquarters of the town's first and only newspaper a fresh coat of paint.

In 1970, his son Neil, clutching a freshly inked diploma from Columbia University School of Journalism, took over the *Pilot*. These days, however, the seductive siren call of $1,000,000—the most recent sum offered by a regional daily not just intent, but *fixated* on buying him out—keeps getting harder to resist.

Neil, who had never found himself inclined to marry, was beyond exhausted. He hadn't been able to schedule a single vacation in four decades. Except for two underpaid stringers, Neil did everything at the *Pilot*—from taking photos to writing editorials to sweeping the floor.

Revenues kept dropping off as advertisers fled to the cost-free classified-ad websites on the Internet. Old Man Lewis was barely hanging on—depending almost entirely on publishing legal notices, printing the *Cabrillo High Foghorn*, the *Santa Lucia University Light* and the occasional engraved wedding invitation.

"Good morning, Mr. Lewis," said Anne.

"Have you seen my glasses, young lady?" said Lewis, his ill-fitting dentures causing an annoying whistle as he spoke.

"Up here, sir, as always," she said, tapping the crown of her own head.

"Ah," he whistled, feeling for the plastic spectacles. "Here they are!"

The office didn't look or smell any different than it had when she served as his copy editor—twenty-five years ago. The only thing missing from this frozen-in-time scenario was the ear-damaging racket created by the offset printer now gathering thick brown dust in the back room.

"Would it be alright if I did some research in the morgue?"

Neil nodded in the affirmative and returned to his computer. Anne headed back through a veritable maze of workspaces. Freestanding cubicle partitions jutted out, willy-nilly, from the interior walls of the century-old warehouse.

The *Pilot* archives were little more than towers of musty newsprint. Neil, like his father before him, simply heaped representative copies of each thirty-two-page tabloid as the spirit moved him. He hadn't even bothered to organize the pillars by year. He basically allowed them to climb as high as possible before they threatened to collapse under their own weight. If a would-be researcher needed to look up a particular name or keyword, his best bet would be the Port Cabrillo Public Library where an indexed collection was preserved on microfiche.

From time to time, the stacks did more than threaten—a fact of which Anne was well aware. She gingerly stepped over the pools of slippery newsprint, being cautious not to lose her footing. She had hoped a *Pilot* article moldering away somewhere might present her with a clue as to Cesar's need to flee. She was positive that fear had been the motivating factor but fear of what?

Both Emily and Charlotte believed Cesar was a deceased John Doe—the victim of foul play soon after the bachelor party. Yet when Charlotte expanded Miller's search to include the Los Angeles County Morgue records as well, it didn't appear that Cesar had died—at least not locally.

The rank-smelling mildew, powdered grime, and insect bodies covering the stacked-up newspapers sent Anne into allergy-attack hell, but she couldn't allow her drippy nose and watering eyes to sidetrack her from her mission. With intuition as her only guide, she made a beeline through the stacks for a newspaper pile that *just felt right*. She also grabbed the first chair she spotted and dragged it along with her. While she wasn't all that confident in its ability to support her, she felt fairly safe as she attempted to distribute her 140 pounds over its four spindly legs.

The newspaper pile in question yielded a *Pilot* published during the last week in August 1971. It was crammed full of features about the San Perdido County Fair, the Sand Sculpture Contest at the Beach Festival, interviews with locals about the passage of the Twenty-sixth Amendment to the U.S. Constitution, and the gruesome murder of an Santa Lucia University sophomore named Truman Carpenter. Old Man Lewis had included two grisly photographs with the article: one of the bloody baseball bat and the other of the spray-painted word "faggot."

The two-page story on the Carpenter murder mentioned the address of the Hot Spot—a cabaret that featured female impersonators—as 210 West Bay Boulevard. As Anne shuffled through later newspapers, she discovered articles detailing the arrest, trial, and conviction of Andres Aguilar. One of them mentioned the address of the Gutierrez Family Restaurant—209 Via Pacifica—because of the owner's role in reporting the Norman Mortenson murder to the police. *Hadn't the Gutierrez Family Restaurant been Cesar's place of employment?*

Having lived so long in Port Cabrillo, Anne didn't need a map to realize that not only must the two businesses have shared the same alley—but the addresses indicated they had to be situated directly across from one another. *There are no coincidences in mystery novels. What if Cesar witnessed the Truman Carpenter murder, and that's why he took off? He must have known the killer was after him.*

The fact that Aguilar was found guilty of both the Carpenter and Mortenson homicides, however, did bring her hypothesis into serious jeopardy. If Cesar had seen somebody kill Carpenter, then he had no reason to be afraid once Aguilar went to prison. He could have safely returned home. *So why didn't he?*

It's obvious, thought Anne—*because Aguilar didn't kill Carpenter.* Reopening the Carpenter murder case was the key to solving Cesar's disappearance, but how could she convince Emily? As far as the Port Cabrillo Police Department was concerned, the Carpenter homicide had been solved and the killer brought to justice. *I need more information about Truman Carpenter.* She wondered if the *Santa Lucia University Light*, also published by Old Man Lewis, might prove worthwhile.

She would have to pinpoint the appropriate mound of newsprint but then she had already been reading for hours. In fact, her back was starting to spasm, her eyes felt like she'd been caught in a sandstorm, and her feet were heading in the direction of home all on their own—when it happened. An inexplicable force nudged her toward some newspapers stacked next to an unplugged dehumidifier. What she discovered proved to be the proverbial gold mine.

While Anne noticed that Truman Carpenter's byline frequently appeared on the opinion pages of the school newspaper, it was a photograph in the September 8, 1971 edition that gave her an amazing insight. It was the uncropped version of his mug shot and it revealed a light-haired young man with gentle blue eyes, a bit of an overbite, a meager moustache, and a flock of freckles burnishing the bridge of his upturned nose. His glasses were those frameless half-spectacles affected by John Lennon, but his attire, which had not been entirely visible in the thumbnail, was strictly collegiate. Although finely featured, Anne did not perceive anything in Truman's expression or dress that would readily identify him as a homosexual.

Matthew Tannen, who had penned Carpenter's obituary, noted that Carpenter hailed from the Midwest—Lima, Ohio, to be exact—and that his Lutheran parents farmed corn and raised livestock. He also observed that his subject, who had been awarded a Presidential Merit Scholarship, had already distinguished himself by becoming the first sophomore to win the editorship of the university literary journal. Tannen wrapped up his tribute by mentioning that not only had the young scholar served as the founder and president of the university's Jane Austen Society, but he was also employed as a writing tutor under the supervision of Professor Morgan Hunter.

The words "Morgan Hunter" seemed to morph into 48-point Times New Roman right before Anne's eyes. In fact, she sat back on the rickety chair with such force that she cracked off the two back legs, and, almost immediately, found her derriere on a swift downward trajectory.

Landing hard on the dirty wooden floor, Anne became painfully aware of a large splinter that had poked its way into the seat of her polyester pants. And as if that particular indignity weren't enough, as she used the remnants of the broken chair to pull herself up, she found herself farting long and loud.

Whether she would respond with sobs or snickers was a toss-up at this point. Yet she had to admit, this *faux pas* wasn't even in the same league as the worst moment of her life—the moment when Morgan walked out. Besides, this event had gone totally unobserved. *To hell with it, she allowed—let the snorting begin.*

It had been a decade since her father had been able to invade her thoughts, but now, here he was—popping up unannounced, prompting stabs of grief, and ushering in a familiar ache that she had been able to anesthetize with work.

Why don't I just give Daddy a call? As much as she yearned to hear her father's voice, even if it was ostensibly to seek information about his former student, she realized she must resist. He wasn't good for her. He wasn't good for any of them. *I can get the information elsewhere*, she told herself, as she attempted, once again, to banish Morgan from her mind.

Her theory about Cesar running away after witnessing a murder might prove a tough sell with her sisters, but the more Anne studied the Carpenter and Mortenson homicides, the more the differences seemed to overshadow the similarities. Anne was convinced that somebody other than Aguilar had murdered the college sophomore. As she drove home, she outlined the major arguments in her mind.

First, the perpetrators were different. The killer in the Carpenter case left absolutely no forensic evidence at the scene. He seemed, if anything, overly cautious—wearing gloves and parking blocks away so that neither fingerprints nor tire tracks could lead back to him. Yet, with the assault on Mortenson, the killer's behavior was just the opposite. He was, if anything, reckless—bringing along his friends and parking his vehicle in the middle of the crime scene.

Second, the victims were quite different in age, appearance and occupation. The thirty-eight-year-old Mortenson, who impersonated Marilyn Monroe for a living, was also well known for his flamboyant behavior offstage. The nineteen-year-old Carpenter, on the other hand, appeared to be nothing more than a shy college student. He hadn't adopted attire or mannerisms that would readily identify him as a homosexual. The spray-painted word "faggot" could have been a false clue planted by the real killer to distract the police.

Third, although the murder weapons in both cases were, on a superficial level, both baseball bats, they were significantly different in age and appearance. Were the dissimilarities significant enough to indicate two different perpetrators? According to the newspaper article, the first bat was quite old and made of hickory. The second bat, however, was brand new, and because it was a Louisville slugger frequently employed by Little League players, it would be readily available at local stores.

Fourth, even though Aguilar admitted beating Mortenson to death, he denied knowing Carpenter. Since he would have to pay the same price for one murder as for two, Aguilar had nothing to gain by lying to the police. No interrogator, according to the newspaper coverage of the trial, had ever been able to shake Aguilar's claim that while he may have been guilty of beating up Mortenson, somebody else had killed Carpenter.

Fifth, Detective Miller may have been incredibly thorough, but he had also been incredibly overwhelmed. Once the Castillo disappearance started demanding his attention, Anne believed Miller couldn't waste his time pursuing other suspects—especially after the Aguilar arrest.

Anne couldn't blame him.

Chapter 19: The First Big Breakthrough

April 15, 2011

"I think you argued your case quite well, Anne. I vote we reopen the Carpenter homicide."

"Me, too, but be aware that we can no longer access the actual physical evidence."

"You mean like the baseball bats?" interrupted Anne.

"Correct."

"Oh no, Emily!"

"Take it easy, Anne. The Aguilar homicides, as you know, were closed forty years ago, so any physical evidence is long gone. We do, however, have clear digital photographs—especially of the crime scene."

"But no DNA evidence, fingerprints or anything else forensic?"

"That's right, Charlotte."

"Do you have Detective Miller's report?" said Anne.

"I can pull it up right now on my laptop. Still, I must caution you that Miller stopped investigating after Aguilar's arrest as you so cleverly pointed out. Exactly what do you want to know, Anne?"

"I want to know if Miller mentioned any other persons of interest in the Carpenter homicide."

Emily speed-read through the report and, after a moment or two, replied, "I can tell you right now that Miller may have liked one other suspect for the murder but he had an unassailable alibi."

"Who was that?"

"A football player by the name of Jenks—Humphrey "Jenks" Jenkins. He played tackle for the Santa Lucia Vikings. He was apparently a hulk of a guy—stood six feet, four inches, and weighed 220 pounds. Apparently he publicly called Carpenter a 'fag' on at least two occasions. After Carpenter reported him to the school administrators, however, Jenkins was reprimanded immediately. In fact, the dean benched him for four games. According to, let's see, Larry Winterbaum—Truman's roommate—the bullying stopped instantly. Jenkins kept his nose clean after that."

"So what made Jenkins's alibi so unassailable?"

"His girlfriend, her name was, um, Sarina Knight, swore she was with him at the time of the murder. They were at a movie at the Pacific Cove Mall."

"That's on the other side of town from the crime scene."

"If we've learned anything about Miller," said Charlotte, "it was that he loved doing interviews. Who else was on his interview list?"

"Let's see. It looks like he contacted Carpenter's parents, several dorm-mates, all four of his professors, his major advisor, members of the Jane Austen Society, and the staff on the university newspaper."

"Would it be possible for us to access his report and interview notes?" asked Anne.

"I don't see why not." Emily typed a few commands into her computer, and said, "Okay, check your email. And by the way, Annie, I haven't seen you this energized in years. What's going on?"

"Well, if I had to guess," said Charlotte, "I would think it has something to do with adolescent angst. Don't you remember what a huge crush she had on Cesar Castillo? I think it started the first time she saw him mowing our lawn—without his shirt."

"Wh-wh-what's wrong with you, Charlotte? Why do you have say something like that?"

"Something like what?"

I th-th-think." Anne paused, took a deep breath, and finally blurted out, "I th-th-think investigating is something I just might be good at, that's all, and I don't understand why you always have to be such a sp-sp-spoilsport. Are you scheming to wear me down so you can bring in somebody else? Somebody more professional?"

"Oh Annie-Fanny," said Charlotte.

Emily cut in. "Someday, Charlotte, you will have to eat your words. You couldn't be more wrong about Anne." Turning to Anne, she said softly: "Please believe me, Anne. I *can* see that you are good at this. Actually, you are good at a lot of things."

Chapter 20: Foul Play—Off the Field

April 16, 2011

Anne pored over the interviews. She wanted to believe that something in the sixty-seven-page report would paint a bulls-eye on the killer. The key to solving Truman Carpenter's murder was motive. *Who had the most to gain from Carpenter's death?*

"Jenks" Jenkins made an outstanding suspect. She could envision the football player biding his time until the ideal opportunity arose to exact his revenge. Not being able to play in four games during his senior year provided a dandy motive. And spray-painting the word "faggot" next to the body might have been Jenkins's way of signing his name to the payback—without giving the police enough evidence to send him to jail.

Still, Jenkins as a cold-blooded murderer didn't feel quite right. In addition, he did possess an alibi. Yet Anne knew that Sarina Knight wouldn't be the first girl who lied to protect her boyfriend. When Anne wondered if she could locate either Sarina Knight or Humphrey "Jenks" Jenkins through the Santa Lucia Alumni Association, she had no idea she would get so lucky. Not only could the association provide a phone number for both Knight and Jenkins, but it also turned out to be the same number.

When Anne asked if she could drop by, Sarina, who answered the phone, was all smiles and giggles. "Come by the office. Our business is located on the corner of Bollard and Port View. Do you know how to get there?" Anne would have no trouble finding their accounting office—it was only a few blocks away from Surfside Drive. "And it would be helpful if Jenks could be there as well," Anne had said.

"Your timing is perfect, Miss Hunter. We are just finished up with tax season, so we will have plenty of time to visit with you."

When Anne entered the office door with "Jenkins and Jenkins Accounting" stenciled on the glass, there was nobody at the receptionist's desk. A small table held a coffee machine, Styrofoam cups, sugar, creamer and a glass cake keeper that was empty—save for a few colored sprinkles.

Damn, donuts with sprinkles. My favorite. The narrow hall just ahead offered three closed doors from which to choose. Since

Anne didn't feel like playing *The Price is Right*, she hollered "Anybody home?"

A female voice hollered right back. "We are back in the conference room—the last door on your right." Sarina and Jenks had been hovering over a map of the South Pacific. "We are planning our dream vacation to Bali," explained Sarina, a much-too-perky brunette in a color-splashed plaid tunic, worn over opaque black tights. As she bounded across the room to shake Anne's hand, "head cheerleader" sprang to Anne's mind.

"Lucky you!" Anne replied.

Jenks took his time ambling over to offer his hand—and what a meathook it was. Although he probably hadn't stepped on a gridiron since college, he had kept himself in excellent condition. Not a square inch of flab was visible. Anne tried to act blasé as Jenks released her fingers from his vice-like grip, but the ache he left was intense. She paused to give her sore digits a mini-massage.

Anne was prepared for some icebreaking chitchat, but after asking, "How long has Jenkins and Jenkins been in business?" she learned that not only had the couple married the day after graduation, but, instead of staging an elaborate wedding, they took the ten thousand dollars her folks had salted away for her Big Day and invested it in themselves.

Furthermore, while they worked grueling hours during the week, they enjoyed weekend getaways on a boat moored in the Channel Islands Harbor. Once tax season was over, they could also schedule jaunts to exotic locales. The couple didn't seem intent on hiding a thing.

"So you met as accounting majors at Santa Lucia?"

"Yes, but some people find Jenks as an accountant quite difficult to believe," she said, running a tiny gold megaphone back and forth on the chain around her neck. "He was an interior lineman for the Vikings, so everybody just assumes he's nothing but a big dumb jock."

" 'Big dumb jock?' I beg your pardon, Sarina," he said in a false soprano. He took one look at Sarina's confusion and guffawed—he knew his wife meant no disparagement. "No, you are spot-on—as usual. I do admit, however, I *played* the big dumb jock role to the hilt. I so wanted to be accepted by my teammates, I allowed myself to, let's say, participate in a number of imprudent pranks." Jenks' show of self-deprecation surprised Anne.

"Did any of these imprudent pranks have to do with Truman Carpenter?"

"Why, yes. What insults I didn't hurl at that poor guy! I was just trying to show off, you know—play the BMOC in front of my pals. I knew I could always get a rise out of him by calling him a 'fag,' but I never laid a finger on Truman. Never."

"You didn't have to," interrupted his wife. "Just look at you—your size is intimidating enough."

"Yes, Sarina is correct once again. Intimidation was also my stock in trade. I did eventually see the error of my ways. I apologized to Truman and took my punishment like a man."

"What punishment was that?"

The dean of students called me in for a little lecture on the unintended consequences of bullying. To help speed up my learning curve, he informed me that my coach would be pulling me out of the next four games—four games we lost, I might add."

"Jenks," cautioned his wife.

"It was only a week later when his bloody body was found in an alley—the word 'faggot' spray-painted next to it. Frankly, I still don't know why anybody would beat up that defenseless little guy."

"Besides, my darling, *you* knew he wasn't a homosexual."

"Well, after I talked to his girlfriend, I knew. I still don't get why Tru and Ginny decided to keep their relationship such a big secret."

"Of course you do," said Sarina. "You know how strange Frank MacDonald became after Ginny broke up with him."

"Ginny," Sarina said, looking directly at Anne, "had been going out with another football player. But they split up long before she got together with Truman."

"Oh, you mean Frank," said Jenks. "I had forgotten about him."

"But don't blame Ginny," said Sarina, her voice growing more strident. "Truman was everything that Frank was not. Truman was both smart and sensitive. Ginny considered him her 'soul-mate.' "

"You don't really think Frank murdered Truman, do you?" asked Jenks.

"Don't know," said Sarina. "His behavior got very scary whenever anybody crossed him. I could see him not really meaning to kill Truman—but completely losing it—especially if he found out about Ginny. With Frank's muscles and a baseball bat . . .." She left the last sentence unfinished.

Anne waited a few beats before asking, "Do you know where Frank is now?"

"I have no idea," replied Jenks.

"Or Ginny?"

Oh, Ginny is still Virginia Peabody, as far as I know. The last time I heard from her, she was living in Los Angeles. I think she's a deputy district attorney or something," said Sarina.

"Huh, it is a small world . . . "

"After all."

"Damn, that tune is going to rattle around in my head all day," said Jenks.

"Sorry, Jenks."

"Anything else?"

"No, I don't think so. I seem to have everything I need. Thanks so much for your help. And—"

"And?"

"Have a wonderful time in Bali!"

*****

Virginia Peabody was so elated when Charlotte asked her to lunch, she accepted without even consulting her calendar. When the two women met at the trendy Beverly Hills restaurant—one blonde and one brunette—they were shocked to find themselves decked out in identical burgundy two-piece suits. A discreet ruffle set off each jacket neckline and the matching skirt appeared as hip hugging as possible. Furthermore, without realizing it, they also mirrored each other's actions—from parking their designer bags on the back of their chairs to carefully smoothing linen napkins over their size 2 laps to taking microscopic sips from their generous appletinis.

"I wonder if you can help me solve a mystery?" Charlotte began. Ginny fingered one of a pair of one-carat stud earrings she had given herself as a thirty-fifth birthday present. "I understand you graduated from Santa Lucia University."

Ginny's jaw dropped. Why had *the* Charlotte Hunter gone to all the trouble of researching her undergraduate education? When no answer came to mind, she stammered, "I l-l-later attended law school at Berkeley—after I had worked and saved enough to pay the tuition."

"Worked and saved?" said Charlotte. "What kind of job pays law school tuition?"

"The position wasn't glamorous, but it *was* lucrative."

"I'm intrigued," said Charlotte, as she leaned forward. "Tell me more."

"It's kind of a lengthy narrative, Charlotte. Are you up for it?" said Ginny, already warming to the task.

"Of course."

"During my freshman year, I met a very popular football player. He kept telling me how beautiful I was, and since I wanted so badly to believe him, I ignored all the warning signs."

"Warning signs?"

"From the first date, I was afraid of Frank MacDonald. Not only was he physically menacing—standing well over six feet and built like a Mac truck—but emotionally menacing as well. By Christmas vacation, I had permitted him to take over my life."

"In what way?"

"He told me how to dress; what to say; how to act. While I'm not one bit ashamed of my mom, she was a single mother. She could only afford—well, we lived in a forty-foot trailer. The only reason I could attend Santa Lucia was because my scholarship paid for everything. Frank, on the other hand, came from money. Big Money."

"So the MacDonalds were wealthy?"

"Incredibly. Not only did Frank attend a prestigious prep school, but he also had more cash than brains. Here's an example. Frank never bothered to reconcile his checkbook. The bank had been instructed by Frank's father to cover all his checks."

"And he probably gave you a number of expensive gifts."

"So many, I stopped counting. Every Thursday—that was the day we met—he would present me with a beautifully wrapped box. Say, during the week I was taken with an exquisite scarf or a stunning bag in a shop window? It became my Thursday gift. We were also well known at all the top spots in Los Angeles. On weekends when he wasn't playing football, we drove up the coast in his gold Chrysler convertible. He stuffed my closet with chic clothes. But after awhile, I started feeling so uncomfortable, I wanted to return everything he had given me—and break up. But I couldn't. I felt like—I don't know—like I owed him something."

"You mean sexually?"

"No, sex was never an issue. When I told him I was saving myself for marriage, preserving my virginity seemed a point of pride to him. It wasn't my virtue he was after, he said, he just wanted to have me all to himself."

"So he asked you to give up your friends?"

"No, he demanded it. Claimed I hung around with 'low-class skanks.' If the girls came to my dorm room to visit, he would insult them—mock their clothes or their makeup. Once, he even slapped my best friend across the mouth. One by one, they just drifted away."

"Sounds like he was trying to isolate you."

"That's what I thought too. He also used tantrums—major-league tantrums—to control me. When almost anything I said or did seemed to trigger a blowup, it was time to leave."

"Did he ever hit you?"

"No, nothing physical. It was all emotional abuse. But with all the out-of-control rage attacks, I figured it was only a matter of time."

"Sounds like you were wise to get out when you did."

"But you would be wrong. I jumped right back into the flames one year later."

"You didn't actually go back to him?"

"No, not to him—but to his parents. The MacDonalds, you see, were even more manipulative than he was. Because they were so rich, let me just say, they usually got their way."

"Please don't take this personally, Ginny, because Santa Lucia University is a great school, but I was just wondering how a kid like Frank, with all his advantages, ended up at SLU."

"No offense taken, and you're right to wonder. They could have sent him anywhere."

"What kind of Mom and Dad were they?"

"I wouldn't look on the mantel for any parenting awards. He was barely out of diapers when they turned the job over to somebody else."

"A nanny?"

"No, they shipped him off to boarding school. Frank once got all weepy about the time when he was five or six and they put him on a plane for Massachusetts. I think he ended up staying at Haines Academy up through high school—even during the summers. Yet, according to Frank, he used to *live* for the field trips. Haines students were able to tour all sorts of historic landmarks on the East Coast—learning, firsthand, about American history, art, and literature—subjects that still remain, I would think, close to his heart."

"So, where is this Haines Academy?"

"It's in Concord."

"Lots of American history there."

"But something very bad must have happened in Massachusetts."

"Really? Like what?"

"I don't know the specifics. Something about his parents being summoned. An accident? All I know is he ended up back in California."

"So how did he arrive at Santa Lucia?"

"Well, that's another long story. Since Frank's father attended Harvard, there was no question that his son would attend the old *alma mater* as well. Unfortunately, Frank was kicked out. I have no idea why he chose Santa Lucia, but he always claimed that Sully changed his life."

"Sully?"

"Coach Sullivan discovered that Frank could play football. And Frank discovered life as a BMOC."

"Big Man On Campus. Haven't heard that acronym in ages."

"Guess that must date me, but BMOC really fit Frank. Those were heady times for a guy with such low self-esteem. Unfortunately, for Frank, big men on the campus of Santa Lucia were also expected to pass their classes. They were to be 'athlete scholars'—with the emphasis on 'scholar.' While he did well enough in the courses he enjoyed, the ones he didn't—well, let's just say that after two years of failing to maintain a "gentlemanly C" average—he was on his way out the door once again."

"That couldn't have pleased the MacDonalds."

"Charlotte, you are the Queen of Understatement. Alicia insisted that Frank just needed to find himself, but his father, who had had quite enough of Frank, laid down the law. 'Up or out,' Loran told Frank. Either his grades went up or he was out on the street. When Alicia found my name on the Dean's List, she hired me as Frank's tutor."

"So how did *that* go?"

"Surprisingly well. At first, Frank wanted to take up where we had left off, but when he found out that the power base had shifted—he actually buckled down and worked on his studies."

"So tutoring was the lucrative job?"

"Tutoring paid well, but no, lucrative wouldn't arrive for two more years. In the meantime, during May of 1971, I think it was, Frank was only four final exams away from picking up his sheepskin."

"There's a 'but' coming, right?"

"A professor—I think from the English Department—accused him of cheating. Frank, of course, denied the charge—but more vehemently than he should have."

"What do you mean?"

"Frank possessed a hair-trigger temper. So did the professor. What started out as a shoving match, escalated into a fistfight, and, no surprise, Frank was also asked to leave SLU."

"By any chance, do you know where Frank is now?"

"No clue. After I graduated, Loran employed me to sell cars. He owned a Chrysler dealership in Westlake Village."

"You sold Chryslers?"

"New Yorkers, Newports, and Imperials."

"Commissions must have been quite substantial. Those cars were never cheap."

"Bolt Law School got most of it, but, and I've just got to say this, peddling cars was the ideal internship for an attorney."

Charlotte laughed so hard at Ginny's last remark she had to haul out a tissue. She knew she would be sporting raccoon eyes even before she opened up her compact. "I want to thank you for the most entertaining lunch I've had in a long time. You are one hell of a date."

"But what about the mystery? Didn't you need my help?"

"Ah, right you are. Let me see. I wanted to ask you about a couple of classmates of yours. Did you ever run across a Truman Carpenter?"

"Oh, my God," said Ginny. She took on the expression of somebody who had just taken a serious blow to the *solar plexus*. "I haven't even allowed myself to say his name for so long. Why it must be nearly forty years since he died. Please, Charlotte. I'm so sorry about this, but I'm going to need a minute. Do you have another?" she said, holding out a trembling hand for a tissue. A whole box of tissues, however, weren't going to stem the mascara tide inundating her cheeks.

After dabbing her eyes and clearing her throat, Ginny finally replied: "Truman was the love of my life. In fact," she paused to sop up a few more tears, "his murder was the reason I became a prosecutor." She smoothed out the charcoal-smudged tissue, refolded it, and blew her nose. "Why are you bringing him up now?"

"My sister—her name is Emily—she's the Port Cabrillo police chief."

"I know Port Cabrillo—that's where Santa Lucia University is located."

"Of course you do. In fact, my father taught at SLU, but that's another story. When our mother was dying, Emily, who worked for the LAPD, decided to return home. Becoming a police chief in Port Cabrillo was her ticket to ride. She also recently won a grant to start a cold case unit. She asked Anne, my other sister, and me to help her tackle a 1971 missing-persons case. Anne seems convinced that the missing person, Cesar Castillo, decided to take a permanent powder after witnessing a murder."

"Witnessing a murder? Whose murder?"

"Truman Carpenter's."

"But Andres Aguilar was convicted of Truman's murder. In fact, he is still in prison."

"While that's true, based on significant inconsistencies, Emily decided to reopen the Carpenter homicide. If Anne is right, Aguilar was unjustly convicted. The defendant, as you might have known, went to prison maintaining he was innocent in the Carpenter homicide."

"But Charlotte, you and I both know the prisons are overflowing with 'innocent men'—at least according to them."

"Yet with DNA—surely you've heard of Project Innocence— DNA is now proving that some of them were actually telling the truth."

"So there's DNA evidence that exonerates Aguilar?"

"We will never know. Unfortunately, once the case was closed, only photographs were stored. Still, no other theory seems to explain Castillo's forty-year disappearance. Cesar could have been sitting in his parked car when Truman was murdered and witnessed the entire attack."

"I can see where you are going with this. If you can locate Castillo, he could testify against the real killer. Or if you can locate the real killer, you could find out what happened to Castillo."

"That's our thinking—exactly."

"You must believe that I could provide assistance in some way. How can I be of help?"

"What you told me about Frank MacDonald was extremely useful, Ginny. We were wondering if you might still keep in touch with his parents."

"Loran is deceased, but Alicia is still alive. Actually she lives in a nursing home in Port Cabrillo. Do you want me to find out if she knows anything about Frank's whereabouts?"

"It certainly couldn't hurt. To tell you the truth, Ginny, we are getting pretty desperate. For all intents and purposes, Frank seems to have fallen off the grid."

"No, I'm the one who is sorry, Charlotte. It now appears I've doubled your workload."

"What do you mean?"

"Now you need to find *two* missing persons."

Chapter 21: You've Got a Hit

June 29, 2011

Emily scooted her wheelchair over to the table to answer her phone, which had been programmed with the jazzy ringtone from *Law and Order*. "Hello, this is Chief Emily Hunter."

"Good Morning Chief. This is Theodore Bronson."

"Good Morning, Mr. Bronson."

"Did you enter a DNA sample into the national missing persons database about six months ago?"

"That's correct."

"Well, congratulations, Chief. You've got a hit."

"On Cesar Castillo?"

"Yes. No. Wait a minute—the name I have is Santiago Gomez Castillo. At least that's what it says on his driver's license."

"Is there also a thumbprint on file with the DMV?"

"Yes, there is."

"Hmm, thumbprints weren't required until 1982. This guy, however, has been missing since August of 1971."

"So, okay. That's interesting."

"I'm sorry, Mr. Bronson. I was just thinking out loud. Hmm. The different name looks like he might have successfully established a new identity."

"I wouldn't know about that, Chief Hunter."

"Of course not, Mr. Bronson. I apologize for the second time. So where did you finally locate Mr. Castillo?"

"On a slab at the San Perdido County morgue."

"He's dead?"

"Yes. Quite dead."

"And you are sure that it's the same guy?"

"Yes, his thumbprint and the DMV thumbprint are an exact match."

"Wow, Mr. Bronson. I never saw *that* coming. When exactly did he die?"

"I think it was last night. I can check on the exact time if you need the information immediately."

"No, it can wait for your report, but I'll admit, right now, I'm having trouble trying to wrap my head around this. So Cesar Castillo or—what did you say his name was, again?

"Santiago Gomez Castillo. Do you want the address on his driver's license?"

"Sure."

"It's 211 San Gabriel Valley Boulevard, Apartment F."

"What's the city?"

"Alhambra."

"Alhambra?"

"Actually it was also unclear to the Sheriff's Department as to what Castillo might have been doing here in San Perdido County."

"So let me get this straight. According to your information, my missing person has been living under an assumed identity for the past forty years. His last known residence is eighty miles away—in Alhambra. This morning, however, he turned up at the San Perdido County morgue. Did I get everything right?"

"Yes."

"Has a cause of death been determined?"

"It was a homicide."

"Homicide? Are you serious?"

"Uh, well. I really don't know how to answer that, Chief Hunter."

"I didn't really expect you to, Mr. Bronson." Emily was still reeling from the sharp left turn her cold case had just taken but she realized she had better shift into professional mode, and immediately. "I'm going to need a copy of the autopsy, the fingerprints, the DNA results, and anything else you've got. Please? Make that 'pretty please.' Can you believe how astounding this is, Mr. Bronson?' "

"Uh, I don't know," he said, befuddled by yet another personal question. When he first picked up the phone that morning, all he planned on delivering was a simple status report on a DNA search.

"And, if you have the time, could you make getting me those records a priority?"

"I sure can," said Bronson. That was something he could handle with his usual uncomplicated efficiency. Bronson found himself on solid ground once again. "I can shoot everything to your office computer as we speak."

"Thanks," said Emily, and found herself wishing she had applied a little bit more antiperspirant this morning.

Chapter 22: No Such Thing as Bad Publicity—Not!

"Just when I figured we were making progress with this investigation, it's game over," said Charlotte, drumming her manicured fingernails on the mahogany table.

"What's the coroner's official ruling?" asked Anne, a pencil keeping a oily knot of hair off the back of her neck.

"Santiago Gomez Castillo, according to the medical examiner, was very much alive, when a vehicle, presumably a compact car, ran over him."

"It could have been an accident, you know. Maybe he was just taking a walk. Maybe it was too dark for the driver to see him."

"I know why you'd like Cesar's death to be ruled accidental, Anne, but the coroner gave me three good reasons he believes it a homicide."

"Like what?" asked Anne defensively.

"First, the injuries to the body indicate that Cesar was in a supine position when he was hit."

"Supine means he was lying on his back, right?"

"Right."

"Well, couldn't he have fallen? Accidentally fallen?" Anne's feelings for the Castillo family just wouldn't allow for the possibility that Cesar's death had been a homicide. If that were the case, they might also be in danger. On the other hand, if Cesar *had* been murdered, it would actually support her theory about Cesar's disappearance. It meant Carpenter's killer had finally eliminated the single witness linking him to the murder—it had just taken him forty years to get around to doing it."

"What about the other reasons—you know, the medical examiner gave you?"

"Okay, second, the evidence shows that Cesar was hit more than once."

"No, I'm sorry, Annie-Fanny," said Charlotte. "More than once doesn't sound like any accident."

"But why was he already lying on the ground? What's the explanation for that?

"Hmm. Good question, Anne, but the third finding might help with the answer to that."

"So don't keep us in suspense, Emily, what was it?"

"Thank you, Charlotte, for interrupting me but a second time. The coroner found evidence of GHB in Cesar's blood."

"GHB? Isn't that the date-rape drug?" asked Anne.

"There are actually two date-rape drugs—Rohypnol and Gamma Hydroxy Butyrate or GHB. Both depress the central nervous system. Both can be administered as a liquid. And both are relatively easy to obtain on the street. If the goal were to keep a victim from remembering, a perp might just choose Rohypnol. If the goal, however, were to render the person unconscious, he would go for GHB."

"So why would the murderer need Cesar to be unconscious?"

"I think the killer required a physical advantage," said Anne, now scratching the back of her head with the pencil. "Cesar was in pretty good shape, so if the killer were female or elderly—" She decided against finishing her thought, though—for the moment.

"You may be on to something there," said Emily.

"Here's what is bothering me," said Charlotte. "Why did he run over Cesar, back up the car, and then run over him again?"

"Obviously," said Anne, "the killer was employing his vehicle as the murder weapon. And I also think he was making some sort of statement with his choice of car. Otherwise, why would he use a '63 metallic blue-green VW? Wasn't that the exact car Cesar owned but was never found?"

"Exactly, Anne. Keep going."

"I think the homicide, for the killer, was personal. Very personal."

"The personal aspect also backs up Anne's theory," observed Charlotte, somewhat reluctantly.

"What do you mean?"

"Look, if Cesar witnessed a murder but went into hiding for forty years, the killer didn't need to go after him. He or she would have believed themselves in the clear—that the witness knew better than to stick around; much less open his mouth."

"But when Emily chose this missing person's case as our first cold case—"

"And the newspapers made a big deal about meeting the anniversary date—"

"As we hoped they would—to enhance the Police Department's public relations and all— well, as far as the murderer was concerned, I'm sorry to say, we forced him to do something about Cesar," said Emily.

"On the other hand," said Charlotte, "just remember, Emily, that publicity could have also brought us information critical to the investigation."

"I know you are trying to make me feel better, Char, but I just wish I hadn't come off as so sure of myself with reporters. Sure of myself—and our ability to solve this case."

"It wasn't so much your level of confidence, Emily, as it was the killer's faith in DNA," said Charlotte. "That's what forced him to act. I think he believed he had to silence Cesar before DNA led us to him."

"Wh-wh-what DNA?" asked Anne.

"The murderer doesn't know there's no DNA. Everybody watches too much television these days," said Charlotte.

"Do you think Frank MacDonald suspects we've made the connection to him?" asked Anne. "And what about Ginny? Has she been able to extract any information from Alicia MacDonald?"

"When Ginny called on Tuesday," said Charlotte, "she reported that Frank's mother suffers from Alzheimer's, but seems to be in the early stages."

"So why is she in a special facility?"

"That's because Alicia MacDonald also suffers from bitchiness—terminal bitchiness to be precise. She could never get along with any of her home caretakers. According to Ginny, Alicia herself made the decision to move to Sunset Manor."

"I don't blame her. Sunset Manor is more like a luxury hotel than a convalescent home," said Anne.

"How would you know that?"

"Carina rehabbed a short time there, after her surgery."

"Where did she get that kind of money?"

"She told me it was covered by the insurance."

"What insurance, Anne?"

"Come to think of it, I don't know. In fact, I know virtually nothing about her finances. Perhaps we should consult her attorney."

"Not now—we are far too busy dealing with this case."

"I do think, though, that one of us should pop over to Sunset Manor for a little visit. It can't be me—I'm still stuck in this damn chair."

"How about me?" asked Anne. Charlotte, always the drama queen, opened her eyes widely and blinked as if in disbelief. "I could take Chloe over," Anne added. "She is a certified therapy dog, you know."

"I don't think so, Annie-Fanny. Maybe we should just stick with Ginny. She's the one who has already established a relationship with Mrs. MacDonald."

"That may be true, Charlotte, but with Anne, we double our chances."

"If you say so, Emily." Turning to Anne, Charlotte said, "Listen, dear sister, don't take this personally, but I'm putting my money on Virginia."

"You'll probably win, but I think I'll give it a try anyway."

Chapter 23: Birds of a Feather

The report from the San Perdido Sheriff's Department was pretty straightforward. "George B. Grinnel discovered the body of Santiago Gomez Castillo at approximately 15:00 hours on June 28, 2011. Grinnel immediately informed the 911 operator of his location via his cell phone. Grinnel had been watching birds in a copse of pine trees about 500 yards from the 22-mile marker on Lake of the Woods Road."

"Approximately five minutes after he discovered the body lying face-up on the asphalt, Grinnel observed an old, rather large woman climbing into her Volkswagen. She drove south."

"Grinnel identified the vehicle as 'a Sixties-era Bug—blue-green in color.' He did not observe a license-plate number, and could provide no further information."

"You know Emily, I know a little bit about birds."

"Don't be modest, Anne. You know *everything* about birds," said Emily.

"Oh, thank you," said Anne, with both bashfulness and bravado. "Maybe there is something George Grinnel knows—something that he either forgot, or didn't think significant enough to report."

"So you want to question Grinnel?" Emily asked, amazed at her sister's heightened self-assurance.

"Again, trying to mess with business best left to the pros, Annie-Fanny? Are you sure you want to tackle interrogation, Lil Sis?"

"Lil Sis by mere minutes, Charlotte. Besides, why should my wanting to help out bother you so much?"

"Don't mind her," said Emily, fingering the controls on her wheelchair. "Are you willing to drive all the way out to the San Gabriel Valley?"

"I understood that Lake of the Woods was the crime scene."

"Mr. Grinnel might have been bird-watching in Lockwood Valley, but he lives in South Pasadena," said Emily.

"Maybe I should go, Em," said Charlotte, stretching out her chin and vigorously patting underneath. Her biggest fear was that her inactive neck muscles might contribute to a turkey waddle later in life. "I could check the repairs on my loft on the way over."

Without waiting for a response from Emily, she started rummaging through her Coach bag for car keys.

"But you don't know a thing about birds," pointed out Anne, rather petulantly.

"But I do know how to ask questions."

"Please, Charlotte, let me go," said Anne. "You know how much I'd love to spend a little time with a fellow bird-lover. It would be worth the sixty-mile drive. Please, Em?"

"I thought you bird people were called 'twitchers'?"

"Good God, Charlotte, 'twitcher' is a nickname that a real birder would never use. It's not exactly a term of endearment."

"It's not?" said Charlotte, attempting, rather unsuccessfully to hide a smirk.

"Just so you know," declared Anne, who could never figure out when people were mocking her, "It's a term used to disparage those who would turn birding into a competitive sport."

"What's this? Now twitching is a competitive sport? Next, you'll be telling me it's an Olympic event."

"A twitcher, you see," said Anne, getting excited about sharing her passion, "is willing to travel anywhere in the world in order to 'tick off,'" she said, hanging imaginary quote marks in the air, "a new species on his life list.

Charlotte crossed her eyes like a spoiled child. "So why don't they call them 'tickers,' if they are 'ticking' something off a list?" Charlotte also felt it necessary to hang quote marks in the air.

"Good question," said Anne without irony. "Actually, 'twitcher' was the nickname bestowed on a British bird-watcher named Howard Medhurst."

"Medhurst? I've never heard of him."

"Why, that *does* surprise me," said Anne in all seriousness. "Medhurst is something of a legend. You see, he was quite willing to do whatever it took to sight a new species—even if that meant twitching for hours in the snow or the rain or the hot sun."

"Well, Annie-Fanny, it seems that you've given me more information than I'd ever care to know."

"But I haven't even begun, Charlotte." Anne was now talking so quickly, she could barely keep her words from running together. "For example, according to the U. S. Fish and Wildlife Service, 51. 3 million Americans watch birds and—"

"Not listening, dear sister, not listening."

"Not to interrupt this scintillating discussion, ladies, but I just had a thought," broke in Emily, as she closed her laptop and turned her wheelchair around. "Charlotte, would you be willing to combine a stop at your loft with a face-to-face interview with Mrs. Castillo?"

"Which Mrs. Castillo?"

"Mrs. Santiago Castillo. I believe her first name is Pajarita."

"Pajarita? That certainly is an unusual first name. So what are you looking for, Emily, in this particular interview?"

"I need you to start from scratch. The Alhambra police report—I just emailed each of you a copy—is a bit on the perfunctory side."

"A perfunctory police report—imagine that! I'm shocked, simply shocked," said Charlotte, doing an uncanny imitation of Claude Rains from *Casablanca.*

"According to Detective Milo," said Emily, "Pajarita stated that she had no idea where her husband was going on the day he was killed. I can't believe that's entirely true."

"An angle worth exploring. Anything else?"

"At another point, Pajarita mentioned something about a newspaper ad."

"Ah, now that sounds like a promising lead. Perhaps she might still have the newspaper."

"And last, but not least, Pajarita made a reference to Santiago having a brother, but Milo never followed up. Maybe during a face-to-face situation, you can ferret out more information."

"Now that she's over the initial shock of her husband's death, you mean," said Charlotte, checking out her appearance. Charlotte never met a mirror she didn't like.

"Speaking of which, how is the Port Cabrillo Castillo contingent coping?" asked Anne.

"My understanding," said Emily, "is that the San Perdido County Coroner's Office only spoke with Cruz. My plan is to question the entire family."

"By phone?"

"Oh, no," said Emily, "I have to do this in person. In fact, the ACCESS bus arrives later this afternoon to transport me and my trusty wheels to Ocean View Place." During the past twenty years, Gold Coast Transit had provided a special transportation service geared toward the aging population in San Perdido County. At six dollars a ride—door-to-door—ACCESS was an affordable option for those who still needed public transportation.

"Wow, Emily, you're finally breaking out of this joint."

"Hell, yes."

"Then give them my love," called out Anne, as she headed out the door.

"Me, too," echoed Charlotte.

This interview with the Castillo clan is going to be quite a challenge, thought Emily. She couldn't have anticipated just how true that would be.

*****

When Anne finally arrived at the Grinnell house at the top of Redwood Drive, she congratulated her mother's aging Mustang for making it up the seven percent grade. To Anne, the cool breeze whipping her ponytail and the sun caressing her cheeks had to be "California Dreamin' " at its best. Yet as the air grew cooler, she began to develop a Howard Medhurst-like twitch of her own. She hadn't realized how much effort it would take to keep Carina's thirteen-year old convertible from slipping back down the steep hill whenever she was forced to engage the clutch.

Still, she didn't have to wonder why a bird-watcher would choose a residence surrounded by such a wide variety of native trees. The sequoias, ashes, walnuts, and sycamores covering the hillside not only provided welcome shade but lofty perches for the more rare avian species.

Mrs. Grinnel greeted Anne at the door and escorted her out to the back deck. There she found Grinnel inserting a movement-activated camera into a Parasol flower. "You must be Anne Hunter," he chirped. "Welcome to my roost."

"Thank you, George. I didn't mean to interrupt your, uh . . ."

"My work on this device? You don't recognize it, Anne?"

"No, but I suspect it's something ornithological."

"You are quite right. This plastic flower is actually a commercial feeding tube. I'm concealing a camera inside so I can document the activity of my more reticent feathered friends."

"Something in the hummingbird family, perhaps?"

"Have you been holding out on me, Anne? Are you a fellow birder?"

"Yes, ever since I was a youngster, but you, I'd say, were born to birding."

"Born to birding? What do you mean by that?"

"Well, weren't you named after George Grinnel—you know, the founder of the Audubon Society?"

"Ah, I see what you're getting at, and thank you for the enormous compliment, Anne, but having the same name as *the* George Grinnel is strictly a coincidence."

"If you say so, George, but you must know what Freud had to say about coincidences," said Anne, stepping up to the railing. She became instantly captivated by the 180-degree vista.

Grinnel chuckled softly. "Now if Freud had only known something about birds."

Now it was Anne's turn to snort. She should be paying attention to Grinnel—giving him complete eye contact as Carina carefully taught her—but she just couldn't get over the perfect panorama spread out before her. "You have quite a vantage point from up here, George. It's as if the Arroyo Seco had been captured as a vast yet exquisite oil painting."

"The view is quite pleasant, is it not?"

"More than pleasant, George."

"Actually there are 500 other reasons why we purchased this aerie." Anne looked back with a puzzled expression. "And each one of them has now been documented on my life list."

Anne grinned and nodded understandingly. "You've been able to spot 500 different species from this deck?"

"Armed only with binoculars."

"That's truly amazing." As Anne returned to her chair, she couldn't help but ask, "But since you're sitting in the 'catbird seat,' so to speak, why would you travel all the way to Lockwood Valley just to watch more birds?"

"Excellent question, Anne. My friend Ernie—he's got a cabin on Lake of the Woods—he spotted a *Colibri thalassinus* on his property."

"You don't mean a "Green Violetear?"

"Yes, I do."

"I wouldn't blame you for not wanting to miss something like that. So you stayed with Ernie—at his place?"

"No, as a matter of fact, he had other plans, but he provided me with the key to his cottage. I actually spent a couple of days out there, exploring the environs around Lake of the Woods."

"Were there any other birders around?"

"No, each of the residences is almost completely isolated. Ernie told me that every cottage sits on at least an acre of land."

"How fortunate for you, George." Grinnel grinned. He knew precisely what she would say next. "With fewer human beings around," said Anne, "one is able to sight more birds."

"I've got you now, Anne. You must be a birder, a seriously dedicated birder."

"Not as dedicated as you are, George. As for me, I've only seen photographs of *Colibri thalassinus.* What an amazingly colorful hummingbird it is—especially those glittering violet ear-patches."

"And don't forget the iridescent blues and greens in its majestic tail."

"Please tell me you managed to photograph it."

"Unfortunately, not during this trip, but I did hear the '*tsu-tzeek*' call from somewhere high up in the lodge-pole pines—so it still counts."

"On your life list, you mean."

"That's correct. Unfortunately, by the time I got the digital camera out of my vest pocket, he was gone."

"What a shame, George. Please allow me to wish you better luck next time. You did, however, discover something else, did you not?"

"You must mean the body. That, dear Anne, was not a discovery I wanted to make."

"How did you happen upon the corpse?"

"You see, Anne, I had been following a *Pandion haliaetus.*"

"An osprey?"

"Yes, with my binoculars. I couldn't believe how suddenly he was able to wheel around. I watched in awe as he dipped down, crossed the road, and headed toward the lake."

"I'll wager he was looking for a little midafternoon snack. A tasty fish, I'd expect."

"And you'd win that bet. That's when I first noticed the old lady getting into her car."

"First, George, tell me about the car. Did you recognize the make?"

"I don't usually pay much attention to makes of cars but identifying this one was easy. It was a VW—but not one of those cartoon cars Volkswagen started putting out during the Nineties. It was an old-fashioned Beetle from the Sixties.

"What about the color?"

"Well, I'd have to say that it wasn't—well, the color wasn't typical."

"Not typical for what?"

"You know, Anne—not one of those regular—what do they call them? —'stock' car colors. You know, for a Volkswagen.

"Okay, so what color would you say it was?"

"Well, I would say—perhaps only you could appreciate this, Anne, but when the sheriff questioned me about the color, all I could think of was the tail of a Green Violetear. But, of course, had I said that, he would have had no idea what I was talking about."

"Sadly, yes. The iridescent greens and blues in his tail are incomparable with anything else. So it was an iridescent combination of both colors."

"You *do* understand. I knew I felt an instant connection to you—from the first minute you said 'hello.' "

"Why, George. I really appreciate that. Not only are you very kind, but I've been enjoying our conversation as well. Tell me, do you remember anything else about the car?

"The paint is what I remember the most—how shiny it was for such an old vehicle—especially compared to the chrome."

"What do you mean?"

"Even at a distance, I could see that the chrome was quite dull. There must have been a great deal of pitting. So much that it was incapable of reflecting any light at all."

"So have you an explanation? I mean for the disparity between the paint and the chrome?"

"I think the car must have been recently repainted. Quite recently."

"Ah, now that's intriguing. I think you've uncovered something extremely significant." George grinned so widely that Anne could scarcely keep from grinning herself. "Now, what can you remember about the old lady?"

"What do you mean?" said George, trying not to look confused but failing miserably.

"Can you remember what she was wearing?"

"Oh, sure. She had on a pink, green, and black-flowered print dress—with a lace collar," he said, using his finger to circle his neck. "I recall thinking that the lace made the dress look terribly out-of-date. You know—not at all fashionable."

"Like something someone might have discarded years ago?"

"Exactly."

"What about her hair?"

"It was snow white, cut very short, and styled in tight little curls." At this point, he used his finger to make little descending circles. "I remember that the curls shook every time she moved her head."

"What about shoes or a purse?"

"I couldn't see anything below her neck because the vehicle—the Volkswagen—was in the way."

"So she was standing on the driver's side of the car?"

"That's right."

"And you were facing the passenger side?"

"Yes, that's correct."

"Could she see you?"

"No, I don't think so. I was still pretty far away and, well, the woman—she wasn't equipped with binoculars."

"Is there anything else you remember?"

"I don't know—there was just something not right about her."

"What do you mean?"

"I can't really say, Anne. It's not anything specific—not anything I could point to and say, 'that's it.' "

"Okay, let me try to help by asking direct questions. How tall was she?"

"Well, she was above average in height. Especially compared to the car. I remember thinking to myself—that's going to be a tight squeeze. I mean, I wondered how she was going to cram that big body of hers into that car."

"Because the VW was so small?"

"Because she was so big. Hefty, as well as tall. She simply towered over the car."

"How much would you say she weighed?"

"Oh my God, Anne, I never try to estimate a woman's weight."

"Why not?"

"Self-preservation, I guess. My wife is always asking me to guess how much she weighs."

"And you tell her, what—nothing?"

"Exactly. That's why we've managed to stay married for thirty-six years. Look, why don't you just estimate her weight for yourself?"

"How would I do that?"

"My binoculars—they take videos. Don't yours?"

"Oh no, George. My binoculars are 35-year-old Bushnells — all they do is magnify."

"Digital video recorders are standard birder equipment these days."

"They are?"

"Along with special zoom-lenses for our digital cameras, MP3 players to call the songbirds, and illustrated field guide apps for our smartphones. Birding has gone high tech."

"Apparently, so. I would definitely love to see your video."

"Actually, I've already uploaded it to an online birding site."

"No kidding?"

"I wouldn't kid, Anne. You must know how important it was for me to share the sheer size of my *Pandion haliaetus* with the rest of the birding world. You should check out the comments. Nobody else has ever photographed an osprey with such an impressive wingspan."

Anne found Grinnel's camera work quite professional. He kept his subject perfectly framed during the four-minute clip, even though the bird of prey moved at dizzying speeds in every direction. As the raptor dropped down over the road, however, Anne had no trouble clearly making out both the car and driver. She couldn't wait to show it to her sisters.

Decades of birding had not only honed Grinnel's powers of observation, but also bolstered his memory for detail. Anne realized that he had recalled every aspect perfectly—with two understandable exceptions.

First, a lacy white glove, which Grinnel failed to note, could only be seen for a split second covering the old woman's hand as she placed it on top of the vehicle. Anne, however, immediately sensed its significance.

Second, Grinnel's inability to remember the license-plate number reminded her of the classic "dog-that-didn't-bark" clue once utilized by Sherlock Holmes to solve *The Silver Blaze*. When no witness could recall hearing the stable-dog bark, Holmes deduced that the mysterious midnight visitor must have been known to the canine—thus narrowing down the list of suspects to one.

Grinnel's video showed that while a license plate holder had been attached to the back of the Volkswagen, it was empty. There had been nothing for George to see.

Chapter 24: A Warmer, Gentler Charlotte

Charlotte was just about to insert her key into the ignition of her Porsche when she heard Helen Reddy's "I am Woman" coming out of her purse. In fact, the ringtone was obliged to play out in its entirety before she could fish her smartphone out of the brand-new shoulder bag.

The purse had cost $1,200—one Ben Franklin for each of its zippered compartments—but the purchase had not made Charlotte happy. Not only would it take her weeks to relearn where she had now stashed her stuff, but the designer had also failed to make any of the compartments easily accessible from the outside. *Why in the name of heaven, not? Too practical to be cool,* she guessed.

"Charlotte Hunter," she spoke into the phone.

"Hi, Charlotte, it's Ginny."

"Greetings, Virginia. I was hoping to hear from you today."

"I'll bet you want to know what's going on with Mrs. MacDonald."

"Has she been at all helpful as to the whereabouts of her son? There's still a warrant out on Frank you know."

"She's the reason I am calling. She refused to see me today."

"She did? Did the two of you have words?"

"No, the receptionist just handed me a letter. Handwritten. Eight pages. The essence was that Frank was unhappy that we were meeting."

"How would he have known?"

"I have no idea. Apparently, he threatened to cut off all communication with Alicia if she kept seeing me."

"That must have come as quite a shock. Did you have any idea?

"No, I was totally flabbergasted. When we had chatted previously, I got the impression that she hadn't seen him in years."

"Did she specify how long it had been?"

"She told me that the last time she saw Frank, it was right before her husband died. That was at least ten years ago. I feel just awful letting you down like this."

"Don't give it another thought, Ginny. Alicia MacDonald was always a long shot, although I do have one final question."

"Shoot."

"Did you get the sense that Frank contacted his mother by telephone?"

"It had to be by phone. I don't think he's ever visited at the convalescent home."

"Maybe we can get a warrant for her phone records. After all, if she's been in contact with Frank—that's aiding and abetting a fugitive."

"You may be right about 'the aiding and abetting part,' but I don't think phone records will prove very helpful. Frank is one smart cookie. According to her letter, when he wants to talk, he messengers her a burner cell. She also said he instructed her to dispose of it immediately after they hang up. I am just so sorry I couldn't be of more help."

"You've helped us enormously, Virginia. Frank, on the other hand, always seems to be one step ahead of us."

"You're right about that."

"Please know how grateful we are—especially because you did this on your own time. We will have lunch again soon. I promise."

"That would be delightful. Anytime, Charlotte."

"Wish it could be today, but I'm on my way to Alhambra to see if I can get Cesar's wife to remember something she didn't tell the cops."

"You still haven't found the murder scene, have you?"

"Wish me luck."

Charlotte would need more than luck—she would need a personality transplant if she wanted to get any information out of Santiago's wife. She would need to become a warmer, gentler Charlotte.

The San Gabriel Valley Garden Apartments were situated just across the street from a relatively quiet sycamore and oak-shaded park. A cement path meandered through the freshly mowed lawns and separated the old men playing bocce ball from the kids enjoying themselves on the railroad-themed playground.

Charlotte found a convenient place to park under a tree whose occupants, a couple of chestnut-backed chickadees, warbled their greetings. A light breeze whispered through her scarf, ruffled her curly blond hair, and caused the dust motes in the afternoon sunshine to pirouette like tiny ballerinas.

After an easy hike up the stairs to the second floor, Charlotte located Apt. F and knocked. The black-painted door swung open and revealed a tiny sparrow of a woman. She cocked her head, opened her mouth without speaking, and started to weep. But instead of the sobbing sound that typically accompanies such a volume of tears, she emitted an odd "cheep, cheep, cheep." Then, without warning, she disappeared inside, leaving the door slightly ajar.

An itchy twitch traveled up Charlotte's backbone. *Oh, dear, this doesn't bode well for Pajarita's first impression of me.* Charlotte attempted to gather together as much empathy as she could. Never adept at coping with female waterworks, Charlotte found herself wondering what her mother would have done. *Carina would have wrapped her arms around Pajarita.* As Charlotte attempted to simulate compassion in the same manner, she couldn't help but stare at Pajarita's apparel. In fact, she was barely able to stop herself from involuntarily sniffing her disapproval.

Since Pajarita was wearing the same color pants, shirt and sweater, from the crown of her brunette hair to the toes of her sensible shoes, she was a blur of brown. *What could this style-challenged woman be thinking?* And as she held Pajarita, it was all Charlotte could do to keep from checking her watch. Finally, Charlotte was relieved to observe that Pajarita had peeped her last, and was hopping over to the sofa. Charlotte, on the other hand, was left standing in the middle of the room with the front of her expensive silk blouse soaked in Pajarita's spent emotion.

Charlotte was much more comfortable in the role of prosecutor, where hounding and harrying are *bona fide* occupational requirements. In fact, she excelled at playing the bully. In this case, however, she realized that if she didn't switch gears and adopt a "we're-all-sisters-under-the skin" mindset, her long drive to Alhambra would be for naught.

What should she ask first? Charlotte knew full well that her initial question would set the tone for the rest of the interview. As she was gathering her thoughts, though, it was Pajarita who broke the silence. She pulled a tissue out of her sweater sleeve, blew her nose, and asked, "Who killed my husband?"

"I think that's something we both want to know," said Charlotte. She recited the condensed version of Cesar Castillo's missing person's history—including Anne's "witness to a murder" theory. "We think that's why he ran away," she finished.

"Then why didn't he try to return home? Hasn't it been forty years?"

"We think the killer must have also threatened Cesar's wife and child. We believe that he had no choice but to stay away for good."

"To keep them both safe?"

"That's the theory."

"I understand."

"I know I'm giving you a great deal to process right now. Let's switch roles. Do you have any questions for me?"

"Are you saying Santiago is still married to somebody else?"

"If you are worried that your husband is a bigamist, don't be. I'm a lawyer. Cesar's first wife, Maricela, had him declared legally dead. She did so after he'd been gone for ten years."

"Did she marry somebody else?"

"Yes, she did. She married Cesar's twin brother."

"I'm confused. Why do you keep calling Santiago by this other name?"

"We believe that when Cesar disappeared, he assumed the identity of a brother who died as an infant. The dead brother's name was Santiago. Cesar must have used Santiago's birth certificate to get a Social Security number, driver's license, passport, and anything else he needed to establish a new identity."

"What happened to Santiago's son?"

"Cesarito? Cruz adopted him. He now heads up the family flooring business. I need to know more about Santiago, Pajarita."

"Of course, what would you like to know?"

"What did he tell you about his family?"

"*La familia* was a forbidden subject with Santiago," said Pajarita. "He admitted that he had a mother and brother living somewhere else—he never would say where—and that he was forced to leave home at nineteen. He never said why."

"Weren't you tempted to find out more?"

"At first I was—but the topic made Santiago so angry, I just had to stop asking to keep peace in the family. He was a good man, but if he needed to keep that part of his life secret, then that's how it would be. To fill in the information void, however, I decided to invent a past history for him." Charlotte smiled. "In my version, Santiago and his father have this big fight. His father throws him out of the house. In fact, his father is so angry, in my story, he tells Santiago, 'if you ever try to contact anybody in the family again, I will kill you.'"

"You weren't that far from the truth. Santiago was threatened with death—but not by his father."

"Being banished is a familiar story with many Latino men. Sometimes fathers allow the whole *macho* thing to get out of hand—to where there's no turning back. In the heat of an argument, words, unfortunately, can divide *la familia*. Permanently," she said, with a meaningful sigh. "As the years flew by, though, knowing Santiago's history became less and less important to me."

"Don't you think Santiago ever tried to contact somebody from his family?"

"I can only tell you what I saw. Once a year, always at some point during our summer vacation, Santiago would look for a pay phone. Then he would call."

"Who?"

"I think he would talk to a friend of his mother's, if I'd had to guess—and he or she would keep him apprised of his family."

Charlotte immediately thought of Carina. Despite the age difference, she and Angelica were more like sisters than friends. If it had been Carina, Charlotte thought, she would have been the perfect choice. Carina would have taken Cesar's secret to her grave. She probably did.

"Sometimes, he would return from the pay phone and start laughing to himself. Sometimes, he would have no expression on his face at all. Once—this was the most memorable time—he jumped back behind the wheel and started whistling this funny little tune. I asked if his song had any words, and he said, 'No, I made it up when I was a little kid.' During all those years, he never said another word about those phone calls."

"When was the last time he called?"

"It was just two weeks ago—when we were in Washington, D. C. This time, after he returned to the car, he just put his face in his hands and wept."

"Why?"

"I didn't ask," she said, and the cheeping started all over again. *Maybe he was told that Carina had died, that his one and only informant was gone.*

"I'm sorry to bring up what seem to be such painful memories, Pajarita. Why don't we speak about happier times? Exactly how did the two of you meet?"

"We met at Alhambra High School." Remembering that day not only brought Pajarita peace but also a measure of joy. "He was the new history teacher," she said, as the image of a handsome young Hispanic appeared before her closed eyes. *Santiago es muy guapo*. Do you know what that means?"

"Not literally, but from the way you said it, I'd guess you were immediately taken with him."

"Was I! Yet I was sure that he would never notice me."

"What year was that?"

"1982."

"But I take it he *did* notice you."

"Yes, he did," she said softly. "Santiago was—he seemed much more mature than the rest of us."

"In what way?"

"For one thing, he was much older, I mean, than we were when we first started teaching."

"Why was that?"

"We earned our teaching credentials during our fifth year of college. It took Santiago twice as long to get to that same point."

"Do you know why?"

"Two reasons. Not only did he have to work full time in order to support himself, but when he first arrived in East Los Angeles, he didn't even have a high school diploma."

"I'll bet it was his perseverance and determination that impressed you," said Charlotte, with a wink, "even more than his good looks."

"You are quite right, Charlotte. When it came to earning a degree, I had it easy. Even though I was the first person in my family to graduate from college, my father paid for everything. All I had to do was study."

"Did your parents like him?"

"They said he was too old for me."

"Really? How much older was he?"

"Eight years, but, to me, the gray at his temples just made him look distinguished."

"Instead of just old?" said Charlotte. Hearing Pajarita giggle pleased her. "Did he ever tell you how he supported himself while going to school?"

"He worked at a wide variety of jobs. Construction, for one, and waiting on tables—but that kind of work didn't pay very well. There was a stint at an electronics store for awhile, but it was plumbing that paid off most of his bills. He claimed he could make enough money in one year to pay for four years of courses."

"But ten long years—he must have gotten pretty discouraged at times."

"He did. I think the only thing keeping him going was his dream of becoming a high school history teacher. Later, he would also be tapped to serve as the football coach. Coaching, he liked to say, was the icing on the cake. Only last week, he told me, 'you know, *mi amora*, I am doing exactly what I was born to do.' "

"So Santiago was a happy man?"

"We had a good life."

"And everything was perfect?"

"No, nobody's life is ever perfect. Perfection, as you well know, wouldn't have included those vacation phone calls."

"So he felt like something was missing?"

"I don't really know. What I do know is that over the years, *mi familia se convirtió en su familia.*"

"That sounds beautiful, Pajarita. What does it mean?"

"It means 'my family became his family.' "

"Tell me more about the annual vacations."

"See all those photo albums over there on the bookshelf? Every year we would choose a new historic locale to visit. Sometimes it was a Civil War battle site. Sometimes, a California mission. One year, we actually followed Route 66 all the way from Chicago to Santa Monica."

"Each trip sounds like an education in itself."

"Precisely."

"And you have a degree in American history."

"Summa cum laude, no less."

"Kudos to you, Pajarita. Teaching and traveling sound like a rich, full life. Which summer excursion was your favorite?"

"I don't know how it all came about, but Santiago started corresponding with a 119-year-old woman from Meridian, Mississippi. She claimed to have been a slave—"

"She must have been born near the end of the Civil War."

"Santiago even wrangled an invitation to visit her. We took along the school's video camera and I taped a couple of hours of Santiago talking with her."

"That must have been a remarkable experience."

"It was. Santiago asked exactly the right questions. You know Charlotte, I've probably read twenty books about slavery, but when you listen, in person, to somebody like Harriett Washington. She had so many moving stories."

"Did you ever show the video to your students?"

"That's exactly why we shot it. Both of us were always trying to find ways to make our classes more meaningful to the students."

"I see a couple of plaques on the wall that attest to your success in that department. It appears you were both outstanding teachers."

"We never had kids of our own, so, in a sense, our students were our kids. I keep a scrapbook full of letters from them."

"That's amazing, Pajarita. I never wanted to keep in touch with *any* of my former teachers."

Pajarita laughed, and then realized she had never offered her guest refreshments. "I am so sorry, Charlotte, I have forgotten my manners. Would you care for some coffee?"

"Thanks anyway, but I must be leaving soon. I do have a few more questions before I go."

"Fire away."

"Did Santiago ever mention that he was a twin?"

"No, but if he and his brother were twins, referring to their 'special relationship' makes more sense now."

"I'm a twin as well—actually a triplet. Emily and I are just as identical as Cruz and Cesar were, but our other triplet, Anne, doesn't look anything like us."

"But the three of you are close?"

"We hadn't been for a long time but that seems to be changing."

"Does Santiago's brother—and mother, of course—know? I mean about his murder?"

"Yes."

"I should have considered how Santiago's death might have affected them. How are they doing?"

"Well, as time slipped by after the disappearance, I think his older brothers became convinced he was dead." When Charlotte caught Pajarita's puzzled look, she added, "Let me explain, Cesar—I'm sorry, Santiago—actually has three older brothers."

"Goodness, do they all live in Port Cabrillo?"

"Two reside in Port Cabrillo—the oldest, Enrique, lives in Texas."

"Is his mother—well?"

"As well as anybody in her late eighties can be. Her name, by the way, is Angelica. I want you to know that neither Cruz nor Angelica ever gave up hope that Cesar was still alive. They both felt a psychic connection to him. And of course, his son Cesarito couldn't help but miss his father—even though Cruz adopted him."

"Do you think I could meet them?"

"I don't know why not. I'll give them a call and let them know. Before I leave, though, maybe you could clear up some things for me. Something you told Detective Milo still keeps nagging at me. Did you mention a newspaper ad to him?"

"Yes, I can't remember if it was in the *Los Angeles Herald-Chronicle* or the *San Gabriel Valley Tribune*. Santiago would always cart both newspapers into the bathroom with him. It would drive me *loco*."

"Because there's only one bathroom, right?"

"You get the picture. I was out of luck if I had to go—as long as he was in there reading."

"How long are we talking about?"

"An hour."

"An hour? My derriere would have fallen fast asleep."

"But now that Santiago's gone, you know, Charlotte, this might sound silly, but sometimes I just close the door and pretend that he's still in there."

"Just reading the paper." Charlotte wisely said nothing more. Anything else would just sounded like some sappy greeting card advice. Nonetheless, Pajarita started to cloud up anyway. Charlotte didn't wait this time for another crying jag to run its course. She realized she had to do something drastic to distract Pajarita so she walked over and pulled the crying woman to her feet. "I have something really important to ask you," she said, as she focused all her energy into holding Pajarita's attention.

"What is it?" sobbed Pajarita.

"Something Santiago read in the classifieds convinced him to drive out to Lake of the Woods."

"Was that where his body was found?"

"Yes."

"The man from the morgue only told me that his remains were discovered in San Perdido County."

"Lake of the Woods is located in the northernmost portion of San Perdido County. Have you ever heard of Lockwood Valley or Mount Pinos?"

"No, I don't think so. I've never been to San Perdido County."

"Well, we don't know why he would have driven all the way out there. It's a good eighty miles from here. Didn't he say anything—anything at all?"

"Yes, I remember now. It was about a car."

"A car he wanted to buy?"

"No, not this time, although Santiago was always checking the 'for sale' ads. He called it 'window shopping.' No, this was a 'lost and found' ad. Let me think. Some man found an old Volkswagen, I believe—and was trying to return it to its rightful owner."

"Did Santiago own such a vehicle?"

"No, I don't think so. He said the ad was actually some kind of code from his brother—just meant just for him. He believed his brother was trying to get in touch with him—you know—through the classifieds."

"Why would he believe that?"

"Because the ad specifically referenced a 1963 metallic blue-green VW. It even gave the right license-plate number."

"Do you remember when the ad ran?"

"Of course—the same day Santiago was killed."

"And was there a phone number in the ad?"

"There must have been, because Santiago called it."

"What happened?"

"The guy's wife answered and gave Santiago directions to their house."

"Did he, perhaps, write the directions down on a scratch pad?"

"No, I'm afraid not. He wrote it on the margin of the newspaper, and then took the entire paper with him."

"That's okay. We can find the advertisement if we have key words and a date. All newspapers are online now, so it should be fairly easy."

"I wish I could have given you more assistance."

"You've given us a great deal of help, Pajarita. Thanks. Oh, and I promise I won't forget about Santiago's family. I'll be in touch.

Charlotte didn't even wait until she was inside her car before notifying Emily of her findings. By the time she reached Port Cabrillo, a deputy sheriff was already combing the Lake of the Woods crime scene for clues.

Chapter 25: Granny Was Really a Grandpa

Anne downloaded Grinnel's video for her sisters. When the osprey swooped down over the road and the old lady was finally visible, Charlotte couldn't help herself. She just blurted it out. "That's a man trying to pass himself off as a woman!"

"Admittedly, she towers over the car but how can you be sure?"

"Well, besides the masculine posture and movements, the white-lace gloves are all wrong," said Charlotte, pointing to the computer screen. "Gloves like that are too formal for daytime wear—unless you're walking down the aisle of a church."

"And she was definitely not a bride," said Emily with a chortle.

"What bothers me even more," said Charlotte, "is the hair. That can't be real hair."

"Why not?"

"Oh that's easy. Those corkscrew curls look like they have just relieved of their bobby pins. Can't you see? They still need to be combed out. It's obviously a wig some foolish man liberated from a wig stand."

"Ah," agreed Anne. "Some man who had no idea what he was doing so he didn't bother to comb out the curls."

"The biggest tell, for my money, is his Adam's apple," said Emily.

"What's he trying to do?" asked Charlotte. "Hide his apple behind that antiquated collar?"

"Well, that cinches it," said Emily. "The perpetrator was a male trying to impersonate an elderly female."

"Do you think he might be a professional hit man?" asked Charlotte.

"Of course not," said Emily. "No pro would have worn such a butt-ugly dress."

"Not even when it was brand new?" asked Anne innocently.

"You mean back in the Seventies?" asked Charlotte snidely.

"So why do you think the murderer dressed as a female?"

"I think," said Anne, "it's because Cesar knew his identity."

"But why disguise himself as an old woman?"

"There's nothing very intimidating or threatening about an old woman," said Emily, "so Cesar would not have been suspicious of a stranger who looks like somebody's grandmother."

The triplets turned to their computers to examine the photographs taken at the crime scene. Astonishingly, they had made the journey from the deputy sheriff's smartphone to their laptops in seconds. The phone number listed in the *Los Angeles Herald-Chronicle* classified ad from the day of the murder led Deputy Jose Estrella to a lakeside cabin belonging to Dr. Bernard Sullivan, a retired English professor from Santa Lucia University.

"This is almost as good as being there," remarked Emily, reaching back and rubbing her sore back. Emily had been bitterly disappointed when a second surgery extended her immobility for an additional six months. The shooting had occurred on January 21, the triplets' 50th birthday, but by Easter, Emily had simply had enough. Her undersized reserve of patience had descended well below E. The only thing that kept her going was her drive to solve the cold case.

The rustic cabin in Estrella's photos had been fitted out with early-American reproductions. Panels of pebbled glass fronted the whitewashed cupboards and a simulated antique hand pump, sink-side, took the place of a shiny chrome faucet. In the center of the great room, a round cherry-wood table was surrounded by ladder-back chairs and laid out with an English bone china tea service painted with lilies of the valley. The enormous fireplace was faced in locally quarried granite and topped with a rough-hewn mantelpiece of ash. The floor-to-ceiling front window framed the mirror-like lake that was, on this particular occasion, a startling aquamarine—courtesy of a clear cobalt sky and a jade canopy of conifers around the perimeter.

"Who doesn't believe that those teacups will show evidence of GHB?" asked Charlotte.

Only one hand shot up, and it belonged to Anne. "I think he put the drug in the chocolate-chip cookies," Anne replied. "They certainly look tempting on that delicate china plate."

"I disagree, Annie-Fanny," said Charlotte. "Cookies would require too much GHB to be an effective delivery system. Besides, while Cesar might have refused a cookie, he couldn't say 'no' to a cup of tea. It would be impolite."

"I have to go with Charlotte on this one," said Emily. "Tea would be the most expedient method of giving Cesar enough GHB to lose consciousness—even if he only took a sip or two."

"Hadn't thought about the quantitative aspect," said Anne. "But check out the cookie sheet in the sink. Those babies were freshly baked. In fact, I can almost taste the Ghirardelli chocolate chips from here."

"How do you know he used Ghirardelli chocolate chips?"

"Is there any other kind?"

"Are you angling for a field trip out to the lake, Annie? Maybe a tasting tour?"

"Just saying that if I were Cesar, I wouldn't turn down a Ghirardelli chocolate-chip cookie—especially right out of the oven. And I would have devoured more than one."

"Okay, let's move on, Ms. Sweet Tooth. What about fingerprints, Emily?"

"According to the deputy's report, the house was thoroughly dusted and apparently only three sets of prints were found—Dr. Sullivan's, his wife Katherine's, and the victim's."

"That doesn't mean that there wasn't a fourth person— especially if he wore gloves," reminded Anne. "Remember the white-lace glove in Grinnel's video."

"So, if we're talking about a fourth person, where is the evidence of a break-in?" asked Charlotte, suddenly craving something sweet.

"Apparently, according to the authorities, whoever killed Cesar must have possessed a key.

"That *does* make it look bad for Professor Sullivan."

"Or the real killer," said Anne, mentally inventorying the cupboard for cookie ingredients, "could have known where the Sullivans kept their spare key. There had to be one."

"Why is that?"

"Just think about it," said Anne. "Keys have a way of slipping out of a pocket when tromping around the woods. I doubt that anybody—especially anybody looking forward to two weeks of seclusion—would relish driving all the way back home just to retrieve a spare key. Also with a second key hidden somewhere on the property—the owner could loan out the cabin to a friend or allow first-responders to enter in case of an emergency."

"I can see that you have really thought this through, Annie-Fanny."

"I sure hope Dr. Sullivan has an alibi," said Anne.

"Why isn't Mrs. Sullivan a person of interest?"

"Katherine has been quite ill," said Anne. "In fact, I think she was hospitalized at the time of the murder."

"Do we have the exact time of death?"

"Thanks to Grinnel who supplied a time code on his video."

"So where is Dr. Sullivan now?"

"He's being questioned at the Lockwood Valley Sheriff's station."

"You know," said Charlotte, "the name 'Sullivan' sounds familiar. Didn't he coach football at SLU? I recall Ginny mentioning a 'Coach Sully.' Do you think it's the same guy?"

"Well, football coaches, especially at the university level, don't coach forever—but with a Ph.D. in, say, English, a coach may be able to negotiate retreat rights back to his academic discipline when he retires from coaching."

"Carina mentioned something about Dr. Sullivan returning to the English Department to teach. I can check," said Anne, now realizing she possessed a second excuse to contact her father. She immediately squashed it, though, like some intrusive insect. She just had to let go of Morgan. After all, her sisters had.

When Anne tuned back in again, Charlotte was saying, "If it's the same guy, he might have had it in for Truman Carpenter."

"Why is that?"

"As I understand it, back in 1970 it was Carpenter who complained to the administration about being harassed by Jenks Jenkins. As a result, the dean of students forced the coach to bench Jenkins during the last four games of the season."

"Four games—that's quite a penance."

"The loss of Jenks put Santa Lucia out of contention for the championship."

"So you really think Coach Sullivan wanted to exact his revenge on Truman Carpenter because of a silly trophy?" asked Anne.

"And why wait nine months?" asked Emily.

"He had to," said Charlotte. "Otherwise, the police might have suspected him."

"Well, you could be right. Don't we all believe the same person killed both Carpenter and Castillo—even though the murders were committed four decades apart?"

"If the killer were Coach Sullivan—that would explain the disguise. Cesar might have recognized him—even forty years later. Sully couldn't take that chance."

"Maybe you should question Cruz about both Sullivan and MacDonald when you visit the Castillo family," said Charlotte. "Wasn't that meeting set up for this afternoon, Emily?"

"Yes, it was, but I had to reschedule when all this evidence started pouring in. Now if you ladies aren't doing anything tomorrow morning, perhaps we can all go over together."

"I'm game."

"So am I, but let's get through the rest of the photos. I do have a question first, though," said Anne.

"What is it?"

"What about the car Santiago drove to Lake of the Woods?"

"The Prius?"

"Was it ever found?"

"Yes, Deputy Estrella saw it parked in the garage."

"In the garage? Well, then our fourth person could have parked it in there."

"No, the deputy had to cut off the padlock. There was no evidence of a break-in."

"Wait a minute, how did he see the Prius without opening the garage door?"

"Apparently in the middle of the door, at eye level, there are three little windows."

"So with no evidence of forced entry in the garage, that's black mark No. 2 against Sullivan."

"I find it interesting," said Anne, and then went abruptly silent. When she realized her sisters were staring at her, she added, "I mean the part about the three little garage windows."

"Now what, Annie-Fanny? Spit it out. I'm starving."

"I'm th-th-th-th-th . . ."

"Just take your time, Anne," said Emily. "I want to hear what you have to say."

"Wh-wh-at if the old lady told Santiago that the V-V-Volkswagen was in the garage—"

"Take a breath, Anne, and slow down. You have something important to tell us and I want to hear every word."

"B-b-but what if the old lady told Santiago that the garage door was locked? She could have invited him to look through the l-l-little windows at the car."

"Well, why would she do that?"

"So he would see the t-t-top of the car but he couldn't see the license plate."

"Oh, I understand what you're getting at," said Emily. "The garage door would have blocked his view."

"The door would have blocked his view of the license plate but the color of the car would have been exactly right," said Anne.

"Of course, that's the reason the paint was new but the chrome was old. The killer had to purchase a '63 VW—but it was the wrong color. He tried to fool Cesar with a new paint job."

"And locating old lady clothes would have been pretty easy," said Charlotte.

"While he couldn't be sure he'd find the right size in Katherine's closet, he could have purchased the dress and shoes at, say, a thrift store."

"But I still think he used Mrs. Sullivan's wig," said Anne. "She had been undergoing radiation treatment for cancer. I think it was a good bet that a white-haired wig would be sitting on a stand right on top of her dresser."

"And the murderer could have suggested that 'she' and Cesar enjoy fresh-baked cookies while waiting for her so-called 'husband' to return."

"To unlock the garage door."

"So Cesar never dreamed that Granny was offering him tea laced with GHB."

"What I don't understand is why Cesar came out of hiding. I mean, after all those years?" asked Charlotte.

"Cesar couldn't resist. There was so much specificity in the ad that suggested Cruz was trying to reach out to him. But I suspect the license-plate number was the kicker. Who else, Cesar must have figured, knew the correct license-plate number but his own brother?" said Anne. "He must have assumed it was Cruz's way of telling him that the coast was clear."

"So how did the killer get the right license-plate number?"

"He could have written it down that night in the alley or he might have read about it in the newspaper like I did," said Anne. "Remember when I visited the *Port Cabrillo Pilot* morgue? After the wrong VW was found in the harbor, the newspaper published both plate numbers as part of the story."

"So how did he know where to place his ad?"

"Didn't your Internet search reveal that the same ad had been running in both the *San Gabriel Valley Tribune* and the *Los Angeles Herald-Chronicle* for quite a while?" asked Charlotte.

"Every day for six months—and the ad started one week after we opened up the Cold Case Unit," said Emily.

"The killer, whoever he is, is clearly very clever."

"And patient. He was willing to troll for Cesar for as long as it took—and he provided exactly the right bait."

"If only we'd figured out that Cesar was using his dead brother's Social Security number sooner," said Emily.

"I suspect the murderer hired a detective who was able to track Cesar all the way to Alhambra."

"He might have even discovered his actual address," said Charlotte.

"But the killer couldn't just walk up and ring the doorbell. He had to figure out a way to get Cesar alone—and unconscious," said Anne.

"Alone, I understand, but why unconscious?"

"The murderer, I believe, has some sort of physical handicap," said Anne.

"That makes sense. If it's been forty years since the Carpenter murder, the murderer would forty years older too. He could suffer from arthritis."

"So what happened to the Volkswagen?"

"The photos tell the rest of the story," said Emily. "This one shows deep tire tracks in the pine needles leading down to the lake. In the next shot, if you look closely, you can actually make out the top of the Bug. It's just beneath the surface of the lake. About, I'd guess, twenty-five feet from the shore."

"Aren't VW's supposed to be airtight?"

"Not if you leave the windows down."

"Here's the VW being pulled out of the lake."

"Now this photo is a close-up of the car's rear end. What do you see?" asked Emily.

"No license plate."

"Just like Grinnel's video," said Anne.

"What about the VIN number?

"Deputy Estrella checked that out, as well," said Emily. "The car is registered to Sam Thomason from Dayton, Ohio."

"Ohio?"

"Yes, but Thomason reported his vehicle stolen in March."

"Of course it was."

"So this could not possibly be Cesar's Volkswagen?"

"Not according to the Ohio Department of Motor Vehicles. Sam Thomason is the original owner. He bought the VW in 1963. The color listed on the registration is 'white.' "

"Has a search warrant been issued for Sullivan's house?"

"Both of his houses. Why?"

"If a sales receipt for either the car or the paint job can be found, he's our man."

"Unless Sullivan was framed," said Anne.

"Who would frame him?"

"Frank MacDonald might. He'd played for Sully so he might have known about the cabin and the spare key," said Emily.

"Come to think of it, an isolated cabin in Lockwood Valley would be the perfect place for Frank to hide out. I don't imagine the Sullivan family uses it much during the summer months," said Charlotte.

"Why not?"

"It's so much cooler in Port Cabrillo."

"That's true."

"So you still like MacDonald for both murders?" asked Anne.

"I do," said Emily.

"But I'm leaning toward Coach Sullivan right now," said Charlotte. "What about you, Anne?"

"I'm not sure that either one of them did it. Some critical information still seems to be missing."

"Something about both murders?"

"Right now," said Anne. "I feel like I'm trying to complete a jigsaw puzzle, but I don't have all the pieces."

"As well as the cover to the box?" asked Emily.

"The cover?" The question baffled Charlotte.

"Yes, the one with the picture of the completed puzzle," said Anne.

Chapter 26: Emily Hears a Confession

Well, I dodged another bullet—not that Emily meant "bullet" literally. When she had initially scheduled her meeting with the Castillo family, she hadn't considered the logistics of rolling herself up five steep front steps. This morning, her sisters would make all the difference. Not only had Charlotte and Anne grown quite proficient at the two-person carry, but also at wrestling her heavy wheelchair over stubborn obstacles.

Emily also realized that the visit to Ocean View Place would require delicate handling. While she had informed Maricela that they were merely paying a condolence call, what she was really after was a private audience with Cruz. She was certain that he would help her build a case against either Coach Sullivan or Frank MacDonald.

In addition, Charlotte had mentioned Pajarita's wanting to connect with Santiago's family in Port Cabrillo. Because of the shabby way Maricela had treated Pajarita at the county morgue, Emily was even more determined to honor Pajarita's request, even if it meant leaving Maricela's name off the guest list.

*****

A black plastic wreath embellished with an oversized black ribbon greeted the triplets at the front door. "Do you hear that?" asked Emily. Trumpet sounds from a mariachi band had made their way to the front stoop. "The Castillo family must be hosting a party."

"Probably a celebration of life—Mexican-style," said Emily. "Please, Anne and Charlotte, follow my lead. This may not be the best time to ask personal questions of the family."

"*Lo siento mucho*," said Anne to the Hispanic man opening the door. He had coarse white hair and thick wire-rim glasses. He introduced himself as Enrique.

"You live in Dallas," said Emily.

"*Si*, we found an ideal retirement community only twenty minutes away from the kids," said Enrique in a disconcerting Texas drawl.

"Do you return to Port Cabrillo often?"

"Not, unfortunately, in the past, but now that I am retired, we'll fly out more frequently. Especially during the summer, when it gets really hot in Texas."

"My sisters and I just stopped by to offer our condolences."

"*Muchos gracias.* You know, we never anticipated anything like this."

"I'm sure Angelica appreciates your coming."

"I don't know about that. She's locked herself in her room. She says she wouldn't attend a memorial service after Cesar went missing, and she won't attend one now that he's dead. She's *testaruda,* you know, like a mule."

The triplets nodded, and Enrique stepped aside so they could move through the door. Emily, who had instructed Charlotte and Anne to circulate among the family members, didn't even have to request a private word with Cruz. He had already appeared in front of her wheelchair—bending down to take her slender white fingers into his large brown palms. As he moved closer to kiss both of her cheeks, she looked so deeply into his eyes he thought she might have glimpsed his soul. "I promise you I will find the man responsible for your brother's death," Emily said quietly.

He silently wheeled her into a side garden where spikes of intensely purple blooms stood out against the weathered grape-stake fence. When Emily moved in closer to sniff the blossoms, Cruz said, "Don't touch it, Emily—it's monkshood." Then he reached for a freshly ironed handkerchief and tried to sponge away the teardrops moistening his cheeks. He finally gave up, bowed his head, and raked splayed fingers through his graying hair. "I want you to do something for me, Emily."

"What is it, Cruz?"

"I want you to stop looking for Cesar's murderer."

"But why?"

"I have my reasons."

"Look, Cruz, I realize this has been a very difficult time for you and your family. Your brother, who has been missing for forty years, finally makes an appearance—but as a corpse. Every time you imagined the day when Cesar would return, you saw the two of you, arms around each other, sobbing with happiness. But that's not what happened. The phone call informing you that your brother had been found, also told you he was dead. Your hopes were raised and dashed in the same instant. You realized that all of the questions you wanted to ask him would never be answered. You understood that your unfailing love for him would never be returned. You felt angry, frustrated, heart-broken, and demoralized. His death was devastating for all of you—but especially for you, Cruz."

The fifty-nine-year-old man took in every word. He started to speak but something—something very painful—seemed to be holding him back. Finally he closed his eyes and stammered, "N-n-no, that's not it."

"Is it Maricela?"

"Maricela says she is leaving me," said Cruz, looking resigned. "She says that marrying me was the biggest mistake of her life, that she has never gotten over Cesar, and that he has always been her soul mate."

"Those words must have been excruciating painful to hear—but you have to realize that it's the grief talking. Maricela isn't herself. She's forgotten, hopefully, temporarily, that you two share a remarkable history together. Your union spans three decades while her marriage to Cesar didn't even last two years. I suspect, Cruz, that Maricela has idealized Cesar in a very unhealthy way. You are going to have to be patient with her."

"Your insights—they are most astute, Emily, but the truth is, I *do* deserve to lose her. I was never completely honest with her during the entire marriage."

"What do you mean?"

"First of all, you must know that my brother is the real hero in this little drama. He was the one who demonstrated the utmost in courage and selflessness. He sacrificed everything for me."

"Cruz, I don't know what you are talking about."

"Look, Emily, I'm sick and tired of lying. I just can't keep up the pretense. Not any longer."

"What pretense?"

"In the past, it may have been necessary, but now? You have no idea how much I hated keeping his secret—but I promised."

"What secret?"

"Look, if I were to tell you everything, would you agree not to pursue his killer?"

"I can't do that. I am a police officer. I've sworn to uphold the law. You know that, Cruz."

"You probably won't believe me anyway."

"Won't believe what?"

"That I am Cesar."

Emily would later consider herself fortunate to have been sitting down when she heard Cesar's confession because if she had been standing, she could have cracked her head on the patio pavers when she fainted. When Emily finally did open her eyes, the intense smell of fish confused her. She would later learn that Cesar had splashed water from the koi pond in her face to bring her to consciousness. Even now, as she opened her lips to speak, she could make no sound.

"I knew you wouldn't believe me."

When Emily finally found her voice, all she could croak was a request that Cesar tell his story—leaving nothing out.

"After the bachelor party, it was Cruz who blew town," said Cesar. "Cruz said he couldn't allow me to forsake my wife and son—not even for a few months. I dropped him off at the bus station right after we got rid of my car. All he had to do was buy a ticket to Albuquerque and lay low for a couple of months."

"Why Albuquerque?"

"A distant relative lived there. *La familia*. That's why he would have had to take Cruz in—no questions asked. And we figured nobody else would make the connection to Albuquerque."

"Nobody?"

"Well, Big Guy wouldn't."

"Who is Big Guy?"

"That's my little nickname for the murderer. I was a witness to a murder. I saw Big Guy kill Truman Carpenter."

"We know."

"You know?"

"You witnessing a murder has been Anne's working hypothesis all along. It seemed to be the only explanation for the disappearance that fit, but we had no way of knowing for sure until this very moment."

"Amazing. How did Anne come to that conclusion when Aguilar went to prison for the crime?"

"She believes that the authorities only saw how much alike the Truman and Mortenson homicides were—while she couldn't help focusing on the more important differences."

"You know I was totally shocked when Aguilar was convicted but, well, I just couldn't come forward. Besides, Aguilar was hardly an innocent man. He did kill Mortenson."

"You know Anne mentioned to me just the other day that we were missing some big puzzle pieces. I suspect she would have figured out eventually that you and Cruz had traded places. Now it all makes sense. You would have to be Cesar."

"You Hunter women are pretty shrewd investigators. I just hope that Big Guy doesn't figure out who I really am."

"So what exactly happened to Cruz in Albuquerque?"

"When I called Ernesto, he told me that Cruz had never arrived. I still have no idea where he went after I dropped him off."

"Well, you might learn something about that from his widow—if you take the time to make peace with her, that is."

"I am more than willing to do that, but Maricela and *Jefa*—never."

"How do you know?

"Well, Angelica might come around eventually, but Maricela—she would never accept 'the woman who married her soul mate.' "

"But you are her soul mate."

"That would require her to believe that I am Cesar. She's changed, Emily. She says she doesn't know who I am anymore, but she's wrong. I haven't changed. The truth is, I don't know who she is anymore. Nobody does."

"But Cesar, don't you owe your wife the truth?"

"It's like she's deaf, Emily. She can't hear anything I have to say."

"Not right now, but in due course. Try to convince her, Cesar. She married you twice—once as Cesar and once as Cruz. Surely, during all those years, she must have suspected something wasn't quite right. That 'something' will be the key to getting her to believe you."

Emily looked at Cesar. She watched his eyes fill with tears and his chin drop low enough to rest on his chest. "I think I understand, Cesar. You are convinced that neither Angelica nor Maricela will *allow* themselves to believe you. If you were Cesar, it would turn their whole world completely upside down. You might get away with fooling other people, but not them. If you could dupe them, what kind of wife or mother might they be?"

"And that's the crux of it, 'Chief Hunter.' "

"You'd better make that 'Father Hunter. I *did* hear your confession."

Cesar laughed for the first time. "I must say, Emily, you are one perceptive lady."

"So how did you pull it off—the con job as Cruz, I mean?"

"Frankly, my mother wasn't too difficult to deceive. She's always been so vain—especially about wearing glasses or a hearing aid. Had she been a little younger, I might have failed. As it was, there was nobody who could impersonate Cruz like I could—not even Cruz himself. Angelica might have told you that we switched places from time to time in high school to find out if we could trick our teachers or girlfriends.

"And you were successful?"

"Better than we ever dreamed. All I had to do to become Cruz was to incorporate, you know, his little mannerisms or drop one of his catch phrases into the conversation. It was easy to do his special strut or rub my forehead that way he did, you know, with two fingers or drape his letterman's jacket over my shoulder everywhere I went. My mother—she saw what she expected to see."

"But what about Maricela and Cesarito? Surely you couldn't hoodwink them as well?"

"They were even less work. Cesarito was only a baby at the time and Maricela spent very little time with me."

"Even though you lived in the same house?"

"Even though we lived in the same house. Besides I was busy living Cruz's life."

"What about sexual intimacy?"

"What sexual intimacy? I slept alone in Cruz's twin bed for ten long years. Don't forget that Maricela didn't fall in love with me until 1981. She had to finish both mourning and wrestling with the decision to declare me dead. In fact, I had abandoned all hope of getting together with her when out of the blue—it happened."

"So during all that time, you and Maricela shared nothing romantic?"

"I was her brother-in-law, not her husband. She didn't think about me that way."

"Yes, I see. She saw you through the eyes of a grieving widow."

"At first, Maricela seemed intent on drowning herself in her depression. It was a black, black time for her. Then, ten years later, well, she had no reason to suspect who I really was."

"Yet back in 1971, you and Cruz lived very different lives. Exactly how did you deceive his teachers?"

"I loved his classes. Our intellectual interests have always been the same. In fact, after I was forced to drop out, I actually envied Cruz his life—so carefree and unencumbered. He was educating himself and excelling at football, while I was waiting on tables and pounding ten-penny nails into two-by-fours."

"So what about the football coach?"

"Yes, faking it on the gridiron was a little tougher than faking it in the classroom—especially playing quarterback. Cruz was a much more accomplished athlete than I was. But don't forget, I had also won a football scholarship. At first, Sully, who had chalked up my dismal performance to grief, gave me a pass. Eventually, I climbed out of my despair and started working hard—especially during practice. Gradually—I guess it's because we share the same DNA—I became Cruz in every conceivable way."

"You know, I can't believe I am saying this, but I believe every word of your story, Cesar—it all adds up. You do realize, though, I am going to have to tell my sisters the truth."

"But you can't tell them, Emily."

"Why not?"

"The more people who know, the more compromised is *mi familia*.

"Not even to hunt down your brother's killer?"

"Not even to put him in prison for life."

"Okay, Cesar—here's the deal. I'll give you a few days before I tell Charlotte and Anne. That's the best I can do. My only hope is that you confess to Maricela and Angelica by then."

"Don't hold your breath."

"Very funny, Cesar. You know I actually came here to ask you about some individuals you might have known at Santa Lucia University."

"You're still not satisfied? Even after hearing my confession?"

"You would think I would be—wouldn't you? But there's so much more I need to know."

"Okay—but no more about Big Guy.

"Don't hold *your* breath."

Cesar found himself chuckling, despite himself.

"Do you remember a football player named Frank MacDonald?" asked Emily.

"Sure. Rich kid. Parents gave him everything—except discipline and self-worth. He was voted 'most likely to end up in jail.' "

"Why was that?"

"He took too many shortcuts—ethical shortcuts. And he also had a pretty nasty temper."

"How nasty? Was he physically abusive?"

"Well, he drew the line at punching out somebody who might actually kick his ass—but women, of course, were fair game. His steady was really sweet but he was always threatening to slap her around."

"Do you remember her name?"

"Ginny. She showed up everywhere. She was on his arm like some kind of eye candy. Ginny was not only beautiful; she was smart. I don't know why he treated her like shit. I can still remember the time Sully had to intervene on her behalf. I think it was right after he saw Frank give Ginny a shove. Coach called him out there and then. But that wasn't the end of it."

"It wasn't?"

"The next day, there was a more serious chat in Sully's office. You could hear it all the way out on the football field."

"So 'Sully' is what you called Dr. Sullivan?"

"Right."

"His name is also on my list."

"What do you want to know about Sully?"

"Anything you can tell me."

"He was, in a word, just great."

"That's two words."

"Right, right. What I meant was, he was everybody's favorite professor."

"Why was that?"

"Well, most of our teachers at SLU did well enough in the classroom, but Sully paid attention to us outside of class. He really cared."

"In what way?"

"He worked very hard at maintaining a personal relationship with each of his students. The good, the bad, and the ugly—so to speak.

"So in your opinion, Sully wouldn't have been capable of beating Truman Carpenter to death?"

"Beating a student to death? You can't be serious. What I most appreciated about Sully was that he made me want to become the best person I could be."

"What about MacDonald? Could he have killed Truman?"

"He might have been capable of murder but why would he do it? What was his motive?"

"Because he found out that Truman Carpenter and Virginia Peabody had fallen in love."

"Tru and Ginny? Now that's pretty heavy, but, you know, I never heard a word about them being an item—not a syllable. That must have been the best-kept secret on campus."

"As I understand it, they were both afraid of what he might do."

"Well, I can buy that. MacDonald's one of those guys, you know, who was born without a conscience."

"So you believe he was capable of killing Truman?"

"He might have been capable, but I'll never admit that he's Big Guy. Look Emily, you have no idea who you are dealing with."

"But don't you want to bring Big Guy to justice?"

"I can't risk it. I'm not going to jeopardize the safety of everybody I love."

"But we can protect your family."

"No, you can't. This guy is rolling in dough. Even if you hauled his ass into court, my testimony alone won't convict him. I doubt that even DNA evidence would—that's how untouchable he is. I have no doubt that his team of expensive lawyers—and he can afford the best—would get him off. And then, if I had testified, and he got off—nobody would be safe. I can't risk it. I just can't."

"But you still owe your mother and wife the truth."

"What good would that do now? Neither of them is inclined to believe me, Emily, and you know it. Take my word —the only viable course of action is to do nothing. Let Big Guy believe he's finally in the clear. Please, Emily. Please allow my brother to rest in peace."

Chapter 27: Chloe Goes to Sunset Manor

"Chloe, its time to go." The dog poked her head out from between the legs of an Eastlake ladder-back chair. "Oh great, you're playing hard to get again. I told the people at Sunset Manor that we would be there at ten. We're already late."

Chloe crept out on her belly, cocked her head at Anne, and seemed to smile. When Anne reached out for her, the Yorkie streaked back to her "safety zone" under the chair. "Well, I guess I'll just have to leave without you," said Anne, sighing dramatically. That did it. The little dog yipped, slid out in front of Anne, and bowed in submission. In fact, she even appeared reconciled to being beautified.

"Let's wear the pink and yellow outfit today," Anne told Chloe, as she adjusted the Velcro fastener over the dog's tiny tummy. "It's quite summery, and the old ladies are going to love the eyelet trim." Chloe submitted to the wardrobe change with as much dignity as a self-respecting puppy princess could muster.

Being a therapy dog was something at which Chloe excelled. She was so effective at meeting people's individual needs, some of her "clients" actually took the time to express their appreciation in writing. But while acquiescing to loving caresses and hearing compliments verging on hyperbole should satisfy any therapy dog, Anne observed that whenever Emily was training the German shepherds, Chloe couldn't help herself. She lived to run with the big dogs.

Sunset Manor was as ritzy as Anne remembered. Between 1871 and 1895, the pink-brick, four-story building had been known as the Demeter Hotel—named for the Greek goddess of the harvest. The bas-relief above the door always reminded Anne of the flaxen-haired deity in Homer's *Odyssey*—the one who separates the chaff from the wheat. During the Demeter's heyday, Port Cabrillo was the second-largest grain-shipping port on the Pacific coast. After the turn of the century, though, the hotel still managed to hold on financially, despite its location adjacent to the noisy docks, largely because it provided an E-ticket view of some spectacular sunsets.

Marianne and Jonathan Peters gutted the interior during the Fifties—reconfiguring the floor space and turning the 140-year-old structure into a medical refuge for the affluent. Three elevators, festooned in burnished copper, provided access to the upstairs residences. Not only did the guests value the inlaid frescoes, marquetry flooring, and mosaic detailing in their suites but they also appreciated Sunset Manor's unspoken promise. No matter in what state they left their apartments, seconds after the door closed behind them, their rooms would be restored to the original showroom state. Guests could return with nary a book, piece of wearing apparel, or scrap of paper out of place.

In direct contrast with the off-putting formality of the lobby's silver and burgundy-striped wallpaper, cold marble floors, and antiques that screamed, "do not touch," Anne found Sunset Manor uncommonly warm and inviting on this particular Monday morning. Apparently, she had been seduced by the fragrance of the freshly baked banana nut bread being turned out by the gourmet cooking class. There, however, no sign of Alicia in the kitchen.

Sunset Manor also provided tastefully decorated spaces for reading, oil painting, board games, exercise with the Wii, and classes in ballet or tap dancing. Alicia occupied none of these areas either.

An auditorium that provided seating for two hundred was also empty. Yet walking down the aisle reminded Anne of the last time she'd occupied one of the seats. She and Carina had attended the Follies, an amateur production in which Port Cabrillo's male movers and shakers donned women's dresses and performed for local charities.

"Chloe," said Anne, as they exited the oak double doors, "I really miss Mommy today." But the little dog didn't cock her head as she usually did. She just lowered her nose and headed toward the aquatic area. Dozens of swimmers were doing laps in the indoor Olympic-sized pool. The spa, ample enough to reduce ten people to jelly-like states of relaxation with its heavy-duty jets and 104-degree temperature was also filled to full capacity. But there was no Alicia.

In a last-ditch effort to locate the elusive woman, Anne inquired at the concierge desk. There she discovered that Mrs. MacDonald hadn't booked an appointment with the esthetician, hair stylist, manicurist, or masseuse. She was just about ready to give up when the little dog pulled her leash in the direction of the gardens.

The first garden, which was filled with rows of vegetables, actually provided year-round organic produce for the guests' meals. The second was a horticulturalist's delight and featured a smooth stone pathway leading to discrete sections of plantings—from a formal English garden to a lily-pad-covered koi pond to a heirloom rose garden.

The roses at Sunset Manor actually outclassed Carina's prizewinners, much to Anne's chagrin. A petite white-haired lady in a white-linen pants suit was pruning a bush loaded with huge pink blossoms. Somebody—certainly not somebody as frail as Alicia appeared to be—had dragged a wrought-iron chair from the dining area so she might clip in comfort. And at her left elbow, a robust man of about seventy was surreptitiously whispering in her ear. He reeked, in Anne's humble opinion, of class and breeding.

She allowed her writer's imagination full rein—bestowing on him such abilities as always knowing the correct wine to order, being able to converse on any subject with genuine authority, and making the woman in his life feel like a gorgeous runway model, whatever her age.

In reality, he was seated in a wheelchair with his left leg sheathed in a dirty-white cast. His hair was mostly white—especially the tufts emerging from two oversized yellowed ears—ears that must have provoked "open-doors-on-a-taxi" taunts during his youth. His face had worshipped the sun for too long, and even though the day was quite warm, his tweed jacket was formally buttoned. A wide blue tie adorned with miniature lighthouses decorated his white Oxford shirt.

"Excuse me," said Anne, as she walked over, "but aren't you Alicia MacDonald?"

"Who wants to know?" answered her companion with an edge he had not intended. His rich baritone voice caused Anne to wonder if he had ever worked in radio. As is often the case with Anne, her thought made the instantaneous leap to her lips—without any awareness that she was speaking aloud.

"No, my dear, I've never worked in radio. My name is Archibald Philip Berylwood—but you better call me Phil if you know what's good for you," he said, crinkling wrinkled lids over eyes the same sky-blue eyes as Anne's prince had possessed. "I recently retired as the executive director of the Port of Cabrillo."

"What an honor it is to meet you, Phil. This is my therapy dog, Chloe. We were told that Alicia was especially fond of Yorkies, so we thought we'd pay a visit."

"Oh my, yes," said Alicia, suddenly wriggling around in her chair, "Let me get this cutie-pie into my lap. Why Chloe, what a darling outfit you are wearing," she exclaimed. "Now please make yourself at home," she told the dog. "The last Yorkie I held was, let me think now, on my birthday," she informed Anne. "A very long time ago."

"Tell me about her," said Anne, relying on the instant bond that Yorkie owners share.

"She died, oh, fifteen years ago. Isn't that right, Phil?"

"Hmm. I believe I recall the beast in question. She was quite a yapper. What was her name again?"

Alicia wrinkled her nose at the word "yapper." "You don't want to know her AKC registered name," she told Anne. "I can't even remember the whole thing myself. To me, she was just 'Taffy.' "

"Did you used to show her?" asked Anne.

"Heavens no. Taffy was a one-person dog. She was miserable whenever she was separated from me. Show dogs spend so much time with other people, you know—being trained, groomed, transported to competitions and all that. No, Taffy was my personal lap-warmer and face-licker—like this one," she said snuggling up to Chloe.

"Taffy was definitely your dog, Alicia. Me, on the other hand, she wouldn't give the time of day."

"You shouldn't take it personally, Phil. I was her whole world."

"And she was yours, my pet."

"So, if it's not too impolite to ask," interrupted Anne. "How did you injure your leg, Phil?"

Alicia started to giggle.

"So you think that's funny, Alicia?"

"Yes, I do. A man of your age, climbing to the top of a sailboat mast."

"Well, the sheet was fouled. Somebody had to untangle it. It was no big deal—something I'd done dozens of times."

"Apparently, the last time was one time too many, if I might make an impertinent observation."

"And who's going to stop you, dearest?" Alicia smiled warmly at Phil. "At any rate, I fell, rather unceremoniously, I might add," said Phil, "and broke my femur. Apparently it takes three times longer for somebody of my advanced years to heal, so I booked myself a six-month stay here at Sunset Manor."

"And weren't you astonished to find me in residence as well?" asked Alicia.

"Delighted, my dear. When you and Loran started globe-trotting I lost track, you know."

"Yes, Loran finally made good on his promise. You know, to take me around the world. He had always been so busy before—business, and all. But when the doctor gave him the ultimatum . . ."

"Ultimatum?" asked Anne.

"The doctor told him that if he wanted to keep living, he'd better retire immediately."

"Loran is MacDonald Motors," said Phil, by way of introduction. "I think he once owned something like eight different car dealerships."

"Ten," corrected Alicia.

"Ten different car dealerships. Since the Port of Cabrillo brings in many of the makes he sold, that's how Loran and I met. He was having trouble with one of the vehicle-distribution companies."

"What's a vehicle-distribution company?" asked Anne.

"They prepare cars before they're transported to regional dealerships."

"Prepare? Aren't these brand-new cars?"

"Well, even though longshoremen are careful, vehicles sometimes get scratched. They also get fairly dusty on their long ride to Port Cabrillo. The vehicle-distribution company inspects, washes, and repairs. That's so, when they arrive at the car lots, they're good to go."

"I always wondered how they get the cars out of the ships. Do they use cranes?"

"Good question, Anne. Actually they are driven down the gangway ramp."

"Of course, that would be the easiest way."

"Have you ever encountered a car covered in paper—except for the windows of course—chugging down the road in Port Cabrillo?"

"Why, yes."

"It probably just came off a ship."

"I seem to recall long, long lines of cars."

"That's right—we hire dozens of drivers at a time."

"And that's why everybody avoids the corner of Harbor and Seashell."

"What do you mean?"

"Since there is no traffic light there, you can get stuck forever. You know—waiting for an opening in the line."

"Don't let the City Council ever hear you say that. We are not supposed to be on Port Cabrillo streets during peak traffic hours."

"Well, I must say you had a strong supporter in my mother. She used to tell us that every one of those cars meant two dollars going into the town coffers."

"Your mother sounds like a very practical woman."

"If, by 'practical' you meant she counted every penny—she was *über*-practical." Alicia and Phil chuckled.

"Now I have a question for you," said Phil. "We know your dog's name, but we don't know yours. What should we call you?"

"It's Hunter. I'm Anne Hunter."

"Or course, your mother is the famous mystery writer."

"She was. We lost her this Christmas to cancer."

"Oh, I am very sorry. I am such a huge fan," said Alicia.

"And you live at Thomas House, don't you?" said Phil.

"Yes. Carina and I spent thirty years bringing her back from the dead."

"Yes, and that's exactly what you did—you brought a splendid Victorian lady back to life again. I haven't been inside her since I was a little boy."

"Well, I can certainly remedy that. You'll have to stop by for a personal tour."

"I'd love to."

"Now that that's settled, I have a question for you. I've always wondered about Scott Berylwood. What can you tell me about him?"

"Besides the fact that he's my favorite uncle?"

"I mean about his furniture."

"Yes, as you might have heard, he specialized in Eastlake-style pieces. In fact, his handcrafted furniture became extremely popular on the West Coast."

"So he truly followed the Eastlake philosophy?"

"How does somebody your age know about Charles Eastlake?"

"My mother found an Eastlake rocker in our attic. It became my favorite place to read books. Over the years, the two of us refinished specimens we rescued from thrift shops all over San Perdido County. Perhaps we have a piece your Uncle Scott crafted with his own hands."

"Well, I know his mark very well. I would be happy to identify it for you. And, of course you noticed the spindles on your front porch. You probably already know that Uncle Scott turned them on his own lathe."

"No, we didn't. We only knew they were added when the porch was enlarged. Now, you must definitely dine with us and fill in the blanks. Mommy and I had so many questions about the house but there was nobody around to answer them."

"Uncle Scott loved to work with his hands. I remember once, when all of the cousins—two dozen of us from all across the country—were invited to a big family reunion at Berylwood Mansion. That year Uncle Scott fashioned a baseball bat for each of us—including the girls. We played on a baseball diamond he constructed in the middle of the south meadow."

"You aren't going to believe this," said Anne, "but I found four small baseball bats in the attic. An expert in baseball memorabilia told me that they were handmade from a hickory tree but there were no markings on them. To whom would they have belonged?"

"Tiberius, Thaddeus, Timothy, and Theodore."

"Oh, I recognize those names. They were all killed on D-Day, weren't they?"

"It was incredibly tragic for Aunt Claire—losing four sons on the same day. You know she never recovered from the heartbreak. But you are wrong about the bats having no markings."

"Really? I couldn't find anything."

"On the outside edge of the knob, you know, the little ridge on the bottom that keeps your hands from sliding off?" Anne smiled knowingly. "Look there. The letters are very small. They were burned into the wood with an engraving tool."

"What do they say?"

"Our nicknames. Each bat was labeled so we could tell them apart."

"So yours said, 'Archie?' "

"You are a very wicked girl. No, mine said 'Phil.' "

"You know, Anne, just for that, I'm not giving this little dog back to you," teased Alicia.

"No, you are giving Chloe to me, Alicia. It's my turn," said Phil.

"But Phil, she reminds me so much of Taffy. I wonder if my Frank remembers Taffy. I'll have to ask him when he visits." Annie looked up, but said nothing.

"Alicia, you know how much I love you, but I can't let you talk about Frank as if he were still alive." Now Anne sat straight up in her chair.

"But he is. He sends me messages."

Now Anne leaned so far forward, her behind was barely resting on the chair. "How?" Anne finally blurted out, against her better judgment. She was afraid the old lady might clam up as she had with Ginny.

"He sends me a cell phone, so he can talk to me."

"So why doesn't he just use the landline? Isn't there one in your room?" asked Phil.

"Oh, Phil. You know that poor Frank's out on the lamb. If the police were to catch him, they would put him in the pokey and throw away the key."

"Alicia," said Phil, resolutely, as if he were speaking to a difficult child. "Look at me. Look into my eyes." Alicia obliged him. "Frank is dead. He died in Bogotá decades ago. He doesn't call you. And he doesn't send you cell phones."

"They're called 'burners,' " corrected Alicia.

Turning to Anne, Phil said, "I suspect Alicia watches too many crime shows on television." Then turning back to Alicia, he took her hand and kissed it—as gently as the Black Swallowtail butterfly had kissed the purple verbena behind them, before they watched it soar over the wall.

Not only has Berylwood been passionately in love with Alicia ever since they first met, reflected Anne, *but he has never told her how he feels*. Yet on this particular occasion, Anne actually had the presence of mind to keep her thoughts to herself.

Chapter 28: A Blast from the Past

When it came to breakfast, the triplets usually fended for themselves—grabbing a bagel or bowl of instant oatmeal. Each skipped lunch unless compelled to dine out for business reasons. Dinner was the only time they ate together so they made a big production out of the meal. Each night one of them was charged with providing a three-course dinner complete with candles, wine, and a freshly ironed linen tablecloth.

Charlotte loved all things pasta, so when the rotation came around to her, she toted home big brown bags imprinted with the names of Italian restaurants located in either Los Angeles or Port Cabrillo. Nobody cared if they contained lasagna, eggplant Parmesan, or chicken cacciatore—the triplets just started to salivate the minute their noses detected the pungent aroma of roasted garlic or cheese in tomato sauce. An antipasto and a tiramisu were typically included in Charlotte's sacks as well.

Emily, on the other hand, knew every joint that delivered within a ten-mile radius. She tended to gravitate toward ethnic eateries, especially those that specialized in Thai, Mexican, Brazilian or Filipino fare. Although she didn't realize it, she was probably paying homage to the "international nights" instituted by Carina. During the years the triplets studied other cultures in school, Carina would prepare a meal based on authentic recipes while the girls were charged with researching and reporting their findings about each foreign land during dinner. They were also encouraged to pull together something vaguely resembling native garb from the "dress-up rack." Since Carina had always been big on acquiring gently used attire during periodic sweeps of thrift stores, if nobody could integrate a purchase into her wardrobe, the item would be consigned to a "dress-up" clothesline in the attic.

Unlike her sisters, Anne, however, loved to cook from scratch. She would always shop at the farmers markets held in Port Cabrillo or San Perdido. Her specialty was entree-sized salad boasting at least ten raw vegetables or fruits—to which she added chunks of chicken or tuna, along with her homemade Vidalia onion dressing. An ice cream sundae frequently topped off the meal.

Tonight, however, she would be preparing her special lobster ravioli in vodka sauce. In fact, she was eyeing a suitably plump lobster when Dave walked over to the tank and asked if she needed any help.

Dave, whose father actually owned the seafood market, had been only two years behind Anne in school, but he looked almost as ancient as Andy, his ancient mariner father. The deep creases crisscrossing his leathery face attested to more hours spent on their boat than behind the counter.

"So how's that cold case coming, Anne?" he asked. "It appears your missing person wasn't so much missing—as missing a pulse."

"Nice one, Dave—but not really very funny. Try to imagine how difficult this whole thing has been for the Castillo family."

"I'm sure that's true. Cesar finally came home—after how many years?"

"Nearly forty."

"But he came home in a body bag."

"Again, I'm not laughing, Dave. Have you always had such a compelling way with words?"

"Now don't get me wrong, Anne. I know exactly how it feels to lose a kid." His statement was appallingly true. Dave's son Greg had been blown up by an IED only last year.

"Okay, I'll pull in my sensitivity feelers for now. You know how sorry I was to hear about Greg. It's not the same, you know, without him behind the cash register."

"Thanks, Anne. I miss him every day. Just like you must miss Carina."

Anne nodded as she attempted to extricate her wallet from the ancient leather purse. It had been Carina's, so it meant the world to Anne despite the worn leather strap and broken clasp.

"I read that the coroner ruled Cesar's death a homicide. Have you girls arrived at a suspect yet?

"You know I can't talk about specifics, Dave. It's still an ongoing investigation. I can only say that we have identified, let's see, two persons of interest," said Anne, unaware that an elderly man was leaning in a little too closely. Originally he had been standing a foot behind her.

"Well, best of luck to you. Have you figured out which lobster is going into your world-famous ravioli tonight?"

Before Anne could answer, she felt a tug on the sleeve of her sweater. She tried to ignore it, but when it happened for the second time, she turned around and faced the individual with the intrusive fingers.

He was a big brute of a man but so visibly old—probably in his eighties—that Anne did not find him at all intimidating. His fleshy body sagged everywhere and she could detect alcohol on his breath. She guessed that the only light his face, which was an unnatural shade of gray, had seen of late had been fluorescent. He probably couldn't recall, she thought uncharitably, the name of the last doctor who had given him a clean bill of health.

"Excuse me, miss, but aren't you Miss Anne Hunter?" asked the man.

Anne studied his facial features. Surely, she could spot something about him that was familiar—but she came up empty. He was a complete stranger. "I'm at a disadvantage here, sir. You seem to know me, but I don't know you."

"I know it's been a long time, Anne. I can't believe that you don't recognize me."

"How long has it been? Give me a hint."

"I'm Morgan, Anne. I'm your father."

Anne had hoped that if she ever swooned, she would have done so with her hand to her forehead like a lady in a Victorian novel—but as she made her unhurried descent to the dusty floor of Andy's Seafood Emporium, she felt more like the downward-spiraling white feather that introduces *Forrest Gump*.

Of all the scenarios she had envisioned of encountering her father again—this had never been one of them. Morgan Hunter remained motionless—except for his eyes, which flitted around the room, unable to settle on where to focus first. Finally, still shaken by the fiasco his intrusion had caused, he walked over to Anne and helped Dave get her seated in a chair.

Positioning himself opposite his daughter, he asked solicitously, "Would you care for a glass of water?" When Anne nodded in the affirmative, he motioned Dave toward the kitchen. But before he would leave, Dave stopped to whisper in Anne's ear, "Do you want me to call the cops?" Anne vigorously shook her head "no."

"I must apologize, Anne. I had no idea my name would precipitate such a fainting fit," said Morgan.

"I just never expected to see you again."

"Well, since none of you chose to attend Santa Lucia University. . ." Morgan intended to say more about this personal slight, but decided to take a different tack. "Besides, I retired from teaching in 1980."

"Wasn't that the same year Grandma and Grandpa were killed?

"That's correct."

"We attended their funeral, but we didn't see you."

Stanfield and Eugenie Hunter died as the result of a traffic accident in Naples, Italy. They had been sightseeing in a cheap rental car. When they stopped for a red light, the driver of the heavy delivery truck behind them kept going, virtually flattening their vehicle. Although heroic measures were employed, the Hunters were pronounced dead even before being loaded into the ambulance. The truck driver, who no longer held a valid driver's license, didn't even require a bandage.

The memorial service was held on the eighteenth green of the Newport Shores Country Club since Stanfield liked to joke that a golf course was the closest to heaven he was ever going to get. Morgan's failure to show up for the funeral, however, prompted considerable clucking of tongues among the mourners. How sad, people thought, that Morgan, the sole heir to the entire Hunter fortune, couldn't be bothered to say a few kind words at the service.

"At that time," responded Morgan, "I was shepherding a dozen students around Oxford. I couldn't very well leave them unsupervised. Stanfield and Eugenie would have understood."

Oh, your parents understood you quite well, dearest Papa, thought Anne. *Luckily, for the three of us, our college education money had been placed in an irrevocable trust.* Nobody doubted that Morgan would have pulled the plug on the funds had he been provided with the option. The triplets would have been forced to leave college in the midst of their sophomore year. Anne, however, mentioned none of this. What she finally sputtered was, "S-s-s-so, s-s-spring of 1980 was your last s-s-semester of teaching?"

"I never really enjoyed working with students, Anne. I'm an author at heart. That is my true calling. My inheritance simply gave me the opportunity to work on my *magnum opus* full time."

"So when was your *magnum opus* published?"

"It will be soon. Every time I think I've finished writing, an additional chapter begs to be added."

"So what's the book about?"

"It's the definitive history of nineteenth century British pre-Victorian writers. All the research is based on original sources, you know, personal letters and diaries."

"Hmm, sounds intriguing. Whom did you study?"

"You mean the authors?" Anne nodded. "Well, I started out with Percy Bysshe Shelley, Mary Shelley, and Robert Southey. Then I added John Keats and Lord Byron. I was going to end the book there, but realized I really couldn't leave out Jane Austen, Samuel Taylor Coleridge, and William Wordsworth."

"Oh, I know those writers. Actually I've read all of them."

"You have? I wasn't aware that you even attended college. I expected to hear that you were still collecting baseball memorabilia."

"That pretty much ended when I was ten, Morgan."

"Oh?" he said, a smug look on his face.

Anne's complexion blazed with shame. She didn't know how to respond. *What should I say? Should I tell him about my literature degree from UCLA? Should I mention my ten years as a manuscript reviewer?* But Anne said nothing. She just kept her eyes closed. Her first priority, as she saw it, was to center herself.

"I'm sorry, I seem to have offended you somehow. I certainly didn't mean to. I've kept up with your sisters' accomplishments by reading about them in the newspapers. None of the articles, however, ever mentioned you."

If Anne had chosen to speak at that moment, anything she said would have been obscured by her stammer. She had wanted to stuff her emotions someplace safe, but she just couldn't overcome her incredible anger at Morgan—anger for abandoning his daughters, for his snide insinuations, and for defining her, apparently during the past forty years, by her handicap. Carina had never placed limitations on Anne. In fact, she didn't even mention the word "Asperger's" until Anne had already celebrated her thirtieth birthday. By then, Anne had disproved every one of Dr. Samuelson's predictions.

Dr. Edward Samuelson was the high school psychologist for all of San Perdido County. Students referred by their teachers visited his Conejo Valley office where they waited on uncomfortable benches in a room with neither windows nor magazines. They found every wall, however, covered with dark wooden frames that held row after row of dead butterflies or moths that had been pressed between panes of glass.

Most of the specimens on display were fairly nondescript— colored only in shades of brown or gray—the occasional black border outlining a wing. Anne, who preferred such flamboyant specimens as the rainbow-like blue butterfly known as *morpho didicus* once asked Dr. Samuelson, whose bright yellow bowtie reminded her of a *Phoebis trite*, why there were no Monarchs on his walls, but he didn't answer her.

Even more boring butterfly displays could be found inside Samuelson's office—on the two walls that weren't filled with floor-to-ceiling bookcases, that is. Carina was horrified to find Samuelson's shelves jammed with more volumes about lepidoptery than either psychology or childhood behavior. Anne, however, was most disappointed to discover two even more bottom-numbing wooden chairs face Samuelson's massive teak desk instead of the comfy couch she had anticipated.

Carina nearly went mad every time Dr. Samuelson asked a question. He would click his pen—not just once, but exactly three times. And instead of looking into Anne's eyes while she spoke, he would swivel around in the squeaky chair and pretend to study the three framed diplomas displayed behind him. She also thought it odd that Samuelson had never considered autism as a diagnosis for Anne. Her personal research had immediately led her to Bernard Rimland, who published the breakthrough journal article on the subject more than sixteen years previously. As far as Samuelson was concerned, though, Anne had been brain-damaged from birth. He was flabbergasted that she hadn't been placed in an institution.

After the last session, Dr. Samuelson informed Carina that her daughter would never be able to graduate from college, would never be able to support herself, and would never find a spouse. Carina wisely kept this information to herself until Anne had earned a degree at UCLA, secured full-time employment with a New York publisher, and became engaged to Martin Bordeaux.

But alas, Martin didn't prove to be the prince with the purple feather. When Anne returned his ring, she explained that it wasn't his mood swings that troubled her most, but rather his constant criticism and controlling behavior. She just didn't like the way he made her feel about herself. Her family members, blasé from the beginning, turned downright celebratory when the couple parted ways. Anne would later conclude that being personally so ill-equipped to compete in the dating game, she had best settle for embracing a life that didn't require a life partner.

Anne, now looking directly at Morgan, finally found her voice. "While I admire most of the authors you mentioned," she said, "my favorite, by far, would be Jane Austen."

"It's been my experience that adolescent girls go through a phase I call 'worshiping at the *Pride and Prejudice* shrine,' " he said, "but eventually they grow up. Even though I've been forced to lecture about Austen for decades, I still consider her nothing more than a lightweight author."

"A lightweight? Who, then, would constitute a heavyweight, in your humble opinion?"

"Ah, dear Anne, how about the poet who wrote, 'And then my heart with pleasure fills, and dances with the daffodils?' "

"Crusty old William Wordsworth? While I did find his *I Wander'd Lonely As A Cloud* quite lyrical—maybe even transcendent in places," stated Anne, without a stutter, "he's certainly no Austen."

"There's no way you can defend such a ridiculous statement."

"Your other writers, with the exception of Mary Shelley, were male. Women writers during the pre-Victorian era, as you well know, were distinctly disadvantaged—due strictly to gender. That's something they could do nothing about."

"Such a broad generalization, Anne. Surely you can do better than that."

"First, take the schooling available at the time. Wordsworth and Coleridge were educated at Cambridge. Southey was an Oxford man. Females like Jane Austen, though, were barred from the great universities. Why? Just because they were women.

Second, ladies, especially if unmarried, were not allowed to travel—that's why Shelley's wife was such a notable exception. While he took her everywhere, women, especially women without spouses to accompany them, were barred from experiencing foreign lands for themselves. That only left them the option of *reading* about other writers' experiences—writers, I might add, who were also exclusively male.

Third, male writers were encouraged to seek out mentors among the ranks of published authors, while women, confined to home and hearth, held no such access. Yet Jane Austin did not allow such entrenched cultural limitations to hold her back. She became more respected and renowned than any of your other *magnum opus* authors. In fact, without counting your yet-unpublished work, more than twice as many volumes have been written *about* Austen than the seventeen books she penned herself."

"Of course your argument is riddled with logical fallacies, yet, I must admit, I do admire your passion. Perhaps you would be interested in a piece of mine published by the *Literary Quarterly*. Have you ever run across "Homerun, Or A Run Home?" It traces Austen's previously unknown association with baseball."

"Baseball, you say?"

"And it further explains why Austen remained a spinster all her life."

"And I should certainly be able to identify with spinsterhood."

"No, you misunderstand, Anne. That's really not what I meant."

"Look, Morgan, I've got too much to do today to waste any more time on you."

"Allow me to mail you a copy," Morgan said. Then he added, "Please?"

"Don't bother. I'm sure I can access it online if I'm interested."

With that, Anne walked to the counter, paid for the lobster, and left without saying 'goodbye.' If turnabout is really fair play, Anne's unexpected reunion with Morgan would prove neither fair nor play.

Chapter 29: Anne Makes Lobster Ravioli

"When's dinner?" asked Emily." I've been trying to work, but with that alluring fragrance emanating from that crockpot—all I can think about now is your *molto delizioso* ravioli."

Anne's big wooden spoon was creating a sweet-scented whirlpool in the rich red sauce that had been simmering since dawn. Although her sisters had dubbed it "Anne's Secret Sauce," there was nothing secret about it. The traditional recipe required several cans of crushed tomatoes as well as plenty of chopped onion, garlic, celery, and carrots. To spice it up, she threw in a handful of sea salt and freshly ground pepper, along with some dried bay leaves and fresh basil from her herb garden.

With the lobster and ricotta stuffing nearly ready to seal into her homemade pasta dough, it was now time to add the vodka infused with red-pepper flakes, the heavy whipping cream, and the Parmesan cheese. The kitchen table was already covered by a twenty-by-twenty-inch square of thinly rolled dough.

A grid of lobster/ricotta mounds marched five down and five across. After considerable experimentation, Anne had discovered that a little cognac and an abundance of chopped shallots made all the difference in her lobster stuffing mixture. She was ready to paint the dough around each seafood mound with beaten egg when Charlotte called her to the telephone.

"Take a message, for God's sake," trumpeted Anne from the kitchen. "I'm at a critical juncture in the process. I can't stop now."

"But it's a man," said Charlotte with a naughty lilt. "You don't want to risk telling a red-blooded male that you are too busy to take his call."

"Damn it, Charlotte," exclaimed Anne. "You just never give up, do you?"

"You're not getting any younger, Annie-Fanny."

"Are you willing to come in here and finish these?" asked Anne, knowing full well that the Hunters would starve if Charlotte were to cook.

"Sorry, sir," Charlotte told the caller, "would you be willing to hold for a few minutes?" Apparently he would. Anne gently lowered the twin top over the bottom dough, pressed lightly around each heap of filling, and deftly employed her cutter wheel to crimp the sides of each three-inch by three-inch square. On her way to the dining room, Anne grabbed a dishcloth, rendered her hands free of semolina, and grabbed the handset from the Charlotte.

"This is Anne."

"This is Morgan, Anne." Anne almost had the receiver back in its cradle when she heard Morgan beg, "Wait, don't hang up. Please. Hear me out." Since Anne had remained silent, he continued but without stopping to take a breath. "I'm so sorry, Anne. I know I got off on the wrong foot with you. Are you still there?"

"Yes," she hissed through clenched teeth.

"I really want a relationship with you. I was so impressed with the ardent way you defended your views. You reminded me, in fact, of my most gifted students."

"Uh, huh," she said, as if responding to a telemarketer.

"Well, my dearest daughter, I'd like to spend some more time with you. Maybe we can go out to dinner—just you and I."

"What on earth would we talk about?"

"Oh, anything, Anne. Whatever you want. If nothing else comes to mind, we could discuss my *Literary Quarterly* article."

"Are you serious? Why would you want to waste your time discussing a lightweight like Jane Austen?"

"Okay, we don't have to talk about literature. I was just giving you an example. What I really want to know about—is you. I want to know what my little Annie of Green Gables has been doing all these years. I need to know about your life."

"Please don't call me that."

"Why not? Wasn't that my special name for you?"

"Now I'm special—but not special enough to call, or write, or—"

Morgan cut her off before she could finish the litany of his many sins. "And I regret not keeping in touch with you, Annie. I was such a fool. I know I can never make up for all those lost years, but if you would just be willing—if you would just *consider* the possibility of forgiving me, I could go to my grave a happy man."

His grave? Like a bolt, it hit her. If she had turned fifty this year, he must be over eighty. He certainly hadn't looked all that healthy at Andy's Seafood Emporium. A 360-turnaround at life's end? Isn't that the plotline to every redemption novel? Once the protagonist feels the breath of the Grim Reaper tickling the hairs on the back of his neck, he decides to change his ways, make up for lost time, (insert your favorite redemption cliché here).

Despite all her misgivings, she really wanted to believe Morgan was telling the truth. She'd have to test him, though, to make sure. "What did you have in mind?" she finally answered.

"Consider this proposal for a moment," said Morgan. "I need to drive to San Diego to take care of some business, but I will return to Port Cabrillo by Friday afternoon. I'll stop by Thomas House around six-thirty. If you decide to see me, then we can go to any restaurant you choose. If you decide you are not ready, just inform me at the door, and I'll drive away without saying another word. Is it a deal?"

Anne wasn't willing to send her father away—but she wasn't going to make it easy for him, either. She responded the way most women respond when they need to hedge a bet. "I'll think about it," she said after clearing her throat.

"That's all I can ask, dearest Anne. I'll see you on Friday," said Morgan with obvious relief, and hung up. Anne, however, just stared at the receiver—until Charlotte's voice broke her reverie.

"Who was that, Anne? Was it Merlot? Or was it Sirah?" Charlotte thought herself hilarious—feigning memory loss with respect to the name of Anne's former fiancé.

"Very funny, Charlotte. His name was Bordeaux. Martin Bordeaux."

"Oh that's right, Martin Bored-oh," quipped Charlotte, circling her finger and thumb to drive the pun home.

"Why can't you just stop, Charlotte? What is wrong with you? Why must you be so deliberately cruel?"

"You've got me all wrong, Annie-Fanny. I was just kidding around. Tell her, Emily." The look Emily shot Charlotte couldn't be mistaken for anything but rebuke. "Well, okay. Guilty as charged. I'm sorry, Annie-Fanny, if I hurt your feelings. Really, I am."

"Fine, Charlotte. Don't give it another thought. The man on the phone? No, it wasn't Martin Bordeaux."

Anne was just about to identify Morgan as the caller, but something held her back. She had also anticipated sharing the episode at Andy's and the prospective Friday dinner date with her sisters but now she wasn't so sure. Was it because she realized that unless she spoke his name, unless she made the situation real—she could still continue to fantasize about her father? Because once she told them, they would feel duty-bound to wail, like some sort of Cassandra duet, that he was up to no good. Their prediction would be so predictable: "Once he gets what he wants, he will break your heart all over again." And they would be right. *But for now . . .*

After returning to the kitchen, Anne set Emily to tossing the salad and Charlotte to setting the table. The ravioli was exquisite, they all admitted as they sopped up the remaining sauce with leftover hunks of Italian bread.

"Is everybody finally finished gorging themselves?" asked Emily, after banging her spoon against her water glass. "I have been waiting to tell you something—something I learned at the memorial service."

"Oh, did you find out anything helpful?" asked Anne.

"Helpful doesn't begin to cover it," said Emily, "but first let me recount the call I just received from Deputy Estrella. You both remember that Coach Sullivan lacked an alibi for the time of Cesar's murder?"

"Yes, but I don't think he really did it," said Anne.

"Actually, now we can be sure."

"Really?" said Charlotte, straightening up as she unloosened the chain belt digging into her waist.

"Dr. Sullivan maintained that he was taking a nap on the afternoon in question," continued Emily. "He had been up all night in the emergency room after his wife suffered a transient ischemic attack—a mini-stroke."

"First cancer and now a stroke?" asked Anne. "Poor Katherine."

"At any rate, although Estrella interviewed the neighbors, nobody could give Sullivan an alibi. But Michael Mott couldn't be reached because he was in Bermuda. When he returned, however, he found Estrella's message on his answer machine."

"So what did he say?" asked Anne.

"Mott places Sullivan's car in the driveway during the time of death. In fact, since the front room-blinds on Mott's side of Sullivan's house were open, he actually saw Sully sacked out on the sofa. All afternoon."

"So, we're down to a single suspect, right?" asked Charlotte.

"If you mean Frank MacDonald, I'm afraid I have equally bad news on that score as well."

"What do you mean, Anne?"

"Chloe's visit to the convalescent home also proved quite fruitful. Apparently, Mrs. MacDonald is a touch on the delusional side. While she believes that her son communicates with her via burner phone, a friend of the family, Phil Berylwood, told me what really happened to Frank."

"What?"

"Frank MacDonald was murdered in Bogotá. Phil wouldn't share the particulars. Apparently, Loran MacDonald kept the whole thing quiet."

"And if Frank died abroad, that's the reason the arrest warrant is still on the books," said Charlotte.

"Colombia suggests narcotics—do you know if Frank was involved in drugs?"

"Well the file mentioned distributing cocaine."

"Then where does this leave us?" asked Anne.

"At the proverbial square one," said Emily. "Unless we can persuade Cesar to talk."

"You mean Cruz, don't you?"

"Well, I certainly buried the lead on that one," said Emily. "What we didn't know is that forty years ago, the twins switched identities."

"What did you say?"

"Cruz wanted to spare Cesar the pain of being separated from Maricela and Cesarito, so—before Cesar dropped Cruz at the bus station, they traded clothes, wallets, and lives."

"Now, let me get this straight. Cruz ran away, while Cesar stayed home and pretended he was Cruz?" said Charlotte.

"Even if Cesar could have pulled this off at school, he couldn't possibly have tricked his own mother and wife," said Anne.

"You wouldn't think so, Anne, but the way Cesar explained it to me, it made perfect sense. Angelica was getting to the age when she couldn't see or hear as well as she used to. You remember how Carina refused to get bifocals?" said Emily.

"Okay but—" said Charlotte.

"As Cesar so succinctly put it, 'people see what they expect to see.' "

"So Cesar just walked into the middle of Cruz's life?" asked Anne.

"Basically. The upside for Cesar was that it was a much better life. As Cruz, Cesar didn't have to juggle jobs. He was only obliged to study, play ball, and play his role as uncle and brother-in-law."

"But not as husband and father. It would have been impossible to deceive Maricela—especially during sex," said Charlotte.

"That's the thing. As Cruz, Cesar wouldn't be expected to be intimate with Maricela. He was the brother-in-law. It took ten years for them to start a romantic relationship. During all that time, Cesar was forced to exercise incredible restraint—and patience. He had to wait for his wife to fall in love with him all over again," said Emily.

"Imagine how fearful Cesar must have been to allow a killer to upend his life as well as the life of his brother," said Anne.

"And that's the nitty-gritty of the matter. Fear, even if irrational, can be a formidable motivator."

"So Cesar can identify Truman's killer?" asked Charlotte.

"Yes, he can," said Emily, pulling Chloe on her lap. "But he refuses to do so. All he would say is that the man he calls 'Big Guy' can afford an army of attorneys to get him off. He is also convinced that Big Guy would execute anybody who testifies against him."

"Well, attempting to try a murder case after forty years is really going to be problematic anyway," said Charlotte, about to apply lip gloss, but then realizing it was almost time for bed. "Even though there's no statute of limitations on homicide, it will be very difficult to gather evidence, witnesses and forensics. Why even the murder weapon was thrown away. Yes, Cesar can serve as an eyewitness, but the deputy district attorney will require additional proof to corroborate his testimony."

"I think the biggest problem is going to be providing a motive for the Carpenter murder," said Emily.

"Obviously, Cruz was killed because Big Guy believed he could identify him," said Anne.

"Does Cesar know why Big Guy killed Carpenter?"

"I have no idea," said Emily, tickling Chloe's tummy. "But, even if he knows, he definitely won't tell us. He's afraid it would put his family in danger."

"And, although I hate to be the one to bring this up, you can expect blowback with respect to Cesar's credibility too," said Charlotte. "Big Guy's attorneys are going to keep reminding the jury that Cesar lied about who he was for four decades."

"Oh, Charlotte," said Emily, now completely disheartened.

"But the lying can be explained," said Anne, rearranging the salt and pepper shakers to help her think. "He did it for the best of reasons—to protect his loved ones. Juries should readily identify with that reason."

"I think we need to get Cesar's family involved," said Emily. "Perhaps *they* could persuade him to testify. Also, they could testify as well."

"They could corroborate his story and speak to his character. Yes, they might be the only ones who can persuade the jury to believe him," admitted Charlotte.

"But I suspect Cesar is right about Maricela and Angelica. They will be most reluctant to accept him as Cesar," said Anne.

"I wonder if there's some piece of evidence—one stubborn fact that would convince them that Cesar is telling the truth."

"What about the car—the VW?"

"What do you mean, Anne?"

"Can't we check out Cesar's Volkswagen?" asked Anne. "As much as he loved that car, he would have hidden it away somewhere where it wouldn't be damaged by the elements."

"I understand what you are saying," said Emily. "You hope that forensic evidence of some kind might have survived."

"It's a long shot, but if the car were protected from the weather—I don't know, in a garage or barn somewhere—maybe we can still discover something that proves that Cesar is telling the truth," said Anne.

"Do you think he will tell us the location of the car, Emily?"

"Let's find out." Emily called the number, and Cesar picked up on the first ring. "This is Emily. Is this a good time to talk?"

"Sure, I'm in the garden—smoking a cigarette."

"I'm going to put you on speaker."

"Smoking is bad for you, Cesar."

"Oh, Annie-Fanny, not now."

"I understand you won't give us Big Guy's identity, but would you tell us where you hid your car?" asked Emily.

"You mean *Señor Escarabajo?*"

"*Señor Escarabajo*, that's pretty funny," said Anne.

"What do you mean?"

"He's calling his Volkswagen 'Mr. Beetle' in Spanish."

"So where is *Señor Escarabajo?*"

"I don't suppose it will make any difference now. The car Big Guy showed to Cruz couldn't have been *Señor Escarabajo*. What I don't understand is why Cruz didn't realize it right away."

"First of all, we believe that Big Guy was dressed as a woman."

"Are you serious?"

"We think he disguised himself, so that you—"

"Or the person Big Guy thought was you wouldn't recognize him. You know, sisters, this is getting way too complicated for me."

"Anyway," said Anne, picking up the story. "Cruz only saw the VW through a tiny garage-door window. Big Guy wanted to make it impossible to see the license plate, you know, on the back of your Bug."

"Because while he had purchased a '63 Volkswagen to show Cruz," continued Emily, "it was the wrong color, so he had to have the car repainted—you know, your special metallic blue-green."

"We think," said Anne, "the disguised Big Guy probably told Cruz that 'her husband,' who had the only key to the garage, was on his way home. That's how 'she' got Cruz to come into the house."

"While they waited, Big Guy served homemade chocolate-chip cookies and tea laced with a knockout drug."

"And while Cruz was unconscious, Big Guy drove him up to the road, threw him out of the car, and then, you know, ran over him."

Cesar was silent for a long time. "Where did this happen?"

"The scene of the crime was Dr. Sullivan's cabin at Lake of the Woods."

"I know that place. Sully took players up there every year after football season."

"We were wondering how Big Guy knew that the VW would make the perfect bait for Cruz."

"The thing you forget," said Cesar, "is that Cruz didn't actually know Big Guy's identity. Only I did. And I never told Cruz, not even when we saw Big Guy's black Mercedes idling in front of our own house. And by the way, Big Guy deliberately crashed his Mercedes into *Señor Escarabajo* in the alley that night."

"So there might be paint transfer on the rear end of the Bug?"

"Could be—but Big Guy would have traded in his Mercedes decades ago."

"Okay, Cesar. Where's *Señor Escarabajo?*" Without further argument, Cesar gave Emily specific directions to the tunnel of the Lexington gold mine. Emily immediately persuaded the San Perdido County Sheriff's Department to start a search.

"You know," said Anne, "fingerprints might provide the proof Cesar needs to convince Angelica and Maricela."

"Good point," said Emily. "As twins, even though Charlotte and I share similar ridges and whorls, our prints are not identical."

"So, if I wanted to know which sister borrowed my silver bracelet last week, I could catch the culprit with fingerprint powder?"

"Okay, Annie-Fanny. I confess. I took your bracelet. But I returned it in one piece. No harm; no foul, right?"

"Except you failed to ask my permission."

"Oh puh-lease. Sisters don't have to ask permission."

"You know who gave me that bracelet, don't you?"

"That Bordeaux chap. Am I right?"

But she wasn't right. Morgan had given Anne the bracelet. In fact it was the last present she had received from him. Anne, however, also decided to keep that information to herself. "I guess my special things are not very special to you, Charlotte," she said instead.

"Oh Anne, why do you always make such a big deal out of everything?"

"Everything?"

"If we could return to the fingerprint issue," said Emily, now fed-up with both her sisters. "The point I was trying to make is that while twin prints are strikingly similar, they can always be distinguished on closer examination."

"In fact, before modern genetic testing, fingerprints were used to determine whether twins were fraternal or identical," said Anne.

"That's right. You must remember the classic fingerprint study with the Dionne quintuplets?"

"But all five of them weren't identical," said Emily.

"They were and they weren't," said Anne. "Three sets of monozygotic twins were conceived. Émilie and Marie were one set. Annette and Yvonne were another. And Cécile, it was believed, lost her twin to miscarriage. Their relationship to each other, however, could only be determined by fingerprints."

"Then when the shrinks started studying the quints," said Charlotte, who had minored in psychology, "they found out that each Dionne sister had become emotionally closest to her identical twin. Cécile, however, whose twin never got the chance to be born, remained a loner."

"And you would suppose, Charlotte, that I most identify with Cécile," said Anne.

"Well, duh."

"Just shut up, Charlotte. You're not at all humorous—just annoying now," said Emily. Then turning to Anne, she added, "You know, when we were kids, Charlotte and I were sometimes very thoughtless—especially when it came you. We tended to leave you out because we were so focused on each other. We didn't really try to get to know you."

"And I am still a jerk," admitted Charlotte. "Sometimes I can't help myself. I'm just trying to be funny—but it's usually at your expense, Anne."

"Tell me about it."

"Please, Annie. I do promise I will do better."

"Both of us are going to try to be more sensitive to your feelings," said Emily.

Anne turned away so they wouldn't see her tears. "Try not to give it another thought," she blustered. "I certainly won't."

"But we must, Anne. You are the superglue that holds this family together.

"Oh, sh-sh-sugar," said Anne, stumbling up the stairs. *Worse than not being appreciated enough is being appreciated too much.*

"So what you are saying, Emily, is that the Dionne study predicts that while identical twins like Cesar and Cruz might share the same DNA—they possess unique fingerprints?"

"That's correct. And wasn't it just ducky of Mother Nature to make each of us, including identical twins, singularly different?"

"That's assuming, of course, that she didn't make fingerprints solely as an aid to law enforcement," said Charlotte.

"She didn't?"

"Oh, Emily, get a grip."

"Will you look at all those dishes piled up in the sink? Fortunately, it's your turn to wash," said Emily.

"No, you're wrong, Em, it's clearly your turn," said Charlotte.

Emily rolled her wheelchair out of the kitchen.

"Oh, hell," said Charlotte, "Where's Annie now that we really need her?"

Chapter 30: Charlotte Gets Called on the Carpet

"It's only been a couple of days, so we have to relax," said Emily, as Anne glanced down the driveway for the fifth time. "What are you looking for?"

"I'm looking for Charlotte's red convertible." Early that morning, Charlotte had been summoned downtown by the district attorney—"the only one elected by the voters of Los Angeles County" as he continually reminded his staff. Charlotte hadn't looked pleased after she hung up the phone. She shrugged into her red power suit, and took off in the Cabriolet.

"Be patient."

"But I don't want to be patient," whined Anne. "I want to know what the forensic unit found in Cesar's car."

"It may be nothing. It's been forty years, after all. Besides, I doubt that processing the VW is the sheriff's highest priority today."

"But this is evidence in a murder case."

"Technically, you're right but it's still a cold case to the forensic unit. Besides, what if the fingerprints you're counting on have simply evaporated over time?"

"But Volkswagens are airtight."

"That's a myth, Annie. It's not like *'Señor Escarabajo'* was hermetically sealed. Even if Cesar *did* remember to roll up the windows, they could still find *nada*."

"Well, I'm not giving up hope," said Anne.

"Hallelujah," said Emily, Here's Charlotte now. I wonder what sort of Italian dish she's carting home tonight."

"My money is on a scrumptious seafood risotto."

"Still, I wouldn't turn down gnocchi with chicken and garlic cream sauce."

"Wait a minute, that's not a bag from any Italian restaurant we know. First of all, it's too small, and second, there's no fancy name on it," said Anne, looking like she discovered a lump of coal in her Christmas stocking.

"Hush, hush, sweet sisters," said Charlotte. ""I didn't feel like Italian tonight. I picked up three California burritos, homemade *pico de gallo*, and an order of *carne asada* fries."

The women had the Mexican food out on plates in less than two minutes. The air was so scented with cilantro and roast pork, they were forced to make use of their napkins even before sitting down.

"Did you remember flan?"

"Oh crap, I forgot. I guess I have too much on my mind."

"I'll say—especially if *you* forgot dessert."

"Give me a break, Anne. This day was worse than the day I lost my first case."

"So what did your boss have to say?"

In the midst of a historic third consecutive term as the Los Angeles County district attorney, Stephen Chamberlain had already established his office as the premier prosecutorial agency in the nation. "If you don't believe that's the God's honest truth," Charlotte used to say, "just ask Stephen."

Actually Chamberlain's major claim to fame resulted from his smart practice of recruiting bright young lawyers from Ivy League law schools and pairing them up with court-tested veterans like Charlotte. She was especially fond of mentoring newbies. During the past five years, however, there had been no time to introduce newly minted *doctors of juris prudence* to the legal combat zone. Her promotion to No. 2 might have nourished her bank account, but when she slowed down long enough to catch her breath, she found her passion for the law was being starved by both her job and her life. Charlotte found herself asking the same question as her favorite philosopher, Miss Peggy Lee—namely, "Is That All There Is?"

Before her six-month leave, Charlotte was engaged in daily turf wars with the superstars heading up DNA evidence, public corruption, foreign extradition, animal cruelty, high-tech crime, fraud, and gang prosecution. Charlotte now realized that progressing from a courtroom career (that pivoted on the dynamic give-and-take between prosecution and defense) to the stress-filled life of a glorified paper-pusher might have been a mistake. *A Big Mistake*. Only after she joined the Cold Case Unit had she felt, once again, alive. "I really don't want to talk about it now," she said.

"You can't leave us in suspense. Spill the beans."

"Don't have to. They're already in the burritos."

"Okay, enough of the standup routine. Out with it."

"Well, the repairs on my loft have been finished for a month now. I really should move back."

"Sure, I get that, you need to return to LA, but why today?"

"Because my boss informed me this morning that I would be getting no more leave—paid or otherwise. Apparently he doesn't need a part-time No. 2. How did he so eloquently put it? 'Look Missy, either you quit wasting your time and talent on that nothing-burger case or I will be accepting your resignation.' "

"Oh Charlotte, I'm so sorry," said Emily. "I never expected you to stick around forever. Now I see that I have taken advantage of your considerable expertise for far too long."

"But it's been the happiest six months of my life. I loved the brainstorming, chasing clues, the delicious dinners."

"Especially the Italian ones, right?" asked Anne.

"But it's more than that. It's this town. When I was a teenager, I couldn't wait to get out of here—but now I can't wait to see what color the ocean is going to be every morning. It's silly I know, but I'm going to miss Port Cabrillo."

"At first, I wasn't crazy about moving back here either," said Emily, "but the most welcome difference in my life has been the pace. While it's much, much slower . . . "

"It's much more satisfying," said Charlotte. "Come on now, you two, I have no intention of turning on the waterworks."

"You can't—you'd have to apply your makeup all over again, said Anne.

"Well, since there's no dessert, said Emily, "let's fire up the Hunter brain trust. The topic for tonight's discussion is—'What do we still need to know?' "

"I think we should have an official murder board."

"A murder board, Anne?"

"Yeah, like on my favorite crime show. You know the one with the sexy writer. We could start with a timeline."

"Fine, what's the beginning date?"

"That's easy. August 31, 1971. Put down the murder of Truman Carpenter and the disappearance of Cesar Castillo."

"What's the end date?"

"June 29, 2011 with the murder of Cruz Castillo."

"Okay, now we've got a forty-year timeline. What goes in between those two dates?"

"Well, Kate takes different-colored pieces of yarn and links the suspects to the victim."

"But we have two victims," corrected Emily

"Okay, we can link the suspects back to our two victims."

"But, all our suspects have been exonerated," said Charlotte.

"But we have a witness."

"But the witness won't talk," said Emily.

"Well, we can still write known facts about the murderer under a huge question mark." said Anne.

"So what are the known facts about Big Guy?"

"We know he likes to dress as a woman."

"He's not a transvestite, Charlotte. That was just a disguise—not a lifestyle choice."

"I certainly hope not. From what I've been told, cross-dressers have better taste than that."

"Always the fashion maven, Charlotte."

"Jest if you will, but I would estimate the size of Big Guy's flowered dress as a 3X," said Charlotte. "Now if he stands around six feet tall—he did tower over the VW—he could easily weigh 300 pounds. Wait a minute, the fabric, especially around the waist, seemed to be straining at the seams. Let's say 325 pounds. I just can't imagine why he didn't invest in some tummy-trimming undergarments."

"Heavy-duty tummy-trimming undergarments."

"Santa Lucia University," said Anne, who indulged in non-sequitors on occasion.

"What about it?"

"There has to be a connection to the murderer."

"So was he a professor or a student?" asked Emily.

"Or she—we still haven't ruled out a woman."

"I'm leaning toward a professor," said Anne. "Somebody who is now retired."

"Because of the mobility issue, right?" asked Charlotte.

"Don't forget that the murderer knows Coach Sullivan very well."

"Because of the frame job?" asked Emily.

"Yes but I would say the frame was more opportunistic than personal," said Anne.

"Why opportunistic?"

"Lots of people knew about the Sullivan cabin. I don't think the murderer was trying so much to implicate Sullivan as the killer as he was in taking the bulls-eye off of himself. But there's definitely a personal connection between our killer and each victim."

"Why do you say that, Anne?"

"Because each murder weapon was unique."

"I don't follow—how were the weapons unique?" asked Charlotte.

"The murder weapon used on Truman was no ordinary baseball bat—it was an antique hickory bat. Why that might be meaningful to Big Guy, I haven't a clue, but he took the time to bring it with him to the murder scene. We just have to figure out why.

"I think you are on to something Anne. When he killed Cruz, he duplicated Cesar's VW. Big Guy must have hated that car. That was the car that allowed Cesar to escape the first time Big Guy tried to kill Cesar."

"So you're saying that with Big Guy, the murder weapons speak to motive?" asked Charlotte.

"Exactly. The weapon tells us exactly why each individual was killed."

"What about Cesar? Did he provide any hints as to the identity of Big Guy?" asked Charlotte.

"He claims Big Guy has unlimited funds," said Emily.

"And unlimited patience," added Charlotte.

"And drove a high-end Mercedes back in 1971," said Emily.

"The $64,000 Question is—how can we persuade Cesar to testify?"

"We need to bring his entire family onboard," said Emily. "Before we can do that, we have to persuade Angelica and Maricela the Cesar stayed in Port Cabrillo."

"And once that happens," said Charlotte. "I think the family will pressure Cesar into doing the right thing."

"After all, Big Guy did kill Cruz," said Anne. "But I'm not so sure that the family will agree to stay in witness protection."

"Especially for the rest of their lives."

"One step at a time, dear sisters," said Emily. "Otherwise we will start drowning in an overwhelming number of 'ifs.' Before we head upstairs, though, I want to share something a very smart LAPD detective once told me. He said, and I quote, 'every murderer eventually gives himself away.' "

"What did he mean by that?"

"He meant that either guilt drives a killer to confess or his arrogance does it for him. I believe that Big Guy has already told us exactly who he is."

"But how could we have missed it?"

"Sometimes the hardest thing to see is something right in front of your nose."

Chapter 31: Almost the Whole Damn Family

"I miss Charlotte."

"So do I, Anne, but guess what I'm holding in my hot little hand?" asked Emily.

"Is it the forensic report on Cesar's car?"

"Yes, it is, and it's a fascinating read as far as I'm concerned."

"In what way?"

"First, only two sets of prints were discovered.

"Inside or outside the car? '

"Inside. Those on the steering wheel and the ashtray belong to Cesar. Those on the glove box, passenger-side door, and passenger-side window belong to Cruz."

"How about the ashtray— any cigarette butts found?"

"Yes. And you won't believe this but one still contained intact DNA.

"But, since twins share the same DNA, that doesn't really help. How about the paint transfer on the back of the Volkswagen?"

"Stock black for a 1971 Mercedes SL—just as Cesar reported. Nothing unique to identify the owner, but the paint transfer from the Mercedes SL does support Cesar's story. There was also paint transfer from a California license plate as well."

"Could it lead to a number?"

"No such luck. Still, we could do a registration search on black Mercedes SLs in Port Cabrillo in 1971. I don't believe the list would include more than one or two cars. I'll make a note to contact the California DMV today."

"Perhaps, Emily you should invite the whole damn Castillo family, including Pajarita, to the police station. You could tell them you want to disclose the information the forensics unit found with respect to Cesar's car."

"That's an excellent idea, Anne."

"Wait a minute, you can't tell them about the fingerprints, though."

"Why not?"

"Didn't you promise Cesar that you'd wait—give him time to confess?"

"Well, when I summarize the report, I could merely identify the prints as belonging to Subject A and Subject B—that would allow Cesar to step up himself and tell the truth.

"Or not," said Anne. "Do you really think he will?"

"I have faith in Cesar. He's a good man. I'm going to set up the meeting for later this afternoon. Will you be available around five?"

"Is today Friday?"

"All day, Annie. Why? Do you have a hot date?"

"Now you are starting to sound like Charlotte."

"Somebody has to keep an eye on you."

"Not a hot date, but I do need to get back to the house by 6:30."

"Shouldn't be a problem. You can take Carina's car and I'll call ACCESS. I was planning on sticking around the station afterward for a few hours anyway."

"Are you also thinking about moving out of Thomas House?"

"*No*, Annie. Why would you think that? In fact, I've already given notice on my apartment and arranged to have all the belongings I don't need moved to a storage facility. I wanted to surprise you with the news this weekend."

"Really?"

"I can't leave you to rattle around this old house by yourself. There was also a second announcement, but I suppose that I could tell you now."

"What is it, Emily?"

"My doctor says that I'll be out of this damned wheelchair by next week."

"Then crutches?"

"No, actually I should be able to get around with a cane."

"That's terrific, Em."

"Now I can start earning my paycheck as chief. I've been so frustrated lately with how slowly this leg has been healing."

"What's going to happen to the Cold Case Unit?"

"You really love it, don't you, Anne?"

"You bet I do, but with Charlotte gone, it's not quite the same."

"Don't worry, we will find an alternative *modus operandi*."

"Why are you staying late tonight?"

"I need to spend more time with my officers. You see, telecommuting has its disadvantages—lots of them."

"Charlotte learned that lesson the hard way, didn't she?"

"When managing people, the only way to head off personnel problems is by paying attention. And you can't pay attention unless you spend enough time with the people you are managing."

"Why is that, Emily?"

"Most of what you need to know comes to you nonverbally."

"And here I thought it was just because you were addicted to donuts."

Emily chuckled, "Right, as well as really bad coffee."

"I'll wager what you really miss is your German shepherds."

"I certainly do miss the dogs. Attending their weekly training sessions was always the highlight of my week. But it's the men I'm responsible for. The dogs are there to make the men more productive."

"So how do you pay attention?"

"The best way to explain is to give you an example. What I've had to forgo is what I call the 'bitch and moan' sessions."

"But can't you get the same information by reading all the reports they email every day?"

"No, what I'm talking about are the spontaneous remarks officers make at the end of a shift. Most of it is bitching and moaning, but the comments allow me to take the emotional temperature of the squad. Every day."

"So what you need is information that isn't contained in the written reports."

"Exactly."

"Do you think we can wrap up this cold case before the anniversary date?"

"August 31st? That was the unwritten deadline, wasn't it?"

"Well, that's what Charlotte thinks."

"But what do you think?"

"I think that if the case won't stand up in court, there's no sense in trying to push Cesar to talk."

"Good point. We could be placing the entire Castillo family in jeopardy by merely getting the killer, but not the conviction."

"And right now, we've got absolutely nothing."

"But maybe—if Cesar tells us *everything* he knows—we could uncover enough evidence to convict Big Guy. The murderer, you know, always leaves something behind."

*****

Emily assembled just about everybody in the Cabrillo family around a black rectangular table. Only Rafael and Jorge were missing. They were otherwise occupied—gambling away their retirement checks in Laughlin. While the table was large enough to accommodate six leather-upholstered swivel chairs, it was far too large for the conference room. Both Anne and Emily could sense the tension building up in the claustrophobic space. In fact, the animosity Maricela held toward the sparrow-like Pajarita radiated out from her in toxic waves.

Maricela could never gain enough weight to pad bones that were now riddled with osteoporosis. At the age of fifty-nine, her sunken cheeks and frozen frown lines had hardened into permanent facial fixtures. She fumed all of the time. The extravagantly lush black curls that had softened her angular face forty years ago, had been replaced by an unflattering headdress of bottle-blonde frizz. Maricela had evolved into an acrimonious old scold, who, although she held her entire family responsible for her sorry state, saved an extra-large portion of blame to heap on the newest member.

Cesar's forty-year old son, who took over the flooring business from his bachelor uncles, was seated next to his grandmother. His transition lenses glowed green under the florescent lighting. He was successfully promoting a pencil moustache, soul patch, and the two-day stubble that passes for "cool" these days. As he absentmindedly ruffled his right hand through his curly hair, his left hand reached under his glasses to pinch the bridge of his nose. He was trying, but again, to clear away a migraine, but his technique, while recommended by various acupressure experts on the Internet, had rarely proved effective.

As Cesar shifted Angelica's oxygen tank, fluffed the goose-down pillow behind her back, and scooted her straight-back chair (hastily borrowed from the squad room) toward the end of the table, he shot Cesarito an SOS smile. Glancing at Pajarita, he silently approved of his brother's selection of spouse. He was grateful that his twin had been able to find love, and a life—even though any further contact with his brother had excluded him. He would have given anything to reverse the course of events that started with Cruz's words, "Don't worry, Bro. I have an idea."

Since he promised Emily he would transport Angelica to the police station, Cesar was forced to show up as well. It was his intention, however, to remain silent—unless the topic of his VW came up. His hope had been, once the investigation was over, to find a way to wake *Señor Escarabajo* from his forty-year slumber. *Perhaps, I should give some consideration to renaming him "Rip Van Winkle,"* he thought.

Although her ballooning weight propelled her blood sugar numbers into the diabetic range, eighty-seven-year old Angelica defiantly popped a caramel-flavored candy into her mouth. She couldn't wait to watch the fireworks. While Maricela and Angelica had once been close, Angelica realized she wouldn't shed any tears if Maricela decided to move out. She despised Maricela's behavior toward her son.

Angelica wasn't exactly independent, but she was gratified that she had still been able to get around without a wheelchair. Nevertheless, her family found her emphysema distressing— especially when they saw her permanently tethered to an oxygen tank. Yet, she thanked God everyday that she could still take a breath. Sucking loudly on her sweet, she turned her attention to Pajarita. She could see why her son had fallen in love with her— she possessed the posture and presence of a *baile folklórico* dancer.

Instead of donning an ensemble in various drab shades of brown, Santiago's wife had selected a multihued flowered skirt and a colorfully embroidered peasant blouse. She sat quietly— smoothing out the gold-satin fabric covering her photo album and observing the Castillo family dynamic. She had been hesitant to come at all, given the distasteful business with Maricela about her husband's body at the morgue, but her curiosity managed to trump her timidity. She also had the feeling that the fiction she had concocted with respect to Santiago's past was going to pale in comparison with the truth revealed this evening.

As Emily surveyed the group, the Margo Channing line from *All About Eve* sprung to her mind. "Fasten your seat belts, ladies and gentlemen, it's going to be a bumpy night." Instead of Channing's more appropriate words, though, Emily took the conventional way out and said, "I want to thank you all for coming. I realize your hearts are still heavy with the loss of your loved one, but I expect that you would appreciate knowing where we are in the process of solving the murder."

"I thought you said something about finding Cesar's automobile," interrupted Maricela, looking as brittle as a cockroach. "If that *puta* over there thinks she's going to get her hands on his car—"

Cesar's eyes, usually the color of mocha ice cream, blackened in a split-second. Just about everybody in the room saw his fist come up from under the table. He deliberately stopped the trajectory, however, and turned his hand over so the palm was now open and poised in the slapping position. Yet, just to make sure she got the message, he also said, "Another observation like that, Maricela, and you will be leaving this room one way or another."

Maricela started to open her mouth, another insult at the ready, when she felt a stab of pain. The cracking sound as her fragile kneecap bore the brunt of the unseen blow echoed throughout the conference room. It took Maricela a moment, but she finally realized that it was her mother-in-law who had delivered the well-aimed kick. As Maricela started to whimper, the entire table looked away, leaving her to nurse her wounded knee without even a soupçon of sympathy.

"The 1963 Volkswagen registered to Cesar Castillo was located in a gold mine tunnel in Lexington, California," Emily read from her report.

"Isn't that a ghost town?" asked Cesarito.

"That's right. And that's where the twins hid the car. After they boarded up the entrance, the vehicle remained undisturbed for forty years. Fortunately for us, the rolled-up windows preserved the fingerprints in the interior."

"Was there anything else in the car?"

"Yes, a couple of cigarette butts in the ashtray and a black apron that had been folded up and left in the trunk."

"With DNA?" asked Angelica.

"Yes, with DNA, but you should be aware, since twins share the same DNA—neither sample helps. While we assume the waiter's apron belonged to Cesar, we can't really identify the smoking twin with the DNA evidence alone."

"Don't twins share identical fingerprints?" asked Cesarito.

"Actually, they don't."

"Were there more than one set of prints in the car?"

"Yes, there were."

"And they belonged to Cruz and Cesar, right?" asked Angelica.

"Right."

"Don't forget about the paint transfer, Em."

"Thanks, Anne. We also know that a much heavier car hit the Volkswagen from behind. Forensics identified the paint from the larger vehicle as a stock black from a 1971 Mercedes SL."

"How did Cesar's vehicle get hit?"

"Do you want to jump in here, Cruz?"

"Not at all—you're doing fine, Emily."

"Our theory is that the driver of the Volkswagen witnessed a murder. A Santa Lucia sophomore named Truman Carpenter was beaten to death with a baseball bat the night your son disappeared. We think the murderer drove the Mercedes. We also believe he deliberately crashed into Cesar's VW. We think he was trying to silence Cesar as a witness."

"So Cesar saw the murder and that's the reason he ran away?" asked Angelica.

"He ran away," interrupted the man known as Cruz, "because he saw the killer's Mercedes parked in front of your house. He ran away because he was afraid that if he didn't, the killer might start wiping out members of his family."

"So he disappeared in order to protect *la familia?*" asked Angelica

"Yes."

"But then why didn't he come back?" asked Cesarito.

"We think he wanted to return, but he couldn't take the chance. We learned from Pajarita that he did keep track of his mother and brother by making yearly phone calls to a family friend.

"But nobody ever told me that my son was still alive," said Angelica.

"We suspect that she—we believe it was a woman—was sworn to secrecy. She kept her silence, we think, because she, too, believed that if the murderer ever found your son, he would kill him."

"As it was, even though he never came back, he was murdered anyway. What I want to know," added Angelica, "is why now? Why was my son killed now?"

"Probably because of the publicity. The papers gave the Cold Case Unit all sorts of coverage. If I hadn't picked the disappearance as our first case, your son might still be alive. I have to live with that."

"How did the murderer find Cesar?" asked Cesarito.

"We don't have all the facts, but we believe he ran a newspaper advertisement in the 'lost and found' section of the classifieds. We do know that he ran the same ad for six months in both the *San Gabriel Valley News* and the *Los Angeles Herald-Chronicle*.

"If I can interrupt, I think I can add something here," said Pajarita. "When my husband finally ran across the ad, he believed it was from his brother, and that his brother was trying to get in touch with him. The ad listed a telephone number, and when Santiago called, the woman who answered gave him directions to a cabin at Lake of the Woods. He left around one o'clock that afternoon but," here Pajarita faltered for a moment, "he never returned."

"A witness at Lake of the Woods provided a videotape that clearly shows a man disguised as an old lady getting into a metallic blue-green Volkswagen," said Anne. The video didn't record the actual murder but a tox screen showed GHB in your son's blood. From the coroners report, we believe he was unconscious at the time the car hit him."

"So, all you have to do is find out who owns the cabin at Lake of the Woods," said Angelica.

"But the killer didn't use his own cabin. He framed a retired university professor by including his phone number in the ad and by leaving incriminating evidence at the scene."

"The owner of the cabin, Dr. Sully Sullivan," said Anne, "was initially arrested on a charge of first-degree murder but then when his alibi held up, he was released."

"Because he wasn't the killer?" asked Angelica.

"A neighbor was able to provide him with a solid alibi," said Anne.

"The problem," interrupted Emily, "is that while we know *why* the murderer killed your son. . . "

"To shut him up, of course," interrupted Angelica

"But what we don't know is why he also murdered the Carpenter boy."

"So if you knew the motive in the Carpenter murder, you could identify the killer?" asked Cesarito.

"We believe so."

"So, what's the problem?" asked Angelica.

"It's been forty years. I think you all know from watching courtroom dramas on television how much documentation is needed to prove murder in the first degree," said Anne.

"Like witnesses and evidence, right?" asked Angelica.

"And forensics, of course," said Cesarito.

"Primarily linking the murder weapon to the killer," said Anne.

"Fingerprints and tire tracks—stuff like that, as well?" asked Angelica.

"Exactly, but since Andres Aguilar is already in prison for the Carpenter homicide—the evidence from the murder was discarded years ago."

"So Andres Aguilar didn't actually killed Carpenter?" asked Cesarito.

"That's what we now believe."

"Then why did Aguilar go to prison?" asked Angelica.

"Because he was caught in the act of beating up Norman Mortenson only one week after the Carpenter homicide," said Emily.

"In the very same alley," said Anne. "And even though the evidence was circumstantial, the jury didn't hesitate to convict him for both murders."

"The wrong man went to jail," concluded Angelica.

"That's correct."

"So what can we do to help?" asked Cesarito.

"What we are worried about is that if any of you help the police, you may be placing a target on your own back. This killer has no conscience. He will do anything—absolutely anything—to avoid detection. He's smart and rich and treacherous."

"I'm not afraid," replied Angelica. "Why don't you use me as bait? You know, like they do in the movies?"

"Not a chance, *Jefa*," said her son.

"I am not afraid of dying. I'm already an old lady. I've led a very full life. If I could help find Cesar's killer, I could rest in peace."

"I won't hear of it," said her son. "In fact, I forbid it."

"So who are you to forbid me?" asked his mother. "I'm the one who changed your dirty diapers, *Hijo*."

"So what is this plan of yours, *Abuela?*" asked Cesarito, diplomatically changing the subject.

"I know this polite young reporter for the *Port Cabrillo Pilot*. His name is Raul. Apparently he has much better manners than my own children. I was thinking that I could give him a call. I could tell him I want to reveal a big secret about my son's disappearance."

"What secret is that?"

"I could say my son witnessed a murder and before he left town, he told me the name of the murderer. Since the same bad man came back forty years later and killed my Cesar, I will tell the newspapers everything I know."

"But that's not true, *Jefa*."

"That's okay. I can lie with the best of them."

"If you say so, *Abuela*."

"I'll really have to think about your offer," said Emily, trying not to roll her eyes.

"I know," offered Cesarito. "You could set up a sting—fix up my grandmother with a wire. They could talk for a while. She could get him to confess. But a SWAT team would be ready to rush in, you know, so she wouldn't really be in danger. Is that what you had in mind, *Abuela?* "

"If the point is to get the murderer to confess on tape, your grandmother would be taking a huge risk. What if the killer got suspicious? What if he decided to shoot Angelica even before she gets a word out of him? No, it's just too risky."

"You could give her a Kevlar vest," said Cesarito.

"Goddamn it, Cesarito, stop this shit now," said Cesar. Then he turned to face the chief of police. "You should be ashamed, Emily. You can't fool me. I know you put Angelica up to this."

"Put Angelica up to what?" asked Emily. "Are you accusing me of manipulating a private citizen into risk her life in a sting operation? Let me set the record straight right now—I never intended to implement Angelica's plan. In fact, I think it's a really bad idea—on so many levels. Can't you see that I was just trying to be polite? To hear her out?"

"No, you were deliberately encouraging her. You were doing it for leverage. So you could get me to talk."

"Emily was doing no such thing," said Angelica. "It was all my idea."

"What do you mean—for leverage?" asked Cesarito.

"Emily has been after me for days now—to tell you the truth."

"What truth?" asked Angelica.

"The truth about Cruz and me."

"Aren't you a little mixed up, *Papi?* Your name is Cruz!"

"No, I'm not Cruz."

"Are you *loco?* Of course, you are Cruz," said Maricela.

"Okay, Emily. I certainly hope you are happy now. I have no choice. I have to go through with it."

"What are you talking about?" asked Angelica.

"It all started that night at the bus station. You know, right after we got rid of the car."

"What started?"

"Before Cruz and I parted, we agreed to exchange identities."

"This is nonsense, Cruz!" shouted Angelica.

"No, *Jefa*, I'm not Cruz. For forty years I've been pretending—but all this time, I've wanted to tell you that I'm Cesar. It was Cruz who did the disappearing act."

"I don't believe you," spat out Maricela.

"I didn't expect you to. That's why I never told you. The only evidence I had up until now," said Cesar, removing a blue Swatch from his pocket, "was this."

"You could have gotten that anywhere. That's no proof," said Maricela.

"Besides, you couldn't possibly deceive your own mother," said Angelica. "Especially for forty years."

"But I did, *Jefa*. When Cruz and I swapped our belongings, I forgot about this watch. When you came into Cruz's room where I was sleeping, I realized the Swatch was still on my wrist. But you never even noticed it. It was then I knew—"

"Knew what?"

"How easy it would be to fool you. Think about it, *Jefa*. You know that Cruz could never have worn a watch."

"That's right—he always hated anything around his wrist— even a long-sleeved shirt. When I would ask him to wear his dress shirt to church, he would roll up the sleeves, you know—up to the elbows." Parjarita looked up. She wanted to tell them that her Santiago also refused to wear long-sleeved shirts too, but decided to bide her time. Things were heating up.

"So here's my forty-year-old Swatch. But now there is even better proof. Isn't there, Emily?"

"Yes, the fingerprints in the VW. They definitely prove that this man here," she said, "is Cesar. His prints, and his prints alone, were found on the steering wheel of the car."

"And you all know that I never allowed anybody, not even Cruz, to drive *Señor Escarabajo*," said Cesar.

"Could this be true?" asked Angelica. "Could you really be my Cesar?" She looked confused and started sobbing into a tissue.

"Eres uno pinche mentiroso," said Maricela, her voice croaking with rage.

"I am not a fucking liar."

"Yes ,you are, you *cagada*."

"Now I'm a shit? Make up your mind, Maricela."

"You are *loco* if you think that you fooled me, Cruz. I am your wife. I am the mother of your child."

"Ves lo que esperamos ver, Maricela. You saw what you expected to see."

"What does that mean?" asked Maricela, the venom dripping over every syllable.

"In your mind, it was always the perfect Cesar you loved. I just want you to know that your perfect Cesar doesn't exist. He never did." Maricela was poised to interrupt, but after spotting Cesar's blazing black eyes, she stopped short. "You made him up, Maricela. You know, after the disappearance. The perfect Cesar became your god. No human being—no *hombre de verdad*—could have ever lived up to your Cesar."

"I'm not surprised that you would lie to us. *Tu esta desesperado*. So desperate, you would say anything. I'm still going to divorce you, Cruz. I won't change my mind." Cesar shrugged. Then Maricela turned to Cesarito. "Take a good long look at this *cagada*, Cesarito. He's nothing like your real father."

"But *Mamacita*, he's the only father I've ever known. He taught me how to ride a bike. He practiced with me so I could catch a pass. He is the reason I know how to tune up a car. He sat with me when I was sick. He cheered for me when I graduated high school. He has always been there for me."

"But if he's really your father, how can you forgive him for lying to you all of these years?"

"*A veces una mentira mantiene a salvo de la familia.*"

"We were never in danger, Cesarito. He's speaking falsehoods—and to *la familia*."

"You couldn't be more wrong, Maricela," said Cesar. "If Cruz didn't fear for our safety, why would he have been willing to disappear? He gave up his whole life for us."

"Don't speak to me, *cobarde*."

"None of you know this murderer like I do," said Cesar. He has no respect for *la vida*. He has no respect for *la familia*."

"How do you know he wanted to harm our family?" asked Angelica.

"Because Cruz and I both saw him. He stopped his Mercedes right in front of your house. The same house where our little Cesarito was sleeping." It was at that precise moment that Cesar realized how long he had been paralyzed by his fear of Big Guy.

"But if you know who murdered Uncle Cruz, *Papi*, why don't you tell the police?"

"Because I just can't." But his words sounded empty— especially when he saw their effect on his son's face. They were the words of a child.

"We will help you," said Angelica. "But you must tell Emily so she can put this *hombre malo* in jail."

"Cruz was a hero," said Cesarito. "Please, *Papi*, you can't allow him to die *por nada*."

In desperation, Cesar turned to his sister-in-law, "What about you, Pajarita? Do you think your husband would have wanted to put all the others at risk to find his killer?"

"Only Santiago can answer that."

"But surely you have an opinion?"

"I came here to learn more about my husband's family. I imagined that we might exchange information. You would tell me about the boy you knew and I would tell you about the man I knew. That's why I brought our family album, Cesar. To show you who Santiago had become after he left you at the bus depot."

"Who cares about this *pendejo* you married," screeched Maricela. "I could give a shit about your *estúpido libro de fotografías*. You can shove—"

"Maricela." At this point, Emily grasped the hysterical woman's right arm and, in an even voice, ordered her to control herself. Maricela looked across the table, half-expecting another kick from Angelica, but was still unable to control her virulent tongue. "Why should I?" she asked belligerently.

"Because I intend to ask *you* a couple of questions."

Maricela set her wine-colored lips into a pout, but said nothing more about Pajarita.

"I want you to give my inquiries," continued Emily, "some serious consideration before you respond."

"And you'd better answer Emily with the truth—if you know what's good for you," piped up Angelica.

"Did Cesar ever smoke?"

"Cesar?"

"Yes, Cesar."

"Maricela, I'm warning you."

"Yeah, yeah, he did—from time to time."

"Oh hell, Maricela," broke in Angelica. "When you caught him sneaking cigarettes in the car, you blew your top. I remember. You said he was wasting good money—money that should go to *la familia*. You used to call them 'cancer sticks.' "

"Fine. I admit it. It's true."

"Now, before the disappearance, did Cruz smoke?"

"Absolutely not. He was a quarterback, and as he always told me, 'I'd never put a poison like nicotine into my body.' In fact, he and I used to gang up on Cesar. We promised that we wouldn't leave him alone until he agreed to quit smoking.

"Does your husband smoke now?"

"He says he's under a lot of stress."

"But you just admitted that Cruz would never smoke. You said, and I quote, "As he always told me, 'I'd never put a poison like nicotine into my body.' " " Isn't that just what you said?"

"People change."

"But their fingerprints don't change. The ones we found on both the cigarette butt and on the ashtray belong to the same person."

"So Miss Emily, are you trying to tell me those fingerprints belong to my husband? Are you saying Cesar and my husband are the same man?"

"I'd stake my reputation on it, Maricela."

"What do you say to that?" asked Angelica.

Maricela didn't say anything. At first, she just looked around the room. Then she looked at Cesar. Without anger and bitterness as her default position, she didn't know what to do. Should she come up with a smart remark? Should she leave? Should she break into tears? Finally, she just threw herself on the ground, squealing, as if a thousand pins were piercing her voodoo likeness.

"You'd better take Maricela home, Cesar. We can talk tomorrow."

Chapter 32: Anne Does a Little Reading on the Pier

By the time Anne arrived at Thomas House, it was five minutes of seven. But even if her father had arrived on time, she would have missed him by more than twenty minutes. Although she had not intended to dine with Morgan that evening, she wanted to tell him in person, rather than have him ring the front doorbell and find nobody at home.

She honestly wasn't sure about allowing Morgan back into her life—especially considering how badly he had hurt her before. Still, what was weighing heaviest on her mind right now—Anne being such a conscientious person, and all—was not having finished Morgan's article. While "Home Run, or Run Home" had been downloaded from the Internet, with all the recent developments in the Castillo case, the fifteen pages of manuscript were still sitting on top of the printer.

Chloe did her customary dance of welcome as Anne stepped through the entryway. She couldn't remember the last time the high-energy dog had been taken out for a decent walk. Since Emily was still tied up at the station, Anne decided she and Chloe would grab dinner at the fishing pier. And they would enjoy a Chamber of Commerce-endorsed sunset for dessert.

They loved the fresh-caught fish and chips at the Surf Shack and since Ol' Sol wouldn't finish daubing the sky with summer-only shades of pink, purple and lavender for nearly an hour, she could read while they ate.

Sprinting the two short blocks along Surfside Drive, both Anne and Chloe arrived a little out of breath at the pier. Individuals and families, who had begged the ocean to share its bounty all day, were starting to pack up.

Fathers cautiously rolled red kids' wagons loaded with fishing gear behind them; while mothers pushed strollers or baby buggies in which a plastic bucket—usually filled with spider crabs or sardines—took the place of an infant.

Anne was amazed by the agile fishermen who tucked long poles with heavy tackle under one arm while they maneuvered overloaded bicycles down the uneven wooden planks.

Eight-hour anglers had cleverly fitted out the backs of their bicycles with coolers—their Styrofoam containers initially loaded with bologna sandwiches, while by day's end, jam-packed with halibut, white croaker, thornbacks and guitarfish.

Those opting to rig snag lines for small smelt, perch and queen fish awaited the opportunity to clean the day's catch in the stainless-steel sinks located on the eastern side of the pier. Anne watched as dogs and seagulls competed for discarded innards or luncheon leftovers. Those treats, though, held no absolutely interest for her spoiled pooch.

Anne knew that the most professional gear showed up on the octagon-shaped pier's end where the prime fishing spots could be found. Here, the ocean bottom dropped down twenty-two feet, and, because of the adjacent underwater canyon, the temperature never rose above fifty degrees. In addition to the usual mix of fish, these elite fishermen snapped up all manner of mackerel as well as bonito and barracuda well into the evening hours.

While the harbor seals and dolphin pods swimming on the far side of the pier usually attracted her attention, this particular evening Anne chose a bench close to the entrance. Although Chloe never minded the mile-long stroll down to the Cabrillo statue, she balked at trotting just a few hundred feet down the fishing pier. Not only did she feel apprehensive as she peeked through the wide cracks between the planks at the deep water roiling around mussel-covered pilings—but she also loathed the stench of kelp and seaweed, whose growth warped into overdrive during the summer months.

The current fishing pier was nothing like the wharf erected by the Honorable some nine years after Thomas House. At 44 feet wide and 1,500 feet long, the nineteenth-century structure was so massive that its two warehouses could accommodate an entire local harvest. The wharf also provided anchorage for dozens of coastal schooners.

For more than two decades, Port Cabrillo had been a leading shipping point between San Pedro and San Francisco. By 1898, however, when the railroad decided to snub Port Cabrillo and locate farther inland, the original wharf found a new purpose. For the next four decades, it would serve as a popular recreational fishing spot.

A 1939 winter squall, however, sounded the death knell for the Honorable's wharf. The natural enemy of all wooden piers is the gribble worm. While the tiny wood-boring species of marine isopod plays an important ecological role by degrading and recycling driftwood, it also weakens wooden pilings and renders wharves highly susceptible to heavy winds and towering waves. To add insult to injury, an enormous barge broke loose from its moorings during the storm and ended up cleaving the obsolete structure in two. The citizens of Port Cabrillo, however, simply constructed a new pier.

The sun had begun sinking behind a cloudbank piling up over the Channel Islands. As soon as Anne got her takeout settled on the rigid metal bench, Chloe sat up and shamelessly begged for a bite of the deep-fried halibut. While Anne was blowing on the steaming piece of fish so it wouldn't burn the dog's tender mouth, a seagull decided to land right next to Chloe. He kept hopping sideways, inch-by-inch, until bird and canine nearly became one. "How cute is that," exclaimed Anne, as she retrieved her smartphone and engaged the video function.

She propped it up so that the viewfinder would frame both dog and bird. Dividing the remaining halibut into two portions, she threw out half to Chloe with her left hand and half to the seagull with her right. Anne was astonished when each claimed her prize without moving an inch. After she slipped the phone back in her pocket, she fed the remaining fries to a flock of freeloading gulls. The noisy rush of their wings, however, compelled Chloe to claim the security of Anne's lap.

Anne wished she had picked up a few more napkins at the Surf Shack. Her fingers were depositing unsightly oil stains all over the *Literary Quarterly* manuscript. When Anne finally finished reading, though, she decided that Morgan's piece, on the whole, was quite ingenious. Her father had chose to tell his story from the viewpoint of a baseball bat—one that had once belonged to Jane Austen.

According to "Home Run, or Run Home," while Austen's sister, Cassandra dutifully burned correspondence between Austen and Tom Lefroy after Austen's death, Cassandra couldn't bear to put the bat handcrafted by Austen's lover to the flames.

Cassandra presented the artifact to a younger relative named Edward, but neglected to disclose its real significance. The boy grew up to become an amateur historian, baseball fan, and the first Baron Brabourne. He would also publish the 1884 edition of *The Letters of Jane Austen*.

Curious about the bat's origin, Edward got nowhere when interviewing his own relatives. When he turned to the Lefroy family, though, he uncovered the love affair between Lefroy and Austen that inspired *Northanger Abbey*—the Austen novel in which the word "baseball" appears twenty-eight years before the Knickerbockers ever took the field against the New York Nine.

According to "Home Run, or Run Home," Austen not only fell in love with Lefroy but also with the game of baseball. Morgan explained that Austen's affection for the male-dominated sport was quite understandable, given that six brothers dominated the Austen household. He argued that not only did Austen feel more comfortable in the company of the opposite sex, but her ability to identify with the masculine mind was the reason *Sense and Sensibility* as well as *Pride and Prejudice* remain classics.

While, initially, Austen's parents rejected Lefroy as a suitor because he had no financial prospects, they grew even more dismayed, according to her father's article, when instead of pursuing gainful employment, Lefroy frittered away his time with bats and balls. His worst offense against the family, however, was persuading Austen to pull on men's britches to play a sport from which women were specifically banned.

Instead of leaping to his beloved's defense, however, Lefroy fled to Dublin—and without delivering the marriage proposal Austen had been awaiting. As a result of his rejection, Austen swore she would never wed.

As Anne set down the manuscript, she couldn't help thinking about Carina's firmly held belief that every cloud eventually yields a silver lining. As the result of Lefroy's betrayal, Austen threw herself into her writing and subsequently provided remarkable insights into the psychology of unrequited love. She chuckled to herself as she recalled her father's rather impolite remarks about her favorite author. "Home Run, or Run Home," thought Anne, was a veritable tribute to Austen.

The freshening wind not only freed a few strands of hair from Anne's drooping ponytail, but also whipped them across her half-open mouth. As she spit out the taste of strawberry-flavored shampoo, she looked around and realized how immersed she had been in her father's essay. What little sunlight that still lingered was being chased by the deep shadows from the pier lights sidling across the weathered wood.

Searching the pier from one end to the other, Anne couldn't find another soul. The water, which, only moments earlier, had reflected the colors of a summer sunset, was now a deep indigo. Suddenly Anne was startled by a flock of blackbirds shooting up in front of the multihued clouds like a fountain of fireworks in the negative. As the subtle tang of brine teased her nostrils, Anne listened carefully. *Somebody is calling my name.* But it couldn't be. The pier was deserted.

During the hour she had been absorbed by Morgan's article, every fisherman had departed, including the eternal optimist known as "Murphy John." The snowy-haired retiree in the Land's End fishing vest was a venerated pier institution. Despite returning home empty-handed every single night, he never gave up hope that today would be the day he would bag a Pacific Jack mackerel. As Anne looked east down Surfside Drive, she could still make out the taillight of his ancient bicycle as it followed the curving road toward Civic Center.

Twisting back around, she was staggered to find the bulbous nose of Morgan Hunter only inches from her own. He pivoted on his good leg and he maneuvered his supersized derriere down next to her on the aluminum bench.

She noticed that although his gray hair was conservatively cut around the ears, the back straggled rebelliously over his starched white collar—totally negating the classy look he'd been going for. He had obviously dressed for dinner—complete with an English sports coat and maroon silk tie. The full-length London Fog raincoat draped over his shoulders not only accentuated his height but would be much appreciated once the settling fog started to liquefy. He carefully placed his brass-knobbed cane at his feet and asked Anne with exaggerated civility if he might join her.

Chloe's growl was centered so low in her throat; it was hardly audible—especially when it had to compete with the purple, red, orange, and yellow boardwalk flags snapping in the wind. "Your mother would have never abided such a nasty little dog," he said pompously.

"Actually, Chloe *was* her dog," said Anne, suddenly too tired to confront his rudeness.

Yet, Morgan, who seemed to be itching for a verbal altercation, continued to harass her. "Why Chloe's not a dog—it's some sort of furry rodent."

"I'm aware of just how upset you are with me, Morgan. I want you to know that I fully intended on being there when you arrived."

"You decided to join me?"

"No, Morgan, it's too soon. You told me you would understand if I wanted to wait. I just wanted to tell you that in person."

"So I did. I'm sorry. I don't want us to get off to another bad start. It's not that I don't understand. I realize my showing up so unexpectedly and wanting to become a part of your life must have come as quite a shock. But tonight, please believe me, all I desired was a delectable repast and lively conversation."

"I considered calling you from the police station, but then I realized you had never given me your phone number."

"What a dreadful oversight, my darling. I should have—how thoughtless of me." Morgan tried his best to appear sincere as he stared out at her from sinisterly shadowed eyes. Anne couldn't help feeling uncomfortable. *What was he looking at? Had her hair become a rat's nest in the wind? Was he concentrating on the lines around her mouth? Did he find her attire too mundane?* She simply wasn't up to batting away the next insult he'd be tossing her way.

"Just so you know," he finally said, "I wasn't upset."

"Well, that's a relief," responded Anne with recognizable sarcasm.

"What were you doing at the police station?"

"We met with the entire Castillo family. It ran much longer than expected."

"And more stressful too, I'd speculate."

"Yes, it was, but, as you know, I really can't talk about it."

The obese old man nodded as if he understood. When she didn't respond, he added, "Of course not, Princess."

"I'm glad you understand," said Anne, ignoring the nickname she once treasured, "but I do have a question for you."

"What's that?"

"How did you find me tonight?"

"This bench was always your favorite place to think. You and that thousand-yard stare. Whenever your face would adopt one of those vacant looks, I knew I could find you here. I have never ceased to wonder exactly what transpires in that mysterious brain of yours."

"I was probably thinking about baseball cards," she mocked.

"Baseball cards?" he said, missing the derisive jab.

"Tonight, however," she said, shifting gears, "I literally do have baseball on my mind. I just finished reading your essay in the *Literary Quarterly.*"

"You did? How flattering!"

"Well, don't be too flattered. After all, you did give me the assignment as homework."

"Oh, now you are poking fun at me, dearest Anne. Actually, I came here tonight to talk about you."

"The essay," said Anne, ignoring his attempt to butter her up, "reminded me of something. Can you guess what it is?"

"I haven't a clue."

"The four baseball bats I found in our attic."

"Did they also belong to Jane Austen?"

"How droll, Morgan."

"As I recall," said Morgan, realizing Anne didn't find him as witty as he did, "you found out from an expert that the four bats were worthless."

"Not entirely worthless."

"No?"

"Not as historical artifacts. I may yet donate them to the Port Cabrillo Museum."

"You mean that half-assed collection of old junk in the bank building?"

"There's no need to be uncouth, Morgan."

"Now where to display your bats?" he asked, allowing his hands to imitate the mincing mannerisms of a museum docent. "I wonder if we couldn't find a home for them *here* next to the broken *Port Cabrillo Pilot* printing press—or maybe tucked into this room with all the tacky salt and pepper shakers?"

Anne ignored her father's pathetic attempt at humor. "Not only did I find out to whom the bats once belonged, but also who crafted them as well.

"Really? Do tell."

"Phil Berylwood told me all about the when we met at Sunset Manor."

"One of the Honorable's kids?"

"No, Morgan, his kids are all dead. Phil was a grandson. Phil's father was Dr. Archibald Berylwood."

"The brain specialist?"

"The one and only. Phil is no slouch, either. He just retired as the executive director of the Port of Cabrillo. He was at the helm for something like thirty-nine years."

"So what does Berylwood have to do with the baseball bats?"

"According to Phil, his Uncle Scott made them. Scott Berylwood was also a famous furniture craftsman.

"Would I know his work?"

"He specialized in Eastlake-style pieces."

"Of course, I actually know a great deal about Eastlake furniture. If your mother could have, she would have furnished the entire house in it. Do you think Scott Berylwood might have crafted any of our things?"

"Phil promised to answer that question once his leg heals. He did inform me that Scott also turned all of the spindles on our front porch.

"No kidding."

"But the best news concerns the baseball bats. I now know to whom they once belonged."

"I'm breathless with anticipation, Sweet Princess. Please don't keep me in suspense."

"A total of twenty-four bats were crafted by Scott. He made them for each of the Berylwood cousins—both male and female—so they could play a baseball game at a family reunion. In order to tell the bats apart, Scott engraved each cousin's name at the bottom of each bat."

"Imagine that," Morgan said, shifting his considerable weight on the bench.

"I'm sure that when I get the bats down from the attic, the names 'Ti,' 'Tad,' 'Tim' and 'Ted' will still be legible."

"Whose names were those?"

"Not names, nicknames. They were the four Thomas brothers whose parents were Claire Berylwood and Trey Thomas. Claire and Trey owned the house, you might remember, before we did. All four of their sons were tragically killed on D-Day."

"Ah, Carina's research. Now it is beginning to come back to me."

"Would you be interested in seeing her notes? She planned on writing a history of Port Cabrillo, you know."

"I couldn't think of a duller subject."

"You know, Morgan, I'm getting quite tired of this," said Anne.

Time to change the subject, thought Morgan. "So how did you run into Phil Berylwood?" he asked.

"I took Chloe to Sunset Manor on a therapy visit. Phil was convalescing from a sailboat accident."

"You mean to tell me an upscale facility like Sunset Manor permitted this ridiculous little dust mop through the front door?"

Anne glared at Morgan. "Chloe, for your information, is certified as a therapy dog. Carina had planned to visit hospitals or old-age homes with her once she retired, but then she got sick."

"Despite what you may believe, I was sorry to hear that your mother passed away."

"Hundreds of people showed up at her memorial service."

"I didn't know about the memorial service. I must have been abroad."

"Even a contingent from Santa Lucia University dropped by to pay their last respects."

Morgan was stunned. "Was Coach Sullivan there?"

"No, I don't think so. Why do you ask?"

"He replaced me in the English Department, you know—after I resigned."

"Oh, I didn't know that. I've never met him. His wife Katherine, however, was a close friend of Carina's. They met during intraperitoneal treatments at UCLA."

"She had cancer, too?"

"Both Katherine and Carina shared the same oncologist."

"Didn't I read somewhere that Cesar Castillo's body was found at the Sullivan cabin?"

"That's correct."

"And that Sully was arrested for the murder?"

"He was a person of interest, but isn't anymore."

"No? Why not?"

"He had an alibi—a neighbor vouched for him."

"An alibi? Really? I didn't know that."

"Well, if you knew Coach so well, you couldn't possibly believe he was capable of killing anybody."

"Of course not. And besides, what would have been his motive?"

"Truman Carpenter."

"Did you say Truman Carpenter?"

"Me, and my big mouth. Please, Morgan, you have to promise to keep that to yourself."

"Don't worry, Princess. I actually knew Truman Carpenter. In fact, he was one of my most promising students. I was simply devastated when he died. But wasn't a man named Aguilar convicted of his murder?"

"Yes, he was, but we believe that his conviction may have been a rush to judgment."

"What do you mean?"

"I can't talk about this any more, Morgan. I've already said too much."

"Well, from what I remember," said Morgan, ignoring Anne's plea, "it was an open-and-shut case. The homosexual slur—right next to Truman's body. Then Aguilar, caught in the act of beating another homosexual to death only days afterward."

"But Truman wasn't a homosexual."

"How do you know that?"

"Please, Morgan. I'm just not confortable talking about this. Let's find another topic before I get into serious trouble."

"All right Princess. I don't want you to suffer your sisters' wrath. How about this? Since that's my manuscript lying facedown on the bench, why don't we discuss *it*?"

"Sure. Before we go any further, though, I would just like to say that you respect Jane Austen much more than you are willing to admit. In fact, I believe you are a huge fan."

"Oh, do you now? What makes you say that?"

"Last time we discussed Austen, you said she was a literary lightweight but—"

"But?"

"But the fact that you selected her as the subject of an essay you submitted to such a prestigious literary magazine—"

"Wait a minute, the subject of my essay was baseball."

"Fine, fine, since you told the story from the viewpoint of Austen's baseball bat, you are technically correct."

"Is that all you have to say?"

"Well, I considered the article exceedingly clever."

"Clever, how?"

"First of all, the strategy of employing an inanimate object as the narrator was brilliant. That allowed you to pre-empt the real argument. After reading your essay, nobody will question whether or not Jane Austen actually played baseball; instead they will be questioning the social mores of the day."

"Nicely done, Anne. I'm delighted with your analysis so far."

"Thank you."

"What about Tom Lefroy?"

"Again, choosing him as Austen's real love was equally brilliant."

"Don't stop there."

"You selected Lefroy to resolve a century-old literary controversy. How many researchers have written about Austen's decision to remain single?"

"Probably, a dozen or more."

"Yet most scholars look to Harris Bigg-Wither as the only man capable of stealing Austen's heart. Am I right?"

"Yes."

"But scholars seem to differ as to her motive for breaking off her engagement to Bigg-Wither."

"So why is that important?"

"Some maintain Austen sister's needed her more. Cassie, as you well know, was inconsolable after her fiancé died."

"Settling for being Cassie's companion would have meant an enormous personal sacrifice. Marriage, at that time, you well know, was critical to a woman's status."

Anne nodded. "Other scholars argue that Austen chose spinsterhood because she feared the perils of pregnancy and childbirth."

"A realistic concern, given the state of medicine in those days."

"But most modern critics contend that Austen must have realized *Pride and Prejudice* would have never been completed had she become Mrs. Harris Bigg-Wither."

"That's the most frequent feminist claim."

"But they all missed the point. Austen never really loved Bigg-Wither. She only loved Lefroy. You are the only one who knew Austen's heart. Furthermore, you managed to put your finger on the only real obstacle to the couple's future happiness."

"You mean Austen's parents? But Anne, wouldn't they have perceived Lefroy as quite the catch? Austen, you know, was the dowry-less daughter of an impoverished preacher."

"But you weren't fooled, were you? You figured out the most plausible reason that such hyper-class-conscious parents as the Austens were forced to reject Lefroy."

"Which was—?"

"Baseball."

"But surely you must have considered that Lefroy could have matured during his period of self-banishment to Dublin? Become more acceptable financially?"

"He could have, but that wouldn't have mattered to Austen's parents. He had already stepped across the line they had drawn in the sand—one backed up by years of social convention, I might add."

"And that line was—?"

"Persuading their daughter to don men's trousers."

"But you can't lay the blame for that entirely on Lefroy. After all, Austen could still have exercised her free will."

"But I can. He used women's cumbersome clothing to manipulate her behavior. He knew that she would find her gown too heavy for running bases. He may have even coaxed her to pull on pants with the words, 'nobody will ever know.' However, when her social set came down hard on her for violating their Victorian sense of propriety, he didn't stick around to defend her reputation. He ran away."

"Excellently argued, Princess. I am truly impressed. My only regret is, of course, the awkward title."

"You didn't supply it?"

"No, it came from my editor. I always felt "Home Run, or Run Home," was too—I don't know—pedestrian."

"Pedestrian?"

"It sounds like something an undergraduate might come up with. The play on words—it simply falls short. But there's always the danger that people like you might miss the point if it were any more artfully nuanced."

"People like me? Are you serious? Don't you remember comparing me to one of your most promising students? I can't tell you how glad I am that I never got the chance to enroll in one of your classes," Anne shrugged. "The only thing you seem to value intellectually is the ability to nitpick obscure literary points to death."

"They don't have to be obscure."

"Another *bon mot*, Morgan?"

"But I do adore a stimulating debate."

"So do I—but with somebody who scores his points by using logic; not insults."

"Oh, poor little Annie—offended again. May I remind you, my original intent has always been to find out more about you?"

"As flattering as that may be, it makes me wonder why you didn't contact Emily and Charlotte as well."

"Because, I already know everything there is to know about them."

"Then what could you possibly learn from an old brown shoe like me?"

"No matter how hard I try, Annie, I will never convince you that you're special. Only you can do that. I do admit, however, that I have seriously underestimated you."

"Well, thank you for that. But you know what really bothers me, Morgan? Why *now?* Why after all this time?"

"Do you think you might call me Father?"

"Do you think you deserve it?"

"No, I suppose not. You're right. I realize I have to earn your respect—and that's likely to take a great deal of time."

"So, let me pose my question again—'why now?' "

"Why does this have to be such a big deal? You remind me of your mother in that regard. Why not just be gracious? Why not accept me for who I am?"

"You mean—who you *say* you are. You know, Morgan, being abandoned by you proved to be the defining moment in the lives of all three of us."

"It seems to me that all three of you have done quite well for yourselves."

"When I said 'defining moment in our lives,' what I really meant is that we're all still haunted by the question you continue to leave unanswered."

"What question might that be?"

"Why did you go?"

Morgan looked down at his high-priced shoes. He was obviously mulling over a wide variety of answers. Anne searched his fleshy face for a clue. Was he going to tell the truth or continue to lie? Morgan then looked at her and flatly announced, "I don't know."

Anne just shook her head. She wasn't going to let him off that easily. "Don't know, or won't admit?"

"Look, my sudden departure had absolutely nothing to do with you."

"If that were true, you could have made an effort to stay in touch."

"But I couldn't. I had to make a clean break."

"Look Morgan, I can understand ending a marriage, but a father doesn't forsake his children. Not if he cherishes them like he should."

"Please Anne, let's discuss something else."

"Okay, Morgan—have it your way. By the way, where's your car?"

"My Mercedes is parked in the lot."

"Mercedes?"

"Don't you remember? I purchase a brand-new Mercedes every other year. It's my only vice."

"Quite an expensive vice, I'd say, but if you don't mind my asking, is it always the same color? Your Mercedes?"

"Just like Henry Ford's Model T. What was it he used to say? 'Any color you want—as long as it is black.' Why do you ask?"

"So you only purchase black Mercedes cars?"

"I thought I just said that."

Anne stared into the gray gloom that presently defined sea, sky and pier. Her brain was in the process of scanning dozens of mental file folders.

As the contents of each started flashing before her eyes, all Morgan perceived was one of Anne's thousand-yard stares. He wasn't even aware of the moment in which her facial expression transitioned from puzzlement to satisfaction. Or when her mouth finally arranged itself into a serene smile.

"Why do you want to know about my car?" he asked, a little perplexed. "Do you need a ride home?"

"No, I don't believe so. I don't take rides from strangers. Or murderers."

"Murderers?"

"It me took too long, but I finally figured it out. *You* killed both Truman Carpenter—and Cruz Castillo."

"Don't you mean Cesar Castillo?"

"No, Morgan. I'm afraid you flattened the wrong twin."

Morgan slowly yet painfully pulled himself to his feet. As a shaft of moonlight temporarily pierced the shifting shadows, Anne caught sight of a glinting metal muzzle pointed directly at her heart. She couldn't help herself. "A gun, Morgan? I can't believe that you, of all people, would stoop to using a gun."

"What's wrong with a gun?"

"Don't you remember all the protest marches you used to drag us to? You were always preaching mandatory gun control. It topped your list of pet peeves. Whatever happened to making America a gun-free nation?"

"Old age happened. I needed an expedient way of getting rid of you. All I'm looking for, Anne, at this point in time, is ease of operation. With this, dear girl, all I have to do is point and shoot."

"Chloe, run home. Run home now," said Anne, silently praying that just this once, the willful little dog would do as she was told.

"Run home, Chloe?' What's *that* all about? Are you imagining that your mangy mutt is going to save you? Do you fancy she will run home and bring Emily and Charlotte running?"

he said, waving the pistol at the trembling Anne. "I don't think so, you stupid girl."

All Anne could think about was *Murder by Numbers*. She couldn't remember exactly what Sandra Bullock did to keep Ryan Gosling from strangling her, but as her fingers brushed against the pocket outlining her smartphone, her fear proved a little less paralyzing. While her father would have already shot her before she could complete dialing 911, she still felt reassured that she wasn't totally without resources. Tracing and retracing the phone's outline, in fact, seemed to calm her down and allowed her to make eye contact once again. "So, Morgan, would you have no trouble shooting your own daughter?"

"No trouble at all."

"But you couldn't just leave me here, could you?" Her father shrugged his shoulders. "Didn't you plan on throwing my body over the side of pier?

"Now that's an excellent idea."

"But that's so—what's the word? Pedestrian?"

"Quit stalling."

"When you murdered Truman, you used an antique baseball bat. That was such an *elegant* way to kill. Your weapon told the world exactly *why* he had to die."

"And what was my motive, Princess Know-It-All?"

"Truman was going to inform the Santa Lucia University administration that you had submitted his work under your name. He was the actual author of 'Home Run, or Run Home,' wasn't he?"

"Good guess."

"And when you discovered that your daughters were investigating a cold case involving Cesar Castillo, well, you didn't want anybody to awaken that sleeping dog."

"That canine had been snoozing for forty years."

"So you were forced to act because DNA might have led us to you." Morgan nodded again. "You had to entice the witness to reveal himself, so you could eliminate him as well."

"But how could I do that? Nobody knew where he was."

"That's easy. You employed a first-tier private eye. I suspect he was so good, he was even able to give you the exact address in Alhambra—not such a difficult task since he had been using his dead brother's Social Security number."

"So why didn't the police locate him, Annie, if it were such an easy task?"

"Good question. I'm afraid I don't have the answer."

"Well, I do. Statistics. Missing persons cases are rarely solved. And the detective assigned to locating Cesar Castillo was probably swamped. Didn't Cesar's disappearance occur during the same week as the Carpenter and Mortenson murders?"

"You know that it did. But it was your classified ad that demonstrated how astutely you could zero in on your target. You used an old Volkswagen to make him come to you. The kicker, of course, was including the actual license-plate number."

"But how would I have known that?"

"Also a cinch. You read it in the newspaper."

Morgan motioned with his revolver for Anne to continue.

"In fact, I recently read the same article at the *Port Cabrillo Pilot* morgue. Both plate numbers were included because the VW that ended up in the harbor was only one number away from Cesar's."

"You know, Anne, I really had no idea if I could actually pull it off. But it was so effortless—fooling Cesar with my old grandmother disguise, that is. He wasn't even a bit suspicious." Morgan was clearly envisioning the scene at the Sullivan cabin. "I think I had him the minute he got a whiff of my chocolate-chip cookies."

"We know you put the GHB in the tea, Morgan, but what was Plan B, had he declined to share a cup with you?

"Please, don't be so dense. If it came to that," said Morgan, cackling like a madman, "it would have been a 'Got milk?' moment. Get it, Annie? Don't worry, I had it covered," he said, fanning out his fingers and moving them over an imaginary problem.

"Did you have to bring the wig, dress, and gloves with you?

"Katherine and I aren't exactly the same size, as you may have noticed, but I did borrow her wig. Radiation therapy can be so brutal to one's tresses, you know."

"But a disguise wasn't even necessary, Morgan."

"No? Have I changed that much over the years?"

"Because the twin you were entertaining was Cruz. He actually had no idea who you were."

"Don't be idiotic—it was Cesar I ran over—not Cruz."

"No, Morgan. The twins traded identities. It was Cruz who ·left Port Cabrillo."

"No, that's not right. Why would he do that?"

"Because that's what brothers do. Cesar had a wife and son. Cruz did not. You killed the wrong twin."

As Morgan gnawed on Anne's words, confusion was clearly getting the better of him. "You know what distresses me most?" he finally said.

"What, Morgan?" said Anne, her voice properly solicitous.

"When I killed Truman, Andres Aguilar went to jail. But when I killed Cesar—"

"You didn't kill Cesar—you killed Cruz. You can't argue with fingerprints."

"Now, who has things confused? With identical twins, fingerprints are also identical, my dear. Everybody knows that."

"Everybody does not know that, but you can believe whatever you wish, Morgan. You would still be wrong."

"Everything," said Morgan, ignoring Anne, "was going so well with the Castillo murder—with one minor exception. Do you know what I found most disconcerting about all this?"

"Why don't you tell me, Morgan?"

"I was counting on the police to pin the murder on Sully. That's how I planned it. Now, with him exonerated, well, I'll just have to think of something else. It seems to me, Anne, I just can't catch a break."

Poor Morgan, what I find most disconcerting is how you make everything about you. But Anne stopped herself from speaking—just in time. Her present situation was too precarious to take a cheap shot at her narcissistic father. "Yes," she simply responded. "I see what you mean."

"So if you are right, and I killed the wrong man, why doesn't Cesar report me to the police?"

"He would have, but he fears that with all your money, there's a good chance you could get acquitted, and he won't gamble on you coming after him or his family."

"Smart man. Too bad you aren't that smart. You never could learn to censor your thoughts. Whenever you had one; out it would come. Like vomit."

"Something I know only too well," said Anne, as the evening's chill brought up goose bumps.

She now realized that shock was setting in. She really had to stop shivering. Anne decided to picture herself cradling a favorite mug filled with hot cocoa. She even floated miniature marshmallows on top. And as she warmed her hands around the ceramic cup—the comforting aroma filling her nostrils—the shakes left, at least momentarily.

"Just remember, this isn't personal, Princess. I simply won't spend the few years I have remaining in some hideous orange jump suit. One has to keep up appearances, you know, when one is a Hunter."

Chloe, who had been slowly padding down the pier, kept pausing to glance back at her mistress. She had been told to go home, so she was trying her best to obey—but something was not right. As she looked up toward the road, however, the scent of a very familiar vehicle caught her attention. It was K-9 police car. Chloe gave a sharp yip, made an abrupt U-turn, and streaked back into the lap of her mistress.

"Oh Chloe," said Anne, hugging the shaking Yorkie. "Why didn't you listen to me?"

"Look at her," said Morgan. "She's so scared; she isn't even pretending to protect you. It will be my pleasure to rid the planet of both of you."

With his attention focused on Anne and Chloe, Morgan was unaware of Ranger leaping out of the squad car and bounding down the cedar pier—that is, not until the well-trained shepherd knocked the revolver out of his hand.

Cradling Chloe, Anne stood up and dispatched a perfectly aimed kick at Morgan's arthritic knee. He collapsed on his back, writhing in anguish. Before Chloe could cover Anne's face with sweet Yorkie kisses, however, Officer Carver had Morgan in cuffs. The cop and his clever canine accompanied Morgan on a perp walk down the pier, where, unfortunately, no paparazzi were present to document his shame.

Anne was pleased to see her father hobbling along with a much-deserved limp. Only after the back door to the squad car slammed shut, did she allow herself the luxury of tears.

Chapter 33: The Demon Jigsaw Puzzle-Solver

"Neither one of you would have allowed yourself to be alone with him," said Anne, tossing a spinach salad with a raspberry and walnut vinaigrette dressing. "I wasn't brave; I was just plain stupid."

"Come on, Annie-Fanny, don't be so hard on yourself. Why would we ever suspect our own father?"

"My tendency to talk without thinking is why Morgan chose me to pump for information. He knew that I'm incapable of reading people. You two would have instantly picked up on any suspicious speech or mannerisms."

"Maybe we would and maybe we wouldn't," said Emily, shoving her wheelchair out of the way. "The point is moot. You were the only one who could complete the puzzle. You figured out what the missing pieces looked like, and then you fitted them together."

"Okay, I'll take the compliment but my only real gift, if I do say so myself, is my photographic memory. It's what makes me such a demon jigsaw puzzle-solver, you know."

"When was the moment you figured out it was Morgan?" asked Charlotte, hefting squares of steaming three-meat lasagna, fragrant with Asiago cheese and basil, on three dinner plates. She had driven all the way over to Thousand Oaks to satisfy Anne's craving for traditional Tuscan cuisine.

"My 'light bulb moment' was when Morgan said, 'Look, my departure had nothing to do with you.' That was the only time during the entire evening that he told the truth. He wasn't leaving us; he was being forced to leave."

"What do you mean?"

"Every week, Cesar mowed our lawn and washed our car—the new black Mercedes, in fact. If Cesar hadn't recognized Big Guy—he would have eventually recognized the car. Morgan couldn't afford to let that happen."

"But why couldn't Cruz return once left Port Cabrillo?" said Charlotte, fishing pungent garlic bread out of the bag. "Morgan would have had no way of knowing."

"It wasn't about Morgan finding out. It was about the twins' terror. They gave Morgan all his power. And seeing the Mercedes idling right in front of their home only sealed the deal for them."

"What *was* Morgan's car doing in front of the Castillo house?" asked Emily.

"It was just a coincidence. Morgan was taking Angelica home. He kept the motor running while he made sure she got safely inside. Remember the timeline? Angelica babysat us that night so that Morgan could take Carina out."

"To tell her he didn't want to be married anymore," added Charlotte.

"So the night Morgan walked out was also the night of the Carpenter murder? I never put that together," said Emily.

"Why would you?" asked Anne. "But Morgan couldn't have merely vanished after the murder. He had to find a legitimate reason for moving out."

"Of course. Otherwise, his disappearance might have drawn attention to him as a suspect. He needed something that would keep Detective Miller from connecting the dots," said Emily.

"So not wanting to be married anymore was as good a reason as any?" asked Charlotte.

"But we still took it personally, didn't we?" asked Anne.

"Just for kicks, do you remember what Morgan's 1971 Mercedes looked like, Anne?" asked Emily.

"Sort of—big and black. But I couldn't have told you the make. I was only nine years old and had absolutely no interest in cars."

"But when Morgan mentioned the series of black Mercedes automobiles, did something click for you?"

"You know, Emily, when he talked about the car I could actually picture it sitting in our garage."

"Can you picture it now?" asked Emily.

"Sure. In fact, I can even see the license-plate number."

"You can?"

"The background is blue and the letters are yellow. It read '365AXY.' "

"Do you think," giggled Charlotte, "we could actually locate the automobile graveyard where the compacted Mercedes rests in peace?"

"You never know," said Anne, neatly folding up her napkin.

Now Emily started laughing—especially when she realized how ridiculous this conversation would sound to a squad room full of actual cops.

"Yet finding the 1971 Mercedes pales in comparison with getting Morgan's confession. I wonder if the video will hold up in court."

"Video?" asked Charlotte.

"Anne assumed she had merely taped Chloe and a seagull. Apparently, her finger, greasy from the fish, slid across the touch screen without actually disengaging the record button."

"So," said Anne, "not only did I manage to document the inside of my jacket pocket for all posterity—"

"But you also captured Morgan confessing to two first-degree murders—as well as his intention of killing you," said Emily.

"I know it sounds irrefutable, but, I must caution you, any high-priced defense attorney would move heaven and earth in order to get that video suppressed," said Charlotte, reaching for the Parmesan cheese. "And he might well win if the right person doesn't represent the people of San Perdido County. Too bad I won't be allowed to prosecute the case."

"But you work for the Los Angeles District Attorney's Office—LA doesn't have jurisdiction here," said Emily.

"News flash: I no longer in the employ of Stephen Chamberlain."

"I don't believe it. Did you quit?" asked Anne.

"It was bad enough when he called me on the carpet, but when he issued his so-called 'ultimatum,' well, enough is enough."

"Especially considering how good you always made him look, Charlotte."

"I just couldn't do it anymore—even my understanding has limits." Charlotte wiped marinara sauce from the corners of her mouth.

"While the district attorney in San Perdido County—" said Emily.

"Offered me a position today at lunch. Not only will I be back in the courtroom again—which is something I've really missed—I'll be spending a significant portion of time mentoring new recruits."

"But what about your condo with the spectacular view?" asked Anne.

"Peter already put it up for sale."

"Who's Peter?" asked Emily, as she popped the last bite of bread in her mouth.

"Peter Burnett is my accountant-slash-financial planner."

"I think he's more than that, Charlotte," said Anne.

"And you claim you can't read nonverbal cues," said Charlotte, blushing as crimson as her designer suit. "If I know you, Annie-Fanny, you probably realized how I felt about him even before I did."

"No, I didn't read any secret body language, Charlotte. You know that I can't do that. It was after the fire that I just asked myself why he would have been your first call."

"And what did you answer yourself?"

"Let me just say that I see a visit to Kauai in your future."

"It seems like you have been holding out on us," said Charlotte, with a grin. "Confess Annie-Fanny!"

"Confess to what?"

"Along with those four baseball bats, wasn't there also a crystal ball in the attic?"

"As a matter of fact, there was," said Anne, with a couple of snorts.

The laughter continued as the Hunter triplets finished up the rest of their celebratory feast. Carina's spirit, present in her daughters' love for one other, joined in as well.

The End

About the Author

Beverly Merrill Kelley, Ph.D. recently retired from teaching communication courses after thirty-five years in the department she founded at California Lutheran University. She has instructed so many local attorneys, she is rarely permitted to serve on a jury.

She previously published three nonfiction books that explore the relationship between politics and film as well as numerous scholarly articles in the fields of argumentation, persuasion, credibility, interpersonal communication, television, and film history.

A former radio and television talk-show host and frequent contributor to the Ventura County Perspective pages of the *Los Angeles Times*, she continues to file a biweekly opinion column for the *Ventura County Star*, a position she has held for the past fifteen years.

She resides in a sleepy little beach town on the California coast, accompanies her therapy dog to weekly visits at a day care center for mentally challenged adults, and tutors in the literacy program at her local library.

Her only vice is overindulging her two adorable grandsons.

Connect with Me Online

beverlymkelley.com

beverlykelley.typepad.com

Facebook Page:
https://www.facebook.com/beverly.kelley.148

Smashwords Page:
https://www.smashwords.com/profile/view/kelley2013

Other Books by this Author

Reelpolitik: Political Ideologies in 30s and 40s Films
Reelpolitik II: Political Ideologies in 50s and 60s Films
Reelpolitik Ideologies in American Film

Made in the USA
Monee, IL
03 March 2022

92187275R00154